Shadow of Doubt

Judith Erwin

Published by
Emerald Cat Press

ISBN 13: 978-0-9863367-0-6

Library of Congress Control Number: 2015902258

Published by:

Emerald Cat Press

Jacksonville, Florida

First Printing 2015
Second Printing 2018

Other Books by Judith Erwin

Shadow of Silence

Dedicated to

all women who had to build

a new life after divorce and

to Perry Duggan

Acknowledgements

I wrote the first draft of this book in 2001 but stored it away, unread, for twelve years, promising myself that when I had time, I would read and revise the manuscript. In 2006, the inspiration for Annie Cameron's story captured my creative juices. While four-hundred pages of Ansley's story languished on floppy disks and in notebooks, I focused my efforts on my new heroine. When Shadow of Silence was completed, Ansley beckoned. With the phenomenal support and contributions of those named below, the manuscript was substantially revised; however, the story and events remain the same.

I am, once again, overwhelmingly grateful to my editor, John Boles. His contributions, knowledge, and keen eye for detail took Shadow of Doubt from rough draft to polished manuscript. To my writing group: Julie Delegal, Jennifer Grannis, Keith Gockenbach, Erika Valenti, Michael Huebeck, and Marcella Beeching, I say thank you for all your astute and valuable input.

As before, a gigantic thank you to Nancy Duty for her cover painting of Nick's estate and her patience in putting up with and interpreting my mental perception of the grand manor house in the Cotswolds. Likewise, to Cheyenne Knopf who worked diligently to transition the manuscript into a finished book.

To the best family a writer could have: Bill, Allison, Judson, Sarah, Trevor, Brooks, Caroline, Amelia; and my family by marriage: Lynda, Marshall, John, and soon to be Keri. And to a best friend of over sixty years and former sister-in-law, Eleanor, I am eternally grateful to you all for your love and support.

An extra big thank you goes to the expert consultants who helped maintain the accuracy and integrity of many sections of this book: John Boles for his vast knowledge of the entertainment industry; Marcella Beeching for her infinite knowledge of horses; J.A. Wilson and Raymond Crews of the Jacksonville Sheriff's Office for their vetting of scenes involving law enforcement; Heath O'Shea, Blake Crenshaw, Dave Westberry and Stephen McManus of Engine Company #51 of Jacksonville Fire Rescue for their consultation on the accident scene;

and to Van Cleef and Arpels Americas, Gail Lee, Education & Heritage Assistant Manager, for her assistance with the authenticity of the shopping scene.

Finally, to two talented poets who shared their knowledge and passion for the magic of language when my goal of writing a novel was no more than a dream: Reverend Deacon Kevin Bezner, PhD and Mary Sue Koeppel, former editor of Kalliope, a journal of women's art. Thank you for all you taught me about writing and for your faith in my writing ability.

Acknowledgements could not be complete without thanking the fantastic body of readers of Shadow of Silence for their support, complimentary ratings, reviews, comments, and expressed desire to read more of my work.

PART I

CHAPTER ONE

Tuesday mornings were always slow at the boutique. Alone in the shop, Ansley took the opportunity to begin unpacking a shipment of couture clothing that had come in for the Christmas season. The slender blonde manifested an air of professionalism in her requisite black dress; low-heeled, black pumps; and a single strand of the best fake pearls her budget had allowed. Her hair was sleeked back in a bun, like the one she had often worn during her brief career in ballet. Although the austere ensemble complimented her green eyes, porcelain complexion, and classic bone structure, her husband, Mark Dixon, had scoffed at the attire.

"You look like my mother," he said, the first time Ansley dressed for work.

"I'm not working at Queen Anne's Closet to impress anyone. I'm there because it pays more than any other shop in the mall," she had responded. "I was lucky to get the job."

As Ansley carefully removed each designer dress from the box that morning, she caressed the fine fabrics, admiring the exquisite detail and wondering what it would be like to wear such a garment. The sound of a bell, signaling the entry of a customer, caused her to quickly hang a dress on the rack and proceed to the showroom. However, it was only the shop owner. Hardly acknowledging the young clerk, Delia Stewart went straight to her office next to the workroom.

Minutes later, a voice came over the store intercom.

"Ms. Dixon, please come to my office." It was Stewart.

Panic seized Ansley. Stewart's tone had been harsh. Had a temperamental customer lodged a complaint? Her hands grew clammy, and her knees felt shaky as she walked into the office. *I can't lose this job.*

Delia motioned for her to take a seat in a folding chair against the wall in the stark room. Like Ansley, the owner wore black with her silver hair fashionably short. Stewart's pearls were real. A super-model some thirty years before, she was imposing with the air and posture of her former profession. Her desk was stacked high with catalogs, invoices, and assorted correspondence.

"I'll get right to the point," Delia said, a sharp look in her eyes.

Ansley felt her hands go weak, an involuntary flush rising on her face.

"Sally has given her two-week notice. She is moving to Chicago. If you're interested, the assistant manager position is yours."

Speechless, relief raced through Ansley's veins like the air escaping from a punctured tire. A smile crept across her face and her emerald eyes sparkled.

"The job carries more responsibility, but the raise in pay will compensate you for the inconvenience."

The magic word *raise* resonated in Ansley's mind as she struggled to contain her excitement. Recent medical expenses and car repairs had put a strain on the Dixon marriage. *Thank you, God. A raise could get us through until Mark graduates.*

After clocking out that afternoon, she virtually floated to her car in anticipation of relaying her news. Driving toward SW 34th Street, her mind was on how to celebrate. *I'll pick up a good steak, a key lime pie, and a six-pack of beer at Publix. Mark will be so thrilled about the money that he'll forget I blew the budget.*

Leaving the supermarket with her purchases, large drops of rain began to pelt the pavement. "Darn it," she whispered. "But nothing is going to dampen my spirits." She had hardly stepped off the curb when a heavy downpour drenched her clothing.

Once in the car, she turned the ignition key. A cool breeze from the air conditioning struck her wet skin, causing her to shiver, but she was still too excited about her promotion and the thought of giving the news to her husband to let it bother her.

Driving the short distance to the tiny apartment on West 34th Street, a coy smile brought a glow to her damp face as she contemplated the positive affect her promotion would have on her marriage. After two years, the honeymoon was definitely over. Mark seemed to be critical about everything she did, causing her moments of near regret at having walked away from her career. Ten days before, when denied a withdrawal at the ATM, Mark had stormed into the apartment.

"I guess I'm going to have to trash my degree and get a job," he said. "Obviously, *you* don't know how to budget money."

He didn't give her a chance to explain how rent, utilities, and auto insurance had devoured the bank balance.

"Don't worry. We'll be okay. With the Christmas season coming, I'll get overtime," she had said, hoping to placate him.

Ansley hated conflict and avoided arguments if possible. She rationalized that he was under stress because of the demands of grad school and the demise of their savings account. She clung to the hope that once Mark finished his degree in architecture, a large firm would hire him, and the marriage would be like before. They needed only one more year.

Turning into the apartment complex, her anticipation accelerated. Despite his recent attitude, Ansley still loved Mark. Thoughts of making him happy swirled around in her head.

She was home early, having switched her half-day-off at the request of another clerk. Mark would still be in class. She hoped he would not go out with the study group and be late. *Maybe I'll call and leave him a message.*

As she turned a corner at the back of the complex, her heart skipped a beat. Mark's car was parked in front of their entrance. A smile spread across her face.

He's home!

Taking the empty parking space next to his car, she juggled umbrella, purse, and groceries to make it through the rain, up the steps, and into the building. Once inside the hallway, she let the open umbrella drop in front of their first-floor unit. The sound of music was coming from inside the apartment, and butterflies tickled Ansley's stomach as she pictured his face when he heard the news.

She wriggled the key into the slot and felt the click of the tumbler. The music grew louder as the door cracked. Inside, the drapes were drawn across the sliding-glass doors, putting the room in semi-darkness. She reached for the light switch.

As the door swung open, Ansley gasped—groceries crashed to the floor. On the living room couch, Mark was poised over their upstairs neighbor. Clothing and shoes were askew on the floor.

The light and clamor of groceries hitting tile brought his head instantly around. For a moment, they stared at one another, each with an expression of disbelief. A bullet through Ansley's heart would have been merciful.

"Turn that light off! What the hell are you doing here!" he shouted, shifting guilt with his accusatory tone.

Stunned, Ansley stood frozen for several seconds, unable to speak.

3

The smell of raw sex permeated the room. Without thinking, she turned and ran out of the building, leaving the groceries where they fell—the umbrella rocking in the doorway.

As she turned the car out of the complex, Ansley had no idea where she was going or what she would do. Driving aimlessly, with the image she witnessed tattooed on her brain, the full-blown rainstorm pounded her windshield with a vengeance, rendering the wipers nearly useless. Streaks of lightning crossed her path, followed by an angry clap of thunder. Ansley felt as though she were swimming in a sea of setting cement as she tried to sort out her life and reconcile what had happened.

As she drove, she mentally scrolled though the history that led to this nightmare. She had sacrificed her youth for ballet, and then her career for Mark—her first and only romance.

Handsome Mark, with his tousled mane of chestnut hair, flirtatious blue eyes, and sexy body, had come along at the close of her second year in the company. Only a week before they met, she had been given a contract to dance in the corps for another season—not the demi-soloist contract she had expected. To soothe her disappointment, she travelled home to Jacksonville to spend the weekend with her family and old friends. During the visit, her best friend, Elaine, had arranged the blind date with Mark. He was a fraternity brother of Elaine's fiancé. When Mark proposed within two months, the excitement of marriage and children overshadowed Ansley's career disappointment.

I should have listened to everyone. Mother, Dennis, even Jean-Claude, cautioned me to not rush into marriage.

When she tendered her resignation, Jean-Claude, the mince-no-words director of the National Ballet, ranted about what an error she was making. His words echoed in her ears as she wiped fog from her windshield.

"You are giving up what you've worked so hard to accomplish— sacrificing your *rare* talent for a *man*?" His face had wrinkled in disgust. "You have the potential to become a prima, mon cherie. Think hard about this. Take him as your lover. It will increase the passion in your performance. Don't discard your destiny." He rose from his chair and walked around the desk. Facing her, he put his hands on her shoulders and looked her straight in the eyes.

"You will regret this. The bloom will fade and the career gone— poof!" He snapped his fingers.

"But you didn't promote me," she had responded.

"Lentement, mon cherie. One does not become the prima so quickly. The flower, it needs to grow. You have much promise. The technique: it is superb; the artistry—c'est si bon—but your attack? It needs the work. Don't throw your gift away for a man!"

Jean-Claude was right. The bloom faded, and now it is dead and buried. The bastard has been living on my earnings and sleeping with someone else.

Rain veiled the windshield; tears blurred her eyes. She drove on autopilot, responding with no awareness of traffic and street signals.

Out of nowhere, a car cut in front of her. Ansley pumped the brake, but her Corolla began to skid.

CHAPTER TWO

The brakes made a futile attempt to stop the Corolla but sent it hydroplaning instead, sideways, into the path of oncoming traffic. The first impact came on the passenger side, spinning the car across the road like an air hockey puck. As the car spun nearly 360 degrees into its original lane, the driver's side, front fender glanced off the right rear of a pickup truck. The airbag shot out, filling the car with a powdery smoke and impacting Ansley's torso. As the car came to rest, rain blew inside the vehicle through the broken window on the passenger side. Ansley was conscious, but disoriented. At some point during the accident, she had closed her eyes. As they opened, her head throbbed and her chest burned from the impact of the airbag. Everything seemed quiet and out of focus for a few seconds.

"Call nine, one, one," she heard someone shout.

As she cut her eyes around, trying to orient herself, she was unwilling to move her aching head and could not tell where the car had landed. She couldn't see the vehicles she had collided with, but saw a few people beginning to gather, even though it was still pouring rain. A man was walking toward her.

"Ma'am, are you alright?" he shouted through her closed window as he tapped against the glass.

Ansley tried to push the button to lower the window, but there was no power. She couldn't respond, partly because she couldn't make herself speak and partly because she did not know whether she was okay.

The man attempted to open her door, but it was jammed. Sirens flared out of what seemed to Ansley like nowhere. They came from both directions as a police car and fire truck arrived simultaneously. The airbag had deflated, but Ansley remained frozen in place. She could see that a crowd of umbrella-bearing pedestrians had congregated. EMTs rushed through, waving onlookers back.

"The door is jammed," someone shouted, presumably the man who had tried to open it.

She heard the sound of metal against metal as the first responders pried the stubborn closure loose.

"Ma'am, don't move. Are you in pain?"

"I can't feel my feet. I'm a dancer. . . . I can't feel my feet." She began shaking.

"Take it easy. You're going to be fine," the deep voice said as he slipped a blood pressure cuff on her arm and put cold fingers on her neck. "We're going to take care of you." He turned to a colleague. "Bring the oxygen. Her breathing is shallow. She may be going into shock."

"I can't," Ansley whimpered but could say no more.

"Relax and breathe." The EMT put the oxygen cup over her nose. "We're going to get you out of there. Just relax and let us do the work." He lifted her head slightly, put on a cervical collar, and then wrapped a blanket around her. Seeing her purse on the floor, he reached over and removed it from the car. Passing it to another member of his team, he asked Ansley, "May we take your ID from your wallet?"

She nodded.

Ansley felt something wet on her cheeks, as the team gently lifted her out and onto a hard, board-like surface. She wondered whether the liquid was rain, blood, or tears. One of the rescue team tried to shield her from the rain, but she could feel it. She closed her eyes and yielded to the circumstances.

Once she was loaded into the ambulance, the EMT, who had done the communicating with Ansley, removed the oxygen cup and asked, "Where is your pain?"

"My head," she whispered. "It hurts."

He held up three fingers and said, "How many?"

"Three," she responded.

"Who's the president?"

"Hillary's husband."

The EMT laughed. "Well, I don't think you have serious brain injury."

"Are my legs paralyzed?"

The paramedic lifted the blanket and slipped off her shoes. "Try wiggling your toes."

Ansley's toes slowly moved.

"Looks to me like you'll still be dancing."

"You wouldn't lie to make me feel better?"

"He's not lying," a second EMT said. "Your toes are moving."

"Let's get this oxygen back in place. You look like you're doing well, but let's play it safe."

Ansley held his hand back. "I don't dance anymore. I just want to know that I can."

The paramedics both smiled.

By the time the ambulance arrived at the emergency room, Ansley's color had improved, and she was calming down from the trauma. The paramedics rolled her gurney into one of the ER cubicles under the direction of the triage nurse. Once in the room, she tried to sit up, but the team insisted that she allow them to move her onto the hospital bed.

Taking the chart from one of the EMTs, the nurse glanced at it and then at Ansley.

"Ansley.... That's a pretty name."

Ansley looked at the woman without responding.

As the EMTs left, the nurse took her vital signs while Ansley watched. During the ambulance ride, thoughts had darted around inside her head like agitated goldfish in a bowl: the helpless feel of the car careening, the trauma of impact, the scene at the apartment, and the uncertainly of what to do next. Her brain was a mass of confusion. The expression on her face resembled a cornered fawn, separated from its mother.

"Is there someone we can call for you?" the nurse asked, sensing that Ansley was fragile.

Pulling herself together, she said, "No, no one," and then turned her head away.

"You don't want me to call your husband?"

"I'm not married," Ansley said, covering her left hand to hide the ring, which the woman had likely seen.

The nurse paused, but was intuitive enough to realize that the husband might be a sensitive subject, and moved on without probing.

Ansley acquiesced to the examination as the woman completed her routine procedures, although she continued to profess that she was fine. Once alone, she removed the wedding ring from her finger and tossed it into a nearby trash container. As it struck bottom, it hit against the lined plastic container with a thud. With the gesture, Ansley ended the marriage with the finality of a judicial decree.

Once her condition was considered stable, the nurse asked if Ansley was up to speaking with the traffic investigator.

"I suppose I am."

As the police officer entered her cubicle, Ansley was pleased to see the investigating officer was a woman.

"I just need to get some information from you, Ms. Dixon. Witnesses on the scene have given me a good description of the car that cut you off, causing you to lose control of your vehicle, but I need you to tell me what you remember."

"Does that mean that it was not my fault?"

The officer nodded. "It looks that way from all the information I've gathered."

It did not take Ansley long to give her version of the circumstances, because she remembered very few details. "It happened so fast that I don't know much between stepping on the brake, the car skidding, and ending up in a mangled mess. I couldn't even describe the car that cut me off. I only know that it was a car, not a truck or SUV."

The officer had barely completed recording the essential facts on her report when an orderly came to take Ansley to radiology.

After a battery of x-rays, a tactile examination, and multiple questions, a physician, whose name Ansley never recorded, pronounced her okay for release. However, he warned that there would likely be an aftermath of soreness the following day, and if nausea, extreme pain, or other signs of injury were to arise, Ansley should either return to the ER or consult her private physician immediately.

Free to leave, the question became—how? Her car was towed, her husband eradicated, and she was not willing to engage in conversation with any acquaintances. Her parents, who lived seventy-five miles away in Jacksonville, were not an option. They would immediately ask where Mark was, and Ansley was not ready to explain.

As a nurse's aide helped her dress, Ansley asked, "Could someone call a cab for me?"

"Why sure, honey. Do you have a preference?"

Shaking her head, Ansley then contemplated where she could go and how she would pay. There were only a few dollars in her wallet, but she had an ATM card and a credit card on her parents' account for emergencies. Her current circumstances certainly qualified as an emergency.

In the cab, her head cleared a little, but still throbbed. Her body ached all over. She directed the driver to take her to the motel where her parents had stayed when visiting, and to stop at a bank on the way so that she could withdraw money from a machine. She decided to take the maximum amount permitted since she had no idea what the next few days would be like. Fortunately, the monthly bills had not yet been paid, therefore she was confident that the account could bear the withdrawal.

At the motel, she wondered what the clerk thought about a young, disheveled woman checking in after ten o'clock at night. But she couldn't dwell on it. She would not be staying in Gainesville, so it didn't matter. With no makeup or change of clothing, she would look no better the next day.

Once in her room, Ansley curled up against the headboard of the queen-size bed. Hugging one of the pillows to her abdomen, she sat for hours, not turning on the television or the lights. Her mind replayed the repulsive scene at the apartment over and over. She knew the woman lived in an apartment on the second floor of their building but had no idea that Mark knew her. Her first name was Beverly, which Ansley had learned one day when they arrived home simultaneously. She was a law student, but looked one layer of lipstick short of a hooker. It was hard not to notice how well-endowed nature, or silicone, had made the woman—just Mark's type. He was always commenting on the chests of women on TV, which had made Ansley self-conscious since her bra was the typical ballet dancer *A-cup*. He had even suggested that she might consider implants. As much as she wanted to please him and improve her self-esteem, it wasn't going to happen.

A little after eleven, her mobile phone rang. She ignored it.

Although her world had imploded in that one instant, she hardly cried. It was as though she was in shock. Sitting upright the remainder of the night, she slept intermittently—her dreams filled with images of his paramour, with and without clothing. Instinctively, she wanted to pack up and run home to her parents. She was not scheduled to work that next day, but had two classes at Santa Fe Community College. Without her books or fresh clothing, she couldn't go, and there was no way she was going back to the apartment and risk a confrontation.

Shortly before daybreak, she woke for the last time, thirsty, but uncomfortable about leaving the room. She settled for tap water.

Picking up her cell, she saw that the one call had been from Mark. *Did he leave a message? What could he say? Tell me it was a mistake? Had only happened the one time? Beg me to come back?*

Turning the phone round and round in her hand, she tried to muster the courage to check the messages but couldn't just yet. She laid the phone on the scarred night table and walked to the bathroom.

"I've got to do something. I can't stay here, but I can't go back to

11

the apartment." She talked to herself, trying to sort out her next step. "I've got to go to work tomorrow. I can afford to miss classes today, but I have to work all weekend. If I quit my job and go back to Jacksonville, I'll forfeit this semester, plus, my name is on the lease; and it's not up until June."

Standing in front of the bathroom sink, Ansley looked at herself in the mirror. "Well, I look about as bad as I feel." She pulled the pins out of her bedraggled bun and shook her hair loose, splashed cold water on her face, and then went to her purse for a comb. *I need a toothbrush,* she thought. After combing her hair and putting it back up in a ponytail, she opened the curtain over the air conditioner and saw that dawn was breaking. *I'll go out for a Coke and a toothbrush in about ten minutes. It should be reasonably light by then.*

Looking over at her cell phone, she decided to bite the bullet and listen for messages. The cold water had done a fair job of washing away the mental hangover. She dialed voice mail, but put the phone on speaker to avoid intimacy. There was one message. She hesitated before letting it play.

"The apartment is yours. I've moved upstairs with Beverly."

That was it. No apology, no explanation, no remorse. *Where have I been? I've been sleeping with a man for over two years who I don't know. I gave up everything—sold my soul—while he screwed around.*

Up until the last thought, she had not cried. But remembering the baby brought overwhelming guilt and sorrow.

After having her cry, she used the cold-water trick again. Ansley left the motel room and told herself that if she didn't go back to the apartment immediately, she might never go back. Somehow, with self-meditation tricks she used to control stage fright, she managed to anesthetize her brain long enough to return.

The apartment was eerily quiet as she slowly opened the door. She looked around as if afraid that despite his message, he might still be there. He wasn't. It was safe.

Laying her purse on the kitchen counter, she went to the refrigerator for a Diet Pepsi, having failed to get a drink at the motel because the vending machine was out. The key lime pie was there, albeit the filling was smashed, the crust broken, and the tin bent from the fall. The beer and steaks were gone. She took the pie out and threw it in the garbage. She wanted to throw it across the room. "I hope they choked on *my* steaks. How I would love to smash that pie onto both of their faces and grind it in," she said aloud. "And that sofa…. It's out of here today."

Walking over to the one chair in the living room, she sat and stared out the sliding glass doors at the swimming pool in the center of the complex.

How stupid am I? He wanted to be caught. If not . . . they would have been in her apartment.

CHAPTER THREE

After forcing herself to eat most of a grilled cheese sandwich, Ansley called her dad. She had to report the accident to her insurance company, and her father, Mike Sheridan, was her agent. Keeping her voice upbeat, she was able to avoid any discussion about Mark.

"Your policy will pay for a rental car, honey," Mike said. "I'll call Enterprise in Gainesville and then get an adjuster out to assess the damage. Are you sure that you're okay?"

"I'm fine, Dad—just a little sore, and I have a slight headache. They checked me out at the hospital," she said, rubbing her neck.

The first twenty-four hours were the hardest. Anger alternated with grief. She managed to get through three days by focusing on her work. At the shop, she smiled at customers and chatted with the other two clerks as though everything was normal in her life. However, at home, she was miserable. Coming and going, she feared a confrontation with either Beverly or Mark. While inside, the rooms taunted her with memories of him and that last image of the two of them naked. She kept the TV on all the time, hoping it would be a distraction. Studying was impossible. Her mind refused to comprehend the text and constantly returned to thoughts of either the horrific betrayal or panic over how to face the future.

The day after the accident, the insurance adjuster called and told her that her car was a total loss. She would have to find a way to replace it, which would be impossible without help.

I've got to tell Mom and Dad.

She asked Delia for Monday off and drove to Jacksonville immediately after closing on Sunday evening. She arrived at her parents' home shortly before eight o'clock.

"Honey, what are you doing here? Are you okay?" Laura asked

15

as Ansley walked in, suitcase in hand. Mike was sitting in his recliner, reading a mystery novel, which he closed at the sight of his daughter.

"The marriage is over." It was all she could say for several minutes. She hadn't cried since Friday, but speaking the words brought forth a torrent of tears.

Laura's face was a mixture of shock and bewilderment as she shepherded her daughter to the couch. The faint smell of Sunday's fried chicken lingered in the room. Mike remained silent.

Once she regained her composure, Ansley described the discovery of Mark and Beverly to her parents. Mike's face turned red with anger.

"The bastard," he said, his teeth clenched. "He ought to be castrated."

Sitting next to Ansley, Laura put her arms around her daughter, held her tight for several minutes, and then said, "I'll go back with you tomorrow, and we'll pack up your apartment. You'll come back here."

"No. I've thought it through, Mom," Ansley said, wiping tears away. "I can't leave my job, school, or the lease on the apartment. I've talked to the manager, and she will let me move to a vacant unit on the other side of the complex."

"Honey, you can't stay down there by yourself. You need to come home."

"I've got to stay there for a few months at least. It's going to be tight, but I think I can make it."

Laura paused for a few seconds, shaking her head. "If you're determined, Dad and I will help." Mike nodded.

"I don't want to take any money from you, but I may have to until I can get a student loan. I've got to get a degree so that I can support myself, and my car was totaled." She began crying again.

"Don't you worry about the car, honey. I'll help you with that tomorrow," Mike said with a serious look on his face.

"You're going to be fine. Give it some time, sweetheart, and you'll find someone else—someone worthy of you. Forget about that jerk," Laura said, rubbing Ansley's back.

"Never," Ansley responded—her green eyes flashing. "I'll never depend on a man again."

"You're hurt now. You'll change your mind."

Ansley shook her head. "No, I won't."

*****

Other than her parents and the apartment manager, Ansley told only her friend Elaine about the breakup of her marriage. Either her colleagues at the shop had failed to notice the absence of the wedding ring, or they were too discreet to pry. She had no friends at the college, having been too busy with Mark, work, and studies to socialize."

"I can't believe he did that to you. I feel horrible," Elaine said when Ansley called her. "I feel like it's my fault. If we hadn't introduced you to Mark, you would be a star in New York." Elaine's husband, Greg Davis, had finished his MBA the year before and was working for a bank in Jacksonville. They were expecting their second child.

"Don't be silly. He didn't come with a warranty. As much as I would love to blame someone, it's my fault. I let my silly ego and chemistry trump rationality. I've got no one to blame but me."

"I still feel partially responsible. When are you coming to Jacksonville? Let me treat you to lunch and a movie."

A cinema day had been a tradition with the two women since their early teens. They had managed to sustain a close relationship even though Ansley's life in ballet had taken her to New York before high school graduation. She had finished her secondary education at the Professional Children's School after being accepted into the National Ballet at sixteen. During the three years she lived in New York and toured all over the United States and Europe, she and Elaine stayed in contact. They always got together when Ansley was home on holiday.

It took six weeks before she told Dennis Devlin, her former partner in the ballet company. Ansley and Dennis had stayed friends after she left the company. She couldn't bring herself to make the call. She knew what he would say. He had been as upset as Jean-Claude when she resigned from the company. He never liked Mark. The feeling was mutual. Despite the fact that Dennis was gay, Mark had been jealous of Ansley's continued friendship with the dancer. When her phone rang shortly after nine on a Sunday night in December, she was in bed, nearly asleep.

"Merry Christmas, pretty lady."

It took Ansley a second to become oriented enough to recognize his voice. "Dennis! How are you? Why aren't you dancing? It's *Nutcracker* season."

"It's Sunday, silly goose. We don't do a Sunday *evening* show, just a matinee."

"Right. So... are you the Cavalier this season?" she asked.

"Hell, no, sugar. But, I'm dancing the friggin' you-know-what out of 'Russian'."

Ansley smiled. "I'll bet you are. It's so good to hear your voice."

"And how are you? Is that handsome hunk you married lurking? I didn't interrupt anything, did I?"

Ansley paused. For a moment, she considered not telling him, but decided that his support was more important than her pride. "He's not around anymore."

"Whoa…. Does that mean what I hope it means?"

The smile faded as she said, "Yeah…. It does. Please don't say you told me so and don't ask me to tell you more than busty redhead with a jiggle in her walk."

"Ugh! You know I want to, but I won't. All I can say is dig those satin torture boots out of your closet and get your butt back up here."

"You know that's impossible." Her smiled returned at the ludicrous thought of dancing again.

"My dear…nothing's impossible. Jean-Claude loved you. We all loved you. A couple of weeks of class, and presto, you can whip yourself back into shape."

"Dennis, get real. Three years out? No way. That little sailboat went down the stream. Besides, if Jean-Claude loved me so much, how come I never got anything better than a corps contract? You got a promotion the year I left."

"You would have, darling, you would. You were dancing demi-solos. You would've gotten the contract, especially if you gave a certain favor to our lord and master like a certain Latin lady in the company. But, even if you didn't, you would have made it, love. You just needed to be patient. You haven't gone all fat on me have you?"

"By ballet standards? You bet I have. I probably weigh one-o-five. But, you know that's not the point. A year of classes wouldn't get me close to the level of going on a stage again. That career is dead and cremated. I'm concentrating on my education now so I can have a future. I had my chance in your world and blew it. Now, it's on to a regular day job."

"I don't agree, but I have to accept your decision. Just know that I'm here for you, sweetie, whatever. And if you change your mind, I'll tell JC that if he doesn't hire you back, I'll quit and go to City Ballet."

Ansley laughed.

After talking about holiday plans and company gossip, they said their goodbyes. Ansley placed the receiver in its cradle and blinked away a tear.

PART II

CHAPTER FOUR

October 2001

"Mark and the hussy are in town," Elaine said, as she pierced the crème brulée at the Cozy Corner tearoom with her spoon. "Greg and I had dinner with them Wednesday night at Ruth's Chris. You don't know how hard it is for me to be civil."

Ansley took a few seconds before responding. "You'd think that after five years I'd get over it, but the thought of them still makes my stomach turn."

"Well, you can take pleasure in the fact that she's fat. She eats like a pig and her slacks look like she's packing two watermelons. Mark doesn't look so happy," Elaine said, giving Ansley a you-know-what-I-mean look. "I want to throw up when I think of what they put you through. I know she's uncomfortable around me, but she had the gall to ask me how you are doing. I *loved* telling her how successful you are in your law practice, especially after she dropped out. I wanted to say, 'stick *that* you-know-where, tramp'."

"I don't know how successful I am, but at least I graduated. Did I tell you that I met a lawyer at the courthouse who was in her class at UF?"

"I don't think so. Did he or she know the home-wrecker?" Elaine's eyes opened wide in anticipation of gossip.

"He did. He laughed when I told him that she was my wife-in-law. He said that she flunked out because she got caught cheating."

"That doesn't surprise me," Elaine said, grinning. "You either have integrity, or you don't."

Ansley smiled. "Let's change the subject. We don't get much fun-time anymore, and I don't want to waste it on past misery. You said on the phone that you have some news for me. I hope it wasn't *just* about that dinner."

Elaine put her spoon down and picked up her napkin to blot her mouth before speaking. Taking a deep breath, she looked up with a sheepish smirk and said, "I'm pregnant."

"Oh my gosh! That's great...isn't it?" Ansley asked, with an apprehensive expression on her face. "I know you said you were done with diapers after Keri."

"Right. Three was my limit. I finally had the last one in preschool and life was good."

"So...what happened?"

"All I can say is the attack on the World Trade Center had such an impact on me. It was so horrible, and I felt so...I don't know how to describe it...emotionally raw and clinging to Greg. I just didn't think about missing birth control pills."

"How does Greg feel?" Although Ansley had resolved to never re-marry, hearing that her friend was expecting again sent a pang of envy, but she refused to dwell on it.

"You know Greg. He's so laid back. He says it'll all work out. I kind of hate it when he has that attitude. I want him to worry more, like I do," Elaine said as she scraped the last of the custard from the bowl. "But—what about you?" What's going on? You wanted to tell me something. Don't tell me you've finally found a guy you like?"

"No. Absolutely not. It's just that I think I'm going to New York around Thanksgiving," Ansley said, tipping her chin down with a mischievous expression on her face.

"Wow! What do you mean *you think?*"

"Dennis has invited me up for his debut of the principal role in *Carmen*. I don't know why I said *think*. I've got my plane ticket."

"Aren't you a little nervous about New York after the terrorism?"

"A little, but I'm more nervous about going back and seeing all the people I knew in the company. I don't have any idea how I will feel watching them dance and remembering my days on that stage." Ansley folded her napkin and put it on the table. "But I've got to go. Dennis wants me there. He paid for my ticket and has a house seat for me. I'm staying at his apartment. How could I let him down? You know how supportive he's been for me."

Elaine was quiet for a minute or two. Breaking out in a wide grin, she said, "I know what we should do. You need a killer dress. Nothing boosts a woman's confidence more than knowing she looks great. Let's blow off the movie and head to the mall or, even better yet, to that shop in Gainesville where you used to work."

Ansley frowned. "Elaine, I shouldn't."

"Cut it out. Of course you should. What have you done for the past five years other than work yourself silly?" Picking up her purse, Elaine motioned to Ansley and said, "Let's go buy the most extravagant dress at the Queen's whatever it was called. You're going to make your New York entrance like the *queen* of fashion—who just happens to be an attorney."

When they arrived at the shop, Ansley felt self-conscious.

"I can't believe I let you talk me into coming here."

Delia was on the floor and spotted Ansley instantly. "Ansley, Ansley. How are you?"

"She's great, and she needs a knock-'em-off-their-feet dress," Elaine said.

Ansley shook her head. "This is my closest friend, Elaine Davis— meet Delia Stewart."

"Very nice to meet you," Delia said.

"I can't afford anything here," Ansley said. "I don't know why I let Elaine talk me into coming, but it's great to see you and the shop again."

Delia smiled. "Don't be so sure. I think I've got some nice mark-downs, and you are eligible for the former-employee discount."

"It can't hurt to look, Ansley."

"Make yourself at home. I'll be right back." Delia then disappeared to the stockroom.

"This is insane," Ansley said, picking up the tag on a dress and pointing it out to Elaine.

"Maybe, maybe not. Delia looked like she might have an idea."

Within a couple of minutes, Delia returned, carrying several choices. Elaine reached for an emerald-green, silk cocktail dress.

"Ansley, wait, this is it. I don't even need to see it on you. This one is perfect."

The draped fabric of the sleeveless bodice crossed in a wrap design to form the V-neckline; the skirt was gathered on the left hip, carrying through the wrap effect. Skirt and lining were slit to the thigh.

"How much is it?" Ansley asked, pulling one side of the skirt out to reveal the opening.

"Don't ask. Just try it on," Elaine said. Delia nodded.

"Elaine…I have to ask."

"Just try it on," Delia said, thrusting it forward.

Picking up the tag, Ansley grimaced. "This is pointless. I can't pay that much for a dress. It's more than I spend on clothes in a year."

Taking her by the shoulders, Elaine began pushing her toward the dressing rooms.

"Okay, okay. I'll try it on. But it's a waste of time."

As she slipped into the dress, Ansley could feel the quality. The silk flowed gracefully with each movement. Her heart began to race. *This is crazy. I can't spend eleven hundred dollars on a dress.*

When she walked out onto the floor, Elaine gasped. "You've got to have it. You're drop-dead gorgeous. Sell your soul, sell drugs, but you've got to buy that dress."

"Perfection," Delia added.

"You know that you're a bad influence, don't you? Does Greg know this side of you?" Ansley said, looking at Elaine.

Delia smiled. "Ignore that tag. I can make it work for you."

Once back in her St. Augustine condo, Ansley immediately removed the plastic cover from the dress and hung it on the closet door in her bedroom. Caressing the fabric as she had done so many times when working at the shop, she removed the price tag and tucked it inside the nearby dresser drawer. Delia had reduced the price to less than wholesale, but with tax, it was still over five-hundred dollars. *I'll be eating hotdogs for six months, but Elaine was right. I could conquer Rome in this dress.*

CHAPTER FIVE

Ansley's plane landed at LaGuardia shortly before noon on the Monday before Thanksgiving. Passengers began unbuckling belts and standing before the captain turned off the seatbelt light. Watching others scramble to exit the aircraft, Ansley remained motionless, waiting to take her cue from her seatmate who occupied the aisle seat. When he rose, he motioned her out. Although in no hurry, she accepted the invitation. Opening the overhead compartment, the man took down his carry-on, and then turned toward her.

"Which bag is yours?" he asked. It was the first words he had spoken since takeoff in Atlanta, having been absorbed in spreadsheets and work-related materials.

She pointed to her small duffle bag, and he pulled it down for her as the muffled sound of a bell rang, signaling permission to release the seatbelts. *This is it—New York.*

Over eight years had passed since Ansley exited a plane in the city. So much had happened in the intervening time, but arriving somehow felt the same. Her stomach began to flutter; whether from fear or excitement, she wasn't sure. The feeling was reminiscent of her first venture to New York as a starry-eyed thirteen-year-old with a head filled with visions of Sugar Plums and Swan Queens. As her feet crossed the threshold to the terminal ramp, panic struck. *Why did I agree to this?* Looking around, she had a sudden urge to turn around and go back home. *I don't think I can watch what I might have been. Damn Mark.*

She wanted to cry, but fought the urge. Dennis had insisted on meeting her, and she didn't want him to see her depressed. Taking a deep breath and adjusting her shoulders, she told herself to remember that she was an attorney. She had made it through law school and the Bar Exam. *I may not be the dancer I set out to be, but I have an identity.*

Exiting the gate area, she spotted the eager face of Dennis among a blur of strangers. Wearing the familiar Devlin uniform—tight jeans and ivory, cable-knit turtleneck—he was the same Dennis that she met as an ambitious teen. The thick head of blond hair was still perfectly layered with a single lock that always fell down on his forehead and caused him to flick his head back in an attempt to toss it into place. Of course, he had the sleek, toned body of an athlete with the regal demeanor of a well-trained dancer. His glowing face had less of the New York pallor than she remembered—maybe it was spray tan. She had indulged in a salon session before leaving.

At over six feet tall, Dennis stood out in the crowd and could easily have passed for a Calvin Kline model if not for the splayed feet that betrayed years of ballet class. *He's still the quintessential Adonis,* she thought. Long, toned muscles defined the shape of his tight jeans. He had a body that members of either gender would lust after. *You're a loss to the female population, Dennis Devlin.* Never lacking for attention from his circle, he had never remained faithful to a partner with the exception of William Cabrerra, a relationship that ended badly.

"I don't do commitment," he said, anytime questioned about a breakup. One lover had the tagline painted on a plaque that Dennis told Ansley was on display in his living room. She would soon see.

The instant he spotted her, his arms opened and his face broke into huge grin. She felt the excitement soar, eradicating her qualms. She was back in New York with all its culture, entertainment, and filth. She felt almost like she was still a dancer. Her step quickened as she navigated the congested path, almost tripping over a woman's bag just as she reached Dennis.

He threw his arms around her and in his standard jovial tone said, "Still a clumsy dancer I see." He squeezed until she could barely breathe, the fragrance of his cologne wiping away the aroma of the terminal. It was so familiar, the same fragrance he wore when they spent so many hours sweating in the studios to perfect a piece of choreography. Clinging unabashedly, like long separated lovers, they were oblivious to the bystanders rushing by on either side of the corridor.

"I am so glad you're here, scissor girl. New York needs a ray of Florida sunshine. My tan is growing deeper from just the sight of you."

"I'm so glad to see you too." Her anxiety instantly evaporated. "Thank you for making it possible and for convincing me to come."

Dennis took her duffle bag and linked his other arm with hers. Arm in arm, they proceeded to the conveyer belt to collect her larger bag. Ansley wanted to catch the bus into Manhattan, but Dennis insisted they take a cab back. "We don't need a cab. I still know how to ride a bus," she insisted. But he was adamant.

"My dear, I'm a principal now. We stars do not take the bus." His eyes twinkled.

"Excuse me, please. I forget who I am associating with." They both laughed.

On the ride to his Westside apartment, they talked nonstop, first about her new job, then about his most recent failed relationship, and finally he filled her in on the latest gossip about company members she knew. At the apartment, Dennis made sandwiches while she unpacked. After eating, they walked across to Central Park where Ansley soaked in the city. When they returned, Dennis suggested they each take a power nap to prepare for the long evening ahead. Ansley doubted that she could lose consciousness, but she was tired from the trip. To her surprise, despite the sounds of the city coming through the open window, she fell sound asleep on Dennis's bed. He napped on the couch.

Waking first, Dennis was practicing his Yoga when Ansley woke. She decided to grab her shower. When she finished, he showered while she did her makeup and touched up her dress with his steam iron. Being with Dennis and settling into the apartment, she was glad she came despite the knots in her stomach over how much she charged on her credit card for a garment that she would never wear again. Having the killer dress was like a shot of adrenaline to her self-esteem.

Although there was no need for Ansley to leave for the theater with Dennis, he insisted that she dress for the evening so that he could pass judgment. By the time he came out of the shower, she was ready, with hair and make-up complete.

"So, do I pass?" she asked, twirling around so that the dress flared out, exposing her long, slim legs. The green of the garment intensified the green of her eyes. Her hair was pulled softly back and put up in a twist. Gold earrings dangled from her ears.

"Sweetie, you are going to rock this city tonight," he said. "If I were a straight man . . ."

"Hush. You're just trying to boost my confidence."

"Not so...not so. You look sensational."

"I know it's a while before curtain, but if it's okay with you, I'll just tag along. I can always kill time at O'Neal's. It's still there isn't it?"

"Of course. Just don't get drunk and forget to walk across the street in time to see my spectacular *saut de chau*."

"Wouldn't miss it for the world, although I'm going to be greener than this dress that it's Elena and not me dancing the lead in *Carmen*. But then, I might have still been in the corps, watching the two of you."

Dennis frowned at her and cocked one eyebrow in an expression of reprimand. "Hush that. On your worst day, you were better than she can ever be."

"She's a principal."

"You would have been."

CHAPTER SIX

When the cab let them out at Lincoln Center, Ansley walked over to the restaurant, memories flooding her head: lunch with her mother before attending a matinee, a bowl of soup with colleagues after class, a guilty splurge on a dessert following a performance. She ordered a bowl of soup but consumed very little. With a blink of her eye, years vanished and she was back in her youth, feeling the highs of a good show or a coveted role.

Pushing the remains of the lentil soup aside, she drank her cup of tea and shook off the reverie before leaving for Metropolitan Opera House. The crowd was beginning to arrive.

After checking her coat, Ansley bought a program and went up the stairs to the Dress Circle level. An usher led her to a private box. It was the closest one to stage left and held only four velvet chairs. Ansley's assigned seat was farthest from the stage. When she entered, there was a single occupant. An obviously tall man with dark, beautifully feathered hair sat closest to the stage. His swarthy face was cleanshaven with medium-length sideburns. He wore a superbly tailored black suit with a burgundy tie. Traces of his fragrance hung in the air. She didn't recognize the scent but found it appealing, emanating an aroma reminiscent of Europe that suggested it was expensive. He was absorbed in reading his program and did not look up when she sat down.

As she settled in her seat, her purse slid off the program in her lap. The man looked up and immediately moved to pick it up for her.

Embarrassed at the distraction, as he handed it to her, she said, "I'm sorry, but thank you."

"My pleasure." Standing, he said, "Here, take this seat. It has a better sightline."

"I couldn't take your seat. This is fine." She noted both the British accent and his use of theatrical vernacular. He made her feel uneasy but

29

in a pleasant way.

"I insist. I'm afraid that I am wasting two of the seats. My family was unable to arrive in time for the performance. Please, allow me to make this small gesture," he said, moving toward her to exchange places.

"I'm sorry your family is missing the show, but I can't take your seat."

"I can sit in any of the three remaining."

She could see that he was sincere and insistent, so she stood up and moved to the end. The man took the third seat, leaving one empty between them, but he was still close enough to cause Ansley to feel self-conscious. She mentally rebuffed herself and plunged her attention into her program.

Completing a review of the souvenir booklet, Ansley slid it under her purse. Without her attention on the glossy images, she felt uneasy, as though someone were staring at her. Turning her head, she met his gaze. He did not dodge, rather, he smiled, his right eyebrow rising slightly, as if to say, "You caught me, but that's all right."

"Are you a New Yorker?" he asked.

Paradoxically, he made her comfortable and nervous at the same time. "No. I'm from Florida. I'm here just for this performance." As she spoke, she mentally questioned the wisdom of engaging in conversation with a stranger, but reasoned that he was probably safe, given that he possessed three house seats to the ballet.

"All the way from Florida. That's quite a distance. Do you come often?"

"No. This is special. One of the principals is a friend."

"Really? I'm impressed," he said, far more comfortable with the conversation than Ansley.

Why he would be impressed with a girl from the provinces?

The more she observed him, the more she realized that he exuded wealth and polish, which led her to conclude that he must have important connections to the company. Although there was no mistaking the quality of his suit, Ansley decided that with his suave good looks and self-assured demeanor, the man would look good in clothes from Goodwill. He wore no rings, but she had caught a glimpse of his watch when he handed her the purse. It was sleek in design—solid gold with a black face. It resembled those she had seen in ads for Bvlgaria and Cartier. *He must be either a friend of Jean-Claude, a major benefactor to the company, or a sugar daddy to one of the dancers—maybe even Elena.* Trying to avoid eye contact, lest he read her thoughts, she decided that it was unlikely that he dated a member of the cast since he had expected to share the evening with two family members—probably one was his wife.

As she worked through her analysis of the stranger, he asked, "Your friend, Carmen or Don Jose?"

"Don Jose, Dennis Devlin," she said, surprised that he knew the name of the primary male character. He must be an aficionado of ballet or opera—or maybe not. He *had* been studying the program when she arrived.

"Is your friend a very close friend?" There was a subtle undertone to the question.

"You mean boyfriend? No, not at all. We are just good friends. Dennis dates men." *Why did I say that?*

He smiled. "So tell me about Florida."

Ansley paused before responding. There's was something familiar in the way he sounded. His accent was aristocratic British, and his voice had a powerful, but pleasant, timbre. She tried to place where she had heard it before. *Maybe he just sounds like someone I've heard on TV. Or . . . could he be a celebrity?*

"There's not really much to tell. We have a lot of water, plenty of warm weather, too much traffic, and too little ballet—at least where I live. Floridians focus on sports more than arts."

"And you like the ballet a lot?"

"I do. It's one of the primary things I love about New York—ballet and theater." She was becoming more and more certain that this was someone well known.

"Where in Florida do you live?"

"I'm from Jacksonville and work there, but I live near St. Augustine. Where are you from? I detect an accent."

He smiled, nodded, and said, "Pretty obvious, isn't it? I'm from the UK."

"London?"

"A bit north of London."

"What brings you to New York?"

"I have work here. The concert is a little gift to myself."

Nicholas Colton! An image flashed in Ansley's mind. *He looks like the actor, Nicholas Colton.* The thought was incredulous. Colton had been on the front cover of a recent issue of *People*—the issue naming the sexiest men of the year. Although she had not seen many films recently, she knew that Nicholas Colton was a top box-office draw. Elaine was mesmerized by him. *Am I talking to Nicholas Colton? God, what piercing eyes he has! Are they dark blue or brown?* The stranger's eyes were almond shaped and set deep with a twinkle that suggested a bit of a devilish persona.

As she became more and more convinced that she was sharing a box with a major celebrity, she thought about the reaction that both Dennis and Elaine would have if they knew. She wanted to call Elaine and say, "Guess who I'm sitting next to right now?" But was it? Not wanting to appear like a moonstruck teenager, she was afraid to ask for confirmation of his identity. But when she could stand the mystery no more, she said, "You're not–?"

Tipping his head to one side, he smiled, and interrupting her said, "Nick Colton. And who might you be?" He was smooth—confident but not arrogant.

A mixture of awe and intimidation caused her to pause. "Ansley Sheridan."

"Ansley…. That's a lovely name. I don't believe I know another Ansley." The English accent and reserve were thick.

"My mother…she tried to give me a unique name. I'm named after an area of Atlanta where she grew up."

"Well, tell me, what does Ansley Sheridan do in Florida?"

Still disconcerted by his presence, she hesitated, feeling awkward. "I'm a lawyer."

"You can't be a lawyer. You're far too pretty."

Was he flirting? Was the international movie star Nicholas Colton actually flirting with her? She decided it was boilerplate flattery, designed to make plebeian hearts flutter. *He probably thrives on gushing fans. Well, not this girl. I will accept the compliment with grace as though it were sincere.*

"You're very kind, but lawyers are no longer cookie-cutter barristers in navy-blue suits and tasseled loafers." She managed to keep her voice cool, yet polite, moving into her keep-the-guy-at-a-distance mode.

There was no time for further conversation. The house lights dimmed. A spotlight illuminated the conductor as he lifted his baton, signaling the beginning of the overture. Much as she hated to admit it, Ansley felt herself tingling with the exhilaration of sharing the box with a celebrity. Combined with the anticipation of seeing the company again, sitting so close to the man caused her heart to race. However, once the ballet began, she forgot that Nick Colton sat next to her as she watched her old corps role being performed by a young dancer.

When Elena Garrison made her entrance in the title role, Ansley was impressed, albeit nipped by the envy bug.

Elena had joined the company the same season Ansley was accepted, and they often competed for the same parts. Being of the same age, physical conformation and with similar technical ability, they differed primarily in coloring and artistry. Elena was dark-haired with olive complexion and powerful presentation, while Ansley was blond and fair with an ethereal quality that allowed her to move across the stage like a whisper. The aggressive brunette consistently won the better corps positions and minor roles during their maiden season. Watching Elena now, Dennis' prediction so long ago that Ansley would one day dance the title role stung at her heart. *But for my poor judgment, that could very well be me down there*, she thought. A tear struggled to break through, but she swallowed hard and overcame the impulse.

When the familiar "Habanera" music began, Dennis took charge of the sensual dance with grand aplomb. His interpretation of the character was vivid, presenting Don Jose as richly seductive. *He's grown into the league of Baryshnikov, Nureyev, and Villella. I'm so happy for him.* Over the years, Dennis had sent her videos of some of his performances, but this was the first time she had seen him perform live since leaving the company. Ansley had forgotten how sensual *Carmen* was, and Dennis was dancing full out, infusing Don Jose with vitality and virility. Watching him, a woman could forget he was gay.

Suddenly, she was overcome by a feeling that Nick Colton was staring at her. *Oh my gosh. Here I am with one of the world's sexiest men, watching an erotic ballet.* She felt herself tingle with a sudden thought of sex with Nick Colton, imagining what it would be like to be held by him, enveloped by his enticing fragrance, caressed by his strong hands. She blushed. Mercifully, the darkness of the theater camouflaged her reaction.

Five curtain calls after the end of the one-act ballet, the house lights finally came up. There would be a twenty-minute intermission before the program resumed. Ansley was immediately faced with a choice of remaining in her seat, as she would have expected, or meandering through the lobby of ballet aficionados alone—not an appealing idea. However, it was preferable to the awkwardness she anticipated if Colton remained in his seat. As she rose and started to pass him, he spoke.

"Can I entice you to spend the intermission with me? I expect refreshments to arrive shortly."

Caught off guard, her eyes widened as she searched for a response. "Here?"

He smiled. "It's not the best of ideas for me to mingle among the crowd right now."

How stupid of me. Of course. He could be mobbed, even though the ballet audience is not the same as a rock concert crowd, there are likely a lot of young ballet students here that have crushes on him.

"I don't want to impose on you," she said.

"It would be my pleasure. Otherwise, I will sit here alone, bored."

As he finished speaking, a light tap came at the door to the box. "Come in," Nick said. A sharply uniformed usher opened the door, carrying a tray of hors d' oeuvres and a bottle of Louis Roederer Cristal. There was only one champagne flute. Nick immediately said, "Bring us another wineglass, please."

Looking over the tray, Ansley identified small bowls of smoked salmon, pate, and a substance resembling black berries, which she surmised was caviar. While certainly an upscale collection, nothing she saw appealed to her. On the end of tray, to her relief, she spotted a spread of prawns, cheese, and strawberries. *He may have comp tickets to this concert, but his refreshments cost more than my dress.*

Nick poured a glass of the champagne and handed it to her. Ansley fought to keep her hand steady. *Don't make a fool of yourself.* She waited to drink until the usher returned with another glass. Sipping slowly from the thin crystal, she wondered what Elaine would think.

Unaccustomed to drinking, Ansley was terrified of consuming too much, but it went down so smoothly that she drank the portion more quickly than she expected. Although Nick insisted upon refilling her glass, she adamantly refused to drink more.

"Were you pleased with the performance?" he asked, refilling his glass.

"I can't be totally objective, but I thought Dennis was magnificent. And of course, I love this ballet, choreography and score."

"So, you've seen it before?"

"I have. I was lucky enough to see Baryshnikov dance Don Jose when I was a child." She debated mentioning that she was a former dancer, but decided against it.

"Baryshnikov was a brilliant dancer," he said. "I enjoyed seeing him perform several times in London."

"Absolutely," she said, nodding her head in agreement, impressed by his ballet knowledge. Ansley was not used to the men in her life knowing anything about her art form, not even her father. Mark made fun of dance, saying that only ten percent of the population liked it—spinsters and gay men. According to Mark, normal people liked football, wrestling, and NASCAR.

"Do you have a business card?" Nick asked.

"I do, but why?" She instantly hated herself for the comment.

"You can never tell. I might be in Florida and get arrested. It would help to know a good lawyer."

He's patronizing me. Although it was against her better judgment, she took out her wallet and gave him a card.

Looking at the card, he said, "Ansley Collier Sheridan. Now, what if I get in trouble in Florida after business hours, how would I reach Ms. Sheridan?"

Okay. This is over the top. Does he think I'm buying this line? He is playing with me.

"Is that a not-so-subtle way of asking me for my home number?"

He smiled. "I guess you caught me." One eyebrow rose ever so slightly.

"It wouldn't do you much good unless you were arrested for committing marriage under the influence. I'm a divorce lawyer."

"I take it that you would prefer to not release your home number?"

What on earth could it hurt to give him my home number? He's certainly never going to use it. He's just a horny celebrity, with a missing wife, looking for a playmate for the night—and that's not going to be me.

Watching Nick as he spread caviar on a toast round, Ansley thought she was going to refuse either to give him her number, or in the alternative, give him a fake one. But instead, she found herself taking the card and writing her number on the back. *I've lost my mind. It must be the champagne, this dress, and being in New York.*

As he looked at the card, he said, "You have lovely handwriting." He then slipped it into the breast pocket of his coat.

Watching his every move, Ansley wished she had seen his latest film. It would give her something to say. She and Elaine had seen a couple of his movies, but her mind was blank. She did remember that he was attractive in the films they had seen, but he was far more so in person. His swarthy features combined with his aristocratic demeanor and British accent to form a sexually appealing man. While his poise and speech denoted discipline and class, a streak of the wild emanated from his deep-set amber eyes that captured and held the target upon contact.

Breaking the silence, Nick asked, "Would you join me for a late dinner after the performance? I would like to learn more about Florida."

There it was. Nicholas Colton was asking her out. *Keep your cool, Ansley. Don't be stupid. He probably has room service at his hotel in mind.* As much as the idea of being a one-night bimbo repelled her, there was something so magnetic about the man that if not for Dennis, she might have accepted. After all, what could it hurt? She would be back in Florida in two days with no one the wiser—kind of a "what happens in the city, stays in the city."

Taking a deep breath, she smiled and said, "I'm sorry, that's very tempting, but I have plans to celebrate Dennis' debut with the cast after the show."

Nick frowned. "I am disappointed. I was hoping to get to know you. I don't run into pretty lawyers that often."

As he finished the sentence, the usher arrived to remove the tray. There was still a decent amount of champagne in the bottle. Ansley wondered how much the wasted wine cost.

As the door closed behind the usher, Ansley looked at Nick and asked, "What happened to your family tonight?" *Why did I ask that? It's none of my business.*

He wrinkled his brow slightly and said, "My son and my nephew were coming to spend a few weeks with me. Unfortunately, the travel didn't go as planned. Kevin caught a bug and had to delay departure. They won't arrive from the UK until Friday."

It wasn't a wife. Ansley chided herself for being relieved that his date was to have been his son. *What kind of trip am I on? Am I thinking I could actually date this guy? If he has a son, there's a wife somewhere.* "I'm sorry your son is ill. How old is he?"

"Twelve, but thinking he's twenty-five—like most of his generation. I regret to say that I've been able to spend very little time with him."

"Because of your career?"

"Career and divorce. Kevin lives with his mother."

"I'm sorry," Ansley said, looking sympathetic but liking what she heard. "I know divorce is especially difficult with children."

"No need for sympathy. It was mutually agreed upon. Any discord has long since evaporated, but I'm sure that you see your share of conflict in your profession."

"I'm only in my first year, but you're right," she said, nodding. "I've seen a lot of bitterness."

Nick tipped his head, his elbow resting on the arm of the seat and his index finger resting across his mouth. He appeared to be taking an inventory of Ansley as his eyes lingered on her face. "You're quite extraordinary."

She blushed and hoped the lighting did not give her away.

"How long will you be in New York?" he asked.

Mesmerized by his gaze, she paused before answering. "I fly home Wednesday night—in time to have Thanksgiving dinner with my parents."

"Splendid!" he said as though he had discovered a vein of gold. "Perhaps your friend could spare you for a while tomorrow evening?"

He was asking her out. It was really happening. Despite being attractive, Ansley was unaccustomed to attention from men. It was as though she was encased by an invisible and inviolate barrier. One or two brazen young men in law school had been shot down quickly when they approached, as had opposing counsel in one of her recent cases. Not only was she not interested in the lawyer, she was angered by the fact that he was married with children. However, finding herself in the unique position of being hit on by a celebrity, and not just any celebrity, but a sexy, A-list star, she felt her defenses crumbling.

The lights blinked, indicating intermission was nearly over. She needed to answer, but wasn't sure her mouth could form the words to either accept or decline. Her mind raced with possibilities. If she accepted, would he expect her to go to bed? If so, would she? If she turned him down, she might regret it the rest of her life. Every inch of her body wanted to accept; every bit of her wisdom and experience demanded that she decline. Her excuse was ready-made. It would be rude to leave Dennis. He wasn't scheduled to perform on Tuesday. Although they had not made plans, he expected to spend the time with her. *Dennis is an opportunist. He will understand if I go out with Nick Colton.* While Ansley deliberated, she felt as though Nick was inside her head, reading her thoughts.

"I have theater tickets. Don't force me to go alone. You did mention that you enjoy theater," he said, smiling. "I promise you—I'm not dangerous."

Right, said the spider to the fly. She had to answer. The pregnant pause was growing awkward. Just as the theater went dark, she said, barely above a whisper, "I think that Dennis would understand—as long as I don't stay out too late." *Theater and maybe dinner. Nothing more.*

He nodded with a smug smile that was invisible in the darkened theater. The orchestra struck the first notes of the overture.

Hardly two measures into the score, the audience thundered approval of the John Philip Sousa music, many rising to applaud the patriotic theme of Balanchine's *Stars and Stripes* ballet. The reaction was so great that the entrance of the dancers was delayed. Following the lead of the majority, Nick rose as well, clapping his hands in the air above his head in a gesture of salute.

Ansley clapped, but remained seated. As he lowered himself back into his seat, she said, "You're not even an American." But the noise of the audience drowned out her words.

When the five-act ballet ended with the backdrop of Old Glory, the standing ovation was deafening. The appreciative audience demanded more. In a rare event, the company performed an encore of the "Fifth Campaign" after which the curtain dropped, and the house lights came up without a bow taken. As Nick turned toward her, Ansley said, "I was impressed with your show of support for our country."

"I would expect no less of you had the company performed *Union Jack*."

She smiled and nodded, thinking how well he knew ballet. Nick made no move to rise, but feeling awkward once again, Ansley gathered her purse and program and said, "Would you like to go backstage with me?"

Standing, he said, "I would like that very much, but this is your friend's night. I would not want to draw attention from that."

Taking a moment to comprehend the meaning of his statement, she said, "I understand."

"I'll send the car to pick you up at seven-thirty tomorrow evening. Curtain is at eight. I hope you won't be disappointed in the play, it's an off-Broadway production of one of Noel Coward's lesser-known plays, *Nude with Violin*. I'll try to make up for any deficits in the play by dinner and a good wine afterward if you will allow me."

"I'm sure that the play will be excellent since you must know your way around the theater." She had finally remembered something about him. He had begun his career as a classical stage actor.

He chuckled. "I don't know how well I know my way around, but it is my first love. However, I must confess, this is a work assignment. It seems that my director believes that the young actress playing the barmaid might be a good match for a role in my next film. I'm to check her out."

As she started to walk out of the box, Nick said, "I'll need your address, Ms. Sheridan."

A big smile crossed her face. "I guess you will." Taking a slip of paper from a small leather notepad in her purse, she wrote down the

East 82nd Street address and Dennis's phone number and then handed it to Nick.

A few minutes later as she walked to the stage-door entrance, the thought struck Ansley that she had only the one dress in New York. There was no money to buy another, and the chance of finding a suitable garment in time was slim if she could afford it. *What was I thinking? I can't go out with him. That settles it. I'll cancel—tell him Dennis was upset. But how? I don't have a way to reach him.*

CHAPTER SEVEN

Ansley's apprehension about attending the cast party turned out to be misplaced. Because the ballet world is highly competitive, with a major degree of snobbery, she had feared entering her former domain. However, arriving backstage, the smell of rosin and sweat brought back the exhilaration of being a performer. To her relief, upon entering the inner sanctum, her tour roommate, Diana Barton, immediately embraced her.

"Ansley. Ansley Sheridan," Diana squealed, throwing her arms around Ansley, causing the dancer's headpiece to go askew. "I am so glad to see you. You're gorgeous."

Diana was one of a rare breed of ballet dancers who lacked cutthroat ambition, which gave her the ability to develop friendships among the female dancers. A statuesque brunette, she had changed little. Only a few lines around her eyes gave away that she was at an age considered to be fatal in dance. At thirty-three, Diana was simply thankful to receive a contract each year, knowing that it would not be long before her career would move into training the novices.

"You haven't changed a bit. You're still beautiful and did a great job with your solo in *Carmen*," Ansley said, beaming at the sight of the one female friend she had in the company.

"Always the bridesmaid, never the bride, that's me, sweetie. But, I'm thankful to still be in the wedding."

"Don't give me that. You could have been a principal. You didn't want it. You always said that it was safer to do your job in the ranks and let the rest fight it out for the spotlight."

"Yeah. All that petty rivalry just wasn't for me. But no crap, hon, you look terrific. Law must agree with you. Dennis has kept me up with all your success."

"It's way too early to call it success. I've only been practicing eight

41

months."

Before the conversation could go further, Dennis intervened, grabbing Ansley and pulling her to the center of the crowd to announce her presence. Although she caught traces of the old competitiveness from Elena when they hugged, and was certain the now star of the company was sizing her up for weight-gain, it didn't dampened Ansley's pleasure in being in the midst of her former world.

The excitement of being part of the scene put Nick's invitation out of her mind until after the party and in the cab with Dennis, headed back to his apartment.

"You know you were spectacular tonight, don't you?" Ansley said as the taxi turned left onto Fifth Avenue at the corner of Central Park South.

"No way. My feet weren't working. I didn't achieve a single, decent *saut de chat*."

"Knock it off. Don't even try to play modest with me, or have any of that self-deprecating, tell-me-how-great-I-was, ballet attitude. You were magnificent, my friend. Admit it. I was on the edge of my seat." She balled up a fist and punched him gingerly on the shoulder. "Your characterization and artistry were exceeded only by your brilliant technique and phenomenal elevation."

"Very well. If you insist—I was sensational," he said with a smirk. "Let's hope the critiques agree and say it as eloquently."

"If they don't, they don't know what they're talking about. And who cares about them anyway?"

"Jean-Claude and the backers. You know how ignorant those tight-assed, wealthy widows are who give gobs of money to the company. All they know is what they read in the *Times*," he said, raising his nose in the air to indicate snobbery. "But—what about you, girl? You rocked the party in that so-gorgeous-it-should-be-illegal dress."

"I had a blast. It was like time had stood still," she said, taking his hand. "If I am being honest, I have to admit that I did have a few pangs when I wished I was dancing again, but it was okay. I just soaked up the ambiance."

"Your seat was good, wasn't it?" Dennis asked as the cab stopped in front of his building.

"Perfect. I'll tell you all about it when we get upstairs," Ansley said, with a smug smile exposed by the beam of a streetlight.

Catching the look, Dennis froze. "And just what does that mean, fair maiden?"

"I'll tell you upstairs."

Once in the apartment, Dennis immediately demanded information. "Give, girl, give. I know from your expression that *something* happened."

"Calm down. It's probably nothing, especially for you, living here all the time—but you'll never guess who was in the box with me."

"Prince William?"

His eyes grew wider in anticipation, as she said, "Maybe better—Nicholas Colton."

"No...not *the* Nicholas Colton," he said, his face lighting up with excitement. "The actor?"

Ansley nodded, smiling like the dog that ate his master's lunch. "Him—in the flesh. He asked me to have dinner after the performance."

Dennis shrieked, "Oh, my, God! You should have gone. Honey, you hit the lottery. He's royalty—pure gold. Why didn't you do it?"

"Don't be silly. I wouldn't have stood you up," she said, shaking her head.

"Sweetie, sweetie, that was a no-brainer. Never let an old fag stand in the way of the perfect lay. Not only is Colton a sexy stud, God knows, he has enough money after his last few films to finance a small country. You blew it, babe," he said, obviously agitated.

Ansley was quiet for a minute before she softly said, "He asked me out for tomorrow, too, or is it tonight?"

His face relaxed. "Oh, my God. What a relief."

"I'm not going."

Fanning his face with his hand, he looked at her, a scowl crossing his brow. "What...do...you mean, you're not going? That's not an option."

"Get real, Dennis. I can't, and even if I could, I wouldn't."

"Are you out of your frigging mind?" he said, staring at her. "I would kill to screw the guy. Tell me you didn't turn him down." He put his hands together in a mock prayer position.

"Dennis, I can't go. First of all, I have nothing to wear. You think I could go out with him in this dress? That would be real cool, now, wouldn't it?"

"Honey, I can take care of that."

"I don't know how, unless you've started cross-dressing. But that aside, I'm not interested in being the one-night stand of an ego-enhanced celebrity."

"Don't be a prude. Better to have a one-night stand with a hunk like Nicholas Colton, than to die knowing that you could have." He moved closer to her on the couch where they were sitting. "Let yourself go, pretty girl. You deserve it. You're not a virgin; you're certainly not getting any younger; and you're damned sure not going to have another opportunity like this one."

"Thanks for reminding me that I am getting old. But, I don't care what you say; I'm not going to be a nonprofit hooker."

"Trash that thought. You're a beautiful woman. He's a gorgeous man. A night out on the town, a great meal, and a lifetime to savor the memory—you've got nothing to lose. Think of what a great dinner you'll have."

"We had Cristal and caviar at intermission."

"See. Case closed. You're going. Tell me the invitation is still open."

"I told him I would…. But, Dennis. I can't."

"Yes, you can. Forget about the damn dress deal. I've got that covered."

Looking at him with a drop-the-subject expression, she rose and headed for the bedroom, saying over her shoulder in a singsong tone, "It's not happening."

CHAPTER EIGHT

Ansley awoke the next morning wondering where she was. The wine and her exhaustion had made for a hard sleep—the kind where one doesn't move, doesn't dream, and wakes up tired. Although the drapes were drawn, she could tell it was morning by the light seeping through. Attempting to orient herself, she looked around without moving her head. Spotting the green dress hanging on the closet door, it all came back. She was in New York.

Rolling over to stretch, she came nose to nose with a pair of copper eyes and flinched.

"Madeline. What are you doing here?" Ansley asked, drawing back.

The marmalade Persian stood her ground and glared with unmistakable disdain at the interloper in her master's bed.

"I guess you think that I don't belong here," Ansley said, smiling as she drew her right hand from beneath the covers and attempted to pet the cat. Madeline dodged. "I know. I'm not Dennis, but you don't have to be rude." The cat stood up, stretched, and jumped off the bed.

Tossing the covers aside and putting on her robe, Ansley got up and headed for the bathroom but stopped when she heard a voice coming from the living room. The door was ajar, presumably pushed open by Madeline. Dennis was talking on the phone.

"That's right, the navy-blue silk. Ansley would look divine in it. I'm sure the two of you are the same size—I've lifted you both enough to know, darling. She's a designer four or an off-the-rack six. And be sure to bring those heavenly red, suede, red-sole pumps. I'm not as sure about the shoe size, but they would be so perfect if they do fit. Ciao."

"Dennis, what are you doing?"

"Shopping, sweetie, shopping."

"Stop it. I told you, I'm not going out with him, and I'm certainly not wearing someone else's clothes. Who were you talking to anyway?"

He stood up, took her by the shoulders and ushered her to the sofa. "You stop and listen to your *fairy* godfather. You've met Prince Charming, and you are going to the ball. So get out your glass slippers in case the Louboutins don't fit."

"Fairy godfather?" Ansley said, raising one eyebrow.

"If the shoe fits," Dennis said, turning toward the kitchen. "Want coffee or tea?"

"Don't change the subject. Who is coming over here with a dress?"

"I have strawberry and blueberry yogurt and some fabulous granola. Or do you eat a real breakfast, now? I have eggs."

"Dennis, answer me. Who is coming over here and what have you told her?"

"Relax. I didn't say anything other than you met a fantastic guy who asked you out."

Frowning, Ansley said, "You didn't say who. Please tell me you didn't."

Smiling, he walked back over to her and took her hands. "I promise on pain of a cigarette burn on my best Armani that I did not disclose the name of your prince. So relax. You're going on a Queen for a Day venture. Enjoy every second of it."

"If I didn't love you, I would hate you right now. You know that don't you?" Smiling, she shook her head in frustration.

"You're going to love me even more when you wake up tomorrow morning—wherever you might wake up—with 'Man, I Feel Like a Woman' humming in your ear. Oh my God, how I envy you."

"I'm not sleeping with him," she said, jerking her hands away. "And, do you have any aspirin?"

"Two aspirin and a cup of tea coming up. You'd better get used to Earl Grey if you're hanging with a Brit."

*****

Later that morning, three of the company dancers brought dresses to the apartment for Ansley to try. She knew one of the ballerinas from her past, but the other two were new. Rena, the dancer Dennis had been talking to when Ansley woke, had worn the navy dress on the red carpet at the Golden Globe Awards. Between them, they brought five dresses for Ansley to consider; however, the navy silk was the definitive choice. It was a designer, slip-dress of layered chiffon—the kind of "barely there" style. At first, Ansley balked.

"It's just a little too provocative for me—like a piece of lingerie," she said. "I feel undressed, or like I want to be."

"Bullshit. It's exactly the right look for an exquisite evening in the city," Dennis said, throwing his arms out. "Try the shoes."

After the dancers left, Ansley and Dennis ate sandwiches and watched a Nick Colton DVD. While Dennis salivated over Nick, Ansley felt butterflies beginning to swarm in her belly. When the film ended, she excused herself to catch a nap before getting ready.

By seven, she had showered, shampooed, and dressed. Wearing the navy-silk and the red shoes, she emerged from the bedroom, ready for the date.

As she stepped into the living room, Dennis gasped and rose from the recliner where he had been reading. "Oh my God, you're breathtaking. I want to screw you, and I'm gay."

"You're also prejudiced," she said, turning around like a runway model.

"Those legs of yours go on forever," he said, looking her up and down. "And I love your hair sleeked back—so sophisticated," he said, gesturing by pushing his hair back with both hands.

"I'm not sure I can walk in these skyscraper stilettos."

"You danced on pointe for how many years, and you're complaining about a stiletto heel?"

"I'm still not sure I should be doing this. When did I say I would?" She sat on the sofa, arranging the short dress to cover as much leg as the fabric would allow.

"Do *not* go there again. You're going to have a great time, and I want to hear every *erotic* detail when you get back."

CHAPTER NINE

At seven-thirty, the doorman called to announce that Ansley's car was downstairs. As she left the apartment, Dennis gave her a hug.

"Carpe diem! Remember, every detail."

Alone in the back of the limo, Ansley felt self-conscious. Traffic was heavy, which caused the ride down to the East Village to take nearly thirty minutes. Upon arriving in front of the small theater, the driver stopped at the curb, got out, and opened the door for her.

"Mr. Colton is waiting for you inside. You are to give the woman at the ticket window your name, and she will relay the message."

She thanked the chauffeur and proceeded into the lobby. Nick emerged within seconds from a door marked "Private." Taking her coat, he leaned forward and kissed her on the cheek, sending a buzz through her body.

As they walked to their seats on the front row, they exchanged small talk. A man, who Nick introduced as the play's director, took the seat next to the actor and attempted to engage him in conversation at every opportunity. It was a relief to Ansley that she could avoid talking. She busied herself with reading the program.

When the curtain closed on the final act, Ansley's heart began pounding. The real date was about to begin—no more hiding behind the entertainment. When the house lights came up, Nick stood and extended his hand. She gathered her things and allowed him to guide her backstage. As members of the cast realized who was in the dressing rooms, they gathered around in awe. Nick complimented the performance and signed autographs for the young thespians. As Ansley stood quietly by, Nick spoke with the young actress he had come to observe but did not mention his film. Ansley wondered whether the ingénue had passed or failed her unknowing audition. When he finished the conversation, they left by the stage door where his car was waiting.

"How did you like the play?" he asked, once they were settled in the limo.

"Very much—and you?"

"It was a reasonable rendition of Coward," he said, fumbling with access to the minibar.

"Reasonable?"

"Americans don't quite get his sense of humor. But, all in all, I would say the director and cast did a respectable job with the script." Changing the subject and still struggling to open the minibar, he said, "You must be famished. I am."

"A little, but I don't think you're going to find food in there."

He laughed. "No, but I hope there's something to quench my thirst. I don't usually take one of these rolling examples of decadence, so I don't know the combination to the safe."

"I would have thought this would be your only method of transportation."

He shook his head. "Only when I'm trying to impress." He turned to face her. "I hope I've succeeded."

It was Ansley's turn to laugh. "That was an honest admission," she said as he finally managed to extract a bottle of Evian from the small cooler.

He nodded, a glint of tease in his eyes. "Back to the subject of food—I've chosen a quiet bistro that specializes in Indian cuisine. I hope that is satisfactory to you."

She smiled. "I like Indian food."

When they arrived at the restaurant, the chauffeur got out and opened the door for them. She started toward the entrance, but realizing Nick had paused to speak with the driver, she stopped. The drone of street sounds muffled his voice. As she watched, her mind flashed back to the afternoon video and the image of him in a nude scene. A twinge of sexual exhilaration coursed through her body. Ansley felt herself blush and hoped no one noticed. It wasn't something she wanted to explain.

The restaurant was almost empty. Only two tables were occupied. Ansley assumed that the late hour accounted for the lack of patronage.

Once seated, a waiter brought a bottle of Dom Perignon for Nick's approval. He checked the label and nodded. The waiter poured two glasses and left.

"How did he know what you wanted?" Ansley asked.

"I come here often when I'm in New York." He raised his glass to her. "Here's to a lovely evening with an even lovelier lady."

Not sure what to do, Ansley tipped her chin and said, "Thank you. That was kind of you to say." Her heart was still racing; she was fighting to maintain a cool façade.

After swallowing a large gulp of the champagne, Nick spoke. "Tell me about Ansley Sheridan."

She took a small sip of the wine and, holding the glass with both hands, said, "There's nothing to tell. I'm just an ordinary Florida girl who breaks up unhappy homes for a living. You're the one with an interesting life. You should tell me about yourself."

He shook his head. "There's little to tell that hasn't been printed in the media or on the Internet. But, I want to know more about you. Is there, or has there been, a Mr. Sheridan?"

"Mr. Sheridan is my father. But, if you're asking if I am, or have been, married, the answer is no to the first, yes to the second."

He turned his head to the side, quizzically. "And he let you get away?"

"More like he discarded me. But that's too morbid to talk about. What about your son and his mother?"

Nick threw his head back and rolled his eyes upward. "That, my dear, is simply boring. Married too young for the wrong reasons to the wrong person. Divorced when Kevin was still in nappies. But, it's all worked out. Pen—Penelope—remarried well, and she has done an admirable job raising Kevin."

"Is he still coming over here?"

"That he is. I expect Kevin and my nephew by the weekend. Jonathan, my sister's son, is sixteen. Pen would never allow our son to cross the Atlantic alone, nor would I."

The waiter returned and they ordered. Ansley opted for the chicken tikka masala and Nick chose tandoori lamb.

Although the wine was tempting, Ansley rationed her consumption, taking small sips. She was determined to keep her head and not be seduced by the drink or the man.

As the waiter cleared away the dinner plates, Nick leaned in, staring at her. His gaze made her uncomfortable. Without warning, he reached behind her head and pulled out the pins holding her hair. As it cascaded to her shoulders, he said, "There. That's better."

The maneuver was so smooth that Ansley felt as though he could disrobe her on the spot. She sat frozen, fighting the passion that was replacing the butterflies. The restaurant was empty.

I am completely at his mercy. There's no one here but the owner.

Her vulnerability failed to frighten her. While intellectually, she didn't want to be compromised, physically, she was seething with desire.

"Let's have a carriage ride through the park," Nick said, suddenly. Taking her hand, he rose.

She wanted to ask about the check, but thought it inappropriate. Apparently, he did not worry with such details.

"Isn't it too late for a carriage ride?" she asked, looking at her watch.

Nick smiled. "It can be arranged, and it's too nice a moon to miss."

Before leaving the restaurant, Ansley stopped in the ladies room. When she came out, Nick was waiting near the entrance with her coat. Upon seeing her, a wry smile of approval crossed his face, triggering a warm feeling in Ansley.

Don't lose your head, kiddo. It's just a smile.

New York engaged all of her senses as she stepped through the door. The brisk night air was saturated with the pungent aroma of spices emanating from the restaurants. The sound of ethnic music blaring from a small bar competed with the noise of traffic, and the multiple colors of neon clamored for customer attention. As they crossed the sidewalk to the waiting limo, Ansley anticipated the open-air carriage ride and hoped her lightweight, wool coat would protect her against the November chill. For a moment, she considered begging off, but her will-power wasn't strong enough to end the magical date.

With traffic still heavy at midnight, the car moved slowly up 6th Avenue. Ansley gazed out at pedestrians and thought about how many times she had walked the midtown streets, wondering who was behind the tinted-windows of passing limos. The interior of the limousine was silent. Nick had not given the driver instructions, yet the man seemed to know where to drive.

"You're very quiet, Ms. Sheridan," Nick said, breaking the silence. "Would you like music?"

She smiled. "That would be nice." *Maybe that will help fill the awkward gaps.*

As he chose a playlist of classical music, she watched his hands and had a momentary desire for him to take her in his arms. *Stop it. Think of something to say.*

"Do you still live in England?" The words were not out before she realized it had been a stupid question.

"I do, but am there far less than I would like. My home is in the southwest—Gloucestershire County," he said, relaxing and putting an arm around the back of the seat, but not touching her. "It's commonly referred to as the Cotswolds."

"I love it there."

"You know it?" he said, positioning his body to better face her.

"I was there once, a long time ago."

"Then, you must return. I should like to show you about."

Ansley smiled and began to reply when the car stopped at the corner of Central Park South and 7th Avenue. As the driver exited and came around to open the door for them, Nick said, "We can talk more about England in the carriage."

Assisting Ansley out, while the driver held the door, Nick guided her toward a waiting carriage where a man stood, dressed in tails and a stovepipe hat.

"Good evening, sir," the man said, "and madam." The coachman reached into the white, hansom cab and took out a long-stemmed, red rose, wrapped in green florist paper, and handed it to Nick.

"For you, Ms. Sheridan," Nick said, presenting it to Ansley.

She blushed, smiled, whispered a thank-you, and turned to step up into the carriage. On the facing seat was a box of chocolate-covered strawberries—Godiva. *I'm in the middle of a fairytale.*

Once settled, Nick took a neatly folded blanket from near the sweets and spread it across their knees. The act of being under a cover with him was intensely intimate to Ansley. Her reservations were dissolving.

As they rode through the park, the cool breeze striking her face was invigorating. The clip-clop of the horseshoes striking pavement produced a soothing rhythm. With one arm around the backrest, Nick reached under the blanket for her hand. Finding it, he drew it across to his lap and held it, rubbing gently with his thumb. Her heart was pounding so hard that she was afraid he could feel it. Even in the open air of the park, she could smell his fragrance.

"So, tell me about your experience in my homeland. I hope you're not going to tell me that it was on your honeymoon."

"No, absolutely not. I've actually been to England several times. I studied there when I was sixteen."

She found herself telling him about her background as a dancer, having toured Europe with the company, and having spent a summer in ballet training at the Royal Academy in London. He listened intently.

"I should have guessed you were a ballerina. You have the grace and poise one associates with the ballet."

"You mean that I walk like a duck—feet splayed?"

"I haven't noticed the splayed feet, but I will be sure to watch for it," he said, the moon illuminating the smile on his face.

A jogger ran by. Ansley was startled. "I would never have thought anyone would run in Central Park this late."

Nick nodded without speaking. Several minutes passed without conversation. The longer the silence, the more edgy Ansley became.

"Dennis and I watched one of your movies today," she said, instantly regretting the statement.

"You did?" he said with a slight tone of appreciation and leaned forward to look her in the face. "Which one?"

Remembering the graphic scene, she hesitated before responding. "*The Royal Stage.*"

He burst out in laughter. "Well, I guess you saw more of me than you bargained for."

Now she was embarrassed. "I didn't choose it." *I'm making it worse. Why did I open my mouth?* "I mean, Dennis ..." She caught herself. How would it sound that her gay friend had chosen Nick's erotic film?

But Nick was amused. "I didn't mean to embarrass you . . . . But, tell me, my bare bum aside, did you like the film?"

Ansley felt her face burning. "I did. You were excellent, and I learned a lot about Charles II."

He laughed again. "A lot about his throng of mistresses and bastards, you mean. Not my finest cinematic hour, love."

"I learned that besides being the king's mistress, Nell Gwyn was one of the early women to perform on a British stage. It *was* based on a true story, wasn't it?"

"It was. I'm amused that current society holds the monarchy up to such a high moral standard when our history is riddled with amoral rulers. When I read the script and agreed to play Charles, I thought it would be a valid historical drama. However, the only thing it became known for was the erotic love scene. I do hope you give me another chance. My latest film opens this weekend and has a bit more substance and a little less of my form."

Still chuckling, he relaxed against the seat as the lights of the coach caught a pair of eyes on the road.

"What's that?" Ansley said, loud enough for the driver to hear.

The driver, turning his head to the side, said, "Don't worry, ma'am. That's just a raccoon. The park's full of them."

Reacting to the distress in her voice, Nick moved his arm off the seat back to have it around her, clasping her shoulder with his hand. A warm feeling came over her, together with an impulse to lean against him. She resisted. However, she relaxed and found conversation easier. He asked about her law practice and talked about his reasons for being in New York. He was on a promotional junket for his latest film and in the process of negotiating a contract for a summer production of *Richard III* in Central Park.

"You're playing another British king?"

Nick laughed. "I am. According to my sister, I am an actor because it was the only way I could become a king."

When they arrived back at the starting point, Ansley was sorry the romantic excursion had ended but immediately grew apprehensive as to what was coming next. Somewhere along the way, she had accepted that she would sleep with him. Throwing all her inhibitions and principles aside, she had decided to let it happen. As reality grew close, doubts crept back. Could she go through with it? The thought of being undressed— naked—with him brought on a shiver.

This will finally close the door on Mark—but I need more wine— and the lights will have to be off.

To her surprise, Nick had the limo driver go directly to Dennis' apartment. When they reached the building, the doorman was off-duty so the driver once again opened the car for her to exit. Since Nick was not taking her to his hotel, she expected that he would say goodnight and allow her to go in alone, once she tapped in the security code to unlock the entry. But, instead, he escorted her all the way to Dennis's door. As she fumbled with the key, she thanked him for a lovely time. He took her by the shoulders and turned her to face him. For a moment, they looked directly at one another.

Is he going to kiss me?

Leaning forward, Nick took her chin in one hand, kissed her on the forehead, and then said, "The pleasure was mine." Taking the key, he turned the lock for her and left as the door cracked open. She felt simultaneous relief and disappointment.

It was after two as she tiptoed in. Dennis was asleep on the sofa, but despite believing she would spend the night with Nick, he had left a light on in the bathroom. She had just reached the bedroom door when she heard her name.

"Don't even think you're going to bed without telling me what happened."

CHAPTER TEN

Dennis kept her up past three a.m., probing every minute detail of the date. When she finally got to sleep, Ansley dreamed about Nick Colton in an amalgamation of their date and his film, in which she played Nell Gwynne in the erotic love scene. Waking sporadically, at six she took a bathroom trip and then slept soundly until nearly ten.

"I think you made up that part about the ride through Central Park because you don't want to share the juicy dirt," Dennis said as she came out of the bedroom.

"Good morning to you, too."

"Come on, Ansley. You slept with him. Admit it. Your hair was loose. You left here with it up, and you had that satisfied look on your face."

Taking a cup out of the cabinet, Ansley poured herself coffee. "Where is your sugar? I've never learned to drink this stuff black."

"Quit, dodging," Dennis said, lifting a plastic container out from a lower cabinet.

Taking a seat at the small table in the corner of the room, she took a sip of coffee, pointed to the chair on the opposite side, and said, "Sit."

He eagerly complied.

"There's nothing to tell. If it helps, I'm as surprised as you are. I had made up my mind to let it happen, but he didn't make a move. I swear."

Crestfallen, Dennis played with the salt and peppershakers on the table. Then, he perked up. "I'll bet he's one of us. That's the only explanation—he's gay."

Ansley chuckled. "In your dreams. I didn't get those vibes. But, you never know. Seeing you, especially in *Carmen,* a stranger would never believe *you're* gay."

Thinking for a minute, he responded, "Is that why I have a hard time getting dates?"

"Dennis, you've never had a hard time getting dates. Your problem is being faithful."

Shaking his head, he said, "That man has to be gay if he didn't make a move on *you*."

"It doesn't matter. It was a mystical, magical night, and I'm really glad today that he didn't. I can treasure it, unblemished by regret over compromise of my virtue. Let's store it away. And, please, please, don't tell anyone. I really don't want the world speculating on me with Nicholas Colton."

"Say no more, honey." He reached across the table and put his hand on her shoulder. "My lips are sealed. With that man's degree of celebrity, the paparazzi would be on you like a swarm of angry bees."

After having a sandwich, Ansley packed for the flight home. She pressed the rose, wrapped in the green paper, between the pages of a magazine and placed it carefully in her suitcase. At one o'clock, she left for the airport—and reality.

Ansley made it to her parents' home for Thanksgiving dinner. Laura wanted to know all the details of her trip, and Ansley wanted to tell her, but couldn't talk about the date with Nick. She knew her mother well enough to know that any enthusiasm about her daughter having a date would be squelched by pessimism about his celebrity status. It was better to stay discreet and allow the family to assume her Tuesday night date was with Dennis.

Early Friday morning, Elaine called Ansley at work and suggested that they go Christmas shopping on Saturday, have lunch, and see a movie.

"There's a film opening today that is supposed to be really great," Elaine said. "I need a mommy-break, and Greg owes me one. Nicolas Colton stars in the movie, and I saw him talking about it on one of the late shows last night."

"What's it about?" Ansley said, disguising her personal knowledge of the man and his movie.

"It's based on a true story about a murder in England during the Edwardian period. He plays the lawyer defending the suspect and ends up sleeping with her."

Oh, boy. This is surreal. "Sounds like a good plan. What time and where?"

When they hung up, Ansley sat quietly for several minutes, contemplating what it was going to be like—sitting in a dark theater with

Elaine while a gigantic Nick moved across the screen. *Don't even think about telling Elaine.* The office was quiet, with only one other associate working. The firm was officially closed, but since she had been off earlier in the week, she felt obligated to log some billable hours.

Shortly after two o'clock, she left the office. Heading home, she made an unplanned stop at her local video store where she found four of Nick's movies. She had seen one before on TV, but checked it out as well. *This is crazy. I'm acting like a thirteen-year-old groupie.* Despite feeling immature, it was a guilty pleasure that she couldn't resist.

Arriving at the condo, she checked her mailbox and turned to unlock her front door when she saw that a small slip of paper was attached to the jamb. It was a notice of an attempted delivery by a local florist. *What on earth?* The paper said flowers had been left with her neighbor. She went into the condo long enough to drop her purse and videos on the living room couch before going next door.

Jeanette Farmer opened the door and immediately asked, "How was your trip? I have a delivery for you from LaMee."

"Thanks for taking them in for me."

"No problem."

"The trip was really nice," Ansley continued, avoiding the temptation to give away just how exciting it had been. "I really appreciate you and Melissa looking after the cats while I was gone. If you have a date this weekend, I can stay with Melissa to repay the favor."

"Thanks for the offer, but my only date lives between the covers of a hot romance novel that my thirteen-going-on-thirty-year-old child bought. Do you have time for a cup of coffee?"

"I'd better not. I promised Elaine I would spend the day with her tomorrow, so I'd better do my laundry this afternoon. Give me a rain check."

Jeanette retrieved the package from her dining room table and handed the long, slender box to Ansley. "I was a little worried about how the flowers would keep but didn't feel it was appropriate for me to look inside." A wide ribbon, tied in a bow, secured the contents.

"At the risk of being nosy, I have to admit that I am curious as to what is making the box a little heavy for flowers," Jeanette said.

"I have no idea, but I'll let you know." Instinctively, Ansley did not want to share the experience of opening the package.

Once back in her condo, she took the box to her desk and untied the bow. Inside was a single red rose and two smaller boxes—one, a slender, light-blue, signature Tiffany container. Her heart stopped.

Without reading the card, she knew that it could be from no one other than Dennis—or Nick. Excitement began welling in her nervous system as she opened the smaller package. It held a gold bracelet with a single charm—a miniature clone of the Central Park carriage. The other box, wrapped in shiny white paper, bore the seal of Neiman Marcus and accounted for the weight of the package. Tearing away the wrapping, she found an exquisite Baccarat vase.

Hands shaking and heart racing, she removed the small envelope at the bottom of the box and opened it.

"For a beautiful and gracious lady. Please accept these tokens of my gratitude for a memorable evening. Nick."

Is that really his handwriting? How did he know my address? And isn't this just like him? Extravagant, tasteful, solicitous, and unfathomable.

For a few seconds, she stared at the card, savoring the words and reliving Tuesday night. Removing the bracelet from the box, she gingerly put it around her wrist, treating the bauble as though it were ephemeral and might self-destruct if mishandled.

Don't read anything into this. You're never going to see him again. This is just his way of being courteous.

It was one thing to say it was a routine, platonic gesture, but another to avoid the temptation to dream.

CHAPTER ELEVEN

Saturday morning, the mall was packed with shoppers. The spirit of Christmas was everywhere with the background music, the decorations, and pre-Christmas sales. Elaine's shopping list was by far the longer. Ansley had only her parents, her secretary, and Elaine's children to buy for.

As usual, they met at the big-box toy store near the mall. Elaine had asked to use Ansley's condo as Santa's hideaway. Kelly, Elaine's oldest, was Ansley's goddaughter—a spritely-seven-year-old who viewed world as her oyster—full of pearls. She took ballet classes at Ansley's old studio, idolized her godmother, and was in awe of Ansley's former career. "There are pictures of you all over the studio," Kelly had told Ansley over the phone after her first class. The youngster had a dancer's body, and Ansley encouraged Elaine to support her training.

As Ansley was debating between two collector dolls to give Kelly, Elaine said, "Both girls are enjoying dance classes."

Ansley smiled. "I don't know about Keri yet, but Kelly certainly has potential."

"I would love to see her become as good as you were. Keri loves it too, even though all the three-year-olds do is point their toes and run around the room, pretending to be butterflies."

Picking up a Barbie in a lavish evening gown and looking at it pensively, Elaine said, "How am I going to manage four kids?"

"Anytime you want to give one up, call me," Ansley said, her tone jovial, but her heart was a little sad as always when confronted with Elaine's family. *At times like this, I can't help but hate Mark even more. Because of him, I may never have a child.*

Shopping monopolized their attention until well after one o'clock. The morning was productive, and Ansley's car was packed with toys. As they left Dillard's, Elaine glanced down at her watch and made a face.

"Oh, my gosh, it's nearly two o'clock. We'd better finish the rest of my list another day if we're going to have time for lunch and make the movie."

"It's up to you. If you want to eat and finish the shopping, we can always see the movie another time." Although she spoke the words, Ansley hoped Elaine would not agree. Whenever the movie had crossed her mind that morning, her heart accelerated.

"No. I'm done. I can't walk another store. I don't work out like you do."

After a brief survey of nearby food establishments, they decided to leave the mall for lunch at a nearby Italian restaurant, hoping to escape some of the holiday shoppers.

"I never tire of Italian food," Elaine said, as the waitress left the table with their orders.

"Could that be because you're Italian?"

"Touché. But tell me about New York. We haven't had a chance to really talk. How did the dress work out?"

Ansley smiled. "It worked great. I felt so confident. Thanks for talking me into buying it." *If she only knew.*

"Tell me all about everything you did. I'm green with envy. Did you see any shows other than the ballet?"

Ansley took a deep breath, wanting to spill out the story. She could visualize what Elaine's expression would be. *I can't do it. Like Ben Franklin said, "Three can keep a secret, if two of them are dead."*

"It was exciting to be back in New York. In so many ways, it was like I never left. Riding in from LaGuardia, I felt the electricity of the city. And you know Dennis. He cracks me up." She smiled. "Remember when he came with me to dance in the local *Nutcracker?*"

"I remember. I was impressed."

"He's twice as good now—absolutely breathtaking. I knew he would mature into a brilliant artist, and he has."

"But what else did you do?"

"Not too much. We just relaxed on Tuesday and watched a DVD. That night, it was dinner at an Indian restaurant, an off-Broadway play, and a nice ride through Central Park."

"Too bad you didn't have a real date for the Central Park ride. I think that would be so romantic."

Looking down to avoid eye contact, Ansley said, "Yeah. Wouldn't it?" Ansley took a sip of the iced tea the waitress had put down on the table. "What's going on with you guys? Little Greg adjusting to school?"

The rest of the lunch was spent talking about Elaine's family and Ansley's job. During lulls in the conversation, Ansley's mind strayed to anticipation of the film and thoughts of the gifts Nick sent. She had almost worn the bracelet but at the last minute decided she didn't want to risk questions about where it came from.

By the time they reached the theater and settled in their seats on the back row, Ansley was a nervous wreck. The audience for the matinee was respectable, but not overflowing. Elaine tried to carry on a conversation as they waited for the feature to begin, but Ansley was becoming so edgy that she could hardly concentrate on banalities. When the movie began, with credits rolling, Nick stood in a long shot, his back to the camera, looking at a wall of barrister bookcases. Taking a book from the shelf, he turned. Ansley's heart skipped a beat. He was dressed in a costume of the period: a black morning coat, black and gray striped trousers, an iron-gray waistcoat, and a burgundy cravat. He was the consummate Edwardian aristocrat. His deep-brown hair was slightly longer than it had been earlier in the week, layered in thick waves, and almost covering his ears. Except for long sideburns, his face was clean-shaven.

The room where he stood was obviously a legal office, dimly lit, with rich paneling and elegant accessories. As a young law clerk entered and called his name, there was no mistaking Nick's control of the scene. The camera moved in for a close-up of his face, and Ansley shivered, feeling the eye contact as though seeing him in the flesh. *Careful. Don't give yourself away.*

If the theater had not been dark, Elaine might have recognized how agitated her friend was. During the running of the film, Ansley couldn't concentrate on the plot for her fascination with the actor. Scenes he was not in might as well have been commercials. When he was on screen, she was hypnotized and could almost smell his mysterious fragrance. When the feature ended, Ansley would have failed a test on the plot.

"Wasn't it great?" Elaine said as they walked out to the parking lot.

"Absolutely."

"Didn't you love the scene where Pamela was acquitted?"

"I did." Truth be told, Ansley had no clue. Nick had not been in the scene.

After Elaine said goodbye and headed for her car, which was on the opposite side of the building, Ansley decided to return to the mall. Although it was getting dark, she was on a mission. *I'm going to buy some of that cologne—if I can find it and if it doesn't cost more than my car.*

She went to the two most upscale department stores in the shopping center. Smelling every tester on the men's counter, she failed to find what she was looking for. Nothing came close. Disappointed, she went home. *Get a grip, Ansley. You're acting like a lovesick, fourteen-year-old. Grow up.*

As Ansley drove back to her condo, Stevie Nicks was singing, "Players only love you when they're playing."

How right she is. He's got to be a player. Otherwise, he would be married.

Three weeks passed, and no further communication came from Nick.

"I told you I would never hear from him again," she said to Dennis, during a phone call the week before Christmas.

"That's one strange fellow," Dennis said. "He's gay. What straight guy would take a gorgeous girl like you on a date and not go for a base hit, if not a homerun—then send expensive gifts? What an enigma."

"Maybe I'm not his type."

"Bullshit, baby. You're any sane man's type."

"What do *you* know? You're not attracted to women. I'm probably too flat-chested for his taste."

"What's in a boob?"

"Okay, this conversation is degenerating. Are you dancing Cavalier in *Nutcracker?*"

"Alternating with Willie Weiner."

"William? I thought he was dancing with the Royal Ballet for a year."

William Cabrerra was one of Dennis's former lovers. Their break-up had created a tempest in the company three years before, and Dennis had not blown out the torch. William was the only paramour, known to Ansley, to ever leave Dennis. Whether or not it made the rejection more difficult, the dancer had broken off the relationship for an actress, claiming he had discovered that he was straight. Dennis had threatened everything short of murder, including resigning from the company, but settled for a leave of absence.

"Are you dancing in any of his performances?"

"I, bloody well, am not. I would walk before I would stand behind that fag during a curtain call, and Jean-Claude damn sure knows it."

"I can relate," Ansley said.

"I'm proud of you for having the courage to stay in Dodge. You've got more fortitude than I have."

"Say, do you think that if I get to heaven before him that I could block him out?"

"Where did that come from?"

"My dear, it's hard enough being in the same company, I couldn't bear being near him for eternity. I'd rather go to hell myself."

Ansley started laughing.

"What's so funny?"

"I'm sorry. I just couldn't help but picture you flying around heaven, flapping your angel wings, trying to block William from getting in."

Dennis laughed with her.

"Tell you what. If you find out it can be done, I'll help as long as we block Mark, too."

After exchanging affectionate goodbyes, they hung up, leaving Ansley to think more about Nick. Although it was late, she got up and retrieved the DVD of *The Royal Stage* she had ordered online and inserted it into a player underneath her bedroom TV. As the movie began, she took her remote and snuggled under the covers of her bed to watch—fully prepared to fast forward through the boring parts.

I should feel guilty, but what the heck? I'll never hear from him again, so I might as well indulge myself.

CHAPTER TWELVE

Ansley was in the kitchen at ten o'clock on the 23rd of December, finishing preparations for her first Christmas Eve party in the condo. Her parents and her aunt and uncle were coming for dinner and gift exchanges. "This has been a long day," she said to Shadow as she took a pecan pie out of the oven. The black Persian was sitting on the floor, standing vigil over the proceedings as though he were in charge.

With the final item on her list for the day completed, she loaded the dishwasher and prepared to go to bed. Passing through the living room, she paused to admire her Victorian Christmas tree on the table in front of the bay window. Skye, her white Persian, was curled in a ball, sleeping, on one of the green damask chairs flanking either side of the tree. Shadow had followed Ansley and jumped in her lap when she sat in the vacant chair.

"Isn't the tree gorgeous, guys?" she said, relaxing for a moment before going to her room. Closing her eyes, she soaked in the ambiance of her small condo, illuminated only by the lights on the tree. Orange-spice potpourri filled a bowl on her coffee table and saturated the room with aromas of the season. "O Holy Night" played softly in the background.

I've come a long way from Christmas five years ago. Savoring the moment, Ansley felt proud of herself. She had her education, a good job, and although tiny, her own place. Only the second bedroom lacked furniture.

Thirty minutes later, Ansley had finished her shower, put on her favorite pajamas, and turned on her small TV in the bedroom. She was about to lie down to watch the news when the phone rang. Looking at the clock on her night table, she frowned. *Who is calling at ten-thirty?* Reaching for the phone, her expression softened, thinking it was proba-bly Dennis. *He had no concept of time.*

Picking up the receiver, her eyes opened wide with shock when she heard the voice at the other end.

"And how are you tonight?"

She couldn't respond as visions of the caller clamored for confirmation.

"Nick Colton here. I hope I didn't wake you."

"No. You didn't, but you *have* surprised me." Instinctively, she turned around and looked at herself in the full-length mirror, frowning at the reflection as if he could see her in the faded flannel PJs—without make-up. *Wait a second. Is this really him? No, it can't be. It's got to be Dennis goofing off.*

"I've had you on my mind."

"That's flattering." *I'll just play along until he tires of his silly little game.*

"I would like to see you again."

Good job with the accent, Dennis. "That would be nice, but I'm in Florida, and you're where?"

"We're in Florida this week."

We? Oh my gosh. It could be him.

"Kevin wanted to spend Christmas at Disney. If you are free the end of the week, I would very much like to see you"

"How did you get my number?"

"Have you forgotten that you gave me your card?"

It is him!

"Can you come down for the weekend? I'll arrange for your travel."

She was speechless. *There's a right answer to that somewhere, but .*
. . .

"Are you still there?"

"Yes, yes. You've caught me off guard. I'm not sure what to say." She sat down on the bed, curled her lips in, rolled her eyes toward the ceiling, and took a deep breath. *What do I say? What do I say?*

As though reading her thoughts, he said, "You only have to say yes. I'll take care of the rest."

Of course you will. You're an expert at that. "What about your son?"

"The boys are booked to return on Virgin Atlantic to the UK on Friday. Now, tell me you'll come so that we can work out the details. Or, would you prefer that I come to Jacksonville or St. Augustine, wherever it is that you live?"

"No. Not here." *What do I say?* "You need to give me a chance to think this through." Stalling for time, she tried to wrap her head around what was happening. "What made you think of me tonight?"

"My dear, I didn't just think of you tonight. I've thought about you often since our lovely evening."

Sitting next to Cameron Diaz on the late show, I'm sure I was all you had on your mind.

"That's a little hard to believe."

"Come to Orlando, and allow me to convince you."

Who could resist that voice? After a silent pause that seemed longer than it was, she blinked her eyes and said, "Okay. I'll come. But, you don't need to make any arrangements. I'll take care of myself."

He laughed. "Independent are we?"

"Let's say, cautious," she said, nodding her head.

"I'm completely harmless."

Yeah, right. Like Cleopatra's asp. "I'm sure you *are*."

"Would you like references?" he asked, noting the sarcasm in her tone.

Smiling, she said, "Only if you swear that Bill Clinton isn't who you have in mind."

"He was at the top of the list."

With all his British formality, he's still has a sense of humor.

After he tried one more time to get her to agree to stay at his hotel, promising that she would have her own room, they exchanged mobile phone numbers and hung up.

For several minutes, Ansley stared at the phone. *Did that just happen?* Ignoring the time, she picked up the receiver and dialed New York.

Be there, Dennis. I've got to talk.

On the sixth ring, he answered.

"Did I wake you?"

"No. I just stepped out of the shower. What's wrong?"

"I just had a phone call." She closed her eyes and took a deep breath—her hands trembling.

"A phone call? From who?"

"*Him.*"

"Him? That leaves maybe two possibilities—Mark, the monkey's ass or Nicholas Colton, the Prince of Passion."

"*Him.*"

"Oh, my god—say it's true. Colton?"

"Colton. He asked me to meet him in Orlando for the weekend."

"Holy shit. You accepted, didn't you?"

"I've lost my mind."

"Only if you didn't accept."

"Dennis, what am I getting myself into?"

"Let's see," he hesitated as though thinking. "A little slice of heavenly bliss, Elysian Fields, and everything in between."

"Will you please be serious? You're the only person I can talk to."

"I am serious. And, I withdraw my speculation about his sexual preferences. He's *not* gay."

After being lectured about the lingerie she should pack, Ansley promised Dennis she would call as soon as she returned from Orlando the following Sunday.

*****

For Ansley, the usual excitement of the holiday was overshadowed by anticipation of the weekend ahead. Christmas eve, she woke, more rested than expected—having slept sporadically. Every time she closed her eyes, images of Nick appeared like Internet pop-ups. Some were the man she went out with, others were of characters he had played; but there was no chasing him out of either her conscious or subconscious mind.

Before putting her day in motion, she sat on the side of her bed, trying to sort her thoughts.

Noticing that his mistress was awake, Skye muscled his way onto her lap, purring.

"There's no use fighting you, is there?" Ansley said, rubbing his thick fur. "I've got to get my act together and put that man out of my mind." That was easier said than done. Getting up, she went to the TV and removed all of Nick's DVDs from the shelf under the set. Looking over the disk covers, she took a deep breath and stowed them away in the closet.

The Christmas Eve party went well and helped deflect Colton thoughts. Her parents arrived at four-thirty, followed by her maternal aunt and uncle. Other than a scorched batch of rolls, the food turned out well.

After dinner, gifts were exchanged. The Beechams went home early as Sam was recovering from a bout with pneumonia, leaving the cleanup to Ansley and Laura. During the party, she had been so busy that she managed to forget about Nick; but as she stood at the sink, her hands immersed in the hot, soapy water, his voice echoed in her ears.

"I've had you on my mind."

She almost dropped a piece of her good china when her mother's voice startled her.

"I think that's all, honey," Laura said, referring to the soiled dishes she had been bringing to the kitchen. "Let me finish up, and you go get ready."

The plan was for Ansley to go home with her parents. They would attend the midnight Mass, and she would stay over in Jacksonville for Christmas dinner the next day. Up until the night before, she had looked forward to the diversion. The phone call changed everything. She had an overwhelming desire to stay secreted away in her condo. Being with those whom she couldn't or wouldn't share the knowledge with made her uncomfortable and unable to indulge the private rapture. It was as though her secret would escape by osmosis.

Watching her mother take the rubber gloves Ansley had removed, she speculated on what Laura's reaction would be if she knew. *She would say that I am playing with fire.* "He's only after one thing." *That's probably the real reason I won't tell her. I don't want to hear the truth.*

It was after three on Christmas day when Ansley got back to her condo. Laura had wanted her to stay longer, but she begged off, claiming fatigue. The cats greeted her as she opened the front door. "Merry Christmas, guys. Did you take care of the house for me?" After dropping her overnight bag in the bedroom, she went to the kitchen—both cats following. Laura had sent her home with leftovers that she stashed in the refrigerator before taking the cat food container out of the pantry and filling the two bowls on the kitchen floor. Once the cats were fed, she made a cup of tea and retreated to her bedroom, ignoring the Christmas tree and opened gifts still on the floor.

Her first move was to the closet for the DVD stash. *I'm probably crazy, but I don't care. I'm going to indulge in this moment all by myself.* She closed the door to keep the cats out of her room. This was her private moment. Changing into a cozy warm-up suit, she turned off her phone, put her favorite disk in the DVD player, and snuggled down on the bed with her down comforter and cup of tea.

CHAPTER THIRTEEN

The plastic keycard wouldn't open the door to the Orlando hotel room. Struggling with the lock, she dropped her purse, and the contents fell out on the worn carpet. "Damn, I'm going to have to go back to the desk for help. I hate these things!" Laying her tote bag on the floor, she scooped items back into the handbag and then tried the lock one more time, using both hands. It worked.

The room neither failed to meet expectations nor exceeded them. It wasn't dirty, but it didn't generate a feeling of cleanliness. All of the necessities were there: a bed, dresser, lamps, TV, air conditioning—too much air conditioning—but the room was cold in more ways than temperature. Still in attorney attire, she kicked off her pumps and put her suitcase in the alcove that served as a closet. *Luxury this isn't, but it's doable. At least there's a security lock on the door.*

It was a little past three. Leaving her office at noon, she had made good time getting to the Orlando area. Nick had said for her to call when she arrived, but the thought of calling him made her nervous, plus, she wanted time to ready herself before they met. Out of nowhere, the pulsating rhythm of *Habanera* thundered in her head, along with a vivid image of Nick seated beside her at the ballet. *I'm going to see him in just a little while—this is really happening.* No time had been set, and he didn't know where she was staying. She took comfort in her momentary seclusion. "I'll call him after I shower and relax for a little while—maybe take a nap."

Ansley should have known a nap wasn't going to happen. The band of butterflies, holding Olympic tryouts in her belly, would see to that. *A Valium, a Valium, my kingdom for a Valium.* She had never taken a Valium in her life, but the idea was compelling as she fought to control the combination of fear and excitement. *An hour—I'll wait an hour before I call.*

Within thirty minutes, she had unpacked, taken a shower, and positioned herself on the bed for relaxation, if not sleep. Her feet were propped above the headboard as she lay flat on the bed, head near the end; a cold, wet washcloth covered her eyes as a subliminal tape for stress reduction played on her portable cassette player. The allocated time was cut short by the ringing of her mobile phone.

"Are you in Orlando?" he asked as she answered, the wet cloth falling as she swung to a sitting position and fumbled to silence the tape.

"I have." Her face betrayed her excitement at the sound of his voice.

"Good to hear. I need your location."

Calm down. Get a grip. Don't let him know that you're nervous. I'm at the Reasonable Suites and Rooms just off I-4 on the east side of the city." She wanted to ask where he was, but was reluctant. "Has your son left for England?"

"Indeed he has. I saw the boys off earlier and moved from the resort to a hotel with ducks parading in the lobby."

Ansley laughed. "You must be at the Peabody."

"That's it. Damned interesting sight. I've seen monkeys swarm a hotel in Costco Rico, but ducks are a first. The little bastards act as though they own the place."

"Don't tell anyone, I think they do."

"Enough about hotel owners wearing feathers, I'm looking forward to seeing you. Our dinner reservation is for eight o'clock. May I pick you up at seven? We can have a drink before dinner."

"Seven would be fine, but you haven't told me where we are going. I'm not sure how to dress."

"Forgive me. We are dining at Maison et Jardin tonight. Tomorrow, if it meets with your approval, I would like to visit a horse farm in Ocala. I understand it's not too far."

"It's not."

"Ian will drive us. He's quite good with directions. We'll see you at seven."

With that, they hung up. Ansley sat on the side of the bed, looking at the phone. *Who is Ian? Am I going out with two men?*

Ansley's comfort level was not improved with the idea of a stranger accompanying them. *Do I really want to go out with two men?* After mentally debating the issue, desire trumped apprehension and she told herself to stop being paranoid.

With over three hours to fill, she did, and redid, her makeup and hair. Deciding to wear a conservative hairstyle, she twisted it into a low bun. For her face, she decided on a touch of robin's-egg-blue eye shadow, brown mascara and soft-pink blush and lipstick. *He liked my hair loose, but I don't want to be obvious.* She was pleased that she had brought black slacks, a cream silk shirt, and layers of gold chains. At six-thirty, she surveyed her total look and decided that she had accomplished her goal—understated but tasteful. *He hasn't seen the true me. We'll see how that works. In New York, I was someone else in borrowed clothes.*

Her phone rang precisely at seven. "Will you join me in the lobby?"

When she arrived in the Spartan lobby, Nick was standing by the door. He wore heavy, black-rimmed glasses and had a growth of whiskers, not a beard, but enough facial hair to alter his appearance. He was dressed in a black suit and white shirt, open at the neck with no tie.

Clark Kent looking for a phone booth?

"My, my. Je pense que vous regardez belle ce soir," he said, tipping his head slightly.

"Merci." *Why is he telling me I'm pretty in French?*

Without saying more, he escorted her to a car waiting in the circle at the hotel entrance. It was an unassuming SUV rental. A large, muscular man was seated behind the wheel.

Nick opened the back door of the vehicle and assisted her in entering. The thought crossed her mind that he might sit up front with the strange man who was no doubt Ian. But he didn't. Taking his place next to her, he spoke without acknowledging the driver.

"It is very good to see you. I hope your holidays have been pleasant."

"Thank you. They have." She looked at him for a moment. "I have to admit, you look very different."

Smiling, he pulled off the glasses. "Subterfuge. It makes life a bit easier."

"That makes sense. Was that why you spoke French in the lobby?"

He nodded. "It's not that I mind fans; where would I be without them? But it can steal precious time if I am recognized and get caught up in a flurry of demands for autographs. At least, there's a lesser risk of paparazzi away from New York and LA."

He spoke as though Ian wasn't present. *Who is this man?*

"Thank you for the flowers and gifts you sent. They were all beautiful, but totally unexpected. How did you know where I live?"

He smiled and took her right hand, raising her arm to look at the gold bracelet, nodding approval.

I'm glad I wore it. He seems pleased.

"We're living in the information age, my dear. Stephen, my agent, had his staff look into finding your home address. I hope you are not offended at my taking the liberty?"

"Not really."

He lowered her hand to his lap without releasing it. "I'm happy you liked them. Tell me, have you been on holiday, or working, since you left New York? You said that you are a family law attorney. Is that like a barrister or a solicitor?"

"All of the above. Right now, I'm just an associate in the firm. Mostly, I do intake interviews and paperwork. I haven't done any real litigation, only what we call 'show-up' hearings."

"What's a show-up?"

"It's an uncontested hearing. You can't lose, and it only lasts about five minutes in front of the judge."

"Are you looking forward to complicated trial work?" He appeared to be sincerely interested in her career as opposed to merely making conversation.

"Yes and no. It scares me a little. Kind of like stage fright."

"Well, here we are. Have you been to this restaurant before?" he asked, as the car pulled up to the front of Maison et Jardin.

"Never."

Walking into the building, Ansley looked around for Ian, but he had driven off. *Maybe he's parking the car—but there was a valet.*

"Isn't Ian dining with us?" she asked.

"Not exactly. He'll be around somewhere. I'm sorry. I should have introduced you. He's my security, embarrassing as that may be. I guess you didn't notice him in New York, which is what he strives to accomplish."

"I never thought about that." *So much for your wild imagination, Ansley.*

The restaurant had a neoclassical façade with a formal interior. Elaborate chandeliers and impressive artwork adorned the dining room. It was definitely an upscale establishment, specializing in French cuisine.

"So, did you choose to speak French to carry through the Franco theme of the evening?"

Nick laughed. "Purely coincidental. French is my only alternative language and my best dialect. The restaurant was a recommendation of the hotel concierge."

Throughout dinner, conversation grew increasingly comfortable for Ansley. They had enough privacy for Nick to drop the foreign persona. The reservation had been in the name of Tony Colebridge.

"Do you always use the name Tony Colebridge?"

"It is my name."

She gave him a puzzled look. "So you're Tony, not Nick?"

"I'm both. My birth name is Nicholas Anthony Colebridge—second son of the Earl and all that nonsense. It's not a fact that I publicize, but using Colebridge allows for a shred of anonymity, even though I'm 'outted' on *Wikipedia* and *IMBD*. The family agreed not to disown me if I agreed not to use the family name professionally."

"Does your family call you Tony?"

"No. In the Cotswolds, I'm Nicholas." Changing the subject, he asked, "So why is a beautiful young woman, such as yourself, unattached?"

She bowed her head and paused before answering. "It's not a story worth repeating. But, I could ask you the same question. You said that you've been divorced a long time."

He chuckled. "A true attorney. Turn the question back on the interrogator. If the truth were to be disclosed, I'm single because I'm a male chauvinist, and no modern woman would have me."

"Really?"

"Really. Ready to run, yet?" he said, tipping his head.

"I've been ready to run since the night I met you, but not because you're a male chauvinist."

"I have sensed that." He reached across the table and took her hand, looked into her eyes, and said, "Why?"

"Why wouldn't I be?" As she met his gaze, her expression was as open and vulnerable as that of a puppy begging to be picked up."

"You're doing it again," he said, with a twinkle softening his piercing eyes.

"Okay. . . . You are a walk on the wild side. With you I'm risking a desire for something unattainable—kind of like trying on jewelry at Tiffany's." *I can't believe I said that. Shut up, Ansley.*

"What makes you certain that it's unattainable?"

"Isn't it obvious? You are an international celebrity. I'm a nobody. Falling for you would set me up for failure."

"You're sure of that?"

"I am. I fell in love once and gave up a career for him. Two years later, he was sleeping with a neighbor, and I was trying to figure out how to reinvent myself. That's not going to happen again."

"He was a fool. So you are precluding the possibility that there could be someone who would be permanently committed?"

"Pretty much. But, even if I weren't, and please don't be offended, you would never be a candidate. You live in the fast lane; I'm a spectator at the track. Six months from now, maybe less, you won't remember my name." *Did I just say that?*

"Ouch. I see I have my work cut out for me," he said, kissing her hand and laying it back on the table.

If you knew how much time I've spent watching your DVDs, you'd know how dangerous you are for me. Don't make a fool of yourself, Ansley.

"When did Kevin arrive in America?"

His right eyebrow went up in concert with the corners of his mouth. "Changing the subject are we?" She ignored the comment and waited for him to answer her question.

"The boys arrived last Friday. I wasn't certain until the last minute that Anne would allow Jonathan to be away on Christmas, especially in the company of her notorious brother."

"Why would she consider you notorious?"

"To my family, one patronizes the arts but doesn't participate. Further, one adheres to tradition, or one is an infidel. In the Colebridge Bible, there's an addendum to the Fourth Commandment requiring progeny to pay homage to Lord and Lady C on all religious holidays. Dutifully, the family gathers about the Christmas tree for an eve of mirth and merriment, finishing with a midnight pilgrimage to the village parish. I am an insurgent—conspicuous by my absence."

"Are you absent because of necessity or choice?"

"A bit of both." The conversation was interrupted by service of their entrées.

As the waiter left their table, and they began eating, Ansley asked more about Kevin.

"Did he enjoy Disney World?"

"He did. Had it not been required that he return to his mother for the New Year, he would have liked to stay longer, as would Jonathan."

"Was it their first time in the States?"

Nick swallowed a bite of his beef Wellington before answering. "Jonathan's first, Kevin's second. He and his mother came over two years ago when I was on location in Boston. But, there was nothing like Disney on that trip."

"Your former wife came over here? Did her husband come?"

"Charles doesn't like to travel. He's twenty years her senior and happy with his pipe, brandy, and an evening of cards with his peers. He indulges Pen's fancies as long as his routine isn't disturbed."

"I'm surprised that he would be so liberal with her visiting her ex-husband." Ansley's expression registered her amazement. "I take it that your divorce was not messy."

"Not even a little soiled, actually went smoother than the wedding. Pen and I grew up together: same schools, same salons, and all the rest. We naively fell into a marriage that was essentially arranged by our mothers. She meant to marry a title, or heir to one, but sadly, my brother was taken. Settling for the spare was not supposed to result in the deprived life of a struggling artist. She thought that once we were married, I would come to my senses, take my Oxford degree, and go into a respectable profession," he said, taking a swallow of wine before continuing. "I missed the memo—as they say. By the time she realized that I did not intend to leave the theater, Kevin was well on the way. Shortly after he was born, we mutually agreed to climb out of the marital mess before we grew to hate one another. In divorce we are friends; in marriage we were barely lovers."

As he spoke, he cut his meat, handling his utensils in the British manner. Ansley watched as he speared the beef with the fork still in his left hand. "You're really able to be friends?" she asked.

He nodded. "She's like another sister, who just happens to be the mother of my son."

"I could live life quite happily if I never saw or heard of my ex again. But then, we didn't have a child. What's Kevin like? Does he look like you?"

Shaking his head, he laid down his fork and reached in the breast pocket of his jacket, taking out a slender passport case. He sorted through the contents and removed a photo, handing it to her with a look of pride on his face.

Holding it to the light of a candle on the table, she said, "Nick, he is a very handsome young man, but not at all what I pictured." The image was of a twelve-year-old with a full head of blond hair, bangs across his forehead, and blue eyes staring down the viewer with an air of adolescent authority. He wore what appeared to be a navy-blue school blazer and tie. "He looks like Prince William."

"Favors his mother. A spirited lad—growing into that take-charge-of-the-world phase and probably too much like me for my comfort."

"Does he want to be an actor?"

Nick smiled. "No. He likes visiting me on the set and collecting celebrity autographs, some of which I think he sells, but his main interest at the moment is polo—plays on a school team. That and his rebellious streak are all that came from Colebridge genes."

Looking from the photo to Nick's face, she said, "I'll bet you're a good dad."

"I wish that I were. In truth, I hardly know him. When we do get together, we spend the first twenty-four hours circling one another."

Ansley handed the photo back. "It must be hard."

"It's my greatest regret—maybe my only—outside a few poor job choices like *The Royal Stage*."

"Were you a polo player, too?"

He nodded. "I played. Not too good at it, but loved the raw bonding of rider and horse on a field of competition. I enjoy attending Kevin's matches, when I can. It's one subject that we can discuss."

Ansley looked at him and saw an entirely different person coming out. In New York, he was Nicholas Colton, an A-list celebrity, perched on an untouchable pedestal. In Orlando, He was Nick Colebridge, a very real man, void of glitz. *Conversation has become easy.*

Laying down his fork and taking his napkin to pat his mouth, he said, "We've spent far too much time talking about me. Now, it's my turn to learn more about Ansley Sheridan. What do you look for in your future?"

The question caught her off guard. Toying with her food for a minute, she looked up at him and said, "I'm in search of a future. I have one somewhere, but I've misplaced it."

"Come now, I doubt that's true."

"No. It is true. Twice, I planned my life, and it went totally astray. For now, I'm doing what I do and waiting for act three to unfold."

He raised his wine glass in her direction and said, "Here's to my being lucky enough to be part of act three."

After dinner, Nick called Ian and they returned Ansley to her hotel. As in New York, he walked her to the room.

"Allow me to open it for you," he said as she stopped in front of her room.

Taking the keycard out of her purse, her heart beat a little faster in anticipation of what might come next. *Is this where he invites himself in? Does Ian know to get lost?*

Taking the plastic card, he took her hand as well and pulled her closer. "It has been a thoroughly delightful evening, Ms. Sheridan, and I look forward to a wonderful day tomorrow. Before she could reply, he pulled her against his chest in a warm embrace. She reached around his neck, returning the hug. Her body was pressed against his in the closest encounter of the relationship.

After a minute or so, Nick stepped back and said, "We'll pick you up at eight for breakfast before driving to the farm. Be sure to dress comfortably. We may be walking in pastures." He then took her chin in hand and tipped her face upward, kissing her lightly on her lips. Ansley felt her body lose strength from the waist down.

Nick turned, slipped the keycard in the slot, and whipped it out, releasing the lock without a hitch. Holding the door open, he allowed her to pass into the room and waited for it to close before leaving.

As soon as the door closed, she fastened the security lock and dropped herself onto the bed. *I can't fall for this apparition. I'm a holiday novelty, like a summer romance, and he's going to disappear as fast as he appeared. Keep your wits, Ansley.*

CHAPTER FOURTEEN

On the stroke of eight, Saturday morning, her phone rang. He was downstairs.

As Ansley arrived in the lobby, Nick was glancing over a newspaper at the reservations desk. He wore jeans, a white Oxford shirt, sunglasses, and a New York Yankees baseball cap. He looked up and saw her approaching. A huge smile opened up on his face. His beard, a little longer than the night before, further camouflaged his identity.

"I would never have recognized you," she said.

"Well—I would know you anywhere. You are as enchanting in jeans as you are in silk," he said, leaning over to kiss her on the cheek. With no one around, he spoke in his natural accent.

As they left the hotel, the sun was shining and the temperature was perfect. Ansley wore a peach turtleneck with an ivory sweater tied around her shoulders. Her only jewelry was the gold bracelet and a small gold crucifix.

After a hearty breakfast in one of the national chain restaurants, with Ian joining them, they began the seventy-five-mile trip to Ocala. Ansley had learned at breakfast that Ian had accompanied Nick to the States from England. He had been on Nick's staff for several years and prided himself on his ability to navigate in the U.S., despite candidly expressing his opinion about traffic customs on the west side of the Atlantic.

"You Americans drive on the wrong side of the road and don't have enough round-a-bouts," Ian said as they drove north on the Florida Turnpike.

Ansley laughed. "I felt the same way about the Brits driving on the left. I couldn't even walk across a street correctly in London." Turning to Nick, she said, "How many horses do you have?"

"Seven, if you count Kevin's two that stay at his mother's home. At the manor, I have five. He leaned forward and took his leather passport case out of the seat pocket. Opening it, he pulled out another photo.

"This is my prize, Hamlet." The horse was a magnificent black thoroughbred. "He stands fifteen-one."

Of course, his name is Hamlet. Ansley nodded, acknowledging that it was impressive, although she had no clue as to what it meant.

As she studied the photo, she asked, "Do you breed horses to sell?"

Nick leaned back in the corner of the seat and took off the baseball cap. "No. I am a horse lover, not a breeder.

"I think that horses are one of the most beautiful animals. My favorite Olympic events are figure skating, gymnastics, and equestrian."

"Then we must bring you to Cheltenham for the annual festival there in March. It's the flagship of Britain's steeplechase horseracing."

Can he be serious? Bring me to Cheltenham?

"Do you ride?" he asked as if excited by her interest in his passion.

"No. I've always thought I would like to but never really had the opportunity. Ballet dancers only do ballet. I barely learned to swim."

At the mention of ballet, he took additional interest. "I would have liked to have seen you dance."

Reaching up the sleeve of her blouse to adjust the bracelet, she said, "I wasn't very special. I never made it out of the corps."

"I assume you gave it up for your marriage."

She nodded. "I thought I was in love and wanted to raise a family. When Mark came along, I had been dancing demi-solo roles but didn't get a demi-soloist's contract. I was impatient. Mark was handsome and persuasive—the rest is history."

"And Mark turned out to be a philanderer?"

Ansley nodded her head slowly. "That's an understatement. He turned out to be a nightmare that I never want to repeat."

"I would say that the man was a bastard, but even more, he was a class-A fool. Wouldn't you agree, Ian?"

"I would."

Ansley smiled. She had nearly forgotten Ian was in the car. "That's kind of you both, but you don't know much about me."

Nick lowered his eyelids to half closed and tipped his head to one side, looking at her as though he could see through her clothing. "I know enough."

The trip took less than ninety minutes, but trouble finding the farm caused them to be a little late for the eleven o'clock appointment.

While searching, they passed picturesque farms situated on rolling hills, bordered by white-rail fencing, and sprinkled with grazing horses.

"I understand that some of the most prominent names in America, even the Vanderbilts, keep, or have kept horses in this community," Nick said as they approached the area. "Our host, Colonel William Remington, said that Ocala has terrain similar to that of the states far better known for thoroughbred horses. I can see that he was right."

When Ian found their destination, the manager, Buck Horton, greeted them at the gate in a rugged SUV with the logo of the stables painted on the side.

"The colonel is waiting for you at one of the barns. You can either follow me or ride in my van."

"We'll ride with you," Nick said.

Once Nick and Ansley were seated in the back, and Ian next to the driver, Horton put it in gear and started up the long, private road, while announcing their impending arrival over a static-laden radio system.

"We don't get big-time movie stars out here very often."

Ansley smiled. The contrast in speech was dramatic between Nick's proper British speech and the rural, Southern accent of their guide.

"My missus would love to have an autograph, if that's okay, Mr. Colton."

"I'd be honored. I think Ian has a few photos in the car, right?"

"We do," Ian said.

"I understand you have an outstanding stable of thoroughbreds," Nick said.

"We've had some of the best here," the man responded, a grin crossing his face. "Even had the sire of a Derby winner."

Nick listened intently to the man's bragging about the area's role in the horse world, and Ansley wondered about his opinion of this new slice of Americana.

"The colonel says that you two met up in Kentucky last spring at the Derby," Horton said, as he finished telling how the estate was founded.

"That we did. It was gracious of Colonel Remington to extend an invitation to visit."

When they reached the barn, their host was standing outside.

OMG. He looks just like Colonel Sanders dressed in jeans and a flannel shirt.

As they emerged from the SUV, the owner greeted Nick with enthusiasm.

"Nick, so happy you got down this way. Can't wait to show you my place."

Nick shook hands with the white-haired man and said, "Happy to be here. Thank you for the invitation. This is my friend, Anna and my man, Ian."

The colonel took Ansley's hand and squeezed it, patting her on the shoulder with his other hand. "Happy to have you."

She smiled but her mind was on Nick's introduction. *Anna? Has he forgotten my name?*

"The wife's cooking up a storm. After I show you around Remington Acres, we'll go up to the house for a bite of dinner. She's a great cook."

Horton brought a red, four-passenger golf cart from a building adjacent to the barn. Ansley stared at it. *I'm counting five people here; how is this going to work?*

Her question was quickly answered when Remington climbed into the driver's seat, motioning Nick to join him.

"I'll let Ian ride up front with you. I'll sit on the back with Anna."

"No, no," Ansley said, quickly. "You're here to see the horses. You should be in the front. Ian and I will be fine on the rear seat." She was still smarting from his calling her Anna but not certain how to handle it. If she corrected him, it would announce to everyone that she was so insignificant that he didn't even know her name—it was a slap in her face.

It was a bumpy ride with moments when Ansley had to grasp the side bar. The colonel did most of the talking with a comment here and there from Nick. Neither Ansley nor Ian said anything. She tried to enjoy the perfect weather and the beautiful scenery, but she couldn't shake the feeling of humiliation.

At one point on the tour, the colonel stopped the cart near a gathering of three horses. "There are my prizes," he said, getting out. "Come have a closer look, Nick. I think you'll be impressed."

When the two were out of earshot, Ansley turned to Ian and said, "Nick's got my name wrong. He's calling me Anna." Her expression gave away her disappointment.

Ian smiled. "He's not to have forgotten your name, Ms. Sheridan. He's not wanting to risk exposing you to the paparazzi if these folks be bragging tomorrow about entertaining him," he said, with his Irish accent.

"Oh. I never thought of that."

After the tour, the group went to the two-story, white, frame farmhouse where Mrs. Remington had a full-course meal ready. Ansley couldn't help but smile when she saw the platter of fried chicken, the huge bowl of mashed potatoes, and a dozen dishes of assorted, fresh vegetables. *What else would Mrs. Colonel Sanders cook?*

When the dessert dishes were cleared, Nick asked if there were any stables nearby where he and Ansley might ride. She held her breath, hoping to hear there weren't. However, the accommodating host was quick to give directions to a riding school that rented by the hour and had extensive property for trail riding.

Horton drove them back to their car where Nick signed the requested photos. Following Horton's directions to the Fulton Academy, Ian dropped the couple off and promised to return upon a call from Nick.

The colonel had telephoned ahead and the owner was waiting. Nick introduced himself as Tony Colebridge, complete with American accent, as he had told Remington he would do. However, he suspected from the red-carpet treatment that the old man had managed to reveal his real identity.

Two horses were produced—a mahogany bay for Nick and a small quarter horse for Ansley. Nick's was a retired thoroughbred.

"I'm not sure about this, Nick. I've never been on a horse that didn't have a brass pole to hold on to."

He laughed. "You'll be fine."

After helping her into the saddle, he mounted his ride with the grace and agility of a seasoned horseman.

When they returned to the stable after an hour's ride, Ansley was exhilarated.

"I did it!"

"Of course, you did."

"I would love to learn how to *really* ride."

"That could be arranged," he said as he helped her dismount.

The statement gave her chills.

Back in the car, Nick put his arm around Ansley and pulled her close to him. "Tell me what you thought about your maiden ride?"

"I loved it, once I stopped being scared. But you couldn't have enjoyed it much, having to ride at the pace of an amateur."

"I took delight in seeing you learn. I can ride at home anytime. I'm buying a new colt back in the U.K. I'd like you to name her."

She smiled and said, "That's quite an honor." *If that is a line he gives all women, it's a good one.*

As they rode back toward Orlando, silence settled in the car. Nearing the city, Ian was the first to speak. "Nick, what is my destination?"

"My guess is that Ms. Sheridan would like to stop by her hotel to freshen up before dinner." He turned to face Ansley. "Am I right?"

"I would."

"Afterward, will you join my duck friends at the hotel and me for dinner in my suite?"

She took a deep breath. *What do I say?*

"You're hesitant."

"No . . . well maybe." She looked down, avoiding eye contact. "I'm sorry. It will be fine."

He reached over and took both of her hands. "It's just dinner."

Back in her hotel room, she was nervous as she dressed for the evening. Nick had walked her to the door and said that while he showered, Ian would come back for her, which would take about an hour and a half.

What is the appropriate attire for dinner in a hotel suite? Am I being naive to believe him when he said, "just dinner"? Do I want it to be just dinner?

After deciding on a red silk shirt with the pants she wore the night before, she showered and shampooed.

Ansley stood, looking at her reflection in the bathroom mirror, wondering how to do her hair for the evening. Remembering how Nick took it loose in New York, she decided to let it hang free, having kept it tied in a ponytail all day. As she brushed, it draped softly down one side of her face and over her shoulders, reminiscent of Veronica Lake in the forties. *My hair hasn't been this long since I left ballet. I meant to have it cut when I came back from New York.*

At seven o'clock, Ian picked her up and delivered her to Nick's suite at the top of the hotel. Opening the door, the actor nodded with an impish grin and then said in a low, sexy tone, "I like what I see." He motioned for her to enter with one hand, while lifting a bit of her hair with the other as she passed. "You should wear your hair like that more often. It's stunning."

He wore crisply pressed khakis, a pale-blue oxford shirt, unbuttoned so that about eight inches of chest was exposed, and a pair of Gucci loafers. "Allow me to pour you a glass of champagne before we order."

Ansley looked around the well-appointed room, which was luxurious, but not ostentatious. The bedroom could be seen through a doorway on the right, and a view of the city was visible through a floor-to-ceiling glass wall directly opposite the entry. The sight of a sumptuous, king-sized bed, with a mound of plump pillows, sent a sensation through her. The lamp on the night table was illuminated, casting a soft glow. There was a book and a couple of letter-size packs of paper, three-hole punched and bound with brass brads on the side. She wondered whether the latter were scripts.

He sleeps there—maybe in the nude. What would it feel like to sleep next to him? Oh, my, gosh.

Two hours later, room service had taken away the dinner cart. Ansley stood by the glass overlooking Orlando. "Everything is beautiful at night when you're thirty stories up."

Bringing a flute of champagne, Nick stood behind her for a few moments with one hand on her shoulder, viewing the city lights. "It is lovely."

"My firm is on the twenty-fifth floor on the Southbank of the St. Johns River in Jacksonville. When I work at night, I sometimes look out my window in awe of the lights—sprinkled like precious jewels on black velvet."

"Very descriptive. Night lights are one of the beauties of a city." He opened a door leading to a small balcony. "Would you like a bit of air?"

"I'm fine," she said, thinking about how high they were and how much champagne she had consumed.

"I have little to offer in terms of entertainment, but we could watch a film."

"Sure."

Nick closed the door, crossed the room to a credenza, and picked up one of the hotel brochures. "See if there's anything available that appeals to you," he said, handing it to her.

Flipping through the pages, Ansley said, "Look, they have your new—"

"No. Anything but one of mine."

"Why not?"

"The last thing I want to do is watch Nick Colton on the screen, counting the flaws in his performance—especially with someone I hope to impress."

"I've seen it. I didn't see any 'flaws'."

He took her hand and removed the guide. "If you've seen it, then all the more reason to choose something else. What about the Clooney-Pitt film, *Ocean's Eleven?*"

She looked up at him with a "you're being silly" expression, and then cutting her eyes to the corner with a raised eyebrow, she said, "Clooney and Pitt sound great. I like them both."

"Of course you do. And what a fool I was to suggest it."

Did I hear a note of jealousy?

Tossing the guide back onto the credenza, Nick picked up the champagne glasses they had both put down and handed her one. Taking her free hand in his, he led her to the deep-cushioned sofa in front of the TV. Once they were seated, he rested his wine glass on an end table and set up the film.

"You're good at that. It would take me thirty minutes to get the instructions right to make it play, and then I'd probably have the wrong movie."

"Experience, love—much experience."

As they settled in to watch the movie, Nick used a remote device to turn out the lighting, leaving only the full moon and a dim light from the bedroom for illumination. Putting his arm around her shoulders, he pulled her close as the credits began. Ansley relaxed and allowed her body to lean against his chest. She slipped off her shoes and drew her feet up on the seat as he gently massaged her neck and shoulders.

This is so nice.

Her eyes were on the screen, but her mind was elsewhere. The physical connection between them had moved forward; however, Nick honored invisible boundaries. He seemed content to hold her close, rub her shoulders, and toy with her hair—lifting it off her neck and letting it flow through his fingers. Neither spoke. Periodically, he took a sip from his glass of champagne, but Ansley left hers untouched.

It was close to midnight when the final credits rolled. She sat up and slid her feet back into her shoes. "May I use your restroom?"

"It's through the bedroom."

She felt a little tipsy as she stood—a combination of the earlier wine and sitting for so long. She took a deep breath to steady her walk and went toward the bedroom. *Is this the point where he makes an overture?* Looking at the bed as she passed through, another sensation tingled in personal parts. *Stay cool. Don't encourage what you can't handle.*

Before leaving the bathroom, she washed her hands in the pristine marble sink. Looking around the counter, the only visible sign that the suite was occupied was a leather travel kit on a shelf under the counter and a matte-black bottle adjacent to the cluster of complementary toiletries. After drying her hands, she picked up the bottle and sniffed the top. Without removing the cap, she could smell the familiar fragrance. Turning the bottle so that the light exposed the black-on-black text at the bottom, she read, "Green Irish Tweed." At the top was the embossed logo: CREED. *So that's his fantastic fragrance. I've never heard of Creed.*

Guilt at having invaded his personal space caused her to quickly return the container to its place, suppressing the impulse to wipe away her fingerprints. Coming out, she walked close enough to the bed to read the cover of the book: *Tell No One* by Harlan Coben.

Back in the living room, Nick was watching the news. When she reentered, he immediately rose. "Excuse me for a minute, love, and then I'll see you to your hotel." As he passed by her on the way to the bedroom, he lightly stroked her arm.

He really meant "just dinner."

Back at Ansley's room door, she withdrew the keycard from her purse, and he took it from her. Parking it in the slot, he made no attempt to trigger the lock release. Turning back, he swept her into his arms, pressing her body against his, and kissed her long and passionately, his tongue reaching deep into her mouth.

As he released her from the embrace, he held her firmly at the waist with both hands. His piercing amber eyes locked with hers in a frozen moment in time. Ansley was weak all over, hardly able to think, much less speak. When feeling began to come back in her hands and knees and her thoughts became coherent, she asked, barely audible, "Why haven't you made a move to seduce me?"

A smile crossed his face, and he pulled her against his chest.

"Because, love," he whispered in her ear, "you're not ready yet. I have *no* intention of spoiling this relationship." Stroking her hair, he added, "It will happen when the time is right."

Ansley was at first speechless. Every inch of her craved him—cried out for him to take her to the bed in her room and strip her naked. Struggling hard to place her passion in neutral, she drew back, looked up into his eyes, raised her body as high as her tiptoes allowed, and kissed him on the cheek. "Thank you."

He lifted the keycard and reinserted it, releasing the lock. Holding the door, he handed her the key and said, "I'll pick you up for breakfast at eight."

She didn't respond. She couldn't, simply nodding. Once in the security of her room, tears flooded her cheeks. *Will there really be another chance?*

Ansley was in a dismal mood, driving back to St. Augustine on Sunday. The weekend had been wonderful beyond belief, making the letdown more depressing. Even the weather had turned, with gray skies and intermittent downpours. When they parted, after a buffet breakfast at the nearby Hilton, she had feigned good spirits, but fear that it would never happen again plagued her. She replayed his words over and over. *Was it a line, or did he really mean it when he said, "It will happen when the time is right"? He wanted me. I know he did. I could feel it.*

CHAPTER FIFTEEN

"Where have you been? I've been calling you all weekend," Elaine said, when Ansley answered her phone on Sunday evening.

"I'm sorry. I just went down to Orlando for a couple of days. An old friend from New York was vacationing and invited me."

"Well, next time, let someone know. I even called your mom this morning. I was beginning to worry."

That's going to open a can of worms.

"She said that she had not talked to you since Christmas, but she's expecting you for black-eyed peas and hog jowl on New Year's Day."

"I'll call her when we hang up."

"Do you have to work this week?"

"Yeah. I only have the holiday off. I had so much time off last week." *If only I could tell you about this weekend. You would die.*

After scheduling a girls' day out on the following Saturday, they hung up.

Ansley had barely replaced the phone when it rang again.

"I want all the juicy details."

"Hello to you, too, Dennis Devlin."

"Come on, Ansley. Quit wasting time. What happened?"

"I'll tell you everything as long as you promise not to interrupt or editorialize."

"My lips are zipped."

"First—there was no sex, so don't hold your breath."

"What!"

"No interrupting."

From there, she gave him the instant replay as though it were a computerized recording. When she finished, there was a moment of silence.

"Do I have permission to speak now?"

"Go for it."

"Whoopee!" he shouted. "Triple whoopee. You've got him, babe. The guy's a snared beast—bundled and bound."

"And you think that—why?"

"Ansley, sweet, naïve Ansley, a man that squelches his predatory, hormonal instincts is either a wimp or a man with serious intentions. Nicholas Colton is absolutely no wimp."

"Don't be absurd. He can't have serious intentions. He's seen me a total of five times."

"Mrs. Nicholas Colton—Ansley Colton. Has a harmonious ring."

"Before you start shopping for a wedding gift, get a grip. That's almost too absurd to deserve comment."

"Admit it. The thought has crossed your mind."

"And instantly exited stage left. There's every possibility—likelihood—that I will never hear from him again."

But she did. On New Year's Eve, when she arrived home from work, there was another tag on her door, indicating a flower delivery was left with Jeanette.

"My, you're getting attention from someone. Care to share?" Jeanette asked, handing Ansley the box.

"There's really nothing to share. They're probably from a guy I met in New York, but long distance relationships never work."

The single rose bore a card that read:

> For a weekend indelibly engraved in my memory, thank you. Until I see you again, think of me with warmth and affection as I will, you.
>
> Nick

Ansley had hoped he would call New Year's Eve or the next day, but he didn't. Although there was no contact over the holiday, when she got home on Thursday, there was a small, blue box from Tiffany's waiting in her mailbox. Inside was a gold horse for her bracelet. She immediately attached it with the split ring and sat staring at the charms, exquisite souvenirs of their time together.

On Sunday night, the call came. The caller ID said only that it was an unknown number, but Ansley knew.

"Have I caught you at a bad time?" Nick asked.

"No. I am just folding laundry."

"I was afraid to call earlier for fear of interrupting your day."

After more small talk, he asked, "Is your passport current?"

"*I doubt it.*" *What is he thinking?*

"Best get it renewed as I'm hoping you'll join me in Tuscany for a few days next month."

"Tuscany?" Her heart jumped. *Join him in Italy?* "That's quite a distance."

"I'm there on business and would love to share a long weekend with you."

Her heart was racing. She fought to keep her voice from quivering. "Do you have a specific date in mind?"

"If you can leave Jacksonville on the thirteenth by dinner time, I can have you in Florence by early afternoon on the fourteenth. I think you'll find the beauty of the country worth the inconvenience of the travel."

Valentine's in Tuscany with him. Oh, my, gosh. "I'm sure that it is. I've read a lot about it, but never been there. Can I check with my managing partner and let you know if the firm will give me the time off?"

He agreed and promised to call her the next night at about the same time. Ansley could hardly sleep.

Nick and Tuscany. What if I can't get off work? I'll quit. Wrong. You can't quit. Charles has just got to let me go. Please, God, don't let there be a trial that week.

She had not addressed what to tell her boss, or her family, about where she would be. Her absence in the middle of the week would require some clever fabrication.

The next morning, as soon as Charles Courson arrived at the office, Ansley was at his door.

"Can I speak to you for a minute?"

He motioned for her to come in and then listened to her request.

"Is this something very important? We do have a couple of trials coming up the first of March."

"It really is, or I wouldn't ask. I'll work all of the weekends before and after to make up for the time I'm gone."

"Obviously, it is important. Let me think about it. I'll give you my answer by day end."

Leaving his office, Ansley was panicked. *What if he says no? I could go to Mr. Fontaine, but that will probably derail my career. What am I thinking? I'm not going to let another man ruin another career for me. If*

Charles says no, I'll just tell Nick that I can't. Oh, please don't let him say no.

Waiting for an answer made the day unbearably long. Passing Courson in the hall at lunchtime, she was afraid to make eye contact. *I must be crazy, asking for time off now.* The month of December had been light on the office workload. But January had started with a bang. Not only were old cases ripening for trial, a number of new divorce cases had already come in.

"People must decide to wait until after Christmas to file for divorce," Olivia, Ansley's secretary, had said as she produced the calendar for the week.

"I kind of understand. I waited until after Christmas to file for mine, and I didn't have children. I'm sure most parents don't want to tell their kids that Santa Claus is bringing them a broken home."

It was after five when Ansley's intercom buzzer sounded. Charles summoned her to his office.

With knots in her stomach, she walked the forty feet.

"Come in. Have a seat."

He's going to say no. I know it. He wouldn't fire me for asking, would he? She clasped her hands together to keep them from shaking.

"I've looked over the calendar for the next month. The Sutton trial is coming up and is going to be labor intensive."

He's going to say no. I can't cry. I can't.

"If you can get all the exhibits organized by the tenth, I see no reason why we can't spare you for the days you requested. I'm sure you know that the time will be subtracted from your vacation this year, unless you want to forfeit your pay for the period you're out."

She wanted to shout and hug him as relief soothed the burning in her stomach. "I fully understand. And, thank you. You don't know how much I appreciate this." A tear of joy and relief crept out of the corner of her eye.

When she got home, Ansley could hardly eat. The cats sensed that something was amiss and followed her through the condo like the Peabody ducks. By nine o'clock, she was a nervous wreck, waiting for the phone to ring. *He's not going to call. It's two a.m. in England.* It was midnight when the phone finally rang. She nearly fell over her feet, scrambling to answer.

"I'm sorry to call so late, but I thought it best to wait until I woke because I have to do an interview for the BBC this morning. I should have warned you."

"No need to apologize. I was watching TV." It was true that the TV was on, but hardly accurate that she was watching.

"May I look forward to the pleasure of your company in Florence?"

Doing her best to disguise her excitement, she took a deep breath and said, "You can. I was able to take the time off, and I applied for a new passport today."

"Splendid! I'll book a private plane to take you to New York for your flight to Florence. I'll be at Peretola when you land. It's a short distance to the Villa San Michele where we will be staying."

CHAPTER SIXTEEN

Despite an overwhelming workload at the firm, the weeks between the invitation and boarding the plane dragged by slowly. Anticipation was hard to set aside. Ansley longed to tell Dennis, but she didn't. It was as though revealing the plan might engender disaster.

Curious about the Italian resort where Nick said they would be staying, she ran an Internet search. According to the web site, the hotel offered rooms, suites, and a separate villa. Sample images of each were shown—all appearing luxuriously appointed with sumptuous beds, laden with pillows; exquisite wood furnishings; and plump upholstered pieces—plus amazing views of the Arno River and the city of Florence. Nick had not mentioned specifics as to their accommodations, nor did she ask.

I won't be booking my own reservation this time. As Dad used to say, "This is where the rubber hits the road, kiddo."

The charter plane was a new experience as was her first-class seat on the commercial flight. With a sleep mask covering her eyes and headphones delivering classical music, she was able to nap, in spite of her excitement. When she deplaned in Florence, her adrenalin kicked into overdrive. Passing through customs, her heart throbbed and her hands shook. She needed to use the restroom but ignored the urge for fear of missing him. Traveling in a land where she did not know the language was disconcerting. When the ballet company toured foreign-speaking countries, she had the insulation of the group. Here, she was on her own.

Just as nerves were about to get the best of her, he appeared—swarthy and stately in his unique manner. He wore a black dress shirt, sleeves rolled up, khaki pants, the familiar Gucci loafers, and sunglasses. He seemed darker, as though he had showered in spray tan. A solid gold watch popped on his wrist in contrast to the tanned skin.

When they made eye contact, a spontaneous smile spread across Ansley's face, matched equally by one on his.

As she reached where he was standing, he extended both hands. "You made it—and radiant as always. I hope the journey was not too unpleasant." Pulling her close, he embraced her with gusto. Letting go of her luggage, her arms went around him in kind. After hugging her, releasing her, and hugging her a second time, he took the handle of her rollerboard in one hand, wrapping his other arm around her waist and shepherding her through the facility to a waiting car.

"Where are your elaborate disguises?" she asked, looking at him as the car exited the airport.

He chuckled. "The Italians couldn't care less about a Brit actor, and the tourists don't expect to see me here, so mobility is a bit easier." Whether accurate or not, there had been no signs of recognition in the terminal.

Taking her hand, he said, "Despite your lovely appearance, I know you are weary. I have scheduled a massage for you. That, plus a shower and nap, is guaranteed to ease jet lag."

"Is that a personal trick of yours?"

"I swear by it. By dinner, you should be totally refreshed." He squeezed her hand to punctuate the statement.

As the car pulled up in front of the sixteenth-century structure, its beauty overwhelmed Ansley. A former monastery, with a façade attributed to Michelangelo, it reigned majestically from high atop a hill, overlooking the city of Florence and the river.

"I've planned a cruise for after dinner tonight. I hope you approve."

"That sounds lovely," she said while absorbing the grandeur of the resort. *And I thought the photographs were spectacular.*

A bellman met them at the car and took Ansley's luggage. Not surprisingly, Nick had reserved the villa, located in the former orangery to the monastery. Adjacent to the main building, the separate structure had its own private garden, rich with foliage, and a waterfall with plunge pool. A low wall guarded the side overlooking the slope to the river. A round table and two chairs for outdoor dining were positioned near the wall on the lush carpet of grass.

"I'm staying here with you?" she asked, looking up at him.

"There are two bedrooms."

She looked at him, feeling weak all over.

There might have been two bedrooms, but the intimacy of sharing the villa resonated in her mind. *Don't even pretend to be surprised. You knew darn well that he wouldn't fly you first-class, halfway around the world and not expect you to share his accommodations.*

Taking her face in his hand, he continued, "You'll have all the privacy you desire."

She was speechless, only nodding her head in agreement.

"But for now, you need to prepare for your massage. There is a robe behind the door in your bath. Carlotta should be here shortly. She's very good. I'll leave you to enjoy your afternoon."

"Your business?"

He turned his head slightly, eyebrows raised. "What business?"

"The business that brought you. . . ." A note of realization crossed her face. "Oh. You made that up."

He grinned. "Guilty, counselor." Leaning forward, he kissed her quickly and said, "I'll see you later."

It was five-fifteen and the sun was beginning its descent when Ansley woke from her nap. Nick had been right. The massage had put her to sleep, and she felt quite rested, considering the length of her travel and the change in time zones. Struggling to bring herself to a fully conscious state, she put her feet on the floor and stood up. Opposite the bed was a demilune window, the mirror image of one in the living area. Each went from the floor to near the ceiling. Beyond the glass was the most breathtaking view Ansley had ever seen. *The Internet did not do this justice.* Spectacular is an understatement. The terraced hill held layer upon layer of Italian gardens, flowers, and foliage. *If it is this beautiful in the daylight, imagine what it's like when it's dark.*

Looking around the room, she wondered where her suitcase had gone. Have I been robbed? Noticing closet doors between the bedroom and bathroom, she walked over to check, even though she had not put it there. Opening the double doors, she was shocked to see her garments pressed and hanging orderly. The suitcase was on the floor. *Someone unpacked my stuff.* Turning back to the bedroom, she checked drawers and found her lingerie and other items neatly arranged. *Who did this? Not Nick.* Before she had a chance to fully comprehend the situation, the villa telephone rang. Wondering whether he had returned and might answer, she waited a minute. After the third ring, she was satisfied that she was alone. *What if I answer and the caller only speaks Italian?* Answering, hesitantly, she was relieved to hear the familiar voice.

"Did you have a nice nap?"

At the sound of his voice, the adrenaline increased. "I did. The massage was glorious."

"Was I right?"

"Absolutely. Did you unpack for me?"

"Would I get extra points if I said yes?"

"That was a stupid question, wasn't it? But, you're going have to forgive me. The Holiday Inn doesn't provide such personal service."

He laughed. "You have absolutely no need to apologize. Just enjoy."

"Thank you, but before I expose my lack of upscale experience again, how should I dress for dinner? I feel safe assuming that the dress code doesn't include jeans."

"I would be proud to escort you in any costume you chose to wear."

"You're not being any help. I'm thinking a cocktail dress might be appropriate."

"It would. When you're ready, join me in the lounge of the main building." There was brief silence before he added, "Do me a favor. Don't confine your hair."

Ansley smiled. *He likes long hair.*

Wearing the green dress she wore the night they met, Ansley walked to the entry of the lounge thirty minutes after the phone call. Pausing, she looked around the sparsely populated room. Although there were not many guests in the area, she felt as though she was being scrutinized. *Where are you, Nick. I'm not comfortable in a fancy bar—dressed up and alone like a high-class call girl.* Taking a couple of guarded steps into the area, she spotted him coming from the men's room. He saw her instantly and walked briskly to her side.

"My, Ms. Sheridan, how beautiful you are this evening. A man could fall in love with you."

How am I supposed to respond to that? She smiled and whispered an inaudible thank you, wanting to say how irresistibly handsome he was in his black, satin-lapel dinner jacket.

He put his arm around her waist and directed her to a table in the corner next to the expanse of glass overlooking Florence. Candles, augmented with shaded lamps ringed with flowers and greenery, dimly illuminated the room. In the adjoining restaurant, tablecloths draped to the floor, covering tops decorated with floral baskets and set with gleaming china, crystal stemware, and silver. Cloth napkins were ornately folded on each service plate. Classical music played softly in the background of the bar and restaurant: Shubert and Chopin.

As she sat down at the table, the view took her breath. "Nick, this is the most beautiful place I have ever been."

"I'm glad you like it. It suits you well."

As he poured wine in the stemmed glass in front of her, she asked, "Have you been here before?" *Do I really want to know the answer to that question?*

"Florence, yes—but here, no. I understand it was a favorite of John Kennedy."

Could I be sleeping in a bed tonight that John Kennedy slept in?

Before Ansley could finish her glass of wine, their table was ready. To her relief, conversation was casual during dinner. It was hard to erase from her mind that sometime later they would certainly be consummating the relationship.

The food was superb. When they were done, a driver picked them up and took them down the hill to a dock where they boarded a small boat. The evening was clear—the cruise smooth and picturesque. Like the ride through Central Park, they were alone, but for the boatman. The difference lay only in the physical contact. While Nick had kept a polite distance in New York, in the boat, his hands began to explore, arousing Ansley.

Returning to the villa, Ansley's nervous system was a jumble of both desire and apprehension. *This is it.*

On the table, there was a silver, footed champagne bucket, icing a bottle of Dom Perignon. Adjacent to the bottle was a crystal bowl of huge strawberries, a small chafing dish of toasted nuts, and a tray of caviar, assorted cheeses, and small toast rounds. Nick removed his jacket and laid it across the back of a chair—then poured two glasses of wine, handing one to Ansley. As she took her first sip, he used a remote control to lower the already dim lighting and to turn on romantic piano music. The adjoining bedroom was illuminated only by the light of the moon coming through the expanse of the large dome-shaped window.

This is like a movie—or a dream. I'd better drink extra wine tonight.

Taking a large sip of his wine, and then resting the stem on a nearby table, he turned and said, "Would you like to dance?"

She looked at him, without responding.

"I'll take your silence as a yes," he said, taking her in his arms and sweeping her around to the sultry rhythm of a new-age, piano arrangement of "Love is a Many Splendored Thing." His hold was firm, his movement in perfect time to the highs and lows of the melody. Her body pressed against his, her breasts hard against his chest. It was natural to allow her face to rest against his shoulder, the aroma of his Green Irish Tweed adding to the intoxication of the moment. What began as a hand at her waist became a hand cupping her buttocks, pulling them hard against his groin. She felt the heat through the sheer fabric of her dress. The power of his masculinity at her pelvis was evident. Slowly, his fingers eased the fabric of her dress up until his hand rested on her panties. She turned her face up toward his and his mouth covered hers, his tongue igniting the passion. She felt a flow of warm moisture between her legs and was consumed with a level of desire she had never before experienced. Withdrawing his tongue, he eased his mouth to her ear and whispered.

"Now . . . the time is right." And with that, he swept her off her feet and carried her to his bed.

High above the Arno River, Ansley felt unabashedly naked to the world as Nick slowly removed each piece of her clothing. Without taking his eyes from her nude body, he removed his own clothing. Her back arched, her bare breasts reaching up to him, wanting him to take her completely. Lowering himself down, his hands explored her form as Michelangelo would have explored his work of marble, relishing the perfection. Nick's hands were slow, savoring each aspect of the woman he was taking. The music continued in the background, and when he penetrated her, "Habanera" had begun to play. The magic of the moment took over—all control was lost. Ansley experienced carnal love as never before, taking her to the point of out-of-body rhapsody and simultaneously terrifying her. She was powerless to resist her insatiable desire. When he was done, he caressed her face gently, kissed her, and whispered, "The first time had to be one that you will never forget and one you will not be able tell our grandchildren about."

Lying next to him, Ansley was as weak as a newborn. Her fingers tingled with the exhilaration of what she had experienced. Lovemaking with Mark had never taken her where she had just been with Nick. Thoughts raced through her mind, crashing into one another like a bevy of frightened mice. She wanted to say something, but was afraid to open her mouth, afraid she would regret any words that might escape.

Our grandchildren? A woman he could fall in love with?

For Ansley, making love equated to being in love. It was the only frame of reference she had for an act of passion. But, she could not allow herself to believe that love was on the table with Nick Colton. To even remotely think that he could be in love with her, or even that she could truly be in love with him, was incomprehensible and immature.

He had to be teasing—toying with me. This was lust. Monday, the carriage will be a pumpkin again, and Cinderella will be back at the hearth.

In Ansley's rationalization, no matter how wonderful his words, there was every possibility that it was all an act. Nick Colton lived in a world of make-believe. It would be foolhardy to assume that his innuendos of a serious relationship were valid.

Don't be naïve. This could all be a game for him, but oh my God, he's ruined me for mortal men.

Lying on his side, facing her, Nick slid his arm under her shoulders, drawing her close and wrapping her in the cocoon of his embrace. "Are you okay?" he said softly.

She nodded and reached around him, holding as tight.

Neither spoke. Minutes passed and neither moved.

His arm must be going numb.

Ansley adjusted herself, hoping to relieve the pressure of her weight on his arm, and as she did, he squeezed her affectionately, and then broke the silence.

"Would you like something to drink?"

"No thank you." Her response was based more on a reluctance to emerge from the bed without her clothes than a lack of desire for refreshment.

Sitting up, he said, "Well, I am hungry." Leaning over, he kissed her, long and with unmistakable intensity. As she yielded, he pulled back. "Hold that thought."

He then left the bed. Ansley burrowed under the sheet and watched as the moonlight coming through the window backlit his toned form, igniting her memory of that infamous movie.

After a brief trip to the bathroom, he came out, wearing one of the thick hotel robes and holding another. "I suspect your modesty has invaded the moment." He handed her the robe. "If you like, you may join me. If not, take a nap, and I'll be back in shortly to finish what we've started."

Ansley shivered, feeling like Scarlet O'Hara after her final tryst with Rhett.

CHAPTER SEVENTEEN

The remainder of the romantic weekend was filled with assorted pleasure, in and out of the bedroom. They toured the museums of Florence and ate in out-of-the-way bistros as well as restaurants with gastronomical opulence. Conversation became more and more comfortable as each learned more about the other. They laughed together, stood in mutual awe before ancient art, and discovered common ground in the music they both loved—the only exception being in Nick's distaste for rock, rap, and anything similar, while Ansley defended the modern music. The food and wine everywhere was superb. On Saturday night, they attended the opera, a local production of Verdi's *La Traviata*. Watching Nick immersed in the music, Ansley gained more and more insight into the complexity of the man.

After the performance, they went to a small club before returning to the villa. As they sipped wine and nibbled on cheese, they watched the locals perform a zesty folk dance. Ansley looked at Nick and said, "Outside of the ballet world, you're the only man I've known who truly loves classical music. My ex said that only weird people like ballet and opera—that normal people like sports."

"The fact that he let you get away tells me a lot about his taste and intelligence, however, I won't complain because if he had good sense, we would have never met."

She smiled.

"You must know by now that I'm quite taken with you."

She thought about it for a moment before responding. "I don't think we should talk about anything like that."

"Why not? I don't think you find me offensive."

"Therein lies the problem."

He grimaced.

"I almost wish that I did," she said.

"You're a mysterious creature, Ansley Sheridan. Why would you want to find me offensive?"

"You scare me."

"What, pray tell, have I done to scare you?"

She fiddled with her wine glass, avoiding eye contact and answering.

He reached across the table and covered her hands with his. "Why are you afraid?"

Shaking her head, she looked up. "Liking you too much is equal to high-wire walking across the Grand Canyon."

"Ouch. That's a bit harsh."

"Let's just change the subject. Tonight's my last night here, and I don't want to spoil it with any negativity."

He smiled, released her hands, and said, "I absolutely don't want to do anything to spoil what has been for me, and I hope for you as well, a perfect holiday."

After finishing the wine, they returned to the villa, where Nick made love to her for the last time of the holiday.

When they said their farewells at the airport, he took her in his arms and kissed her far more passionately than she expected for a public place, but she didn't resist. Walking down the concourse, a nasty little thought popped in her mind. *What if I never hear from him again? He said nothing about calling.*

On the plane, she was happy that her first-class seat was in one of the back corners of the section and even happier that the seat next to her remained vacant. It provided the best set of circumstances for napping and secretly reliving the past few days.

It was nearly midnight on Sunday when she opened the door to her condo. Walking into reality seemed to make the previous days feel more and more like a delectable dream. Skye and Shadow were happy to see her. Their bowls were filled with food and water and the boxes as clean as litter boxes ever are. "Melissa took good care of you, I see. Now, what am I going to tell everyone about where I've been?" Looking at Skye who was staring up, she said, "I'll say that I went to Florence to spend the weekend with a friend from New York. Totally true. Maybe if pushed, I'll say Dennis. I'll bet no one thinks of Italy. They'll assume I went to South Carolina. Now, if I can just wipe the cat-who-got-the-canary grin off my face, I'll be good."

Taking her suitcase into the bedroom, she sat down on the bed.

Both cats jumped up, jockeying for a place in her lap as she dialed a number on the phone sitting on her nightstand.

"I hope I didn't wake you," she said when Dennis answered. "But, I thought you would want to know—it happened. I did it."

"I'm not asleep," he lied, his voice giving him away. "What happened? What did you do?"

"I gave away six years of abstinence."

"Nick?"

"Of course Nick."

"You go girl," he shrieked, then lowering his voice, said, "It's about damn time. Tell me about it. Was he great?"

"I'm not giving you details, so erase that thought. Suffice it to say, he exceeded expectations."

"Oh. . .my. . .God. Will you at least tell me where and when?"

"Valentine's in Tuscany."

"Damn, damn, damn, girl. How did that happen? Tuscany?"

"Florence to be exact—in the most beautiful, sixteenth-century villa."

"Oh, my gosh. I can't breathe. I'm hearing bells—church bells."

"Shut up. Don't go there, either. I had a fantastic weekend affair. Don't read anything more into it. And, if you tell anyone, Dennis Devlin, you are a dead man, and I'll put an ancient hex on your soul. Hey, I've got a call coming in. Talk soon. Love you."

Clicking the call-waiting button, her stomach churned. *Can it be?*

"Hello, love. You arrived home safely."

"I did. How was *your* flight?"

"Delightful. All I thought about was the long-legged, sexy American in my bed and her silky blond hair spread across my pillow. Didn't get a bit of work done on my script."

Ansley leaned over, an elbow on her thigh, head in hand, and a huge grin on her face.

"You've become a major distraction for me, I hope you know," he continued.

"I'm sorry."

"You had better *not* be sorry. When can you spend more time with me?"

"I don't know. I don't think I can ask off again for a while." Her heart was pounding, her mind racing.

"Don't you Americans have any holidays coming up?"

"Not for a while. I might take a long weekend at Easter, but

Memorial Day at the end of May is the next legal holiday."

"That's not acceptable."

As he spoke, Ansley got up and went to the kitchen where a calendar hung on her pantry door. "Easter is March 31st. That's just a little over a month."

"I'd like it sooner, but that's better than May. When could you come?"

"Where?"

"I'm thinking Gloustershire. I should be done shooting and I would like to share my part of the world with you. We can iron out details later. Just make sure you can get away. Now, I'd better let you get some sleep. It's late over there."

As she placed the phone in its cradle, she sat down on the bed, staring at the wall, but seeing Nick. *How can I sleep now?*

Walking into the office the next day, Ansley felt like a train had run over her, leaving an invisible tattoo of the word *mistress* on her forehead. *I've got to look different than I did last Wednesday.*

"Welcome back," Olivia said as Ansley picked up her calendar for the week. "Did you have fun?"

If you only knew. "I did. It just went too fast."

"Ted Greene is coming in this morning. Said that he has something really important to talk to you about, but wouldn't tell me."

"Okay. I hope it's not too depressing. I've got a holiday hangover."

The client walked into Ansley's office with a serious look on his face. As his was the first case that she had been trusted to handle alone, Ted was special to Ansley. On intake, his circumstances had appeared to be simple: an eight-year marriage, no children, no real estate, and a successful working wife.

"I'm surprised to see you today. Has something happened?" Ansley asked as he sat down in front of her desk.

"Have you heard from Lila's lawyer?"

"No."

"She's supposed to contact you. They're going to change Lila's petition to ask for permanent alimony."

Ansley could see that he was agitated, because he was breathing hard and had an almost wild look in his blue eyes. "I don't understand. She earns nearly as much money as you do?"

"Not for long. She's sick."

"What's wrong?"

"Lou Gehrig's disease."

"Oh, Ted. I'm so sorry."

He nodded. "What are her chances of getting alimony?"

"This has caught me off guard, but I'm afraid that it does make a substantial difference."

"She can't get it, can she? We haven't been married that long."

"I know, but these are extenuating circumstances." *Certainly, he doesn't want to completely desert her?*

"I can't pay alimony. You've got to make sure that doesn't happen."

"I'm going to have to be honest with you, Ted. With your income and her disability, you'll probably have to pay alimony. It will depend on whether she has any other source of income, like disability insurance or enough money saved to support her. At the very least, the court will award her token alimony to keep the door open in case her needs increase in the future."

"You *can't* let that happen."

Ansley studied his face for a few seconds. The handsome, forty-eight-year-old man appeared desperate. "Why do I have the feeling that there's something you're not telling me?"

He did not respond. Ansley repeated her question

"We've barely been married eight years. I should not have to pay."

"I feel your pain, Ted. But, this puts a whole new light on the case. She didn't get this disease voluntarily." She looked at him, her respect for him diminishing with his attitude.

"I'm serious, Ansley. I won't pay alimony. Can't you stop her from amending the petition?"

"I could try, but it will be a waste of your money. Judges favor allowing amendments, and these circumstances are going to incur ample sympathy to her cause."

"Try." With that, he got up and left.

Great! I get to beat up a sick woman. What's with this guy?

It was nearly eight o'clock before Ansley got back to her condo that evening. She hated coming home after dark, but it would likely be the routine for the next few weeks. The front entry was almost completely dark, but even in the dim light, she saw the familiar note stuck on the door. A smile crossed her face. *He sent flowers again.* Quickly depositing her briefcase and purse inside the front door, she went over to Jeanette's to retrieve the delivery, far more excited to read the card than to obtain the floral gift.

"I think you have scored a winner, girlfriend," Jeanette said as soon as she opened the door. "At the risk of prying, I would assume that the flowers are related to your trip this weekend?"

Ansley blushed. "Assume all you like. My lips are sealed."

"Well, you go for it, sweetie. As hard as you work, you deserve a little recreation. From the looks of it, you've found a great playmate."

"He's a nice guy, but I'm not building any expectations. You know men."

"And don't I? Haven't gotten a child support check from the bum I married in two months. If it weren't for my parents, Melissa and I couldn't hold on to this condo—not on my nurse's salary."

Taking the white florist's delivery from Jeanette, Ansley thanked her and returned home to open both the box and card.

Her hands shook as she laid the box on her dining room table, Shadow jumping up to check it out. Ripping the envelope open, the ink almost blurred as she quickly devoured the words.

"Think of me and our time together as I shall think of you until we can be together again."

It was signed, "With profound affection, Nick."

Ansley closed her eyes and took a deep breath, holding the card as though it were precious metal. *I'm falling in love with this guy. I can't help myself. Please God, help me keep my head or I'm going to be hurt again.*

Her heart was pounding, her skin tingling. The phone rang and she jumped, her heart lurching.

"I've been calling your cell and this number. Did you work late?"

Ansley tried to steady her trembling hand that held the receiver. "I did. I had no idea you would call tonight. It must be late in England."

"Just after midnight, but I didn't want to go to bed without hearing your voice. It's painful enough to not have you with me."

Her mind raced. Words failed her.

"I'm hoping you have a similar feeling," he said.

Stay cool. Don't let him know how much you're beginning to care. "It was a wonderful weekend. Yeah, I do miss you." *That was good. Not too much.*

"I won't keep you. I know you must be tired, so I'll just say good-night and pray that I have a role in your dreams tonight."

After saying goodnight, she hung up. Taking the single red rose out of the box, she took it and the card to the couch and dropped down, eyes closed, head back, and taking a deep breath. She pictured him in her mind and relived the moments of rapture she had experienced in Italy.

When Ansley arrived home from work on Friday, there was a package in her mailbox with obviously foreign postal markings. An immediate glow replaced the strained look of exhaustion on her face. Taking the small box to the kitchen, she carefully slit the seal with a paring knife, her heart racing. Inside, a small velvet box held a miniature, gold replica of Michelangelo's David, exquisitely detailed.

The small card read, simply, "Remember Florence."

"As if I could forget," she said aloud. Studying the charm brought about a vivid image of her hand in his as they stood before the marble statue the week before. She soaked in the memory for a few minutes before putting the charm away and changing into a warm-up suit.

It had rained all day with the temperature dropping drastically. The condo was chilly. Before making a cup of tea, she adjusted the thermostat. As she took a frozen dinner from the freezer, the phone rang. Ansley's heart stopped for a moment. Excitedly, she answered without looking at the caller ID.

"Ansley, it's Elaine. Are you busy tomorrow?"

Darn it. She had hoped it was Nick. "I am. I've got to work all weekend."

After a banal conversation, Ansley hung up and finished preparing her dinner.

All evening, she couldn't help hoping for a phone call from Nick. Each time the phone rang, she held her breath. By eleven o'clock, her mother, her boss, and a wrong number had called. Each time, she was disappointed, but assured herself that she could not infer a lack of interest. He *had* sent another charm, but there had been no phone call since Monday night.

Why would he call the day after I got home and not call again all week?

After the TV news signed off, she gave up hope and went to bed.

On Saturday, Ansley worked until four o'clock. Driving home, she told herself not to be disappointed if he didn't call that night, but the self-admonition failed when the phone remained silent.

By Sunday morning, Ansley was fighting depression. While she rationalized that she couldn't expect him to call frequently, the relationship had moved to another level, and she needed assurance that he had not lost interest. There was so much work on her desk at the firm that she decided to sacrifice her Sunday as well and go to the office, reasoning that it was better than sitting in the empty condo, waiting for a silent phone to ring.

By three o'clock, she was physically and mentally exhausted. The office was deafeningly silent and cold. The heating system did not run in the building on Sundays. No one else was working. She closed down her computer, neatly stacked the files on her desk, and left for home, dreading that her expectations would not be met.

As she turned the key at the front door, she could hear the phone ringing. Nerves got the best of her and she fumbled with the lock. *Don't stop ringing. I'm coming. I'm coming.*

She got there as the phone started its last ring before going to voice mail.

"Where have you been, love? I've been calling all day."

Ansley's face immediately broke into a huge grin—her body relaxed throughout.

"I've been at work."

"On Sunday? I thought actors were the only indentured servants working Sundays."

"I've been away, and my work stacked up."

"Been away, huh? Did you have a good time?"

Pausing for a moment and grinning, she responded, "On a scale of one-to-ten, it was somewhere north of a five." She wrinkled her nose and tipped her head in a coy manner, even though there was no one to see.

"It had better been a hell of a lot north of a *five*," he said, rebuking her.

"It *might* have been."

The rest of the conversation reassured Ansley that she was still prominent in his thoughts. Because of the time difference, he had avoided calling when he was free, believing that she was either sleeping or working. He assured her that he would telephone on weekends if he were unable to call during the week. She thanked him for the charm and told him that she loved his choice.

CHAPTER EIGHTEEN

During the following weeks, Ansley was far too busy at work to think much about her personal life, outside the phone calls from Nick. She had become relatively comfortable with the limited contact, trusting that he called when he could. It was nearly four weeks after returning from Italy before she realized that an important date on her calendar had passed without notice.

Standing in front of the cat calendar hanging on the door of the kitchen pantry, Ansley's stomach turned. *Oh, my gosh. I missed my period. Oh, my gosh.*

She was frozen. Eating was out of the question. All she could think was *what if?*

By eight o'clock, she was a nervous wreck and had to talk to someone. At eight-fifteen, she picked up the phone and dialed New York.

"Dennis, I need to talk. Are you busy?"

"For you, sweet girl, never. What's up?"

"I'm late."

"Late for what?"

"What do you think? Lady late. I haven't had a period since Italy."

For once in his life, Dennis was silent.

"Say something," Ansley pleaded.

"I'm thinking. I'm thinking. Are you sure?"

"Sure that I'm late, of course."

"You couldn't have written down the wrong date?"

"Dennis, I've been home nearly four weeks. Nothing has happened. Even if the date was not marked on my calendar, I would know if I had a period." She was fighting tears as she spoke.

"Have you done one of those drugstore tests?"

"I can't. I just realized the date, and besides, I'm afraid to."

"Before you go off the charts, you need to do that first."

"I can't. I am terrified. What will I do?"

"Calm down," he said, gently. "Let's analyze the situation. Are you on the pill?"

"No."

"Did he use condoms?"

"No."

"Ansley, what were you thinking?"

"Not about this, obviously. Dennis, don't lecture me. I probably thought I was safe because I was just over my period when I left."

"Sweetie, that's why Catholics have so many children. That's not a reliable plan."

"Please, help me figure out what to do if I am pregnant." She was openly sobbing.

"Ansley, you're jumping to conclusions without facts. I'm not a woman, *unfortunately*, but I've heard them talk. There *can* be other reasons why you're late."

"I'm never late . . . never."

"There are choices. Don't panic. You could become a mom. The guy is obviously taken with you. Is it so out of the realm of possibility to consider marriage?"

"No, no," she said, vehemently. "Not even if he were willing. At this point, I wouldn't even tell him."

"Ansley, Ansley. You would have to tell him."

"No way. I see what happens when relationships end and there's a child. Even if we weren't married, he could claim his rights. He could take my baby to England, and I would have no way to fight him over there. With his money, he could hire the best lawyers. No, I would never tell him. I'd just have to break it off."

"You could have an abor—"

"Never. That's not an option." *Never, never again.*

"I think the best idea is to stop dwelling on this until you find out that you have a problem. Go buy a test and call me back." His tone was gentle but firm.

"It's too late to go now. I'll go tomorrow. Will you be home?" Although still upset, Ansley was taking control of her emotions and had stopped crying.

"You set a time, and I'll make certain that I'm home."

Ansley was at the pharmacy before nine o'clock Sunday morning but had arranged to call Dennis at ten-thirty. At ten-twenty-five, she dialed.

Without saying hello, he immediately asked, "Do you have a test?"

"Two. I don't think I could trust just one."

"Have you done it?"

"I've done the first part, but I need you on the phone when I check the results."

"It's going to be alright, Ansley. No matter what those tests say, you're going to be okay. Let's get on with it." His voice was upbeat in contrast to Ansley's.

She smiled, tears in her eyes, and went into her bathroom where the two wands were lying on the vanity counter. Before reaching down to pick one up, she crossed herself with her free hand, still holding the phone to her ear. There was silence as she reached for the first tester, hand trembling. Turning it around slowly, and then looking over at the other one, she sighed.

"They're both negative." She closed her eyes and crossed herself again.

"Fantastic! Do you feel better now?"

For a moment, Ansley was quiet. "This is crazy. I don't. One perverse part of me is disappointed, and another is afraid to trust the answer."

When Nick called later that day, Ansley was remote. He asked if she was not feeling well.

"I'm fine, really. A couple of my cases are pretty stressful, that's all."

"You shouldn't take your clients' problems personally."

"I know, but that's easier said than done."

During the entire conversation, she was preoccupied with the thought of how he would react if she told him that she was late. Would he disappear or step up and support her? *What will I do if the tests were wrong?*

"Ansley, are you there?"

"Yes, yes. I'm here."

"I thought the connection was lost. You didn't answer my question."

"I'm sorry." She was caught. Her mind had wandered and she didn't know what he asked. Clamoring for an excuse, she said, "One of the cats jumped in my lap and knocked the phone askew. What was the question?"

"You are still coming to Gloustershire for Easter."

"Are you sure you want me to come for such a short time?"

"I'll take whatever time you have. It will have been six weeks since I've seen you. Try for as much time as possible."

Confusion flooded Ansley's mind. The thought of being with him was exhilarating; the fear that the tests were wrong—paralyzing. Promising Nick that she would consult with her managing partner, she promised herself that a call to her gynecologist would come first.

At three a.m., Ansley woke with a start and knew from the cramps in her lower back and abdomen that she wasn't pregnant. Addressing the situation, she returned to bed, but couldn't sleep. Tears slipped down on her pillow. *This is insane. I should be dancing in the clouds. I dodged a bullet the size of a cannon ball. Why am I depressed?*

Although it had been four-thirty before Ansley was able to fall asleep, she was at her desk by seven-thirty on Monday. Ted Greene was on her calendar. Her opposing counsel was taking Ted's deposition, and she planned to prep him at ten. However, first she wanted to lock in an appointment with her doctor. The potential trip to England made it even more imperative. To see Nick again, she would be on birth control.

By nine-forty-five, Ansley had approval for two extra days off after Easter. She had barely completed the scheduling of the medical appointment when her secretary buzzed to announce Ted's arrival. She dreaded telling him that the court had granted his wife's motion to amend her petition.

As he walked into her office, Ansley could tell that he was nervous. "How are you today?" she asked.

"I'll be better when this is done." He took a seat in one of the chairs in front of her desk.

"I'm sorry, Ted, but the court granted your wife's motion, and opposing counsel has set your deposition."

His eyes grew vicious as he stood up and slammed his fist down on her desk. "I told you not to let this happen."

Ansley's stomach turned over but her adrenalin kicked in. In a firm tone, she said, "I told you that there was almost no chance to prevent it. I understand your pain in having the burden of alimony, but I can't change your wife's condition."

He sat back down but didn't say anything for several minutes. "Cancel this deposition."

"I can't do that, Ted—at least not without a serious reason."

"Listen to me. I can't be deposed."

He had taken charge of his anger, but the look on his face told her that whatever was bothering him was serious. "Maybe you need to tell me what's going on, Ted."

"I can't do that either."

"I can't effectively represent you if you aren't completely candid with me. What is going on?"

He stood up and walked around the space in front of her desk. He was like a caged cat at the zoo. "What I tell you is confidential, right?"

"Absolutely. You know that."

"I've got to be sure."

"Ted, everything you tell me is protected by the attorney-client privilege. You know all that."

He sat back down, gazing out the twenty-first-story window instead. "I don't need this divorce," he said, pausing.

"I still don't understand."

"I don't need this divorce because I'm not married."

Ansley's face registered immediate curiosity. "Care to explain?"

"I'm not married to Lila because I'm still married to Suzanne."

Ansley tried to hide the extent of her shock. "You're *not* telling me that you've committed bigamy?"

He nodded.

"This is probably over my pay grade, Ted. I think you need to talk to my boss."

"*No.* No one else can know. You have to figure something out."

Relief covered his face. It was as if his burden had been transferred to Ansley. "If this comes out, I could go to jail—lose my job; my kids will have to drop out of college. *Nobody wins.*"

"Wow. I don't even know whether Lila has an alimony claim. You are married, but the marriage is voidable. You've got to let me talk to my boss. He's bound by the same privilege, and you don't want a first-year associate handling this."

Ted shook his head, scowling. "I'll take my chances. You're a bright woman. Between the two of us, we can think this out—find a resolution that causes the least amount of loss. I don't want *anyone* else to know. Are you clear with that?"

"You could just let the divorce go through, pay the alimony, and pray no one finds out."

"Suzanne handles our household accounts. My pay is automatically deposited. She would miss the money and want to know what the deal was."

Ansley thought for a minute or two, looking at the distraught man in front of her. He *was* handsome. The gray in his dark hair was just enough to provide a distinguished look, and his blue eyes stood out against his dark completion. "How the heck did you pull this off?"

"My nomadic life. I've traveled for years, spending many weekends on the road. I met Lila one weekend at a restaurant. She was alone at the table next to mine. I mentioned that I was stuck in Jacksonville for the weekend, and the next thing I knew, I woke up in her condo. I made the mistake of saying I was divorced. Her marriage had just broken up. It just went from there. We always kept our finances separate, as you know."

Ansley listened intently, not sure whether to admire his ingenuity or despise his deceit and his lack of empathy for the sick wife. By the time he left her office, she felt sick to her stomach. *What am I going to do? We have to produce his bank statements, which will show his other family. Can I ethically represent him if this is an ongoing crime?*

CHAPTER NINETEEN

Ian Shaughnessy picked her up at Gatwick on the morning of Good Friday. She had managed to sleep a little on the plane but was wide awake from the adrenaline rush at the prospect of seeing Nick and his home.

"Welcome to the U.K.," he said as he took her luggage.

"Thank you. It's exciting to be here and good to see you again."

"I should have you to the manor before lunch."

Her eyes, wide with excitement, gazed out the window at the picturesque scenery as they exited the A-5 motorway. The rural road wound through the countryside where properties were edged with low stone borders like scenes from a painting. The countryside looked like a patchwork quilt in varying shades of green, gold, and brown. The villages that they passed through were like fairytale scenes, populated with stone houses that boasted multi-gabled roofs, quaint lampposts, and flowers blooming profusely along cobblestone walkways.

It's even more beautiful than I remembered.

When they reached the wall surrounding Nick's property, her stomach began to flutter. She had imagined all sorts of structures. Passing through columns that flanked the opening onto the property, the manor house was visible at the end of a long, narrow, drive that wound through a stand of trees. It was imposing to say the least. From the outside, it appeared to have been plucked from a novel by Fielding, Austen, or Bronte. She could only speculate as to what the inside held.

Nick greeted her at the door, wearing jeans and a white shirt. John, his butler, stood close behind. As Ian took her suitcase from the back of the Japanese SUV and handed it to John, Nick came forward and wrapped his arms around her. Ansley felt a tingle of excitement charge through her nervous system.

I'm at the residence of Nicholas Colton. I really am.

"I'm sorry that I couldn't meet you, but a couple of last minute post-production issues came up. I promise that you will have my undivided attention for the length of your visit."

As they walked through the enormous front door, Ansley looked around like a tourist at one of the wonders of the world. "It's a beautiful house, Nick, but it's huge! How many rooms does it have?"

"Would it be less pretentious to say, 'I don't know,' or to take a guess?" Although flip, he appeared uncomfortable with the question.

"Don't you know?"

"I never counted. The estate agent may have said, but my priorities were not based on the number of rooms. I think it is somewhere in the twenties."

"What do you use them all for?" she asked, overwhelmed with the richness of the interior and beauty of the furnishings. The décor managed to be modern without compromising the integrity of the history of the grand manor. She could see through a large opening on the left of the entry hall into a room lined with row upon row of books rising to the ceiling in built-in cases. A huge Oriental rug covered most of the dark wood flooring. At the far end of the room was a smaller opening that looked like a study, furnished with heavy, ornate wood pieces and leather upholstered seating.

"The truth is: I use very few."

"Then why do you have them?" *Ask a dumb question, Ansley.*

"They came with the house," he said, giving her a devilish look. "My intention was to find a property with sufficient land to provide privacy, security, and room to stable a few horses. My sister found this farm and recognized the potential. On first look, I knew that it was exactly what I wanted. But let's get you settled in. My masseuse is waiting for you."

"Massage, shower, and nap—right?" She smiled.

He squeezed her waist and said, "Of course. I want you *well-rested* for the weekend."

Nick escorted her up the wide center staircase. On the second floor, a six-foot-tall painting of a blond boy in equestrian clothing, standing alongside a horse, greeted them. As he guided her to the right, antique paintings of horses, dogs, and hunt scenes lined the wall, interspersed between closed doors. Ansley wondered if the boy in the life-size work was Kevin. Remembering the photo Nick had shown her, there was a sufficient resemblance. She wanted to ask but didn't. Nick's modern attire was incongruous to the rich formality of the house. Paradoxically, he blended in seamlessly.

I've fallen down the rabbit hole and landed in the middle of Gosford Park.

At the end of the long hall, Nick opened the door to a suite of rooms that bore the unmistakable signature of Laura Ashley, in complete contrast to the dark and somber tone of the rest of the manor. Stargazer lilies and roses in crystal vases erased the musky smell of old wood paneling. This was clearly not Nick's bedroom. They had not discussed her accommodations for the visit, but she was relieved. Having her own space allowed her to feel less like a mistress and more like a respected guest.

The sitting room was furnished with a small sofa of dusty-green velvet; a pair of overstuffed chairs in a muted floral print of coral, ivory, and shades of green; a Queen Anne-styled writing desk with matching chair; and shelves, displaying a mixture of books and artifacts. A tea table on cabriole legs stood between the sofa and chairs. On the far side of the room was a bay window with a cushioned seat and floral throw pillows. The bedroom and bath were to the right of the entry. Ansley could see through to tall, cathedral-shaped windows where sunlight was streaming through, projecting streaks across the carpet. She was instantly captivated by the room.

"It's beautiful, Nick. I feel like a Jane Austen heroine."

"I'm glad you like it. I hope you'll be comfortable during your time here."

"How could I not be?"

A white, distressed-wood nightstand held a Meissen lamp and a crystal vase, containing a single rose. The four-poster bed was skirted and covered by a plump comforter in typical English floral. Her suitcase was already resting on a luggage rack in the corner, presumably placed there by John, the butler.

"I'll leave you to your shower. When you're ready, call down to have Paula come up for your massage."

"I really don't need that," Ansley said, feeling self-conscious.

"I insist. It's the best way to overcome jet lag, and I want you refreshed and adjusted to the time change as quickly as possible since you're here for such a short time."

"Okay, I give up. How do I call for her?"

Pointing to the white phone on a small table next to a chaise lounge in the bedroom, he said, "Push the second button. John will answer. You can tell him what you want, and he will see to it. Don't be hesitant to ask for tea or anything else you would like." He took her by the waist and pulled her close. "I'm very glad you're here. I'll let you get settled and check on you later."

Although reluctant, Ansley made the request for Paula after her shower, thankful that the masseuse was female. While she waited for Paula to come upstairs, she browsed through the books on the sitting room shelves. There were copies of the Bronte sisters, Austen, George Eliot, Joanna Trollope, Helen Fielding, and Agatha Christie. *He knows his women's literature—or knows someone who does.*

It was nearly two o'clock when she woke and took a minute or so to place where she was. Little light was coming through the massive windows as the ivory drapes had been drawn across the glass. Once oriented, she dressed in a pair of jeans and cable knit pullover, following Nick's example. She wondered how to convey to him that she was awake and thought about choosing a book and waiting for his contact. However, after brushing out her hair, she took the initiative and again pushed the second button on the phone. After three rings, John answered.

"May I help you, madam?"

"Thank you, John. Could you let Mr... uh, Nick know that I'm awake." *I don't even know what name they use for him here. Colton or Colebridge?*

"With pleasure, and may I have Martha send lunch up for you?"

Although she was hungry, she thought it better to wait for Nick. "Thank you so much for offering, but if it's okay, I'll wait just now."

It took less than five minutes before there was a tap at her door.

"I hope you're well rested," Nick said, a smile on his face as he stepped inside the room.

She smiled, happy to see him. "I am."

"Have you had something to eat?" he said, gently pushing her hair away from her face and then pulling her close against him by her waist.

"Not yet."

"Martha didn't send lunch up for you?"

"John offered, but I told him I would wait."

"Say no more. Let's get you fed. I have plans for the afternoon."

He called down and instructed Martha to prepare a luncheon plate for Ansley and a pot of tea for two, telling her that they would be down shortly and would take the refreshments on the back veranda.

After lunch, Nick gave Ansley a tour of the house and grounds. His two border collies followed everywhere they went. Although she was hesitant, Nick insisted that they tour the property on horseback.

"You have my word that your horse is docile, and I will keep a pace that is comfortable for you. It's the only practical way to cover the grounds."

After helping Ansley into the saddle, Nick mounted Hamlet. She watched the effortless manner in which he stepped into the stirrup, lifted his weight, and swung his free leg across the majestic animal.

He rides as gracefully as Dennis dances.

Once in the saddle for a few minutes, her apprehension subsided and she soaked in the balmy temperature and scenic property.

It took what was left of the afternoon to cover the land, with only one stop in a clearing along the side of a stream of water flowing through the estate.

"We should have brought a bottle of wine," Nick said, as he lifted her down, her hands on his shoulders. When her feet touched the ground, she looked up at him, and he pulled her against his chest, her arms instinctively went around his neck. Without speaking, he leaned forward. Their lips met and within seconds they were on the grass. Inhibitions vanished as Ansley dissolved in his embrace.

When they arrived back at the house, a white Jaguar was parked near the entrance.

"Were you expecting someone?" Ansley asked.

"No, but that never stopped Pen."

"Your ex-wife, Penelope?" Ansley's eyebrows went up in surprise.

"One and the same. That's her car."

"Oh my gosh. What should I do?"

Nick smiled. "First, let's brush the grass out of your hair and straighten your sweater. Then, we'll go find out what the grand lady is here for."

"I can't meet her now."

"Of course you can. She doesn't bite, just hisses a little."

"Can't I go in a back way and sneak up to my room?"

"No, you can't. You're my guest, and right now, she's the intruder. She may have Kevin with her."

Nick took Ansley's hand, nearly dragging her along, and they entered the house, followed by the two dogs.

"Why, Pen. What an unexpected pleasure. To what do I owe the honor?" Nick said, walking into the vast living room where Penelope was reading a magazine.

Ansley hung behind him like an errant child.

"I see you have company," Penelope said. "Are you an actress from one of Nick's films, my dear?"

"She's not," Nick interjected before Ansley could respond. "Ms. Sheridan is a barrister in the States and my guest for the weekend." Turning, he said, "Ansley, I'd like to introduce you to my former wife, Lady Penelope Bannister-Whyte. Pen, this is Ms. Ansley Sheridan of St. Augustine, Florida."

Out of nowhere came a shout, "Dad." Kevin emerged from the direction of the dining and kitchen section of the house, carrying a can of Coke. "Mummy said that I could spend Easter with you because she and Charles are going to the continent on holiday."

"How nice of Mummy," Nick said, extending his arm to beckon the child. "Even nicer that she gave me notice," he continued, sweet sarcasm exuding from his tone. "Come here and give me a high-five."

"Don't be testy, Nicholas. You haven't spent any time with your son since the Christmas holiday."

"I haven't been in the UK since the Christmas holiday, Pen."

"But, if he will be in your way," Penelope said, looking at Ansley, "I'll trot him over to Katherine and Victor's."

Ansley looked from Kevin to Penelope, and then to Nick. *Yes, he is definitely the boy in the painting, and he looks nothing like his father. He's the spitting image of her.*

Looking around his father's back, Kevin eyed Ansley. Nick turned and said, "Kevin, this is my friend, Ansley Sheridan from the U.S."

Kevin looked at Ansley for a minute before speaking. "She's pretty. Is she your girlfriend?"

This gets more embarrassing by the minute. I wish I could evaporate.

"She is that and more," Nick said, giving the boy a hug. "I'm glad you're here. I'd like the two of you to get to know one another." Turning to Penelope, he said, "You absolutely won't be taking him to Coleridge Manor. He'll do fine right here. You and Charles have a nice holiday. Is it France where you're going?"

"We're doing a river cruise—France, Germany, and Belgium."

"Do have fun and my best to Charles," he said, ushering Penelope to the door.

Ansley could feel Kevin staring at her. *I'm not sure this is good. Thank goodness, my things are not in Nick's room. I don't need a thirteen-year-old speculating about our relationship.*

After Penelope left, Kevin went downstairs where there was a theater room, a workout area, and a game room. Nick called for tea and biscuits and led Ansley to the library.

"I feel like I had sex written all over my face."

Nick laughed. "And how bad would that be?"

"Horrible. That's your son and his mother."

"Well, first of all, I've had sex with his mother or he wouldn't be here. And second, you looked beautiful. I think Kevin might have fallen in love with you as well."

"Nick, be serious. This is a terrible way to meet your child. What do you believe he is thinking?"

"Probably about how to manipulate me into buying him the latest electronic device." He smiled and reached over to squeeze her thigh as Martha came in with the tea tray. Embarrassed, Ansley pushed his hand away.

As soon as Martha was out of the room, Nick pulled Ansley close, lifting her chin upward to face him. "I know this has caught you off guard, but it will be fine. We will include him in some of our activities and leave him either here with Martha and John or I'll send him over to my sister's house some of the time."

"He's going to hate me for interfering with his time with you."

"Let me worry about that. I want *you* to have a good time while here. Kevin's a resilient boy. A trip into London with a little shopping, and he'll be happy. I may not spend a lot of time with my son, but I know him well."

Kevin in the house, despite its size, added another layer to Ansley's level of insecurity. Dinner was served in the dining room at a table that seated sixteen—before extensions. The three place settings at one end appeared almost sad. Although the room was saturated with formality, Nick and Kevin wore jeans. Ansley had changed into an ivory silk blouse, black pants, and black flats but still felt underdressed. John served the meal from a side buffet, opening with a delicate soup and progressing through Boeuf Bourguignon, tender potatoes, carrots, and asparagus, to a light trifle for dessert.

The silverware presented Ansley with near-awkward moments.

She was accustomed to no more than two forks, a spoon and knife, plus dessert pieces. The array of utensils was overwhelming. The only time she felt safe with her choice was with the heavy dinner fork used for the entre. Fortunately, Kevin and Nick were engrossed in endless conversation about the boy's school, sports, and summer plans and failed to notice that she watched intently as each chose his utensil for a course, and thereby followed suit. Kevin seemed oblivious to protocol, but got it right as if it were an indigenous gift. Although not the center of Nick's attention, she was not inclined to complain, taking consolation in her upward movement on the cultural learning curve.

As the meal ended, Ansley contemplated how the remainder of the evening would unfold. Would Kevin be included in their entire evening? She wanted private time with Nick but did not want to interfere between father and son.

After dinner, Nick suggested that the three of them go downstairs to the theater room and watch a film. Kevin immediately asked if they could watch *The Lord of the Rings: The Fellowship of the Ring*.

"Didn't we watch that the last time you were here?" Nick asked.

"Yes, sir. But, I'd really like to see it again."

"Ansley may not be a Tolkien fan."

"It's fine. I would like to see *The Lord of the Rings*," she interjected, anxious to please the teenager.

Nick leaned over and said in a voice little more than a whisper, "You don't have to agree with him. It's a three-hour film."

Ansley looked at Kevin. His eyes implored her to go along with his choice.

"I'm serious, Nick. I would like to see it."

Kevin beamed.

By the time the closing credits ran, it was eleven-thirty. Ansley had been nodding off, but woke at the sound of Kevin's voice.

"That was great. I love that movie. Did you like it, Ms. Sheridan?"

Ansley nodded, hoping he didn't realize that she had been asleep.

Looking at his watch, Nick said, "Glad you enjoyed it, son. You may watch TV in your room until midnight, but I'd better not find any light on later."

With that, Kevin was summarily dismissed. Nick reached for a snifter of brandy that John had delivered earlier, offering Ansley a drink before swirling his own. She declined.

This feels so domestic—like being part of a regular family. Only I'm in a mansion with a man for whom half the female population of the planet would kill to just meet.

During the movie, Nick had sat next to her on one of the reclining, leather loveseats, his arm around her shoulders. Although Kevin was so engrossed with the screen that he would likely have missed a missile strike on the room, Nick took no liberties with discretion. Once the boy was gone, Nick took a sip of the brandy and then pulled Ansley close. When she turned to look at him, he kissed her passionately, with one hand caressing her gently.

Drawing back slightly, he whispered, "Time for bed," and then stood, helping her to her feet.

She started for the stairs in the direction they had come in from, but he took her hand and led her toward the backside of the house where there was an elevator.

I should have realized there would be one somewhere in this castle.

Arriving on the second floor, Ansley was lost. The elevator was in the center of a long hallway—more closed doors on the elevator side and an unbroken wall covered with photographs on the other. Nick gently guided her leftward to the end of the corridor, and then to the right where her suite was located. Opening the door for her, he kissed her, running his free hand down her body. She stiffened, and looked around.

"No one is here, love. Kevin's room is on the other side of the house, behind mine. Martha and John are in their apartment on the third floor. We're quite alone."

"I'm sorry. I'm just a little self-conscious."

He smiled. "Get ready for bed. I'll see you in a few minutes."

"What do you mean?"

"You didn't think that I was going to let you sleep all alone, did you?"

CHAPTER TWENTY

Saturday morning, Ansley woke before six. Nick was sleeping soundly. She watched him for a few minutes and then gently nudged his shoulder. He made a sound without opening his eyes.

"You need to go back to your room," she whispered.

He didn't stir.

"Nick, you've got to wake up and go back to your room," she said, a little louder.

Still, no movement.

"Nick!"

Suddenly, he grabbed her around the waist, opening his eyes and smiling. "Kicking me out, are you?"

"You've got to go. What if Kevin goes looking for you in your room?"

He rolled over, pinning her in place. Raising himself up on his hands and looking down at her, he said, "He's a teenage boy. Left undisturbed, they sleep through lunch. Relax."

"But—"

He put his index finger over her lips. "Hush, woman. I'm going to have my way with you before the cock doth crow."

By seven-thirty, Nick was gone, and she had taken a shower and dressed. When he left, he told her that breakfast would be at eight, but if she wanted tea or coffee, to call for John. Ansley did not intend to ask the man to bring her beverages. She was not good at being an "upstairs" person.

At five minutes before eight, there was a now familiar knock at her door, followed by the door opening. "It's to be an exceptional day, love. Let's take a ride before breakfast and enjoy nature."

"Won't Martha be upset if we don't have breakfast at eight, like you said?"

"I've told her to delay. We'll take a cup of tea on our way to the stables. Paddy is readying the horses."

Kevin was downstairs, having a cup of tea and a piece of toast in a cheerful dining area. The room had a wall of windows overlooking the back of the property. The boy looked as though he had not fully awakened. Nick poured two cups of tea from a pot sitting on a long, narrow built-in cabinet.

"Sugar or milk?" he asked.

"Just sugar," Ansley replied. "Two."

"Good morning," Ansley said to Kevin.

"It's not good, yet," he replied.

"Careful," Nick cautioned. "Be polite, or I'll have your hide." He playfully tousled the boy's hair.

As he sat down with tea, he motioned for Ansley to sit next to him. "I thought we might take in the morning air and perhaps you can show Ansley your competitive skills. I sent for Samson earlier and had Paddy set up the ring."

"That's cool," Kevin said, his expression taking on more life. "He's better than Hamlet, now."

"We'll see," Nick said with a twinkle in his eye.

It was a lovely morning—cool, but not cold. The sun burned away fog as they walked to the stables and the ring that was set for jumping the horses. Ansley sat on the fence as Nick and Kevin took the course. It was hard to tell whether the horses or the riders were more competitive. For Ansley, watching the beautiful animals take to the air in a jump was like seeing a brilliant dancer taking to the air in a grand jeté—grace and power in motion.

After a few rounds of the track, father and son came off laughing and arguing as to who had outclassed whom. It was a perfect moment for Ansley, being a part of Nick's family.

"Let's get you saddled up, love," Nick shouted out to her.

"I'm embarrassed to show Kevin what an amateur I am on a horse."

"That's okay, I'll help you." The boy sounded excited at the idea of being the teacher.

Nick rode up to the fence next to her, leaned over, and said, "Didn't I say that he has a crush on you?"

She smiled, blushing slightly.

After a thirty-minute ride, they returned to the house for breakfast where Nick announced that his sister, Anne, was taking Kevin and

Jonathan to London for shopping that afternoon and the boy would spend the night with his cousin.

"I thought you might want to pick up that new music device—iPod, I think it's called."

Kevin's eyes instantly lit up. "Yes, yes. Thank you."

"If you've finished with breakfast, get ready, and Ian will drive you to Jonathan's."

As soon as Kevin was out of the room, Ansley turned to Nick and said, "Your former wife is going to hang you for that."

Wrinkling his brow, he said, "I'll probably be reprimanded, but her buzz is mightier than her sting."

"She could use it against you in custody dispute."

"What custody dispute? She has custody. I sense the lawyer coming out, Ms. Sheridan."

"I'm sorry. It's just what I do. I don't want you risking anything for me. We'll have other chances to be together if you want them."

"What do you mean, *if* I want them? You know damn well I want them. But, love, I'm not risking anything. Kevin's happy. He's going to get his iPod or whatever—going to spend time with his cousin, and you and I are going to Stratford to see the latest RSC production. Trust me, there's no jeopardy here—familial, financial, or legal. I am fully responsible for Kevin's expenses: school, medical, clothing, supplies, everything he needs and most of what he wants."

Saturday night had been perfect—the play, dinner at a small Indian restaurant, and the conversation. When they arrived back at the manor, it was after midnight. Entering the house, Nick took her by the hand and said, "Your place or mine?"

Pulling on his hand to stop him, she said, "I'm feeling adventurous. I'll come to your place."

Reversing the momentum, he jerked her to him. "You're playing with fire, madam. I can be very dangerous in my den."

"I'll risk it," she said, smiling.

They took the stairs at a quick pace. Arriving at Kevin's portrait, Ansley veered to the right, but Nick pulled her back.

"You don't need to go there."

"But my gown—"

"You won't need it." With that, he picked her up and carried her down the hall and into his massive bedroom.

The next morning, Ansley woke before Nick, again. She cut her eyes around, taking a few seconds to become oriented. The room was enormous with a vaulted ceiling that she estimated to be at least twenty-five feet high at the peak. The décor was a testament to his personality—rich wood paneling, plump chairs and sofa of soft leather, and framed prints of regal horses. The king-size bed was positioned on a platform, two steps above the floor. The frame had a carved motif and heavy ball-and-claw feet. The covering was tailored for a masculine effect in a muted stripe of brown, hunter green, and maroon. A stack of pillows, some solids, others in matching fabric, had been propped against the massive headboard but were now scattered on the floor. Nick's sleep area was as large as the sitting room and bedroom combined in her suite. In addition to the upholstered pieces, there were bookcases; a tea table with a matching pair of chairs; a massive breakfront cabinet, housing equine statuary, family photos, and antiquarian books; a writing desk piled high with scripts; and an entertainment center.

Where does he keep his socks and underwear? There's nothing in this room with drawers.

The cathedral windows, overlooking a view of the property that led toward the entry of the estate, were covered with sheer panels of ivory fabric. The heavy burgundy drapery that hung from wall to wall was partially drawn, permitting a slight illumination of the room.

The trouble with spontaneous passion at night is that you're naked in the morning. Do I redress in last night's clothing to get to my rooms?

Easing off the side of the bed, she took two of the pillows, positioning one behind her and the other in front for the sake of modesty. Nick was asleep, and there was little chance that anyone on the outside could see her.

I must be a hilarious sight—Eve substituting pillows for fig leaves.

In the bathroom, the marble floor felt like ice to the bottom of her feet. Closing the door, she saw a tan velour robe of Nick's hanging on a gold hook. *Problem solved. He can get something else or wrap one of those gigantic, warm towels around his manliness. I'm taking this to wear back to my room.* The robe swallowed her, but served the purpose.

At twenty past eight, without a knock, the door to her suite opened. Ansley was showered, dressed, and stretched out on the sitting room chaise, reading *Emma*. She closed the book and stood up.

"So this is where you are," he said. Approaching her with his arms extended, wearing a black robe and a mock frown on his face. "Slipped out like a little thief in the night, taking my favorite robe. I should spank you," he said, slapping her playfully on her derriere as he wrapped his other arm around her waist.

"First of all, it wasn't night, and second, you wouldn't dare."

Grabbing her tight, he said, "Wouldn't I?" And then as she wriggled to free herself, he forced a kiss on her lips to which she succumbed instantly. "There. That'll do for the moment. Now, bring your book along. You're going to sit in my room while I shower and dress." Pulling her face close to his, he whispered, "Don't ever slip out on me again." The twinkle in his eye and the raised eyebrow gave away the fact that he was teasing.

Kevin arrived back at the manor as they were finishing breakfast. "Are we going to services?" he asked Nick.

"Not today. I thought we might all three go for a ride before lunch. Why don't you go down to the stable and see that the horses are made ready?"

As Kevin left the room, Ansley said, "You're not missing church because of me, are you?"

"Absolutely not," Nick responded. "The Church of England sees little of me, as my mother is quick to point out. But what about you? Would you be in an American church this morning?"

She hesitated as though reluctant to answer. "Yeah, I probably would be, even though it's not quite right for me anymore."

"Why would that be? Forgive me for asking."

"The divorce thing. I'm Catholic—the Roman kind."

"Pope, confession, and all?"

"All the above."

"We're not so far apart. My people just couldn't learn the Latin," he said, smiling. "I guess we're both doomed—being divorced and being absent without leave of the pope or the archbishop."

"Probably. I wish that was my only transgression."

"Don't tell me you ate meat on a Friday."

She laughed. "It was a little worse than that, but it's a story I would prefer to forget. Don't worry, I never served time."

"I know you well enough to know that you *couldn't* do anything illegal. You'll tell me when the time is right."

Martha entered the room with a tea tray, and the subject was dropped.

With Kevin back, they had no time alone. The ride took the remainder of the morning. Ansley was growing more comfortable astride the horse, but not ready to go any faster than a cantor. By the time they returned to the house, Martha had lunch prepared.

"The day is too beautiful to be inside. We'll take lunch over the back lawn," Nick said to the housekeeper.

They were finishing the meal of cold meats, cheeses, and assorted breads when Nick got a call and went inside to his study to talk, leaving Ansley and Kevin at the white, wrought-iron table on the veranda.

"I hope I haven't intruded on your weekend with your father," she said.

"No problem," Kevin said, his blue eyes sparkling in the daylight. "He seems really happy with you here."

"Maybe it's because of you, not me."

"No. I've been here many times when he was not so cheerful. You're the first girlfriend I've met. I think the only one who's ever been here."

"That's hard to believe. Your dad's a very attractive man." Her inner self wanted to probe, but her conscience told her to let the boy say what he wanted to say.

"No. Martha's never said anything about him having someone here, and she would. She's like a mother duck to Dad—bosses him around all the time. No. He's never brought anyone else to the manor." He took a final swallow of his soft drink and then said, "I've seen pictures of him in the *Tattler* and *Okay* with women, but never in real life. Some of them were quite pretty. Are you going to marry him?"

Ansley's face turned bright red. "No. . . no. We've only known—"

"I just haven't had enough time to convince her yet." It was Nick. He had returned without their knowledge and leaned forward to kiss Ansley on the top of her head. "She's too smart to settle for a reprobate like me. That's why I'm keeping her away from your mother, so she won't find out what an ass I really am."

"Flattery and self-deprecation all in the same breath. You're good," Ansley teased. The tension of the boy's question was eased, but Nick's words were etched in her mind.

CHAPTER TWENTY-ONE

Returning home on the plane, Ansley replayed the visit repeatedly in her mind. It had been strange—not at all what she had expected. She left Florida anticipating a repeat of the Italy trip: passionate lovemaking, extravagant activities. The sex had been passionate, but the visit had taken a domesticated turn. Kevin coming into the picture brought an aura of family to Nick and to their relationship. She struggled against wanting to be a permanent part of his life. It had been excruciating to leave.

Reclining in her seat, sleep mask over her eyes, she went through a mental analysis of the relationship. *You're in the deep end without a life preserver. Get your head out of the clouds and dial down this relationship before it destroys you. He's a British actor—life in the UK. You're an American attorney—life in the US. No common ground—sex isn't enough. You couldn't even hold on to a wannabe architect. What makes you entertain for even a second that you could hold on to a celebrity with sex appeal overshadowed only by wealth. You're an olive in his martini. Six months from now, you will be watching his DVDs with Skye and Shadow, crying and hating yourself for letting it happen.*

"It's your fault, Dennis Devlin," Ansley said on the phone. "I would *not* have gone out with him that night in New York if you hadn't pushed me."

"Slow up. What's happened? Did you split?"

"How could we split? We're not together—and never will be."

"What happened in England?"

"Nothing. It was phenomenal."

"Pardon me, Ms. Sheridan, but I don't understand the angst if Sir Sexy was phenomenal."

"Don't be obtuse. This relationship is doomed to vaporization."

"Is that a word?"

"*Dennis*," she was nearly shouting.

"Okay, okay. I've got it. He was spectacular, you had an off-the-charts time, you're miserable, and you want out. Does that sum it up?"

"I'm serious, and you're not. I'm falling so deeply in love with this guy that I can't stand it, and you know it's going to end worse than *The Red Shoes*. How did you let this happen? How did I let this happen?"

"You might want to ask Mother Nature how she made him so delectable. Now calm down. You're not throwing yourself in front of a train. I take it that he's pushed all the right buttons. Right?"

"That's an understatement."

"Okay. You're turned-on and in high-speed. Why don't you just go with the flow and see where it leads? You could find out that he leaves the toilet seat up, doesn't put the cap on the toothpaste, or sleeps with the teddy bear his mummy gave him. Come on Ansley, there's a skeleton in that closet somewhere. And stop selling yourself short. You're a gorgeous woman—smart, kind. You've got just as much going for you, minus a few zillion dollars and billions of fans. But remember, there's a woman out there who tossed that puppy back in the pond."

"I met her."

"No, shit. You met the ex?"

"Her and Kevin."

"You met the kid?"

"It was surreal at first. He didn't know she was coming. She just showed up and left the boy for the weekend—no notice."

"Oh my God! That must have doused cold water on the fire."

"It actually turned out kinda neat. It was almost like family—like I was part of his family. It felt too damn good, Dennis. I cried halfway across the Atlantic."

"Dear friend. I love you as much as this old, gay boy can love a lady, but you've got to stop obsessing. It's either going to work out or it isn't. Life is what happens regardless of your perfect plans. No one . . . no one knows when or how it will end. Go with it, sugar. Snag the stud, and duck the bullets as best as you can. Hell, darlin', whoever thought I would be dancing principal in *Prodigal*?"

"You got it! Oh, my, gosh! You got it!"

"I got it."

"I thought William had that role locked."

"Got him, too."

There was dead silence on the phone for a full minute. "You got *him*?"

"I did. He's back."

"But—"

"I know, I know. He thought he was straight and went for the hetero thing. Turns out he's not."

"Dennis, don't let him hurt you again."

"It's okay, sweetie. It's *all* under control."

Back in her office after the trip, she saw Ted Greene on her calendar. Mediation in his case was scheduled for the following week. They had managed to avoid exposure of his secret, but they were about to hit the wall. She had given the situation a lot of thought and concluded that he needed to tell both women the truth and appeal to their practical natures. To expose him to the authorities could send him to jail, which would benefit no one. He needed to keep his job to be able to contribute to the support of both. It was a gamble, but the only solution she could come up with.

"It's my only recommendation, Ted. If you can't accept it, I think you need to find another attorney. I told you, I'm a first-year associate. Maybe someone with more experience can figure out a better plan, but I don't have one."

He looked at her with an almost contrite expression. "I guess I have no choice."

His response surprised her. The worry apparently had worn him down.

"I suggest you tell Suzanne first. She is going to be upset, but she won't want you to lose your job. Maybe you should take a neutral party with you. Do you have a minister or priest? She may divorce you, too, but she'll want you to be able to pay her alimony and your children's college tuition. We'll deal with Lila at mediation. The mediator will have to know as well. He can help. Lila's attorney can't do anything to harm his client's position, and sending you to jail would certainly do that."

CHAPTER TWENTY-TWO

To Ansley's relief, Ted accepted her plan, and it worked. Both women divorced him, and he paid alimony to both, but he avoided criminal prosecution.

After her weekend in England, the relationship with Nick fell into a pattern. He called several times a week; she traveled to meet him for long weekends every four to six weeks in various locations, always being discreet to avoid the press. She spent a luxurious vacation with him in his seaside cottage on the coast of Wales in late summer and shared Christmas with his family in the Cotswolds. She became quite adept at creating covers for her absence.

Ansley knew that some of her friends and colleagues suspected that she was involved with a married man. While that was not a reputation she enjoyed, the fact that it wasn't true, combined with the stifling effect it had on others prying into details about her personal life, made it tolerable.

In the spring of 2003, Nick signed for a late summer, limited-run of *Hamlet* at the New York State Theater. Ansley planned to spend her two-week vacation with him in the city. To finalize preparations for the production, he would be visiting Manhattan in June. It was a given that she would spend the weekend with him.

When she called Dennis to say that she was coming to meet Nick in New York and would finally introduce them, he was ecstatic.

"When are you getting here?"

"Friday afternoon."

"Am I actually going to meet Sir Steamy?"

Dennis' nicknames for Nick always made Ansley smile. "You bet. That is if you're free Saturday night."

"I am now."

"He is looking forward to meeting you, too. He knows how close we are, and he's pleased that he is finally meeting someone in my life who knows about our relationship."

"That's me—the co-conspirator."

"I've got to run. I'm at work, but I'll have all day Saturday free while Nick's doing whatever Nick does."

"My schedule just cleared. I serve at your pleasure. Call me and let me know where and when."

Friday night, Ansley's car arrived at the luxurious hotel on the Upper East Side a few minutes before eight. Nick wasn't there. She had hoped he would be but had been warned that the auditions for the Shakespeare production could run late. He had considered having her brought to the theater but decided that the hotel would be a better choice, given the time of her arrival.

After the bellman left, she began unpacking, putting her lingerie in one of the empty drawers of the ornate dresser and hanging the other garments in the armoire next to his suits. It took her only twenty minutes to settle in. Glancing at the fancy clock on the night table, she decided to take a quick shower so that when he arrived she would be ready to go out for a late-night dinner.

Before going into the bathroom, she noticed an iPod like the one Kevin bought at Easter. Picking up the small remote beside the device, she pushed the play button and the "Overture from Carmen" began.

Ansley smiled, thinking of the night they met. *He must have remembered.*

She considered checking out what other music was available but didn't know enough about the little device to explore. Further, she liked the score and felt a sense of accomplishment in getting it to work at all. The volume was low. Fiddling with the instrument, she managed to turn it louder.

The bathroom was large with a huge, caramel-colored bathtub complete with brass fixtures on either side in the shape of swans with highly arched necks. Louis XV bombe chests housed the double sinks, accented by gleaming brass and crystal lamps. The Italian marble floor was bare. Electric towel bars heated enormous, thick bath towels. A low light illuminated the area with unlit candles scattered around.

Ansley considered turning on the electric sconces, but decided instead to light the candles. As she suspected, matches were in a small bowl by a sink. Nick's toiletries were in place and had infused the room with the faint aroma of Green Irish Tweed. The smell combined with the musical background to transport her back to the thrill of their weekend in Florence.

She pulled a terry floor mat from one of the chests and spread it out on the floor, stepped out of her slacks, and stood barefoot in her bikini panties and bra. Seeing her reflection in the full-length mirror, a wave of sensuality swept over her body. She looked at the tub, decided it would take too long to fill, and stepped into the glass-enclosed shower stall.

As the warm water struck her skin, the "Habanera" tract began to play on the iPod, enticing the dancer in Ansley to move with its sultry rhythm. The image of Nick in Tuscany flashed across her mind. The music, the water, the soft fragrance, and the thoughts of him were intoxicating. Jets of water came from the heads at three levels. While she lathered, the warm spray of the shower piqued her nerve endings; her hips swayed in time to the music. Completely absorbed by her reverie, Ansley failed to notice him enter the bathroom.

He stood watching her through the brass-framed glass for a second. Although the steam diffused her image, the full outline of her figure was visible. Her slender, delicately curved body moved erotically with the grace of a ballerina. The hum of the water sprays, coupled with the music, drowned out the sound of his disrobing and quietly opening the door.

Stepping in behind her, he murmured in a low and seductive tone, "Mind if I join you?" It was more statement than question.

Startled, Ansley turned and stared at him, unable to speak. His eyes slowly swept her naked body with blatant desire, taking inventory, and then focusing directly on her eyes in a provocative and hypnotic stare. She froze in place.

"Don't stop." His voice was soft, but his words clearly a command. Never losing her poise, she obeyed. His eyes once again swept her body, appraising her with obvious satisfaction. She felt pleasingly vulnerable to his desire, stripped of any ability to protest.

His tan body was long and trim, his muscles firm. Her body retained the slender and muscular tone of the ballerina. They were a perfect match, like corresponding pieces of a jigsaw puzzle. Captivated by her dance, Nick began moving in sync with her—touching her only with his eyes. Although absent contact, she could almost feel the touch of his hands like warm breath tickling her skin as they both swayed with the music. He took her by her waist and gently turned her around. With her back to him, she could feel his eyes comb her body. A new sensation came over Ansley, delivering a sense of pride in her body and a desire to tease his sensual appetite. With the water tingling against her skin, she felt herself compelled to stretch and twist in provocative moves, like Salome or Circe. Her blood was flowing hot and her erogenous zones pulsating. She wanted Nick like she had wanted no one ever before, and she wanted him to first simmer and finally ignite with desire.

The sexual temptress was released—a role she had never played before. It was raw, animal sex. Her ladylike manner fell away, compromised by carnal lust. She was intoxicated with passion and shameless in her pursuit. Nick responded accordingly. He controlled and paced the mating ritual. Turning back to face him, she was once again captured by the hypnotically sexy look he did so well. She had never felt more totally female. His eyes held her mesmerized, penetrating deep beneath the surface. At that moment, she was *both* Salome and Circe, seductress and seduced. The warm water ran over their lean bodies, enticing and titillating. Ansley hungered for his touch, longed to become one with him. He took his time, letting her passion grow to an unbearable level. She wanted him to consume her, but he did not make a move, rather, stood still, allowing his eyes to roam her body with a slight smile on his lips.

Finally, he reached for the soap in her hand. Taking it, he slowly worked a heavy lather between his palms. She anticipated his plans for the foamy substance, tingling even more at the prospect of having him bathe her naked body. She was still swaying to the music as he put his soapy hands on her shoulders and slowly began smoothing the lather over her body, just barely touching her. His touch was electric, charging through her. The warmth of his hands gliding over her stimulated skin was nearly too much to bear.

Working his way down, his hands gently crossed her breasts, barely touching. Refreshing the lather, he moved closer, looking down on her with steely blue eyes. She ceased having a will of her own and became an instrument of his pleasure. His slippery hands continued gliding over her nude body, teasing it with expectation, caressing it as though it were fine porcelain. His control was undeniable. He took her gently, but firmly, by her left shoulder and turned her sideways, holding her firmly around the waist. Although vulnerable under his control, she felt safe within it. Holding her thus, he slowly rubbed the lather over her back, creating circles as he edged downward to her hips where he teasingly caressed her derriere with his hot, soapy hand. Ansley succumbed. Her body begged to join his.

They consummated the union once in the shower and a second

time on warm towels thrown on the marble floor. Each time, Ansley thought she would die from the ecstasy—tears filled her eyes.

When done the second time, he hugged her close, whispering in her ear.

"You're crying."

Her head moved side to side. Her lips were silent.

He gently brushed her hair away from her face. "You are safe, my love. I love you with all my heart."

Weak from the encounter, she could not respond. After a minute or two, she said, "I'm sorry. I didn't mean to cry."

He pulled her even closer and she felt his firm body steady hers as they lay on the towels. "I will never hurt you."

Again, she found no words to respond.

They lay silent for a few minutes longer, and then Nick got up and took two hotel robes from a cabinet in the bath. He put on one and helped her into the other, leaning forward to nuzzle her neck, his arms wrapped around her waist. After a minute or two, he said, "You must be starved. Shall we order?"

CHAPTER TWENTY-THREE

After breakfast in the suite on Saturday morning, Nick prepared to leave for meetings and more auditions for the supporting roles in the summer production.

"I will be done by four o'clock. Will you be okay on your own?"

"Of course. I lived here when I was seventeen. Besides, I'm having lunch with Dennis. Don't forget, we're meeting him for dinner tonight."

Walking over to the sofa where Ansley sat in her pink dressing gown, Nick reached toward her, palm up, inviting her to rise. Taking her hand, he pulled her close and said in a near whisper, "Don't be late coming back here. I have a stop I want to make on the way to dinner."

Before she could respond, he kissed her, squeezed her affectionately, and left.

Ansley went back to the small table where the breakfast dishes remained and poured a fresh cup of tea.

I wonder what that's about.

The tea had chilled to room temperature, but she put in sugar and drank it. After draining the cup, she made a call to Dennis.

"Good morning," she said, her voice giving away her good mood. "I hope I didn't wake you."

"Hardly, gorgeous. I am too excited about seeing you and meeting Sir Sexy to sleep in. Is it to be my place or yours?"

Ansley beamed. "Why don't you come here?"

"I was hoping you would ask. I've never dated upscale, so I haven't seen the inside of one of those luxury suites."

"It's nice. A girl could get spoiled." Her eyes opened wide, as she delivered a reminder. "Hey, don't forget to bring DVDs of your performances."

"Locked and loaded, my love. What kind of premier danseur would I be if I didn't flaunt my fantastic flair?"

"Fantastic or flamboyant?"

"Ouch."

"Kidding, just kidding. You know I think you're awesome."

"Of course you do. See you at eleven."

A call from the front desk announced Dennis's arrival at ten-fifty. Expecting him to be early, Ansley was ready and had placed an order for their lunch. When he knocked at the double doors, she threw them open and they embraced vigorously.

"L'amourette wears well on you, madame. You are ravishing," Dennis said, stepping back to look her over.

"You're not so bad yourself."

The day passed quickly. They watched two of Dennis's DVDs and looked at the spring souvenir program for The National Ballet. Leafing through the pages of dance images gave Ansley a twinge of nostalgia, but she brushed it aside quickly.

Shortly before three, Dennis got ready to leave for a costume fitting. "Reservations are for seven-thirty. Wear dressy casual." He stopped and raised an eyebrow. "That's an oxymoron, isn't it?"

"Pretty much, but I think I know what you mean."

"It's a small, exclusive restaurant, but no one gussies up. The band is hot. You'll love it."

"How do we rate admission?"

"I have connections, sweetheart. And, no, I didn't drop his majesty's moniker to make it happen."

It was four-thirty before Nick arrived back at the hotel. Ansley had been struggling to concentrate on a magazine as she anticipated the evening ahead.

"I need to take a quick shower, love," he said, dropping a briefcase as he entered. "We should leave by five or five-fifteen."

Closing the book, she said, "Our reservations aren't until seven-thirty."

"I told you that I need to make a stop. By the way, is this a formal or casual evening?"

"Nice casual. I'll be ready. But you're being mysterious. Where are we stopping?"

"You'll see," he said, a smug smile curling the corners of his lips.

Cocking her head to one side, she said, "I can see that you're not going to tell me. So, I'll change the subject. Did your auditions go well?"

"Well enough." Kissing the top of her head on his way to the bedroom, he said, "Actually, better than I expected."

By the time he returned to the sitting room, Ansley was ready. Her long hair fell softly over the shoulders of her pale-blue silk blouse.

Nick's interpretation of dressy-casual was a white dress shirt, open at the neck with sleeves rolled up, khaki slacks, and loafers. His hair was still damp. "I called for the car. It should be downstairs within ten minutes." He poured some wine from a decanter on the mini-bar and held up the glass, offering it to her. She declined. He had barely drained the wine before the desk clerk called to announce the arrival of their transportation.

Although Ansley told him that anonymity was not an issue since the bistro was private and catered to the rich and famous, he chose to take an SUV rather than a limo.

"It attracts far less attention," he said as though feeling the necessity to justify the vehicle. As usual, the driver, a New York hire, doubled as a security guard. Ian had remained in England to have dental work.

The man had his instructions and headed downtown to Fifth Avenue, stopping just south of Central Park.

As the chauffeur opened the door, Ansley could see that they were in front of Van Cleef & Arpels. *What is he up to?*

"They're closed, Nick. It's after five."

"It would be a little difficult for me to come during active business hours."

"You're making me nervous. Why are we going to a jewelry store?"

"Humor me."

Don't jump to any conclusions.

When they reached the door, a gray-haired man in a smart, black suit, who was obviously expecting them, opened the door.

"Welcome, Mr. Colton. Mr. Howard is waiting for you in the salon. Lee will show you the way."

The ambiance in the spacious showroom exuded a quiet air of luxury with a gleaming, marble tile floor, chandelier lighting, and soft music. The store was otherwise quiet with Nick and Ansley the only customers.

The younger clerk smiled, looking at Nick with a slight expression of awe, and said, "This way, Mr. Colton."

Nick thanked the doorman before they followed their guide to the first salon, a private room at the rear of the boutique. Ansley stepped lightly to avoid the echo of her heels striking the marble.

Reaching the salon, Nick's personal jeweler met them and led the way to a French provincial table, covered with an array of black-velvet-lined boxes containing diamond rings. He motioned for them to sit in two chairs on one side, while he walked around to a chair on the other.

Ansley froze. *Oh, my gosh. Oh, my gosh.* Her hands trembled.

"Based on your description, I've pulled an assortment for your approval, Mr. Colton. But, if you don't see anything that strikes the right note, I'll bring more."

Nick tipped his head, looking down at the display and said, "Thank you. These look most promising, but it is Miss Sheridan whom you will need to please." Turning to Ansley, whose eyes were taking everything in like a child in a toy store, he said, "Look these over and choose your favorite."

Still standing, she turned her attention from the jewelry and looking up at him said, "What is this about?"

He smiled. "What do you think it's about?"

"Don't do that. Just tell me. Why am I looking at diamond rings?"

"Could you excuse us for a moment, Mr. Howard?"

"Certainly," the jeweler said. Rising, he led them to a second room that was empty.

Once alone, Nick took her hand and said, "I intend to buy a ring for you and would like you to make the choice."

"But, we haven't talked about this. You can't just buy me an expensive ring."

"Of course I can."

"But those are engagement rings."

"And what is wrong with that?"

"Nick, I can't agree to marry you—not yet." There was panic on her face.

"I'm not asking you to. We're here to buy you a ring as a symbol of my feelings for you. No strings attached."

"That's crazy. Prices on those rings have got to be many thousands. I could never accept anything that expensive from you."

He took both of her hands in his. "Of course you can. Call it anything you like. Wear it on your right hand until you decide to marry me. If you come to that decision, switch it to your left, and I'll know that you're ready to spend the rest of your life with me."

"There are things you don't know about me, and—"

"First, I know all I need to know. I'm in love with you and want to share my life with you. Second, I wouldn't want to know everything.

Learning more and more about one another is what keeps a relationship interesting as time passes, and finally, if you had any sinister secret, I would have been told."

She looked at him with a quizzical expression.

He lowered his chin and said, "There are those whose job it is to protect me from risk. They check out anyone who comes close to me—not by my bidding." Taking her hands and putting them together in a prayer position, he continued. "Now, let's get on with it. You're going to select the ring of your choice, and we must not keep your friend waiting."

Dropping her hands, he stood and then extended a hand to assist her in rising. They walked back to the salon.

Ansley felt dazed and fought back tears that she did not understand as she looked over the brilliant collection. There were so many—all beautiful. Her eyes skipped past the ostentatious rings and instantly went to the simplicity of three solitaires with varying sized diamonds. The identical platinum bands were tapered toward the base of the mounting, generating an air of grace. Trembling, she pointed toward the smallest, which was actually two carats. Howard immediately removed it from the box and handed it to Nick.

Taking her left hand, Nick slid the ring on her third finger. It went on easily because it was at least a size too large. "A perfect match to your personality, love."

Ansley smiled.

"And the clarity of the stone?" Nick asked, turning to the jeweler.

"Mr. Colton, the Maison Van Cleef & Arpels uses only FL diamonds. It is indeed flawless."

"And it will be ready tomorrow?" Nick asked.

"As promised. I'll have it delivered to your hotel pursuant to your instructions."

Leaving, Ansley felt nervous and continued to fight back unexplainable tears. As soon as they were settled in the car, she wiped her eyes and said, "I can't wear the ring at home, Nick—not even on my right hand."

"As long as you wear it when you're with me, I won't complain."

Traffic was heavy, causing the car to make little progress. Nick held her hand in his lap, absentmindedly stroking it.

"Why did you choose Van Cleef's?" Ansley asked, more to fill the empty space than out of a need to know.

"If Rainier could choose his ring for Princess Grace there, I felt it a worthy place for my future queen."

His statement left Ansley without words. She looked at him as her brain raced to find an appropriate comment.

Nick smiled and lifted her hand to his lips with the devilish expression on his face that she had become accustomed to seeing.

"Tell me about this club where we're going to meet Dennis," he said, still holding her hand close to his face.

"I don't know much about it either. I'm a little afraid you may hate it."

"Why would I hate it?"

"I don't think they will be playing your type of music. If I know Dennis, there's probably going to be pop and maybe rock and roll, which you despise."

"So, you're going to shock my cultural appetite?" He squeezed her hand and lowered it to his lap.

"Maybe. It's not going to be Paganini or Pachelbel for sure." Ansley was beginning to second-guess what lay ahead. She had looked forward to putting two of the most important people in her life together. However, the differences in the two began to create a fear that the night could be a disaster.

"I'll survive, and you can make it up to me later," he said, winking.

Although he tried to relieve her apprehension, doubts about sharing Nick with Dennis were causing her to panic, especially coming so close behind the emotional turmoil over Nick's purchase of the ring—the latter being a clash of head and heart.

As the car pulled up to the curb in front of the obscure club, Ansley's heart was pounding. From the outside of the building, neither the façade, nor the name, Centre Luminier, gave any indication of what awaited them. A brass plaque on the heavy wooden door read "Members Only." Dennis had told Annie to give his name to the maître d' but added that recognition of Nick would probably be sufficient for entry. Nick held the door for her, following behind. She turned and whispered, "Tell him we're part of the Devlin party."

The black-suited headwaiter summoned an underling to lead them to Dennis's booth. The room was larger than it appeared from the outside. Three-armed sconces and brass chandeliers augmented the candles positioned in the center of each table. Upholstered booths lined the perimeter with white-draped tables scattered around the center. Three-quarters of the way to the back of the room, two steps led down to a small dance floor bordered by a railing. A grouping of musical instruments and equipment was on a back corner of the lower area, and a single musician was playing a familiar love song on the keyboard.

"The music hasn't offended my sensibilities, yet," Nick said, leaning over as they followed the waiter toward the back of the room.

Seeing the couple arrive, Dennis came out of the booth with a huge smile, hugging Ansley and then extending a hand to Nick. "It's a pleasure to meet you, Mr. Colton."

"Nick, please," Nick corrected. "My pleasure as well. I have enjoyed watching you perform."

Ansley relaxed, watching the polite interactions and thinking how the two men were like the set of magnetized Scottish terriers that sat on her grandmother's coffee table, one snow white, the other, ebony. They were of similar height and build. However, Dennis with his blond hair falling across his forehead; his tight, designer jeans; unbuttoned, white shirt; and jangling, gold jewelry was a stark contrast to Nick's swarthy coloring and conservative attire.

Her prior reservations were ill placed. The two men plunged right into conversation—Dennis taking the lead. They dominated the table with comparisons of audiences, agents, and co-stars, leaving Ansley to turn her head from man to man. She watched with smug satisfaction and relief.

They like one another.

Through dinner, only the pianist played. Occasionally, a couple would take the dance floor. Shortly before their entrees were cleared away, four musicians replaced the solo artist, and the timbre of the music ramped up. Ansley eyed Nick, searching for signs of discomfort, but if he had any objection, it was concealed.

When the group began a cover of Bob Seger's "Old Time Rock and Roll," Dennis reached for Ansley's hand. Addressing Nick, he said, "May I steal your lady for a little trip down memory lane?"

Smiling, Nick nodded his approval.

On the floor, Dennis held nothing back with his down-and-dirty jive. It was a momentary throwback to when they were baby ballet dancers, sneaking off from the rigid discipline of their profession to be kids. Ansley did well to keep up with him. It had been so long since she danced to rock and roll, but she loved every minute, forgetting how much Nick disliked the musical genre.

Back at the table when the song had ended, Ansley was out of breath. Nick offered her the glass of wine the waiter had brought, but she declined. "I think I would be far better served with a glass of water right now." She searched Nick's face for signs of annoyance or boredom, but neither was apparent. He was actually smiling with a look of approval.

"I can see that the two of you were quite a team," Nick said, lifting his brandy glass toward Dennis.

"She was the best partner I ever had—and the best friend."

"My sentiments, exactly," Nick said, and as he spoke, the band began playing Marc Anthony's "I Need to Know." "Can't let you outdo me, old man," Nick said, putting his snifter down and taking Ansley's hand.

As they walked down to the dance floor, she looked back up at him and asked somewhat surprised, "You want to dance to *this*?"

"Do you have a problem with it?"

"No, but this is not a waltz or foxtrot."

He smiled and swinging her around said, "I know."

Ansley was astonished. Nick was as in charge of the cha-cha as Dennis had been the jive. She had trouble following, despite her innate abilities. Not only were his steps technically correct, he injected undeniable sensuous and seductive moves.

When they reached the table after the music died, Dennis grinned and said, "I think you guys need a room."

"Couldn't agree more," Nick said, causing Ansley to blush.

"I had no idea that you could dance like *that*," she said.

"I have to give it to you; that was *quite* a routine," Dennis added. "You certainly seemed to know what you were doing."

Nick raised his hands in mock surrender. "Okay, okay. I'm outed. You two have just learned one of my best kept secrets."

Ansley looked at him, wide-eyed.

"In the day, when acting jobs were few and far apart, I earned my rent money in a London dance studio."

Ansley's eyes grew even larger, while Dennis broke into a big grin. "That's capital," Dennis said. "Fat, rich, old widows?"

Nick shook his head, but he was smiling. "That's also confidential. If either of you tell, I'll have to have you killed."

"My lips are sealed," Dennis said, with a chuckle.

"That settled, if the two of you would excuse me for a moment, I'll be right back."

As soon as Nick was out of hearing distance, Dennis leaned toward Ansley and said, "I expected to be turned on by your guy, but I didn't expect to like him so much. He's a real keeper, girlfriend."

Ansley smiled, but looked down, shaking her head slightly.

"What?" Dennis frowned.

Looking up again, her eyes were glassy. "I'm so glad the two of you are hitting it off."

"But what? There's something you're not telling me."

"I don't know if I should."

"Oh, no. You're not doing that to me. Give. What's going on?"

"He bought a ring today." She turned her face away from Dennis.

"And . . .?" He motioned for her to continue.

"And what? He bought a ring—for me."

"You're killing me, girl. What kind of ring? Do I have to drag it out of you?"

"It's a diamond—the kind that is usually worn on the left hand."

Dennis stifled a yelp. "Oh, my God. He proposed and you said yes?"

"He says he wants to share his life with me, but—"

"But, what? You said yes, didn't you?"

"I'm not ready to commit."

"Oh . . . my . . . gosh. Are you crazy?"

"Calm down. People are going to hear you," she said, frowning and looking around.

"Maybe they should. What woman with half a brain wouldn't jump at the chance to marry *him*?"

"And turn into the next ex-Mrs. Nicholas Colton in a few years with a couple of kids to fight over? There's more to it than sex and romance, Dennis."

"Nothing more that matters. And where the heck do you come off thinking it won't work? He apparently thinks it will."

Ansley took a sip of water from the glass in front of her. "Listen and try to understand. What Nick and I have is a cotton candy fantasy. We've never been together enough for the magic to wear off. I have to think sensibly. We don't really know one another. We are still at the stage where we go to sleep at the same time. If he wants Chinese, I want Chinese. If he wants to watch paint dry, then I want to watch paint dry because being anywhere with him makes me happy. Marriage is different. It's more like he wants sex, and I'm tired. It's having an undignified stomach virus—no makeup, bad moods, different opinions. We haven't been there. Dennis, I know what being married is like, and we haven't been anywhere close."

"You're overlooking the fact that the guy is nuts over you. He looks at you like you're a decadent chocolate sundae he is about to devour."

"Hush, he's coming." Changing the subject, she said, "So when is

William coming back from Nebraska?"

Driving back to the hotel, Nick pulled her close. "I like your friend. He's a pleasant chap."

"He is—and has been a source of support for me for a long time."

"Where was his partner tonight?"

"William? He went home to visit his family—his sister's wedding."

"Why didn't Dennis go with him?"

"That's a long story. William's family does not accept his relationship with Dennis. Two years ago, he left Dennis for a woman, which I hated him for at the time."

"To placate his family?"

"That's what he said when he came back to Dennis. William is the only guy that Dennis has ever been serious about, and I'm terrified that William may hurt him again. But, Dennis is happy right now."

"I hope it works out."

CHAPTER TWENTY-FOUR

For the remainder of the year, Nick did not pressure Ansley about marriage, but he insisted that she wear her diamond when they were together. He had no idea how much she wanted to wear it all the time. The two weeks that they had together during the summer piqued his appetite for more of her time. During the late fall, he began pushing to see her more often.

"I'm doing the best I can, Nick. I have a job. I am not my own boss."

"If you were, would you be able to spend more time with me?"

"Maybe. But—"

"No. I don't want to hear *but*. I'll take care of whatever you need to start your own practice."

"That's not happening."

"And why not?"

"I'm not taking money from you."

"We'll make it a business loan. You can make payments. If you marry me, the debt is cancelled."

They argued by telephone for two weeks, but in the end, Ansley gave in and accepted his help. Opening her own practice increased the length of her visits if not the frequency.

In late November, he invited her to spend Christmas in England again.

"I can't leave my parents this year, Nick. It was hard enough to see Mom's disappointment last year. I'm an only child. They would never understand."

"They might if you told them about us. I would be happy to have them come as well."

"Tell my mother that I'm having a secret affair with a divorced movie star. You don't know my mother."

"It's been two years, Ansley. I was in complete agreement with the secrecy in the beginning. I didn't want the paparazzi all over you, but I didn't expect it to be a permanent arrangement. As for the affair, I'm willing to put any legal, religious, or social endorsement on our relationship the moment you say yes and put that ring on your left hand."

"I'll give you Thanksgiving. I'll figure out some story. But I have to stay in Florida for Christmas."

"Thanksgiving is an American holiday. We don't celebrate it."

He wasn't happy, but she would not concede. It was one of the rare times that she stood her ground.

As she put the finishing touches on her Christmas decorations in mid-December, Ansley was pleased with the result. Her tree was exceptional, resembling a Victorian lady ready for the ball. It survived the divorce as the sole marital possession on which Ansley bestowed absolution.

"What do you think, Shadow? Isn't it beautiful?" The black cat scarcely acknowledged his name, but Skye rose and ambled over to Ansley, tail in the air. "Well, at least one of you cares," Ansley said, reaching down to scratch the top of the white cat's head.

To complete the holiday mood, Ansley slipped a Christmas CD into her music system, made a cup of hot chocolate, and curled up on the sofa. As she basked in the contentment of accomplishment, the phone rang, causing her to flinch.

"Hello, love. How is the weather in Florida?"

Recognition of his voice registered instant joy on her face. "I didn't expect you to call tonight." Taking the phone to the sofa, she settled back in the corner, a throw pillow against her stomach, to savor his call.

"I rang earlier, but you didn't answer."

"I went Christmas shopping this afternoon. Since I came home, I've been putting out my decorations. How is the film going?"

"We're close to wrapping and good thing; it's cold as hell here in the Arctic."

"You're not in the Arctic, you're in Vancouver."

"Really, I thought it was the Arctic. You mean there is someplace colder?"

"You're not a sissy are you? Surely you can handle a little cold weather."

"Speaking from Florida, that's easy for you to say. What's the temperature down there? 80 degrees? 85?"

"More like 70."

"Perfect. That's why I've decided to spend Christmas with you."

"Right." Her tone was patronizing. "That's a nice idea, but when are you leaving for Cheltenham?"

"I'm not joking, love. I'm spending Christmas with you."

She shifted around, her attention alerted. "Really. And just how will that work?"

"I'm coming to your flat."

There was silence on the phone. Ansley was momentarily speechless. Where did this come from? Nothing had ever been mentioned about his coming to Florida, much less to her condo. "Yeah, right. You're definitely coming here."

"Lose the sarcasm. I'm coming to Florida. I'll be there on the twenty-third."

"No. . . . You're not." *He's teasing.*

"Oh, but I am. Stock up on your Darjeeling. I've given it a great deal of thought and decided it was about time I see this mysterious place where you live *and* have a go at meeting your family."

Panic shook Ansley. "You can't do that."

"I think I can."

"No, you can't, Nick. That won't work. You won't get to spend the holiday with your parents and Kevin." But it wasn't his missing Christmas in England that worried her.

"I'll make it over there later. Perhaps you will travel with me."

Oh my God, he's serious. "But you can't come here. Someone might see you." While discovery was a major consideration, it was not the only reason that she didn't want Nick in Florida.

"I'll be discreet. I'll come in after dark. I'm fairly clever with disguise."

"Nick, my condo is no place for you. My cats throw up on the bed, and there's a litter box in my bathroom."

"Ansley, I don't give a damn where your cats throw up; you can change the sheets. I'll help you. For God's sake, I'm not royalty. Believe it or not, before I was an actor, I was quite ordinary. On a good day, I can remember that life."

"You were never ordinary. I've been to the mansion where you grew up. Besides, my condo is tiny."

"I want to know the other you, love—the *one* you're always saying I don't know. I want to see the cats you care so much about, meet your family. As for the size of the condo, I feel quite certain that your bed is large enough for two."

"Right, he who lives in a twenty-five-room manor house can fit in a two-bedroom, one-bath condo. Your hotel rooms are larger than my house."

"Twenty-one, my dear, little smart ass. You are damned lucky I'm not there right now."

"You really can't come here, Nick. To be perfectly honest, I am coming down with something. I have a sore throat, and I don't feel very well. I wouldn't want you to catch it."

"To be perfectly *honest*?" he said, mocking her. "Nice try, Miss Sheridan, but you're a pitiful liar. I'm coming. End of story."

He was serious about coming, and he enjoyed making her squirm. She could hear the amused grin on his face and could see that familiar gleam in his eyes. Ansley swallowed hard, surely her throat hurt a little. "No, really, Nick. I think I am getting a sore throat."

"Forget it, love. Arrangements are made. You've been in my life for over two years. Your clothes are in my closet, your toothbrush is in my bathroom, and I've never seen your home or where you work—never met your family or your friends. There's an entire other you of which I know little. I'm coming. End of discussion. You figure out how you want to handle it with your family. I'll take a hotel room under Tony Colebridge for the sake of appearance, but I'm staying with you. You can either make excuses to your parents, which I would hate to see you do, *or* you can take me along."

Although sick to her stomach, she reconciled herself to the inevitable: he was coming. "I'm not telling them who you are, yet. We can say you're an agent that I knew in New York."

"Sounds pretty lame, love, but if that's what you want, give me the script."

"Can you pull it off?"

"Ansley, what do I do for a living?"

"But, they'll recognize you. They've seen your movies on TV and your face on the entertainment news." In her panic, her mind was devoid of his ability to conceal his identity.

"I have a full beard right now for this film. Unless your parents are avid fans, I don't think they will recognize me."

"But your accent—"

"Stop looking for excuses, love. I'll do American, French, German, whatever. It will be fine. You *could* agree to marry me, and none of this subterfuge would be necessary. You can't keep me in the closet forever, you know."

Ignoring his remark, she said, "When will you be here?"

"Finessing me away from the subject, right?"

"Do I need to pick you up?"

"No. I will take a car to your flat. Just have a chilled glass of wine and a warm bed for me."

"It won't be Cristal."

"Victoria's Secret will do. My flight arrives at 7:05 p.m. on the twenty-third, you figure the ground time. I'll stay until the twenty-ninth. Have to be back up here for a retake that Graham wants before Samantha leaves the location to get back to her TV series. I'm off to the UK on the thirty-first. I hope you'll go with me. Check your schedule. For now, I'll let you get to bed. Sleep well, my love, and dream of me."

She hung up and sat down on her sofa in a state of ice-cold panic, sick at her stomach at the threat of exposure his presence in her world would create and the fear of how her home would appear in comparison to his. *What am I going to do? I can't believe he is doing this to me. I have less than a week to get this neglected condo in shape, plan the food, wrap gifts, polish silver, and wash the good crystal and china. What am I going to tell Mother?* She thought about begging off from the Christmas dinner, but she couldn't skip Christmas Eve. Did she dare fake a trip to New York to see Dennis? No. Her parents would be devastated.

"This is going to be awful, guys," she said to the two sleeping cats. "What will I feed him? Southern fried chicken and meat loaf just doesn't seem appropriate for someone who dines regularly on the finest cuisine. And wine? Well, he'll just have to do with grocery store domestic."

She needn't have worried about the wine, because two days later a crate of assorted vintage wines arrived, including several bottles of Dom Perignon.

CHAPTER TWENTY-FIVE

In the days between the phone call and his arrival, Ansley moved like a whirling dervish, whipping the condo into shape. She bought a new bedspread, new sheets, and new pillows for the bed. Fresh flowers were on a table in the living room and in the bedroom. Dozens of candles were scattered through the rooms. When her doorbell rang a little after eight on the twenty-third, she was physically and emotionally exhausted but charged at the prospect of seeing him.

Dropping his Louis Vuitton bag on the floor as he entered, he swept her up, kissing her passionately. She felt her body dissolve against his like butter melting on warm toast. *I hope this feeling never goes away.*

After pouring him a glass of wine, Ansley gave him the short tour of her home. In the candlelight, the imperfections disappeared. Skye and Shadow eyed him with suspicion—one from the bed and the other from the living room couch. Neither cat was keen on the idea of being touched, but Shadow was the more skittish of the two. If Nick started toward him, he fled and then slowly slipped back as if to spy from behind the corner.

"It's a lovely flat," Nick said, standing in the hallway between the two bedrooms.

"Pretty paltry compared to your home."

"It is you, love—warm and inviting—bespeaking well of its mistress. Stop apologizing. I will be quite comfortable here—cats included."

"I've lowered your risk of unpleasant exposure by relocating the litter box to the laundry room for the duration of your stay."

He smiled. "By the way, what happened to that sore throat?"

"It's better."

"So I expected. You say you weren't lying to me on the phone?"

"Of course not, my throat was a little sore."

"I bet it was," he said, mockingly, and threw his head back, laughing. As she started to protest, he grabbed her around the waist. Picking her up, he carried her to the master bedroom. After making love, he showered, and Ansley readied the lasagna she had prepared for their first meal in her apartment. As they sat at the dining room table, he ate with enthusiasm.

"My compliments to the chef. Your talents never cease to amaze me."

"It's just lasagna. The recipe's on the side of the box."

After dinner, they exchanged gifts. She gave him a photo album of French leather, gold tooled and uniquely shaped. She had filled it with photos of their last year together. He gave her a 1989 gold coin from the Isle of Man. It had the image of a Persian cat and was framed in a diamond bezel that hung from a heavy gold chain. Ansley knew that she could only wear it when she was with Nick. It would raise questions she couldn't, or wouldn't, answer in Jacksonville.

Her cats behaved as though they knew there was a guest in the house. Neither threw up, and they honored the litter boxes. Having Nick in the condo did not dissuade them from their appointed positions on Ansley's bed, however. In the morning, when she woke, they were curled together at the foot of the bed. When Nick woke, he kissed Ansley on the forehead and reached to pet the cats. Shadow dodged. Both fixed copper eyes on him. "I get the feeling they might attack if I don't treat you right."

She smiled. "That's right, mister. You'd better be warned. They're *my* security detail."

Over bakery croissants, bacon, and tea, they discussed the holiday plan the next morning.

"Would you be upset if I went to my parent's house alone, tonight? I've prepped them for your coming to Christmas dinner tomorrow, but if I take you tonight, it's going to bring even more questions about our relationship, and they might press for us to attend midnight services."

He reached across the table and patted her hand. "I'll be fine. Ian will find us a quiet restaurant for dinner, and when I come back, I'll take the opportunity to bond with the fur-coat security detail. Enjoy your family, and I'll be waiting."

That night, after gifts were exchanged, Ansley explained that she was meeting her friend for breakfast at his hotel and needed to drive home before it got too late. Laura followed her to the bedroom where Ansley had left her purse and sweater.

"Ansley, this man you're bringing for dinner tomorrow isn't staying with you, is he?"

"Mother, I can't believe that you're asking me that. I'm twenty-nine years old and divorced. But if it worries you, call the Casa Monica Hotel and ask if Anthony Colebridge is registered."

Knowing her mother, Ansley knew she wouldn't call the hotel, but if she did, they would confirm that Nick had a reservation there. It was Ian's room.

*****

Christmas dinner was at the apartment of Ansley's aunt and uncle. Nick blended in far better than Ansley anticipated but managed to give her some anxious moments. When she introduced him, her uncle's first question was, "What do you do in New York, Tony?"

She had told the family that he was a talent agent she had known since her days with the ballet company and that she had caught up with him when visiting Dennis, but didn't anticipate the questions he would be asked.

"I'm an agent," Nick replied.

"Would we recognize any of your clients?" her father asked.

Ansley held her breath, terrified of what he would answer.

"Probably not. My stable comes mostly from the New York theater circle and a few dancers. I don't have any major American names under contract at the moment, but I do represent one British actor who is fairly well known over there."

You just had to add that didn't you?

"What brings you to Florida this time of year?" Ansley's aunt asked.

"My son."

Laura's face immediately registered alarm. Ansley inwardly gasped. *What can of worms is he opening?*

"Your son?" Laura said.

"My ex-wife moved to Florida with her new husband, and I came down to see my boy over the holiday. Obviously, I'm not welcome at her home today. Dennis Devlin gave me Ansley's number, and here I am."

Oh, you're good, Nick. Academy Award good.

Throughout the day, Nick joked with Mike Sheridan and engaged Ansley's aunt in a discussion of Sir Arthur Conan Doyle versus Ian Fleming. His American accent remained impeccable. After eating, the men talked sports and politics. Fortunately basketball season had begun, which was the only American sport Nick could knowledgably address.

After the dishes were done, the women joined the men in the living room. Once settled, Laura looked over at Nick and said, "There's something familiar about you, Tony."

Nick smiled and said, casually, "Nicholas Colton, right? I'm told that I resemble him."

Ansley cringed, wanting to strangle Nick but only able to give him a dirty look. He was taunting her—deliberately flirting with exposure.

However, Laura was oblivious and simply replied, "You're right. That must be it."

"How long will you be in Florida, Tony?" Mike Sheridan asked.

"About a week."

Why didn't you say you were leaving tomorrow, darn it, Nick.

"Why so long?" Laura asked.

"He's going—"

"I can answer," Nick cut her off. "I'm hoping to spend a little more time with Kevin and maybe take in some local theater—always on the lookout for talent."

"Well we're happy to have you," Laura said.

Ansley spoke. "We'd better be going. Nick. . ." She caught herself and felt her face turning pink. "I mean Tony—you all got me confused with your bringing up Nicholas Colton. I know Tony wants to see if his ex-wife will let him take his son out tonight."

Nick smiled, thoroughly enjoying her frustration. "I'm fine. No need for you to cut your holiday short on my account."

I'm going to kill him. I am.

As soon as they were in Ansley's car, she let go on him. "Were you crazy in there? You could have given everything away," she said, cranking her car.

"Well, well, look at the ice princess, getting a wee bit feisty on me?"

"Nick, be serious. I have to hide that you're here for the rest of the week."

"That won't be hard. We'll just stay in bed like John and Yoko." He reached over and squeezed her thigh. "I like that idea."

CHAPTER TWENTY-SIX

They did not stay in bed the rest of the week, but they stayed inside the condo, going out only after dark. Ansley was paranoid and felt certain they would be seen. During the day, they watched videos, played Scrabble, and ran Nick's lines. While he read through a couple of potential scripts, she reviewed deposition transcripts. Ansley was astonished at how comfortable it was having him in the apartment. He wanted to order food in to make life easy for her, but she insisted on cooking, preparing traditional Southern cuisine. Nick hovered around her in the kitchen, helping with both the preparation and the cleanup.

"I wouldn't have thought you would know how to peel a potato."

"You'd be amazed at what I know how to do. I've had expert training on how to look like I'm cooking."

"That's right. You played a chef in that romantic comedy."

"My cooking was the most comical element of the film."

With each dinner, Ansley set the table with her best china and linens. They ate by candlelight and consumed some of the wine he had sent. But Nick insisted that they save a bottle of the Dom for her mother and one for her aunt as thank-you gifts for including him in their holiday celebration.

"They won't know what they have, Nick. No one in my family has ever had a bottle of Dom Perignon."

"Well, it's time they did."

At times, she let her fantasies wander and imagined that they were a married couple. Having him in the condo, especially in the kitchen, was the most domestic scenario she had experienced with him.

Could it work? No. This is not the real life for him. Nicholas Colton in suburban America. Never. Why does everything have to be so complicated?

Ansley called her mother every morning, wanting to avoid the possibility of an unexpected visit, or even a phone call at an inopportune time. She was glad that her condo was over thirty miles from her family and most of her friends. Elaine had called and invited her to dinner, but Ansley declined, saying she had a slight virus and didn't want to expose Elaine's family.

"You're going to hell; you know that, don't you?" Nick said, smiling and grabbing her around the waist as she hung up.

"I think I established that when I first started sleeping with you."

"Ouch. Have I been demoted from king to devil?"

"Probably one of his disciples."

Two days after Christmas, Jeanette called and invited Ansley over to her unit.

"I see your car is home and thought you might come over for a cup of coffee. We never have time to visit."

"I would love to, Jeanette, but I kind of like have company," Ansley said, scrunching up her face.

"Oh . . . ," Jeanette responded with all-knowing tone. "Mr. Mysterious, the flower man?"

Ansley hesitated. Did she dare admit that the man who sent so many flowers was in her condo? "You caught me. Please don't say anything."

"Who would I tell? Melissa? No, sweetie, you enjoy yourself. You deserve it."

On Nick's last full day in Florida, the doorbell rang. They were playing Scrabble on her bed. Ansley froze and glanced at him with a horrified look on her face.

"Don't look at me, love. I'm not expecting anyone."

"What should I do?"

"My first suggestion is that you answer your door."

"What about you?"

"Relax, I'll stay here. Certainly, you aren't going to entertain anyone else in your bedroom, are you?"

She gave him a dirty look and walked to the living room.

"Elaine, what a surprise. What are you doing here?"

"I made some soup from the leftover turkey and thought it would do you good. I should have called but wanted to get out of the house. I'm on mommy-overload and may kill a child if I don't get relief. Are you OK? You look flushed." Elaine looked genuinely concerned and reached up to put her hand on Ansley's forehead.

"Uh . . . yes. I'm fine. Just a little flu bug. You shouldn't come in, you might catch it." The usually calm and composed Ansley was obviously flustered.

"I'm immune. The kids have all had it," Elaine said, ignoring the warning and walking in. "Other than your pink cheeks, you look awfully good to be sick. Is something going on?"

"I'm fine. Don't worry. I really appreciate your coming over and bringing the soup, but I'm really fine—trust me."

"Ansley, I've known you too long for you to fool me. Something is going on. You don't stay home from work unless you are half dead, and you don't even look sick." Elaine looked around the living room as though she expected to see something or someone.

"Elaine, it's the Christmas season. I needed a rest."

"You take time off, stay home, and don't call me? Ansley, I don't buy that either. You would have called for lunch or a movie. And why did you make up the flu business to start with. What are you hiding?"

"Nothing. I just need some down time. I've been working hard lately." At that moment, Nick appeared. Ansley's face turned bright red. Elaine broke into a big smile.

"Tony Colebridge, here, you must be Ansley's good friend, Elaine. She's told me much about you," he said, extending his hand and once again speaking in an impeccable American accent.

Ansley was mortified. He's done it now. He might fool Mother and Daddy with his fake speech and phony name, but this was Elaine, who went with her to all his movies.

"Well, she hasn't told me about you, but nice to meet you, Tony. You're right. I'm Elaine Davis."

"Tony just stopped by on his way back to New York. You caught me. I lied to my parents to have some time to show him around. He's staying at the Casa Monica."

"I understand completely, Ansley. I won't keep you from your guest. We'll get together soon. How long are you here for, Mr. Colebridge?" Elaine was looking hard at Nick, yet she didn't indicate any recognition. She was too busy sizing him up as Ansley's lover to notice that he looked familiar.

"Call me Tony, please. I leave tomorrow. Ansley has been so kind as to act as hostess for me when I got stuck here in Florida for the holiday." Ansley was holding her breath. *Don't push it Nick,* she thought. Her hands were weak and her palms wet.

"Well, I'll be going, but Ansley, we will talk when you are free," Elaine said.

When the door closed, Ansley turned, furious with him. "Damn you, Nick Colton. I am going to get the third degree now. She thinks I'm sleeping with you."

Nick laughed his deep laugh. "You are." He was thoroughly pleased with himself and enjoying Ansley's frustration. "Calm down. She didn't recognize me," he said, pulling her close to him and kissing the top of her head.

"Stop patronizing me. She may have not said that she recognized you. And even if she didn't, I'm still going to be grilled for months as to what there is between us, no matter who you are. It's going to be bad enough with Mother. Now, I'm going to have to deal with Elaine as well."

"I didn't invite her over, love. Remember, you could solve all this intrigue and deception by coming out of the closet and marrying me. Or will I have to remain a secret after we are married as well?"

"Can we not get into that today?"

"If you would stop being so damned stubborn, we could get on with a future together. He stopped abruptly as though thinking. "That's a capital idea. . . . I should make you pregnant—then you would *have* to marry me." His mischievous look appeared.

"How many times do I have to say that I don't want to be the next 'former Mrs. Nicolas Colton'? We have a baby. I get middle-aged and boring. You give into a moment of temptation with some sexy young starlet, and we screw up the child by playing tug-of-war across the Atlantic."

As she spoke, his expression changed. Gone was the playfulness. "Okay, love, slow up. I know your arguments, and I'm not in the mood to fight them. I'll continue trying to convince you. But, you're right, let's *not* spoil the little time we have together."

CHAPTER TWENTY-SEVEN

SPRING OF 2004

It was late spring in England. Ansley had spent Saturday morning with Nick viewing a DVD of scenes from his latest film, and he was in a bad mood.

"Whitfield couldn't direct traffic on a country road," Nick said, turning off the television set. "We're going to have to reshoot thirty percent of that footage."

"Thirty percent? But it was filmed in Hawaii," Ansley said, going to the windows to open the drapes. "Surely you won't go back over there."

"There's no choice if we want to salvage this bomb." He threw the remote on the bed with an unmistakable gesture of contempt. "Where the hell was his head? Or better yet, where was his eyesight? Worst damn camera angles I've ever seen."

She started to say that it wasn't that bad, but decided Nick was in no frame of mind to be placated. In the past year, he had become determined to break free of his heartthrob reputation and build his image as a serious actor. Ansley knew that losing both the Olivier and BAFTA awards earlier in the year had been disappointing, even though he would never admit it.

"Fortunately, we'll need only three other cast members and a skeleton crew, but it's still going to push us way over budget." Nick owned a percentage of the movie, giving him a financial, as well as artistic, interest. "You can go with me. That will at least salvage something by giving us a short holiday."

Ansley hesitated before answering. Walking over to face him, she said, "Nick, you know I can't go to Hawaii. I've got two trials coming up."

His face grew more hostile. "Of course. I should have known."

Reaching out, he took her left hand and held it up. "When are you going to let me move that ring to *this* hand and bring you to live here?"

"This is not a good time to get into that."

Dropping her hand, he put both of his firmly on her shoulders and said, "It's never a good time to get into that, is it, Ansley?"

She looked down at the solitaire on her right hand, biding her time before answering. Since his visit to her condo at Christmas, he had begun asserting more and more pressure on her to set a wedding date–not that she had actually accepted a marriage proposal.

It had been raining all morning, and even with the heavy drapery open, there was not much light in the room. The gray sky showed little sign of clearing. "I'm going to say it one more time. I want you to marry me. I'm fed up with having to schedule time on your calendar like one of your clients and tired of hiding you from the public. I want you on my arm on the red carpet and in my bed every night."

"Do we have to talk about this now?"

His eyes turned darker in one of the sinister modes he used for dramatic moments on screen–but he wasn't acting. "When,   Ansley, just exactly when?"

The bitterness in his tone made her want to back away, but she stood her ground.

"Why is it so hard for you to understand? Marriage is a big gamble under circumstances far better than ours. The application should carry a black-box warning: 'Marriage can be harmful to your emotional, financial, and mental health.' One failure was enough for me."

"And you're damned sure that we would fail?"

"How can I not be? You have love scenes with some of the world's most beautiful women. Temptation overcomes you on the set, and I'm left with a broken heart and no career—maybe an international custody battle for my children. Even if that weren't true, this jet-set life we live is not reality. Reality is me embarrassing you because I don't know the social protocol, disgusting you when I'm throwing up with a virus, disagreeing with you about politics or how to raise our children, getting old and fat."

He looked at her with an almost vicious expression, unmoved by her argument.

She continued, "We could get married and find that it was a mistake, that we didn't really know each other."

"That's a damn circular argument. How do we spend the time together if you don't quit your job? Your logic is fatal."

"If it's meant to be, we will find a way."

"You've got it all figured out haven't you?" His tone was sarcastic, his patience gone. He dropped his hands from her shoulders and threw them into the air as he turned away. "What the hell do you want? Lloyds doesn't sell marriage insurance. I've told you that I'll give you a prenup that will cover you for the rest of your life."

"I'm not for sale."

"I'm asking you to marry me, damn it, not become my harlot."

"I'm probably already that," she said, her face turning red. "You wouldn't be the one throwing away your career."

"Would you like me to move to Florida? We could live in your flat, and you could pay our bills." His toned embodied his disgust.

"Don't patronize me, Nick. You've got to understand how much my career means and how much I need to know I can take care of myself."

"How much would it take to give you a sense of security? Name your figure."

"I've told you. I'm not for sale. Your money can't buy everything."

Walking back to where she stood, he grabbed her by her upper arms; his fingers dug into her flesh as he shook her. Sparks flew from his eyes. "Do you have any idea how much I want to beat some sense into you? You are the most obstinate, vexing woman I have ever known. You deny us a life together because of what another man did. You insult me."

Ansley looked straight into his eyes. She had never seen him so angry.

What can I say? Can I marry him?

She wanted with all her heart to scream yes. But the words wouldn't come out.

Suddenly, he picked her up as if she was a rag doll and carried her across the room to the bed. Startled, she offered no resistance, not even when he tore away her clothing.

When he was done, Ansley lay motionless.

What just happened?

His lovemaking had bordered on brutal. If she had uttered the word "no," it would have been a crime. As abruptly as he had taken her, he redressed and left the room. Feeling violated, Ansley redressed. Subconsciously knowing that he would leave the house, she walked over to the window and watched him walk briskly to the stables. Minutes later, he emerged on Hamlet and rode off in the rain, the mane of the big horse flying.

When he was out of sight, Ansley moved away from the window

and curled up in one of the large chairs with her knees under her chin. She cried for what seemed like hours.

After about forty-five minutes, a soft knock came at the door.

"Come in."

It was Martha with a fresh pot of tea. She took one look at Ansley and put the tray on the table. "Are you all right, Miss Sheridan?"

"I'm fine, Martha."

"Forgive me, madam, but you don't look fine. Does Mr. Colebridge know you're upset?"

"I think he does."

"I noticed he rode away on Hamlet like he was fleeing the very devil."

All of Ansley's reserve collapsed and the floodgate opened. "It's me, Martha. He wants us to get married. He wants me to give up my career. I can't risk everything I've worked for, and he refuses to understand."

The older woman put her hand on Ansley's shoulder, her demeanor sympathetic. "He loves you, lass. I've known him for a very long time and known him to see a lot of women. He never brought any of them here. He's different with you. He eagerly anticipates your visits."

"I believe that he does now, but I'm so afraid he might change."

The room was silent for a minute or two. Typical of British courtesy, Martha said no more. Touching Ansley affectionately on her arm, she left the room.

After Martha left, Ansley put cold water on her face and went to her suite at the other end of the hall. She couldn't stand being in his room. She tried to read, but unable to focus, she cried more. At six-thirty, there was a knock at her door. Blotting her eyes, she went, expecting to see John or Martha.

"Can we talk?" Nick said, no warmth in his voice or body language.

"Of course," she said, stepping aside as he passed.

"I owe you an apology," he said, but his tone bore no sign of contrition. "My behavior was unacceptable."

Ansley was silent, unsure of how to respond. Taking a deep breath, she finally said, "You were upset."

"I'm not sure that should excuse how I acted. However, I won't go back on what I said. I've thought it through, and no matter how I construct the facts, the answer comes out the same. I cannot continue our relationship as it is, and has been, for over two years. Either you're in my life, or you're not. Marry me or live with me—your choice—otherwise, all bets are off." His face was hard, no trace of weakness.

174

Ansley was speechless. For a minute, they stared at one another, and then, Nick turned and headed for the door. "Dinner is at seven-thirty."

The remainder of the weekend was tense. She wanted to say the words he sought, but choked every time she tried. Leaving the firm to start her own practice had given her the flexibility to spend more time with Nick, but he wasn't satisfied.

At dinner, he said little. She watched him cut his steak.

Why can't he understand? How can I sacrifice my career, my family, my identity, even my country?

Nick didn't bring up the subject again during the weekend, but he was not the same. His demeanor was reserved, polite—cold. They slept in the same bed for two nights, but without sex or significant affection. He kissed her goodnight almost as a parent would kiss a child.

When he saw her off at Heathrow on Monday, he hugged her and kissed her with more passion than he had since the hostile encounter on Saturday.

"I'll call you tonight," he said, as she prepared to pass through security.

CHAPTER TWENTY-EIGHT

Nick did call on Monday night, but the conversation was brief. No mention was made of the elephant lurking in the relationship.

Throughout the days and weeks that followed, the calls diminished in both frequency and duration. He always signed off with "I love you," but there was a different edge to it. Ansley felt a dark cloud had descended to envelop her like a death shroud. Their conversations were superficial. The magic was lost. It was harder hiding her depression than hiding her exuberance had been. During more than one conversation with him, she had nearly succumbed and blurted out, "I give. I'll marry you."

Her mother sensed there was something wrong when Ansley went home for dinner a few weeks after returning from England.

"Are you okay, honey?"

"Sure," Ansley chirped, trying to sound happy. "I'm just overworked. Too many balls in the air."

Two months went by. Nick and Ansley had not been apart that long since meeting. His calls were cordial, but without emotion. He asked about her work and talked about his professional life and continued to say, "I love you," when ending a call. She knew that the relationship was sliding down an invisible mountain. She tried to prepare herself for the crash ending, but was not prepared for what happened.

On her way home from work one Friday afternoon, she stopped to pick up a few groceries. As she stood in line to check out, the front page of a tabloid smacked her in the face.

"NICHOLAS COLTON IN COZY TETE-A-TETE"

Beneath the headline was a photo of Nick and a pretty redhead. Both were smiling. He was in the States and with another woman! *He never even mentioned that he was coming over here.*

It was all Ansley could do to flee the market before tears would cause public humiliation. She had no idea who the woman in the photo was and couldn't bring herself to buy a copy.

Why did I let myself in for this? Why didn't I listen to my better judgment? It hurts worse than Mark.

Back in her condo, she snuggled down with the cats. They seemed to know that she was distraught and took turns nestling in her lap. She didn't turn on her TV and hardly ate all weekend. It was over, finished. No more thrilling weekends in exotic places. No more charms for the gold bracelet. But those were not the things she would miss the most. There would be no more touching, kissing, smelling the Green Irish Tweed on his crisp clothing, watching his toned body walk to the bathroom, his sexy amber eyes twinkle mischievously when teasing her—no more making love and no more feeling adored and protected.

Sunday night, a little past ten o'clock, the phone rang. Ansley didn't want to talk to anyone, but curiosity took her to the instrument. "The Pierre" appeared on the caller ID.

It's him. What do I do? I can't talk to him.

Magnetic forces attempted to cancel one another out as Ansley fought the emotional desire to hear his voice and the intellectual desire to avoid him. Emotions won out.

"How are you," he said casually, as though nothing had changed.

She hesitated, carefully choosing her words. "I'm great; how are you?"

"Exhausted. Stephen has me on a hamster wheel."

"Really?"

"Really. I've done eleven promotional appearances in the past ten days in addition to meeting with two directors."

"Did one of them have red hair?" The minute she said it, she wished that she hadn't. *Damn Ansley, you sound like the bitter, scorned woman. Have some pride.*

"No, but an author I met does. Why would you ask?"

I've done it now, might as well finish it. "I saw a nice photo of you on the cover of this week's *Enquirer.*"

"I didn't know it was there, or that you read that particular publication."

"I don't. But it was hard to miss when I was waiting in line at the grocery store." Tears were filling her eyes—a combination of sadness and anger that she was lowering herself to address the matter.

"I told you that all bets were off if you couldn't commit to me. I haven't heard a single word from you in that direction, and yes, I did have dinner with the woman. She is certainly attractive, but don't ask me any question for which you don't want to hear the answer."

"I think I have all the answers I need. How do I return the ring to you?"

"I don't want it. It's yours; no strings were attached. I told you that when I gave it to you."

"I can't keep it."

"Then sell the fucking thing, Ansley. Give it to charity. I don't want it back. But remember, you closed this door, not me. If you change your mind and are willing to put the ring on your left hand, let me know. Otherwise, we're both free to pursue other avenues."

"Goodbye, Nick." She hung up without waiting for a response. *He slept with her. He did. I know he did. Who is she?*

It was nearly eleven o'clock, but Ansley left the condo to get a copy of the tabloid. She found one at the all-night market and took it home without looking at it. Once in the condo, she took a deep breath and unfolded the paper. He looked wonderful, but then he always did. She had never seen an unflattering photo of him. The woman was very attractive. She had short, red hair that fell in a soft wave over one side of her face. It was hard to tell what color her eyes were, but Ansley guessed they were blue and very pretty. Nick looked happy. Scanning the cutline, she saw that the woman's name was Fury O'Quinn. Nick had said that she was an author. The name was familiar, but not a writer Ansley had read. She immediately headed to her computer. *What kind of name is Fury? Must be a pen name.*

Google coughed up a dozen websites. Ansley chose *Wikipedia* where she learned that Fury was the writer's birth name and that she was born in New York, unmarried, and the author of romance novels. The photo on the Internet page confirmed that Fury O'Quinn was indeed a beautiful woman and five years younger than Ansley. *How did she publish so many books by the age of 24?*

Folding the image down, Ansley took the periodical to the kitchen trash and stuffed it in. Starting back toward her bedroom, she stopped, turned around, and retrieved the crumpled paper. Tearing away the front page, she returned the rest to the trash, folded the fateful photo into a small square, and put it inside a kitchen drawer. *If I'm ever tempted to consider him in any way, I'll look at that. Thank goodness, Dennis is the only one who knows about us.*

CHAPTER TWENTY-NINE

Three months passed without speaking to Nick—not that he didn't call, but Ansley could not bring herself to answer. His messages were polite, without emotion.

"Nick here. How are you? Give me a call."

She listened and then pushed the save button on her phone, unable to erase his voice, but unable to respond.

"Maybe you should talk to him," Dennis said in one of their weekly conversations.

"I can't. Not yet. I've got to immunize myself."

"You know that I think you were wrong to turn him down."

Ansley frowned and sat down on her couch next to Shadow, pulling her feet up on the cushion and hugging her knees to her chest with her free arm. "I know you do, you've said it often enough. Let's don't talk about it anymore." Shadow stood up and tried to wedge his way into her nonexistent lap.

"Why don't you come up here? We could take in a couple of shows—do some serious shopping."

She paused for a minute before responding. "Not yet. Too many memories. I would be terrible company."

"Just remember, it's an open invitation, anytime. William and I would love to shower you with love and distraction. We could go dancing. Just think, two partners to help you burn up the floor."

She smiled. "Maybe Christmas. I don't think I want to be here thinking about his coming to Florida last year. Let me think about it."

The Sunday after her conversation with Dennis, the phone rang at three o'clock. Caller ID read, "Unknown number." Ansley knew it was Nick. Her first impulse was to ignore it as she had done the past months, but something changed her mind. Picking up the receiver, she hesitated, instantly regretting opening the telephone line.

"Ansley. Are you there?"

A few more seconds passed before she responded. "I'm here."

"I've tried to call you. I assume you got the messages and chose to ignore them."

"I did. I thought we had pretty much said all that needed to be said in our last conversation. How is Fury O'Quinn?"

"Who?"

"The writer."

"Oh, yes. I have no idea how she is. Why would I?"

"Don't tell me she was just a one-night stand."

"She wasn't a stand of any sort. If you're talking about that tabloid photograph, which I checked out after I talked to you, it was a meeting for her to pitch one of her novels for a potential film. I don't even know the woman personally."

"She's beautiful."

"Ansley, the majority of women I come in contact with are beautiful. I don't sleep with them all."

"Ah . . . but you do sleep with some." *What are you doing? Don't lower yourself.*

"I didn't call you to talk about my sex life. I called because I was thinking about you. I'd like to see *you.*"

"That's a bad idea."

"Why?"

"I am a recovering Nickaholic, and it's common knowledge that an addict cannot drink from the fountain without serious repercussions. I'm cured, or at least in remission, and I'm not going to jeopardize my sobriety." Sliding her feet back to the floor, she started to stand. "Thank you for calling, but I have to go now."

Hanging up the phone without waiting to hear more, she shook off the tears that were flooding her face and went to the bathroom for a wet cloth. Patting her face dry, she gathered up her purse and jacket and left the condo—destination unknown.

He didn't call again. Ansley didn't go to New York for Christmas because Dennis was sick. Instead, she talked her parents into a trip to Williamsburg. It was expensive, but worth the damage to her credit card.

Without the distraction of flights to foreign destinations, Ansley's law practice grew. As time passed, she became less and less introspective with colleagues and was asked out by two single lawyers. While it was nice to feel that she was still attractive to the opposite sex, she turned both down.

"I'm not through the grieving process quite yet," she said to Dennis when he tried to encourage her to plunge back into the dating pool.

In early February, a letter arrived postmarked from the UK. She didn't need to see the return address to know whom it was from. His handwriting was distinctive. Avoiding opening the missive, she laid it on her desk and went to change from her lawyer uniform to sweats. Once dressed, curiosity got the better of her, and she opened the letter. The message, on heavy linen paper with the letter *C* in gold relief at the top, was brief and without embellishments.

> Dear Ansley,
>   I think of you often. I was notified today by the Academy that I'm a nominee for Best Actor and would like to have you share the ceremony with me. No strings. Say yes, and I'll make the arrangements.
>   Forever,
>   Nick.

He certainly knows how to create temptation.
Taking a box of light-blue stationery from the bottom drawer, she wrote:

> Nick,
>   How kind of you to consider me for such an honor. I certainly wish you the best of luck. You deserve to win. However, I couldn't possibly attend as I'm in trial that week.
>   With kindest regards,
>   Ansley

CHAPTER THIRTY

One evening in May, a year after her breakup with Nick, Ansley's phone rang. The caller ID read "Unknown, New York, New York." Expecting Dennis to be on the other end, she answered cheerfully. "Long time, no hear. Where have you been stranger?" It wasn't Dennis. The caller was William.

"Ansley, I hate calling you, and Dennis will probably be angry with me for doing so, but there's something I feel that you would want to know."

His tone told her that she wasn't going to like what he was about to say. She wanted to hang up the phone and not listen, praying that if she didn't know, then it wouldn't be true.

William paused. She could hear his muffled attempt to clear his voice. "Dennis has—"

"Don't say it. I don't want to hear it." Her instinct told her from the tone of his voice that it was serious and likely to be only one thing.

"He's been positive for a long time, Ansley. It's full-blown AIDS now."

"No, no, you're wrong." She couldn't hold back the tears. "I begged him to be careful. How did he get it?"

The phone was silent with no response from William. Ansley put her hand across her mouth as she realized the implication of her words. "I'm sorry, I shouldn't have said that."

"It's okay. I knew you would think that I gave it to him. You haven't forgiven me for hurting him six years ago, but no, Ansley. I didn't give it to him. I'm clean. Dennis first tested positive before we got back together."

Ansley walked to her couch and sat down. "I'm sorry, William. That was off base of me. But, it's not as bad as it used to be, right? They have good drugs these days, don't they?"

"Improved, but they're not working for Dennis. They are very expensive, and his insurance coverage is exhausted. His latest blood work is off the charts, making him ripe for an opportunistic infection. I know you haven't seen him for at least a year. He's lost an inordinate amount of weight and his reserves are depleted in all respects—physically, emotionally, and financially."

"What can I do?" She was on the verge of tears.

"Probably nothing. He is going to be furious that I called you, but I thought you should know."

"I'm so glad you did. I'm coming to New York."

After hanging up, Ansley began preparations to leave. Fortunately, she had only one hearing that week.

Three days after talking to William, she was less than an hour from leaving for the airport when the phone rang.

Thinking it was her mother, she picked up the phone without looking at the caller ID.

"How nice to hear your voice," he said.

Stunned, she said, "Nick?"

"I'm glad you still recognize my voice."

"The entire free world recognizes your voice. Of course, I do. It's just unexpected."

"Did I catch you at a bad time?"

She hesitated, not sure whether she wanted to tell him about Dennis, or even if she could without breaking down. After a moment of silence, she said, "I'm practically out the door on my way to New York. Dennis has AIDS."

"My God, Ansley. I'm sorry to hear that. I was fond of the chap. How bad?"

"Very."

"There are drugs that treat it successfully, aren't there?"

"Apparently it's gone pretty far because he didn't have the money for all the drugs he needed. I can't really talk right now, Nick. I'm sure you understand."

"Of course."

Hearing from him at such a vulnerable time didn't make the trip any easier for Ansley. She tried to read on the plane, but the images of both men kept flashing across her brain. She had lost one and was losing the other. The pain was emotionally excruciating.

Riding through Queens in the cab from LaGuardia, Ansley stared out the window, remembering the exciting trips when she was a dancer, the fateful visit when she came to see Dennis dance in *Carmen* and met Nick, and the subsequent rendezvous in the luxury hotels. This time, there was no limo and no suite, only sorrow and suffering awaiting her.

"The Hudson on West 9th Avenue," she told the cabbie, hopping he understood English. It was the hotel where she first stayed for summer study at the school of the National Ballet.

Why did Nick have to call today and open up that vein—now—when I'm losing Dennis?

As much as she wanted to see her dear friend, she looked forward to the Devlin apartment with dread. For a moment, she wanted to turn around and run from reality.

After stowing her luggage in her room, she took a cab to the co-op. Despite her mental preparation, she was not prepared for the sight that greeted her. When William opened the door and she walked into the familiar space, Dennis was sitting in a recliner, wrapped in a blanket. His eyes were sunken deep in their sockets, his body a shell of its former self. Ansley fought to keep her expression stable while internally she felt razors slicing through her stomach. Gone was the handsome young Apollo he had been.

"William should not have called, but damn, I'm glad to see you," Dennis said. Even his voice had changed within the few weeks since they spoke on the phone. All the zip was gone, replaced by a struggle for enough breath to complete a sentence.

She dropped her purse on the sofa and went to him, arms wrapping around the boney shoulders. "I'm glad to be here." Pulling back, she said, "You think you're angry with William? I should chew *you* out for not calling me."

He smiled and gave a small shudder. "Could you be so kind as to get me another blanket, William?"

William brought a blanket and tenderly wrapped it around his partner and then made a pot of tea. When he returned, the trio sat talking about performances past—Ansley and William bearing the burden of the conversation. Dennis seemed to enjoy the camaraderie but soon tired. Exercising discretion, Ansley excused herself when William picked Dennis up and gently carried him to the bedroom. Once the frail man was settled, William returned to the living room to talk privately with Ansley.

"I know he doesn't have long, and I can't stop the bastard virus from taking him, but I wish that I could somehow find a way to make his last days easier," he said to Ansley.

"I wish that there was something I could do. How much would it take?"

"It's out of reach, Ansley. The meds he needs are thousands a month. His insurance is maxed out, and he's on a waiting list for public funds. It won't come in time. Although he doesn't say it, I think he would like to go home to Indiana. His mom is still living. She said that we are both welcome, but I can't earn enough in Terre Haute to survive, and Dennis doesn't want to leave me." Tears in his eyes as he spoke matched the ones in Ansley's. They were both suffering the impending loss of someone they loved dearly.

Ansley stayed in New York for three days. Each day going to the French bakery that she and Dennis had loved as young dancers and taking him pastries, brioches, and croissants. He tried his best to eat, but his appetite was gone. The day she left, they cried together. As she hugged him, she said, "I'll be back. You eat and take care of yourself." But they both knew that she would never see him again.

The flight home was merciless. All she could think of was the image of the emaciated body, helpless and suffering. *He never did anything to deserve this. He's only thirty-two years old. It's not fair.*

Once back in Florida, Ansley called William almost daily. Sometimes Dennis felt strong enough to speak with her. More often, he did not. She thought about selling Nick's ring, but as valuable as it was, the market for used diamonds promised little more than one-fourth its purchase price. Probably not even enough to cover a week of medication. If she could have cured Dennis, she would have sold it immediately.

Three weeks after returning from New York, her phone rang as she walked in from the office.

"Ansley, it's William. I couldn't wait to tell you. We got a call this morning that some foundation is going to sponsor Dennis. They are paying for his treatment, any equipment he needs, and even a trip to Indiana, if he can make it."

"Oh my gosh, William. That is great news." Her face lit up with joy. "What foundation?"

"I have no idea. I just got this call and followed the instructions. There's a handsome balance in Dennis's bank account now."

"Are you sure it's for real and not a scam?"

"Believe me, I questioned it, but the bank assured me that every-thing checks out."

Despite receipt of all the resources medical science could provide, Dennis succumbed to the disease without seeing his home state. Five months after Ansley's visit, the Foundation paid for transportation of his body to Indiana and his funeral costs. Ansley sat alongside Mary Devlin and William at the service.

After the funeral, the mourners gathered at the home of Mary Devlin. Dennis's father, Declan, had passed away ten years before.

"Dennis loved you," the grieving mother said as the two women embraced upon Ansley's entry into the modest home. "If things had been different, you might have been my daughter-in-law."

William was standing nearby, causing Ansley discomfort at the older woman's remark.

"I loved him, too. He was my closest friend, and I'm going to miss him so much."

After a few seconds, the hug turned into the clasping of hands as they separated. Tears glazed the eyes of both women. Ignoring her other guests, Mary released one of Ansley's hands, but pulled slightly on the other in a silent signal to follow. Leading Ansley down a dim hallway, Mary opened a door to her bedroom. Sunlight streamed through gossamer tiebacks, adding an element of hope to the dismal day.

Dropping Ansley's hand, Mary walked across the room to an antique bureau. She opened a drawer and took out a small, wooden box from which she removed a gold chain with an attached crucifix. The two-inch piece was comprised of a gold corpus mounted on a cross of Connemara marble. "I want you to have this. It's been in the Devlin family for more than a hundred years."

Ansley's face registered dismay. "It's beautiful, Mary; but I couldn't accept your family heirloom."

The older woman looked away. "With Dennis gone, there's no more family." Shaking her head slightly, she turned her eyes back to look directly at Ansley. "He loved you, and he wanted you to have it to remember him by. . . . I want you to have it. Pass it on to one of your children. Dennis's great-grandmother brought it to America from County Galway in 1887." She took Ansley's hand and placed the cross in it, folding Ansley's fingers around the cold stone.

Tears streaming down her face, Ansley put her arms around the woman, hugging her tightly, and whispered, "I'll treasure it always."

William and Ansley stayed with Mary long after the last of her friends were gone, reciting stories about Dennis. They laughed and cried together until nearly midnight.

The morning after the funeral, William drove Ansley to the airport. They promised to stay in touch, but Ansley knew they probably would not. Once settled in her window seat on the plane, she took the crucifix from her purse and gently unwrapped the tissue. Gazing at it, she mentally recounted Mary's words about how the religious ornament had been blessed in an Irish parish and how Dennis wore it to church when he was a youngster. An important part of her life was gone, and she felt as empty inside as she had when she realized the relationship with Nick was over.

CHAPTER THIRTY-ONE

"Time is no one's friend," Ansley said, four months after Dennis's death. One of her hands stirred a pot of spaghetti sauce while the other held a cordless telephone.

"Meaning what?" Elaine responded.

"When you're having a good time and are happy, it speeds by like a NASCAR champion, but when you're miserable, it's as slow as rush-hour traffic."

"You're in a philosophical mood today. Any particular reason?"

"Not really. I guess I've been depressed ever since Dennis died." *And Nick and I split up.*

"You need to change up your lifestyle. All you do is work."

"I like my work."

"That's all good, but you don't want to be alone the rest of your life. What ever happened to that guy from New York? You know—the one I met at your condo two years ago. You never mention him. I think his name was Tony."

Ansley flinched. *Was she reading my mind?* "That was a dead end."

"I always wondered if there was more to his story than you shared."

Ansley braced herself to keep her tone steady. "Not really. He had a life in New York, and I had a life here. It couldn't work."

"Forgive me for asking, and I'm not making any judgments, but was he married?"

Ansley hesitated, not wanting to respond. She had suspected that Elaine did not pry into her mysterious trips because she thought Ansley was involved with a married man. It had made the cover easier to manage, but no longer necessary. "Separated," she responded, pleased with the almost true statement.

"Did he go back to the wife?"

Why is she digging? I don't need the interrogation.

"Not exactly."

"He was damned good looking."

Yes, he is. "He was, but I didn't want to get myself caught in a bad situation. I see enough of that in my practice."

"Oh, like that client of yours with two wives?"

Ansley chuckled. "You remember that?"

"Yeah. I thought the guy should have gone to jail."

"No comment. Back to plans for today. It will take me about an hour to get ready. I just have to put this sauce away and get dressed. Want to meet at the Avenues Mall? We should have time for a quick sandwich and an early matinee."

"That works for me," Elaine said. "There's a bunch of the leftover Christmas movies playing that either look good and or have good-looking guys. We have our choice between George Clooney, Nicholas Colton, Pierce Brosnan, Colin Farrell, and Eric Bana. Want to see the Nicholas Colton one? I can't remember the title, but the review was good, and you like him."

No, I don't. Ansley paused for a minute, hoping to sound casual. "I think I like the Eric Bana one—*Munich*. One of my clients saw it and said it was good," Ansley lied.

After lunch, as the two women walked up to the theater box office, a poster with a larger-than-life Nick startled Ansley. As she paused, Elaine noticed and said, "We can switch and go to that one. He looks awfully sexy."

"No," Ansley responded, trying to tear her eyes away and to stifle the urgency she felt. "Maybe next time. I really want to see *Munich*."

As they walked into the lobby of the theater, Elaine looked at Ansley. "Are you okay? Your face is white as snow."

Fighting her emotions, Ansley said, "I'm fine. It's just that every now and then I get a real depressed feeling thinking about Dennis."

"I don't think I realized how close you were with him."

"We had a special bond. He was always there for me, especially when Mark screwed me over. I'll never forget about when we were both new in the company—living away from home in the big city and pretending we weren't scared. We were just kids in our teens with big dreams. At least some of his came true before he died."

"You did make a lot of trips to New York."

If only I could tell you about those trips, but I can't be sure you could keep my secret.

It was a hard afternoon. Ansley struggled to focus on the movie. Leaving the theater, she was drawn to the poster of Nick like a kitten to catnip. Walking to the car, she knew that she would see his film the next day—alone. *I am such a wimp. He's like a drug addiction. I know the sight of him is going to tear me apart, but I can't resist the temptation.*

That night, she took his framed headshot out of her night-table drawer and positioned it next to the lamp. She then sprayed Green Irish Tweed on a large teddy bear and, holding the bear close, watched a DVD of one of his old films.

This is sick. I've got to get over him. I'll feed my fantasy for the last time this weekend and purge him from my system on Monday.

On Sunday, Ansley traveled thirty-five miles to a theater in Orange Park where she watched Nick on the big screen through two matinee showings.

Monday morning, as she ate a bowl of cereal before leaving for her office, Ansley made a solemn vow to move on. Step one of the Colton cure is to check on a dating service.

Taking a step as drastic as computer-generated dating was not easy. Ansley looked into the leading services and started the registration process three times, backing out before hitting the "submit" link each time. Although she came in regular contact with single attorneys, she continued to avoid interaction, finding none appealing. Weeks went by after she had made the decision to accept male attention, and her social calendar remained blank.

She was reviewing a file, while having a late lunch in a sandwich shop near the courthouse one Tuesday in the spring, when a man sat down at her table. Startled, she looked up to see a pair of pale-blue eyes, like those of a Siberian husky, directly across from her. His hair was light brown with a slight reddish cast.

"Forgive me for being a bit forward," the stranger said, "but I've seen you here several times and hoped we would have the opportunity to meet. If you object, I'll move away."

"You've caught me a bit off guard, but I do remember seeing you."

"I'm Andrew Blake. My office is in the building next door."

Ansley fought the feeling to pull away. *Go with it. You swore you would and you have seen this guy here before.* "A law office?"

He laughed. "No. I'm one of those boring bean counters."

"Oh, right, I recognize the name—the CPA firm, Blake and Blake.

Are you father and son?"

"Our father was an accountant, but he's retired. Now, it's just my brother and me."

Introduce yourself, Ansley. "I'm—"

"You're Ansley Sheridan." He smiled.

Her eyebrows came together in a puzzled look. "How did you know that?"

"You were talking to one of our clients one day, another lawyer. I asked him later who you were and whether you were married."

"Really? And what did he tell you?"

He hesitated.

"Go ahead. Tell me. It can't be worse than I will be thinking."

"Okay, but please don't be offended. He said that you were not attached, to his knowledge, but that you were unapproachable—strictly business."

"He said I was cold as ice, I bet. Who was it?"

"Carl Young."

Ansley smiled. "Carl? We had a nasty case together about a year ago, but I don't really know him personally. I remember him best for saying that he didn't like his client, or mine, and that Judge Miller should order them to stay together because they deserved each other."

Blake laughed. "I bet you see people at their worst."

She nodded, and then looking down at her watch, Ansley said, "I'm sorry, Andrew—"

"Andy."

"Andy. I've got to run. I have a hearing in a few minutes. But it was nice meeting you." Although she was nervous, she managed to keep her tone warm and sincere.

"Before you go, would you give me your phone number—not the one in the book for your office."

A shiver went down Ansley's back. *Don't cower away. Take the plunge. Forget Nick Colton.*

Reaching into her purse, she drew out one of her business cards and was instantly hit with the memory of giving Nick a card that first night. "Do you have a pen handy? It would take me ten minutes to find one in this purse."

Andy whipped a pen out of his shirt pocket, and she wrote her home number.

"Cell number too, if you don't mind."

She wrote the second number and then handed him the card and his pen.

"Thank you very much, Ms. Sheridan. I'll give you a call."

When she returned to her office after the hearing, she immediately booted up the computer and googled Andrew Blake. She found no record of a local marriage license or divorce, but found that he had three speeding violations and owned a condo in Atlantic Beach. His birth date was August 24, 1977, making her three years older.

Maybe I would have better luck with a younger man. His eyes are incredible.

When she got home that evening, she fed the cats, changed clothes, and while her leftovers were warming in the microwave, she listened to her voice mail. There was only one message.

"This is Andy. I'm feeling very happy today for some reason. It may have something to do with the distractingly beautiful woman I had the pleasure of meeting at lunch. I hope that she will be home when I call again later tonight."

She grinned through the entire message and pushed the button to replay it. Hearing his voice gave her a tingle of excitement. After hanging up, she stood by the phone for a minute, ignoring the chime of the microwave timer. *I'm back in the water, so I'd better be sure I know how to swim.*

After eating, Ansley curled up on her sofa with a novel but looked up at the phone from time to time, hoping he would try again. When it rang at eight-thirty, a flash of electricity raced through her nerve endings as the silence was broken.

"I hope I haven't caught you at a bad time," he said.

"No, you're fine. I was reading the latest Nelson DeMille book."

"I like him, too, especially *Cathedral*, but, Steve Berry and Dan Brown are probably my favorite writers."

That's nice. He's a reader. Mark wasn't—but Nick was.

"I don't want to keep you too long. I know it's a work night, but I would like to make plans to take you to dinner, if you're willing."

Hesitating, she said, "That would be nice."

"How about Saturday night? I'm thinking Matthew's if I can get a reservation."

Wow. He goes big. I thought expensive dinners went out the window with Nick. "The food there is wonderful."

"Then it's a go. I'll call you after I check out the reservation situation."

Clearing her thoughts, she said, "Andy, I'm looking forward to going out with you, but I've got to warn you that I move in the slow lane—just so there's no misunderstanding."

"Not a problem. It's taken me many months to finally meet you; I'm not going to rush anything. We'll take our time getting to know one another."

Hanging up, Ansley abandoned DeMille as titillation battled apprehension.

She did not mention her impending date to anyone until Elaine called on Thursday night.

"I've got a date for Saturday night."

"*Hurrah!* Finally," Elaine responded, her enthusiasm nearly rupturing Ansley's eardrum. "It's about time you returned from the land of the dead. I want to hear all about him."

"When *I know* something about him, you'll be the first to hear. All I can tell you for now is that he is an accountant, a little younger than me, and he's got the most amazing, pale-blue eyes."

"Does Mr. Blue Eyes have a name?"

"Andrew Blake—Andy."

"Hmmm. Ansley and Andy—"

"Oh, my gosh. That sounds like a pair of panda bears."

Elaine laughed. "For heaven's sake, don't let that count against him. As Shakespeare said—"

"I know, I know, 'that which we call a rose by any other would smell as sweet.' Don't go making him Romeo, yet."

"What are you wearing?"

"I haven't decided."

"Then let's go shopping Friday night or Saturday morning."

"No, no, no. I've got plenty in my closet. I'm not going overboard with this." The memory of shopping with Elaine, for the dress that she wore the night she met Nick, popped across her mind.

"Do you know where he's taking you?"

"Matthews."

Elaine whistled. "He definitely sounds like a keeper."

CHAPTER THIRTY-TWO

When Andy called to establish the specifics, Ansley insisted on meeting him at the restaurant. She wasn't ready to find herself trapped on a miserable date. The fact that he lived at Atlantic Beach, which was thirty-five miles from her condo, provided a perfect excuse.

"I'll meet you at the restaurant," she said.

"My mother would disown me if I let you drive back to St. Augustine alone."

He's not making this easy. "We won't tell her. I appreciate your concern, but I make the drive all the time, and I'll be fine. See you at Matthew's at eight." Her tone made her position clear, and Andy let it go. He had no way of knowing that she was planning to stay over with her parents, less than ten minutes from the restaurant.

Saturday morning, Ansley went shopping on her way to Jacksonville. Although determined not to give the date enough significance to spend money on a new outfit, she wanted to give the dress she planned to wear a modern boost. Luck was with her, and she found a small, red, Marc Jacobs handbag on sale at Off 5th, the Saks Fifth Avenue discount outlet. The original price had been obscene, but the markdown brought it into the realm of reason. Leaving the mall, she felt satisfaction at having purchased an item on her own that matched Nick's expensive gifts. However, even the glow of consumer satisfaction did not mitigate her reluctance to be interrogated about the date by her mother. She drove to her office and worked until six o'clock to stall the maternal meddling.

I'll deal with Mom's curiosity Sunday when it can't exacerbate my nerves.

Her plan, combined with her mother's intuition, worked. Although Laura insisted on steaming Ansley's dress, there was no probing into details about the date.

"The dress is fine, Mom."

"I'll just run over with my steamer. It can't hurt, and it's no trouble."

Let her do it, Ansley. She needs to nurture.

The dress was hanging on the closet door in her bedroom when Ansley emerged from her shower. Mercifully, her mother was not around. However, as she finished putting the final touches on her hair and makeup, Laura came to the door of her room, knocked softly, and let herself in.

"I don't know what makes me happier—your spending the night here and going to church with us tomorrow, or your *finally* beginning a social life."

Ansley smiled. "Don't get excited, Mom. It's a first date. We may not like one another."

"Well, I'm pleased just the same."

Taking a bottle of cologne from her makeup case, Ansley spritzed her wrists, picked up the new purse, took a quick inventory of her appearance in the full-length mirror, and started for the door before the conversation could progress.

It took less than ten minutes to make it to the restaurant. Ansley's entrance did not go unnoticed. Several men smiled as she waited to be escorted to Andy's table. There was no doubt that her blond hair and red purse contrasted with the simple black-knit dress to set her apart. She had taken extra care with her makeup and felt pretty for the first time since breaking up with Nick. As she walked to the table, the short dress clung to her slender figure. The matching pantyhose and high-heeled pumps accentuated her long legs.

Upon seeing her, Andy immediately rose and extended a hand to guide Ansley to the chair. "I'm the envy of every man here tonight."

Blushing, she said, "There's a gracious reply to that comment, but it fails to come to me at the moment."

"No reply required." His smile was infectious, and his eyes even bluer under the restaurant lighting. A feeling of physical attraction swept over her.

Can this be the man who will make me forget you, Nick?

A waiter stood by the table, exchanging the white napkin by the service plate for a black one and spreading it across Ansley's lap. He then handed Andy the wine list.

"What is your pleasure?" Andy said, looking over the top of the carte. "Red or white?"

"I'll let you choose, but I'll have only a little." *Anything but Dom Perignon.*

Andy smiled again. "You don't have to worry. I have better social graces than to ply a woman with alcohol to have my way with her."

Under normal circumstances, I'll bet you wouldn't need to.

"That's a relief," Ansley said, lifting the water goblet in front of her.

After taking Andy's order, the waiter left, and Andy leaned forward. "Now, I want to know all about Ansley Sheridan, and not just what you put on your Facebook page."

"I don't do Facebook."

He nodded. "I know. I checked. You are a very mysterious woman. It's hard to find out anything about you. No Facebook, no web site. Where have you been hiding? You're not in witness protection, are you?"

She smiled. "I'm not hiding. I'm in the phone book—at least my office number. I'm at the courthouse all the time."

"True. A lot of people know who you are—but nothing else. Is there a husband and five kids hidden somewhere?"

Ansley laughed. Shaking her head, she said, "No husband, no children. Just an ex and a demanding job."

"And how did any man in his right mind let you get away?" he asked as the waiter arrived with their wine.

"That was a long time ago."

"I didn't see any record of a divorce in the Duval County records."

"You have checked me out, have you?"

"Guilty. Please don't tell me it's a deal breaker."

"How could it be? I've checked you out as well and didn't find any divorces."

"That's because I've never been married, but you say that you have."

"It was an Alachua County divorce. We were in school. The payments on the wedding rings lasted longer than the marriage."

"And you never took the plunge again?"

"No. And what about you? Are you the perennial love'em and leave'em guy?"

"Not intentionally."

"Ah! But you do admit it's been true on occasion?"

"Let's just say that I've made my share of mistakes, always hoping to find the *one*, and having no luck."

"Maybe I should be wary."

"This conversation is not getting off to a good start. Let's start over. I'm Anthony Douglas Blake. I'm twenty-nine years old, looking for a soul mate to share my life with, maybe have a kid or two, and join the mortgaged-to-the-max set . . . . Your turn."

Ansley smiled. It was hard not to like him. He seemed honest. "Okay. I'm Ansley Collier Sheridan, thirty-something, divorced, a spoiled-brat-only-child, and dedicated to never trusting another person with more testosterone than integrity." She watched for a reaction. "Does that send you running?"

"Not a chance. I think we're a match made in heaven, Ansley Collier Sheridan."

The rest of the dinner went well. Andy had a good sense of humor and managed to put Ansley at ease. They exchanged some personal history, but she avoided any mention of her last relationship.

Andy described how his partner was his twin brother, identical in appearance, but opposite in personality. "Grant is a typical CPA. He has about as much personality as a can of white paint. But, he has a wife who adores him and three gorgeous kids. I'm definitely jealous. In our practice, I talk to the clients; he buries himself in the paper. I'm not sure that I went into the right line of work, but it was the easy road."

After having a perfect crème brulée, Ansley excused herself to go to the powder room. When she returned, the table had been cleared, and Andy had taken care of the check.

"I'd like to stretch this evening out a little longer," he said. "Would you trust me enough to ride down to the Landing?"

She hesitated.

"The music is usually good. I know you're not interested in hanging out in a bar, but we could sit by the river and get to know one another better." He reached across the table and put his hand over hers. "Stop giving me the rabbit-meets-fox look. I promise no funny business. If you feel more comfortable, you can drive. That way, you can leave me if I misbehave."

"You're on, Andy Blake, but you'd better behave, or I *will* leave your you-know-what."

CHAPTER THIRTY-THREE

It was three o'clock on Sunday afternoon when Ansley got back to her condo. She had wanted to return immediately after Mass, but Laura had insisted on a family lunch at the country club. Walking into the living room, the cats greeted her at the door.

"Are your bowls empty?" Ansley asked, dropping her garment bag across the arm of the sofa and leaving her carry-on case close by. Shadow immediately jumped on the couch, landing in the middle of the bag. "Okay, okay, I know you want attention, but don't claw my things." She reached down and scratched a cat with each hand before going to the kitchen for a soft drink. They followed like baby chicks following the hen.

"I'm going to indulge myself with a nap before I do anything, guys. I'm exhausted," she said as she disposed of the stale cat food and then filled the bowls with fresh morsels.

Changing from her church clothes to a warm-up suit, she curled up on her bed with a throw over her legs and was about to drift off when the phone rang.

Darn it. I was almost asleep.

She considered ignoring the call, but the piercing ring had destroyed her drowsiness.

"Hello."

"Well, how did it go?" Elaine asked.

"Hey." Coming to full attention, Ansley smiled. "It actually went better than I expected. He's easy to be with."

"Any sparks?"

"Elaine, it was a first date." *I'm not going to jinx it by letting anyone know how I'm feeling.*

"You don't have to even go on a date for there to be sparks."

"Granted, but I'm not jumping to any conclusions at this point. We had a nice dinner and then went to the Landing and enjoyed the music, the water, and the wonderful weather. He kissed me goodnight, and it was done."

"He kissed you goodnight?"

Ansley threw her feet over the side of the bed to the floor. "He kissed me goodnight."

"And how was that?"

"Not bad . . . . It was okay." *Very okay.*

"Okay? He kissed you, and all you can say is that it was okay? How long has it been since you kissed a guy?"

Too long, but not as long as you think. "I'm not going to count that up."

"So, are you going to see him again?"

Ansley frowned. "He'll have to ask first." *If you only knew how much I hope that I will.*

"Ah, but you would go again?"

"Yeah . . . . Yeah, I would. But don't get too excited. I don't want to jinx it."

After hanging up, Ansley lay back on her bed, reliving the night before and unable to sleep. There was no doubt that she liked Andy, and it terrified her. Memories of Nick popped in her head intermittently, but Andy was foremost in her thoughts.

The only thing the men had in common was height and proportion—both tall, with slender, well-toned bodies. Nick had piercing eyes, while Andy's were almost translucent and magnetic. Nick was cool, poised, and confident, while Andy was open with an infectious personality. However, the most important difference was that Andy was reality; Nick was fantasy.

Because she hadn't looked at the date as a potential relationship, she had not initially viewed Andy's lack of having been married as a sign of risk. As the evening had progressed and she found herself really enjoying his company, she liked the idea that there was no former wife or children. If his single status gave any cause for doubt, it vanished while sitting on the Riverwalk at the Landing.

"I was in a relationship that lasted over five years," he said when Ansley asked how he had managed to avoid the altar. "We were planning to marry as soon as we had enough money saved to buy a house, but Prince Charming came along in a JSO uniform before the pot of gold was filled."

"I'm sorry. But, I have to tell you, I've had several cases where the wife had an affair with a cop. The uniform seems to be magnetic to female libidos."

"Good way to put it; it yanks the clothes right off," he said and laughed.

"I'm glad to see that you have a sense of humor about it."

"It was around three years ago, so I've long since recovered. Besides, I had the last laugh. He wouldn't leave his wife."

Ansley smiled. "Good for you. Karma is great, isn't it?"

The only negative moment during the date had been when the band played a cover of Bob Seeger's "Old Time Rock and Roll." The image of Nick watching her dance with Dennis flashed across her mind, taking her out of the moment.

"Is something wrong?" Andy had asked, apparently noticing a change in her expression.

"No. I just thought of something from one of my cases," she said, covering for her mood change. "It's a hazard of the trade."

He smiled. "No problem—just as long as it wasn't something I did."

It had been a good date, and as she lay on her bed recounting each segment, she decided that Andy Blake might have a place in her life.

I'll just relax and see what happens, but I hope he asks me out again.

She didn't have to wait long for the answer. At seven-thirty, the phone rang.

"How are you tonight?" Andy asked.

"I'm good. I didn't expect you to call," she said, raising the remote to mute the TV.

"I wanted to tell you again how much I enjoyed your company last night and hope that you're free this coming weekend."

"Thank you. I had a great time as well."

"Then you'll let me take you to dinner in your neighborhood?"

She smiled. "I will. What do you have in mind?"

"If the weather's favorable, how about I come down early? We could roam around St. George Street, playing tourist, and then have a play-it-by-ear dinner."

"Sounds good. I like casual and comfortable."

"Jeans and sneakers—you're my kind of girl."

Ansley smiled. *He could be habit-forming.*

Waiting for Andy to pick her up for their second date, Ansley found that she was excited. She had surprised herself by agreeing to give him her address, but his good manners and easygoing personality gave her a sense of trust.

"Did you have any trouble finding me?" she asked as she gathered her purse and a sweater while Andy stood in her doorway.

"Not a bit. Your directions were spot on."

Andy drove a five-year-old BMW, which, despite its age, was in meticulous condition.

"Nice car," Ansley said.

"What's even nicer is that it's paid for."

"Doesn't that mean it's time to trade?"

"Not a chance. I splurged on these wheels, and they are going to last me a long, long time."

They drove to the heart of the restored section of town, parked the car, and began the trek down St. George Street. It was a perfect evening and the street was alive with the buzz of tourists. After visiting a shop featuring the wares of Ireland, where Andy bought her a coffee mug with the Sheridan coat of arms, they decided to visit the historic fort.

Conversation with Andy was comfortable. He held her hand as they walked, and Ansley found that it felt nice to be out with a man. It had been so long.

When it came time to decide on dinner, he deferred to Ansley to choose the restaurant.

"This is your town, and you know where the good food is."

"If you like seafood, I don't think you can beat O'Steen's. It's not the most glamorous restaurant in town, but I love the fried shrimp."

"O'Steen's it is."

Waiting for their order, Andy looked intently into her eyes. "I've spent two evenings with you and several telephone conversations, but I don't know anything about your history, other than you were married when you were quite young. Have you been in a convent ever since?"

She smiled. "The best place to leave history is in the past. Can I say that there has been a disappointment or two and leave it at that?"

"Ah . . . a lady of mystery."

"Not really. I'd just rather not run the risk of conjuring up ghosts better left buried."

"I concede. No further pressure. The present is what matters, and I count myself lucky to be spending it with you."

The smile crept across her face. "I'll drink to that." She lifted her glass of ice tea as though to give a toast, and Andy met it with his.

The ensuing weekends found the couple sharing dinners, a touring musical, and a concert by a retro pop star. Each night ended with a parting kiss that grew progressively longer and more passionate.

"I'm hoping that we are going to move to the next level soon," Andy said, three weeks into the relationship as they stood at the door to her condo. "I'm beginning to have serious feelings about you."

Ansley pulled back, looking down as she contemplated how to respond. "I like you a lot, Andy. I do. But I'm not quite ready to go where I think you're talking about."

"Well, so far, I haven't gotten past your threshold. Maybe you could let me into your living room. I promise I won't push for the bedroom—at least not yet."

Looking up at his face, she said, "You make me feel like a prude. I'm really not. I'm just cautious."

"I wouldn't want you any other way," he said, putting his hands on her shoulders. "You're worth waiting for."

Ansley smiled. "Thank you." She paused, and then pointed her finger at his chest. "Tell you what. Next weekend, I'll make dinner and let you into my living room. You can even come into my kitchen and help with the dishes."

Grinning, he pulled her close in a hug. "You've got a deal, and I promise that I won't pressure you to do anything until you tell me you're ready."

The dinner date in Ansley's condo went off without a glitch. She made a simple dinner of baked salmon, creamed corn, and sautéed broccoli.

"Amazing," Andy said as he helped her clear the table.

"What's amazing?"

"You are. You're not only one of the most attractive women I've met in a long time, but you're also a smart lawyer and," he gave her a thumb's up, "an excellent cook."

"Flattery will not get you into my boudoir, Mr. Blake."

"Was not my intent. I know my place. Besides, I'm sure those wild cats giving me the evil eye would attack if I dared make a wrong move," he said, grinning and looking in the direction of Shadow who was staring at Andy.

"Keep that in mind," Ansley said, laughing.

When the last dish was put away, they settled down on Ansley's couch to watch TV. Skye jumped on Andy's lap.

"Okay. You must have passed the background check. He doesn't do that with everyone."

"I'm honored. I've never had a cat. You'll have to direct me on what I'm supposed to do."

Ansley reached down and moved the white cat to her lap. "You've never had a cat?"

"No. we always had dogs. I don't have anything against cats, I just don't know much about them."

"It's good to hear that you have nothing against them, because this is a love me, love my cats zone. Cat haters are instantly banished."

He smiled and reached over to scratch Skye's head.

True to his word, Andy remained a perfect gentleman. During the TV movie, they engaged in some exploratory caresses but avoided succumbing to the heat of the moment. When the late news signed off, he left, kissing her passionately one last time.

"I'd better go before I'm tempted to break my word."

CHAPTER THIRTY-FOUR

Arriving at her office on Monday, Ansley was in a good mood. "Judging from the smile on your face, you must have had a nice weekend," Olivia, her secretary, said as Ansley passed by her desk.

"I did, thanks. And you?"

"Not as good as yours, but it was fine."

Once seated at the desk in her office, Ansley booted up her computer to check email. As the browser opened her homepage, a blaring banner appeared next to a photo of Nick.

"NICHOLAS COLTON MARRIES."

Her stomach turned and tears rushed to her eyes. For a moment, she sat paralyzed, unable to click the link to see the full article. Fear that Olivia might walk in and ask questions forced her to fight to regain her composure. After staring for a second or two, she got up from her desk, walked over to her office door, and closed it. Grabbing a tissue from the holder on the front of her desk, she dabbed at her eyes and returned to her chair. Opening the *TMZ* site, she began reading.

> According to inside sources, *The High Street's* Nicholas Colton secretly wed French ballerina, Claudine Cartier in an undisclosed location in the south of France approximately five weeks ago. Attempts to confirm with the office of Colton's manager were met with a routine, "No comment at this time."
>
> Not much is known on this side of the Atlantic about Ms. Cartier other than she is a principal ballerina with the Paris Opera Ballet, noted for her beauty and balletic artistry.

Colton, who has long been one of the most eligible bachelors in moviedom, has not been linked to a serious relationship since his stellar burst on the big screen ten years ago. His swarthy good looks, flair for dramatic, power-player roles, and classy sex appeal have generated media curiosity as to why he was rarely seen in public more than once with the same woman. Rumors aside, it appears that the reluctant bachelor has been signed, sealed, and delivered.

The screen blurred through a scrim of tears. *Why am I reacting this way? I've moved on. He's moved on. It's history.*

Her conscious mind may have believed that Nick was history, but her subconscious was not that easily convinced. Reaching for her purse, she dug through it for her phone to view a photo of Andy. She touched the screen to enlarge his face.

He's handsome, witty—fun to be with. Why am I allowing Nick back into my personal space? Andy is a great guy—a real, vine-covered cottage, picket fence kind of guy. The kind I should be with.

Lifting the telephone receiver, she buzzed her secretary. "Olivia, please cancel my appointments for today. All of a sudden, my stomach is going crazy. I'm going home."

"Can I do anything else for you?"

"No. I'll be fine. It's probably a 24-hour bug. But, I really need to go home."

Scooping up a file and putting it in her bag, Ansley left the office, avoiding face-to-face contact with Olivia, who was busy, following through with Ansley's directions.

Not long after arriving at the condo, the phone rang. Looking at the caller ID, she recognized Andy's number.

Do I answer? If I don't, he might come down here.

She let it ring until it was about to go to voice mail and then picked up the receiver.

"Hello," she said, trying to sound slightly weak without overplaying the situation.

"What's wrong, pretty lady?"

"How did you know that I was home?" Although she asked, she knew that he had called the office and Olivia had told him. "It's just one of those quickie stomach bugs."

"Your secretary told me. What can I do? Do you need any

medication—Imodium, Kaopectate, Pepto Bismol?"

"I'm fine. I've got all the above. It's actually a little better since I got home and can relax, but if you don't mind, can we talk later?"

"Sure, honey. Call me if you need anything."

"Thanks. And thanks for calling."

Ansley felt guilty lying to everyone, but there was no way she could explain the knots in her stomach that had actually created nausea. It seemed that her inner mind could not shake free of Nick. Memories came flooding to the surface—making love, time with his family, the night they met, Dennis, the manor home, his fragrance. It was all tied together in a huge lump of memory.

She went to work the next day, vowing not to wallow in self-pity and depression. A client from one of her more difficult cases came in for mediation prep. The woman was married to a man Ansley believed to be psychotic. Her client had an injunction against the husband for domestic violence. He had made threats during the course of the action, ranging from "If I can't have you, no one will" to "I won't live without you."

"I can postpone the Langston appointment until tomorrow, if you're not feeling up to it," Olivia said.

"No, no. I'm fine, and I'd like to get it over with. The sooner this case is finished, the better."

Andy called while Ansley was with her client. He left a message, asking that she call as soon as she was free. When Olivia handed her the slip with his number, she cringed. Nick's marriage was too new and raw for her to face Andy. He might see her stress and probe. They had become increasingly close. Before that headline, Ansley had been seriously contemplating a consummation of the relationship. It was time—time to put Nick away once and for all. She had told herself that sleeping with another man would close the door to Nick for good.

To her relief, phone calls and appointments kept her busy all day. She had Olivia contact Andy and tell him that she would return his call that evening.

Taking a deep breath, she dialed Andy's cell number shortly after arriving home. "I'm sorry. With being out yesterday, I was tied up so much today. Amazing what a single day away can cause," she said when he answered.

"No need to apologize. I just want to know that you're feeling better."

"I'm much better, but pretty exhausted."

"Then, I think you should have some soup and go to bed early. You need the rest. We'll talk tomorrow."

After hanging up, she looked at the black cat curled up at her feet on the bed—his amber eyes wide in anticipation of attention. "He's a really nice guy, Shadow. I've got to get my head on straight before I mess it up. God please grant me the serenity . . . the courage . . . and the wisdom."

For over a week, she stalled Andy, using her practice and her health as excuses. He seemed to accept her explanations. When she finally went out with him, she told him that something had come up in her personal life that she had to work out but could not talk about, yet.

"Please forgive me. I wouldn't blame you if you ditched me. But right now, there are issues I have to take care of. I don't want to lose what we've established in the last weeks. I really like you, Andy, but I have no choice."

"I hope that's the truth and not just a gentle way of letting me down."

"No, no. Absolutely not. I don't want to stop seeing you. I just need a week or two."

"If you would share what your issues are, I might be able to help."

"If you could help, believe me, I would share. I would turn it all over to you. Allowing me the space is the best help that you can give right now."

She knew he was confused and disappointed, and she hated that she was being evasive.

I need you, Dennis. You could have talked me through this. Andy is a great guy. Nick is dead to me.

It took Ansley two weeks to gather the courage to resume the relationship with Andy. They had touched base in quick phone calls during the interim, and he had sent her a note, expressing in writing his willingness to support her in any situation that she found herself in.

You've come to be very important in my life, and I know you well enough to know that whatever it is that's troubling you is in no way a fault of your own.

When Ansley finally placed the call, she was ready. The pain had worn away slowly, but she had reached the point where she could look at publicity about Nick and Claudine with dispassion. To desensitize herself, she had read every article available about both the couple and Claudine's background. However, the only photo she found of the couple together was taken at the Cannes Film Festival.

"Hi," Ansley said when Andy answered.

"Hi, yourself. Can I hope the zip in your voice means that you've resolved your issues?"

"You can. And I feel so liberated."

"Does that mean I will actually get to see you?"

"It does. And, I'm so thankful you still want to. Someday, I may be able to tell you all about it, but for now, I'm just grateful for your patience."

CHAPTER THIRTY-FIVE

Spring slipped into summer when Ansley wasn't looking. Her first date with Andy after the break had an awkward start, but they soon resumed the previous comfort level. They met after work on Friday in the San Marco district for an early dinner and rekindled their relationship. The following night, Andy picked her up from the condo for dinner near the beach.

"We need to talk," Andy said as they awaited appetizers on Saturday evening.

Ansley felt her body stiffen. How long could she stall this guy and not lose him? Greeting him at The Loop the night before had brought back a rush of pleasure she had when he hugged her. She could feel from his body language how much he wanted to move the relationship forward. However, as it had been with Nick's persistence about marriage, she wanted to give in to Andy's desire, but an invisible force held her back.

"Now that you've worked through your problems, and we've gotten to know one another pretty well, I'd like us to go away for a weekend together."

Ansley hesitated. "You mean share a room?"

"I hope so. Haven't we played the high school thing out long enough? I really like you, may even be falling in love with you, but every time I feel like I move forward in your life, you step back. I told you that I would wait until you were ready, but I need to know that it *will* happen."

"I'm sorry, Andy. The walking wounded are the most vulnerable to additional injury. I'm not leading you on to a dead end. I hope you know that. There is something very special between us."

"Is there a certain sign that you're looking for? What can I do to give you the assurance that you need?"

"You couldn't do any more than you have already. I'll tell you what.

I have a demanding trial in a couple of weeks. I'll need the week after to get caught up with my other cases, but I should be able to take a few days off after that. What if we made plans to go away on the Saturday before Independence Day?"

His face beamed. "Are you kidding? We can *absolutely* make such a plan. Where would you like to go? Want to make a big deal of it and go glamorous, like New York?"

New York rang too many dissonant bells in Ansley's mind. Shaking her head, she said, "How about a quiet place—maybe a cabin in the mountains?"

"Even better. I'm on it first thing tomorrow."

"Tomorrow's Sunday." Ansley grinned at his boyish enthusiasm.

"The Internet never closes. I'll have us a reservation by Monday morning at the latest," he said, reaching across the table to take her hand.

True to his word, Sunday night he called with a web site for Ansley to check. It was a cozy cabin on a North Carolina mountain that was part of a lodge with amenities, including pool, workout equipment, and tennis courts. They could prepare meals or dine at the main building.

"We'll have privacy with perks," Andy said, obviously pleased with himself.

"It sounds perfect," Ansley said, trying hard not to sound apprehensive.

Rustic and quaint should remove all similarities to the first weekend I spent with Nick in Florence.

Her work schedule precluded her ability to dwell on whether she was doing the right thing with Andy. They hardly saw one another as she prepared for her trial.

"It's hard for me to understand why opposing counsel is taking this case to trial. Her client is a certifiable psycho," she said during one of their brief dinners together.

"Have you thought that maybe you've heard only one side of the story?"

Not sure I'm in the mood for your playing devil's advocate.

"Of course. It's conventional wisdom in my field to believe that there's his side, her side, and the truth, which is usually somewhere in the middle. But trust me, this guy is dangerous. One minute, he's professing how much he loves her, and the next, he's beating her up. This is his third attorney, and she hasn't been out of law school long enough to tell fraud from fact."

"You should have no trouble winning the case if the facts are as one-sided as you say."

"Andy, you deal with cut-and-dried numbers. You can't add two plus two and not get four. In my field, nothing is consistent. Judges have discretion, hidden agendas, PMS, and ulcers. They are only human. You never know whether your best point was heard. And then there are the bloody rules of evidence. Ever heard of hearsay?"

"I watch TV."

"Well, they play fast and loose with hearsay on TV. I can't get into evidence anything that the kids have said about this guy because of hearsay. And, all the bad stuff took place behind closed doors. It's my client's word against the husband's. If he comes in all prepped and wearing his best behavior, I will have a hard time getting his true colors out."

"What's the worst that can happen?"

"The worst thing is custody. He's fighting for it. My client believes that he's just doing it to control her, and I agree. But, she doesn't even want him to have visitation unless it's supervised. Unfortunately, he fooled the psychologist who performed the home study of the family."

The week of the trial, Ansley hardly talked to Andy. He sent her short emails, inquiring as to how she was doing; she sent brief replies. Beginning on Wednesday morning, the case took until Friday afternoon to wrap up. Although the judge reserved ruling on the visitation issue, he did award Ansley's client custody, which did not go over well with the husband. The man walked out of the room as soon as he heard the pronouncement. The judge promised a decision on the visitation within a week, stating that he needed time to review the evidence again.

Friday night, Ansley was exhausted, physically and mentally, begging off dinner with Andy at the last minute. She promised to see him the next night. After having a bowl of canned soup for dinner, she showered and changed into pajamas, intending to watch a TV movie. However, she was asleep before the film began. At twelve-thirty, her phone rang, causing both Ansley and the cats to jump. Picking up the receiver, her heart was pounding and her stomach churning. A call at that hour could not mean good news.

Please don't let it be Mother or Daddy.

"Ansley, this is Stephen Miller."

Stephen Miller? Why is Nick's manager calling me—and after midnight?

"Do you remember me?"

"Of course I do, Stephen. It hasn't been that long. But, why are you calling?"

He hesitated, clearing his throat. "This is not easy to say, Ansley. But Nick is in a hospital here in Mexico. He's asking for you."

Ansley didn't respond as chills arose.

"He wants to see you."

"He's in a Mexican hospital? What's wrong? Was he in an accident?"

"He's sick."

"I don't understand, Stephen." She reached over, turning on a light and then flicking off the TV.

"He's very sick—intensive care." Stephen paused and cleared his throat again before continuing. "His life is in danger."

The words stabbed like a dagger in her gut. "You can't mean that. How can he be that sick?"

"He's got hepatitis and his liver is failing. Since you two broke up, Nick has been drinking far too much, which has compromised his liver. It must have been weak genetically. But this disease is putting him in real jeopardy. He wants to see you, Ansley. I'll make all the arrangements to get you here if you'll agree to come."

"I don't know what to say." Tears formed in her eyes. "I can't even process all of this, Stephen. What about his wife?"

"That's a long story, but you don't have to worry about it. Please come. I'll explain when you get here."

"Give me a second. I'm so confused that I need a time to think." She reached for a tissue on the table by her bed and blotted the tears that had formed. The room seemed to turn as cold as ice, and she began shaking.

"I'm begging you, Ansley. Don't say no. He may die."

Can he be telling the truth? Would he lie? Ansley shook her head in disbelief. It was more than she could comprehend.

"Will you come?"

"Yes . . . yes, I'll come. Of course, I'll come."

"Leave for the airport as soon as you can. I'll either charter or get you on the first flight coming this way. You do have a mobile phone, don't you?"

"Yes. Do you have a pen?" He said that he did, and they exchanged numbers.

Hanging up, she could hardly think what to do first. The cats? Her practice? Andy?

"Oh, my, gosh. What am I going to tell everyone? What am I going to tell Andy?"

216

CHAPTER THIRTY-SIX

Her hands and knees were weak and her heart pounded as she threw clothing in a suitcase.

"He can't die. He can't." Tears fell on a blouse as she dropped it in the carry-on. "I'll have to call Olivia, leave money for cat food, have Jeanette and Melissa take care of the cats—no. Mom can pick them up. Where in Mexico is he? I didn't even ask." Ansley talked to herself in an attempt to sort out necessary arrangements. "Make a list for Olivia. She will have to reschedule everything for the next week, maybe longer. If something can't be rescheduled, she'll have to get Bonnie or Sharon to cover for me."

Ansley was avoiding what to do about Andy. Watching Shadow trying to get into her suitcase, she debated choices. *It's over a week until we are supposed to go to North Carolina. I might be back in time. Maybe Nick isn't as bad as Stephen said.* For a second or two she froze, thinking of another possibility. *What will I do if he dies? Stop it, Ansley.*

Lifting Shadow out of the suitcase, where he was trying to make a bed, she said, "I won't be gone long, big guy." She hugged the cat close to her face, wetting his fur with tears. "I'll call Mom when I reach Mexico and have her pick you up. You are going to be fine."

By one-thirty a.m., she was ready. Stephen had not called. She decided to start for the airport regardless but debated whether to drive or to take a cab. Despite the expense, she decided on the latter.

When the cab arrived, Ansley had a sick feeling as she walked out into the darkness. Before getting into the taxi, she dropped a note next door in Jeanette's mailbox, asking that Melissa look after the cats until Laura came for them. As the driver opened the door for her, she took a mental inventory of her checklist. *What have I forgotten? I've got my cell, laptop, the chargers, my passport, my debit and credit cards. Anything else, I'll just have to buy or do without.* The time with Nick had made her efficient with packing.

Her phone vibrated as the cab reached the Jacksonville city limits. Although expecting the call, it startled her.

"Ansley, Stephen here. Where are you?"

"On my way to the airport. I'm about forty-five minutes away. How's Nick?"

"He drifts in and out. There's a charter coming for you from Miami. Check with the airport information desk when you arrive. It's a CFC plane. Your passport is current, isn't it?"

"Barely, but yes. Where am I going, Stephen? All you said was Mexico."

"Cancun. Nick was here shooting when he took sick."

"How did he get hepatitis?"

"They don't know. It has an extended incubation period so he could have picked it up here in Mexico or before he arrived. Contaminated food is the most common source."

"You're sure it's not the *B* strain?"

"No. That's the one thing to be thankful for. It's neither B, nor C. A is the mildest form, but Nick has developed complications. His fever is extremely high. He's had moments of disorientation. It's all speculative at this point."

She closed her eyes and more tears rolled down her face.

The phone was silent for a few seconds before Stephen spoke again. "Kevin told him that you're coming, Ansley. I don't know if Nick heard, but the boy tried."

"Kevin's there?"

"He and Penelope arrived yesterday, along with the senior Colebridges and Nick's sister."

Again, the phone was silent. Ansley's emotions were slipping out of control. "I can't talk anymore. Will you be at the airport?"

"Ian and I will both be there. Be safe, sweetheart, and thank you for doing this."

She pushed the call off and sat immobile, fighting to regain her composure before having to face the public, even though few people were likely to be in the terminal at three a.m.

Once in the air, memories of a trip she and Nick had made to Cancun came flooding back. It had been at the height of the affair and was a glorious weekend of sun, water, and moonlight. They swam, played tennis, and spent afternoons reading and napping. Evenings, they had candlelit dinners and walked on the beach. Nick never drank more than one or two glasses of wine when they had been together.

Was he drinking and I didn't know? Or did he change? She looked out the window of the plane into the blackness of night. She was flying to a man's bedside, a man she had not seen in over two years. *Who are you now, Nick? It doesn't matter. Whoever you are, you can't die.*

Abruptly, Andy flashed across her mind. *What am I going to say to him? I've got to call him . . . . Could I have Olivia call him? No. That would be cowardly of me. What am I doing? Am I ruining the one chance of having a normal life and someone to share it with?*

"Ms. Sheridan, I don't mean to disturb you, but may I offer you wine, coffee, tea, soda, water?"

The flight attendant was talking to her. She had been unaware of him standing next to her.

"I'm fine." Instantly, she changed her mind as he started to turn away. "On second thought, I would like a cup of hot tea."

The young man smiled and said, "Right away."

While waiting for her beverage, she forced herself to type a text message to Andy.

> Got urgent call. Close friend critically ill. Had to leave.
> Best cancel reservations. I'm so sorry. More later.

When the plane touched down in midmorning in a small airport in Mexico, true to his word, Stephen was waiting for her when she cleared customs with Ian and a limo. Ian drove as Ansley besieged Stephen with questions.

"How long has he been sick? What are they doing for him? Has he gotten any worse since you called?"

Stephen took her hand. "Slow down, sweetheart. Let's take your questions one at a time. He'd been sick for a while before he told anyone; no one knows how long. To keep up his grueling film schedule, he used too many over-the-counter painkillers and too much Scotch to combat the fatigue, stomach disorders, and muscle aches and pains brought on by the latent disease. When he collapsed on the set with dehydration, the first doctors on the scene thought it was food poisoning and blundered by giving him antibiotics, making him worse. He's now at the edge of complete liver failure."

"Tell me the truth, Stephen. What is the worst case scenario?"

Stephen took a deep breath and clasped both of Ansley's hands in his. "He's going to beat this. With you here, he's going to have the will to kick this thing in the ass."

"Worst case, Stephen?"

"Seventy to ninety per cent of those with liver failure do not survive." He gripped her hands tighter as he spoke.

Blinking to clear her eyes, she said, "Do the doctors who are treating him now know what they're doing?" As she spoke, she felt as though her entire body was having tremors. Stephen held her hands steady.

"I pray they do. Unfortunately, he's too sick to move right now. If he improves, we will airlift him back to Houston where there are outstanding gastroenterologists. For now, we have to pray that there's enough medical talent in this hospital to keep him alive."

"He can't . . . I can't say it."

"Don't. Let's just get you to the hospital."

"You said his family is here from the U.K."

"Not all—his mother, father, Kevin, Anne, Penelope, and Claudine."

At the sound of Claudine's name, Ansley bristled. "Stephen, how do I walk in with his wife there?"

"Trust me on that one. It's fine."

"But, they are married."

"Ansley, Nick has been screwed up. I told you that he has been drinking way too much. Claudine is part of that package. She's actually a nice lady, but the marriage is a farce. He met her at Cannes a few months ago. In an irrational moment, they got married. She'll tell you that Nick was in never-never land—a Dewar's stupor. Probably in his drunken haze, he believed that if he couldn't have the real thing, he'd take a French stand-in. Claudine was coming off a bitter breakup. She told me in her lovely French language that she thought, 'What the hell? Why not?' I'm pretty sure that she was one glass over the wine line, as well. Nick said that they woke up the next morning, looked at one another, and said, 'What the hell have we done?' It was marriage a la Brittany Spears."

"Are you sure?"

"I am positive. They have kept it quiet to keep the press from making them look like the morons they were. The divorce will be final in a few weeks. Nick gave her a nice settlement. She came here to keep the press from sensationalizing the situation if they discover he's seriously ill. Both of them had hoped the marriage would not be discovered, but in today's world, that's seldom possible. I don't know how he kept you out of the spotlight for so long."

220

"Is there press at the hospital?"

"So far, so good. We've managed to keep the story out of the media. The studio has spent a tidy sum on the cover-up, which is easier done here than in the States."

When the car pulled into the circular drive at the main entrance of the hospital, Ansley's stomach lurched. She felt that she might throw up.

"I'm not sure I can do this, Stephen."

"I'm right beside you."

"I'm not family; I'm an outsider."

"You're less of an outsider than Claudine. She knew no one in the family. And, honey, to Nick, you are family."

Walking through the corridor of the institution, she felt death hovering. *He can't die, he can't.*

Images of Dennis's funeral flashed through her mind, giving her a chill. Her knees and hands lost strength. She envisioned Nick lying in a casket, mourners all around. If he died, would she be at the funeral? *Stop it . . . . He's not going to die. He's young, he's strong, he will recover.* A brief glimpse of Andy flitted across her mind. She had not thought of him since the wheels touched ground in Mexico. *I'm sorry, Andy. God forgive me, but I've never gotten over him. I'm not sure we can work no matter what happens to Nick.*

They entered the elevator, headed for the intensive care unit.

Walking through the hospital corridors, Ansley's legs felt like lead. She wanted to run to Nick's side but felt an equal desire to turn away. *What if I'm too late?*

Reaching the room set up for the family, there was a guard at the door checking identification. Stephen waved him aside. To screen the family from risk of discovery by the press, the hospital had removed the beds from an unoccupied patient room and furnished it with assorted chairs. As she entered, Kevin came to her immediately. She hardly recognized him. The teenage boy had become a young man in two years. He was as tall as his father, with thick blond hair covering his forehead. Penelope was seated in a chair against the wall—a stoic expression on her face.

Kevin embraced Ansley as she fought to keep from breaking down.

"Thank you for coming. Dad has asked for you," he whispered.

Nick's sister, Anne, came up behind him and hugged Ansley as Kevin stepped aside. Katherine, sitting next to Penelope, did not rise, but smiled weakly. The historically stalwart matriarch had aged, and worry was taking its toll.

She might be cold as ice, but he's her son, and she loves him underneath her layers of frost.

Victor had been standing by the window. He came forward to greet Ansley. Of everyone present, he had changed the least—still a very handsome man for his age, distinguished and polished with an unmistakable air of the gentry.

"Nicholas asked for you over and over. It's good of you to come, my dear. I'm afraid that he's not awake, now. I do think that you should go right in," Victor said, putting an arm around her shoulder.

Claudine was not in sight, which was a relief to Ansley. Among those in the room, Ansley felt closest to Kevin and Stephen. It was obvious that Stephen, although not a family member, carried the most authority under the circumstances. To get to Nick, Ansley had to leave the waiting area and walk thirty feet down the corridor.

"Have Stephen go with you," Victor said. "The staff will not challenge him."

As they exited the waiting room, a thin blonde, carrying two paper cups of coffee, passed by. She nodded to Stephen, but ignored Ansley.

"That's Claudine, isn't it?" Ansley asked when they were out of earshot.

"It is."

"This is awkward."

"You're fine. She's fine." He put his arm around her shoulder and gave her a squeeze. "You'd best prepare yourself. His appearance may shock you."

"How many doctors does he have?" she asked in a shaky voice.

"There are two Cancun doctors and one they brought in from Mexico City. We have insisted that they confer with the Houston team. There's a search in the States and down here for an organ donor, just in case."

"A transplant?" An unpleasant sensation ran through her veins. "He could need a liver transplant?"

Stephen tightened his grip on her. "If the liver fails, it might be the only option. But, Nick's not going to need it. We have to think positive."

"And pray."

Stephen nodded.

As she walked into Nick's cubicle, the only sounds were the noise of the monitors tracking his vital signs and the respirator forcing oxygen

222

into his lungs. His face was thin and grayish yellow. He was connected by more wires and tubes than a computer network. Screens displayed his blood pressure, heart rate, and things unknown to Ansley. A bag of dark urine at the foot of the bed documented that he was on a catheter. She felt her knees go weak and fought to maintain control as involuntary tears flooded her cheeks. Stephen held her tight.

"Can he hear me?"

"I don't know, but I think you should try. He was adamant that he wanted to see you before he lapsed into this coma."

Ansley walked to the side of his bed and leaned over. She could smell a combination of antiseptic and body fluid, so different from the Green Irish Tweed that she associated with Nick.

"Nick . . . it's me . . . Ansley . . . . Can you hear me?"

He didn't move. The sight of the handsome man reduced to the emaciated, discolored mortal in front of her was horrifying and rekindled images of Dennis the last time she saw him.

CHAPTER THIRTY-SEVEN

"Nick . . . let me know that you recognize me.

His hands were exposed. One had an IV tube inserted near the wrist, and the other had a pulse oximeter attached to his middle finger. Electrodes connected him to a clicking heart monitor. She reached down and carefully took the hand closest to her. Like the room, it was cold.

"Stephen. I need a rosary and something to play music," she said quietly, tightly curling her lips to fight off her emotions.

He didn't question her purpose. "I'll take care of it."

"The music from Carmen, please," she said, softly, before gaining an air of determination. "I have to stay here, Stephen. Will they give me any trouble?"

"I'll handle it."

Looking around, she saw a chair against the wall. Gently, she laid Nick's hand down on the bed and then retrieved the straight chair. Positioning it next to his bed, she sat and once again took his hand.

"I'm here, Nick. I'm not leaving until you are better. Don't you *dare* go anywhere. I won't let you."

Without further comment, Stephen left the cubicle, pausing briefly at the desk to give instructions that Ansley was to stay with Nick.

ICU visiting times were posted in Spanish and English on the wall of the room. According to the proclamation, visits were limited to five minutes, two family members, and only at designated times.

They will not force me out of this room. She sat alone, holding his hand, murmuring softly to him.

"You will not leave me, Nick Colton. I forbid it. I'll do anything you want if you'll please fight." She reached up to his forehead and could feel the heat before her hand touched his skin. She grimaced.

Sandwiching Nick's hand between hers, she bowed her head and prayed.

"Heavenly Father, I beg of you, please let him live. I know I have sinned and don't deserve your mercy, but please don't punish me by taking Nick, please. I'll do anything if you'll just let him live. I'm not the only one who loves him. Kevin needs him too. Please don't take him. I love him so much." She then began to recite all the prayers she could remember: the Lord's Prayer, multiple Hail Marys, and the Twenty-Third Psalm.

A monitor went off with a grating alarm. Ansley flinched, looking up at the machines with a panicked expression. A nurse rushed into the room, adjusted his IV, and smiled wanly at Ansley as she left.

Thank you, God.

At the appointed time for visiting, Kevin and Anne came silently into the cubicle. Anne immediately went to the chair and put her hands on Ansley's shoulders to offer comfort. Kevin went to the opposite side of the bed.

"Has he moved?" Anne asked.

Ansley slowly shook her head, remaining silent.

"Can we get you anything to eat or drink?" Anne asked in a whisper.

Swallowing, Ansley looked up, tears still glassing over her eyes. "Thank you, but I couldn't eat."

Anne squeezed her shoulder. "I know, my dear, but Nicholas needs you to keep up your strength. I can't vouch for the food here, but we can send Ian out when he comes back with Stephen."

"Stephen left?" Ansley asked, slightly disconcerted.

"He said that he was going for a musical device that you asked him to find."

"Oh."

Kevin's shaky voice interrupted. "Aunt Anne, is he going to be alright?" The young man spoke without diverting his eyes from his father.

"Of course he is," Anne responded without hesitation, her British reserve masking any fear.

Kevin leaned forward, close to Nick's face, and whispered something so quietly that neither Ansley, nor Anne, could hear. He then patted his father on the arm and left the room, obviously distraught.

"He is going to be okay, Ansley. You must believe that," Anne said. Again, she squeezed Ansley's shoulders. "I'm going to see to having tea and a sandwich brought in for you. Even if you're not hungry, think of what Nick would want you to do."

It was late afternoon before Stephen and Ian returned from the errand. It had taken visits to several stores to collect both music and player. In the predominately Catholic country, the religious beads had been the easier item to purchase.

"Any response?" Stephen asked upon entering the cubicle.

"No," Ansley whispered.

He handed her a rosary made of green stones that closely matched the crucifix Dennis's mother had given Ansley, which hung around her neck. "Where would you like this iPod?"

"On the table. I think there is a plug behind the monitors."

Once it was set up close to Nick's head, Ansley turned the menu to "Habanera" and the volume low so that it was barely heard above the sounds of the monitors.

"Anne sent Ian for tea and a sandwich for you. Is there anything else that you need?"

"Nothing. I really don't want the sandwich, but Anne insisted."

"She's right, you know. You have to eat."

"What time is it?"

"A little past six."

"The next visiting time is seven, right?"

"I believe so."

"Do you know who is coming in?"

"Probably Kevin and one of the Colebridges." Stephen watched how intently Ansley was focused on Nick.

"That's an unusual crucifix you are wearing."

Ansley reached up and touched the cool marble. "It's very special. It belonged to my former ballet partner, who died not long ago."

"The dancer Nick created the founda—" He stopped mid word.

Ansley looked at him—her expression startled. "Finish what you were about to say."

"That was a mistake. Forget what I said."

"Stephen, you can't do that to me. Did Nick pay for Dennis's care?"

Appearing uncomfortable, he hesitated before replying. "Ansley, Nick would fire me if he knew I betrayed his confidence." He paused again. "But maybe you should know."

She stared at him, eyes wide.

"The foundation that took care of the expenses for your friend was Nick."

For a second, her eyebrows pinched together—her expression indicated that her mind was racing, trying to sort it out. "Nick paid for

Dennis?"

Stephen nodded. "He did—and swore me to secrecy."

"Why? Why wouldn't he let me know?"

"He didn't want you thinking that it was a disingenuous act—an effort to impress you."

Ansley looked back at the lifeless figure lying on the bed in front of her. "You did that and never let Dennis or me know it was you? Did I never see who you truly were?"

"Although I can't expect you to keep *my* confidence, I would be grateful if you would."

"How can I thank him?"

"He doesn't want your gratitude. Nick wants you."

"He's got to get well, Stephen. *We* need another chance." For the moment, Andy had slipped out of her mind.

"He will. Keep believing that. Would you like to be alone with him?"

She nodded. "If you don't mind."

At seven o'clock, Katherine and Kevin came in. Ansley had been sitting next to the bed, praying the rosary and watching Nick all afternoon. She was exhausted, but adrenalin kept her alert to his every breath.

"You should take a break, my dear. Kevin and I are here. I'll send for you instantly if Nicholas awakes."

"Thank you, Lady Katherine. I'm fine, but I will excuse myself for a minute or two."

As she entered the restroom, she came face to face with a woman emerging from one of the stalls. It was Claudine.

"You're Ansleee," Claudine said—a pleasant look on her delicate face.

Ansley nodded, feeling self-conscious. "I am. And this is awkward. You're Claudine Cartier, Nick's wife."

"Oui. Je ne pense pas . . . I apologize. I mean, oui; I'm Claudine, but non, I do not think that I am the wife of Nicholas. Surely, they have told you that we were married just the five minutes. It will be officially over so soon." She lifted her long, thick hair off her neck as though to obtain relief from the heat.

Long hair. He loves long hair. Ansley reached up instinctively to run a hand through her own short hair.

"My financé—he is here."

"You're engaged?"

"Oui. He, Gérard, he came to the senses when he saw the tabloid photograph of Nicholas and me." The sylph-like dancer extended a hand toward Ansley. "It is nice to meet you, Ansleee. Nicholas, he will be good, no?"

"I certainly pray that he will."

"When he is better, you come to Paree, I dance for you."

Ansley smiled—the first smile since receiving Stephen's call. "I would love to see you dance. I've heard . . . I mean read, that you are brilliant."

"Brillant no, but good." She nodded, agreeing with herself, and then pointed her finger toward Ansley. "You dance?"

She's certainly not modest, but she is nice.

"No. That is, I did, but nothing like you."

Claudine lifted a hand and in a graceful gesture outlined Ansley's body in the air. "You have the physique of the ballerina."

"Not any more. But, if you'll excuse me, I better get back to Nick," Ansley said, walking toward the exit.

That was not what I expected—but what did I expect?

When she reached the ICU, Kevin was leaning against the wall outside Nick's cubicle.

"Has anything happened?" Ansley asked the boy.

"No. Granmama is still there with him."

When Ansley entered, Katherine was seated in the chair by the bed. "He has stirred a bit, but no sign of waking," she said, rising. "A nurse came in and checked on him. If I understood her correctly, she said that his temperature is no higher."

"At least he moved. He hasn't done that all afternoon."

Touching Ansley's arm, Katherine said, "Victor and I are returning to our hotel, but Stephen knows how to reach us. It's rather close by. Send for us if there's any change." She embraced Ansley for a second and then left.

The evening dragged by. At eight-thirty, a doctor came in and checked on Nick. As he left, Ansley followed him to the hallway and asked if there had been any change.

"No, Senora. We will hope better for tomorrow."

"Could he need a transplant?"

"Si. It is possible."

Ansley cringed.

Seeing the distress on her face, Stephen, who had heard the exchange, went to her and put an arm around her shoulders. "Let's pray that he doesn't need one."

After hearing the latest report, most of the family left for their hotel. Penelope offered to stay with Kevin, who refused to leave, but Anne said that she could not sleep and would stay with him.

In Nick's room, Ansley's teacup was empty, but the sandwich was drying out on the table. Shortly after midnight, the beverage had run its course, and Ansley had to use the restroom again. She decided to check on Kevin and to tell those waiting that Nick was moving a little, periodically, but had not regained consciousness.

She was about to return to his cubicle when the code sounded.

"Oh, my, God—it's Nick! He's coding. No, no!" Ansley became hysterical. Stephen grabbed her to try to calm her, and Anne put her arms around Kevin.

"I've got to go, Stephen," Ansley pleaded, trying to pull away from him.

"If it's Nick, honey, they won't let you in."

"But, I've got to be there."

"Stay here," Stephen said, pointing to the trio. "I'll check with the nurse's station and be right back."

As Stephen walked out, Kevin pulled away from Anne and went to Ansley. Putting his arms around her, he whispered, "Dad's going to be fine. That's not him. I know it."

Although it seemed forever to Ansley, Stephen was back in short order. "It wasn't Nick. Everyone relax. It was an elderly woman."

Ansley felt her knees go weak with relief. "I've got to go back to him. I'll let you know if there's any change."

As she passed the elderly woman's room, the staff was dismantling equipment. She had apparently not made it. Ansley crossed herself.

When she entered Nick's room, she went to the bed and reached over, touching his forehead. *Is he not as hot? Or, is it my wishful thinking?*

Resuming her vigil, she noticed the music was off and turned it back on.

Nick stirred and his eyes formed a slit, then eased open, blinking.

Ansley held her breath, too frozen to speak.

"Come here," he managed to get out, struggling to speak in a voice barely above a whisper.

"You're awake. Oh, my, God, you're awake," she said, tears flowing down to her grinning mouth.

"That music." His words were slurred but clearly discernible and the corners of his mouth slightly upturned.

Nodding, she said, "I prayed you would hear it." She stood up and leaned forward to be closer to him.

"Your hair—too short."

Smiling, she said, "You would notice that. It will grow." Drops fell from her eyes onto his sheet.

A little smile crept across his face. "*I'll* see to that." His voice was feeble, but his spirit was strong—the Nick she knew.

"You shouldn't talk. You need your strength."

"His lips curled in a tiny smile."

Ansley was shaking, a huge smile on her wet face. "I've got to let the others know you're awake."

He reached his hand up for hers. "Stay."

"Let me get my phone," she said, putting her free hand over his and squeezing. "I can call Stephen."

Less than a minute after conveying the news, Kevin and Anne appeared in the room.

"You're better," Kevin said, reaching his father's bedside.

"Can't get rid of me that easy."

Anne smiled, blinking away a tear. "I hope you realize how much trouble you've caused—as usual."

"You're here?"

"We're nearly all here, your majesty. And Noel has been on the phone constantly, checking on you." The only family member who had not made the trip was Nick's older brother, Noel Colebridge.

"The earl and her ladyship?"

"They're here, too," Kevin said, "but they went back to the hotel earlier. They want us to call with any news."

Stephen stood in the doorway, ready to block any attempt to evict the small crowd.

Looking around the room, Nick noticed him. "You brought her?"

"He did," Ansley said.

Nick smiled.

Stephen gave a loose salute.

"Now that we know you're better, I'd best get this young man back to the hotel. It's been an exhausting three days since we left the Cotswolds," Anne said.

"Three? Where was I?" Nick asked.

"Hovering somewhere between heaven and hell," Anne said,

smiling, "but I was confident that neither God, nor the devil, was ready to deal with you. Therefore, we are to be stuck with you for a while to come." The glow on her face betrayed the relief she felt.

CHAPTER THIRTY-EIGHT

When the room cleared, a nurse came in and checked Nick's vital signs. She assured Ansley that he was indeed better before she left. They were finally alone for the first time since Nick regained consciousness.

Neither spoke. Each looked at the other, Ansley with glassy eyes, Nick with a faint smile. He tried to talk; his voice was gaining strength, but remained weak. "Nice music."

"You really heard it?"

He blinked his eyes and nodded, slightly.

"Therapeutic memories."

"I prayed you could hear."

"Heard your promises, too."

"You need to rest. Don't overdo it," she said, brushing hair off his forehead.

"Holding you to . . ." His words trailed as he dozed off.

Ansley lowered the railing on the side of his bed and leaned over, resting her head next to him. She was physically and emotionally exhausted but determined to stay with him.

When a nurse finally came in to check him again, using body language to supplement her English, Ansley asked if there were any larger chairs available.

Patting the wooden chair she had been sitting in, she said, "Grand chair, chaise."

When the woman continued to look puzzled, Ansley put her hands in praying position to her cheek, tipped her head, closed her eyes, and then pointed to the chair again.

"Si, senora," the older Mexican woman said, nodding her head.

We'll see if she understood.

The nurse had understood. A half-hour later, two men brought in a lounge chair that, to Ansley, looked like heaven covered in cheap vinyl upholstery.

Nick improved rapidly over the next three days. Ansley left his side only to make brief trips to the hotel for a quick shower and change of clothes. Her appetite returned in direct proportion to Nick's recovery.

Claudine and Gérard left for France the day after Nick regained consciousness. Her presence had been unnecessary since media had not discovered that the celebrity lay close to death. On the fourth day, the physician leading Nick's team announced that through consultation with the Houston doctors, it had been decided that Nick was strong enough to be transported to Texas.

"What a relief it will be to return to an English-speaking country," Katherine said.

Ansley had the distinct feeling that if she was not present, the rest of the sentence would have included "even if it is the colonies." However, she agreed wholeheartedly with the matriarch. The doctors had been reasonably proficient in English, but several nurses were obviously not bi-lingual.

The Colebridge family made the decision to travel to Houston and remain long enough for reassurance by U.S. doctors that Nick's condition was improving and that he was out of danger. Barring bad news, they would return to England shortly thereafter, Kevin included. Nick balked at the idea of Ansley returning to Florida, but she was under pressure from both her practice and her personal life. She had admitted to her mother that she was at the bedside of the man the Sheridans met when Nick came for Christmas in 2003 and begged that Laura allow her to explain when she returned home. She made it clear to Olivia that she would not share additional information about the trip. Andy was her biggest problem.

After the first awful day in Mexico, she sent him a text each day but did not answer his calls. She told him that she was in an area with bad cell service. He asked that she call him from a landline and reverse the charges. She ignored the request. However, she knew that once in Texas, she would have to speak with him. According to his messages, he delayed canceling the North Carolina reservation, holding onto the hope that she would make it back in time. She wanted to tell him that even if she was back in time, she could not go after what had happened. When alone, any thought of Andy cast a shroud of guilt over her. It disappeared when she was with Nick.

Ansley flew with him in the air ambulance. The others flew commercial. They reached the Houston hospital at noon on Thursday. As Nick was checked in, Ansley noticed the day and date on a bulletin board in his room.

How can it have been less than a week since I left home? Last Thursday, I was preparing for court.

The American tests did not begin until Friday but filled the day, exhausting Nick. Immediate results were positive, indicating that not only was the worst behind him but that the healing process was underway.

"There's no reason to believe that he will not have a full recovery, provided he follows the rules," the chief gastroenterologist told Nick and the family. Proper nutrition and the avoidance of alcohol were absolute requirements. Nick insisted that Ansley be present as he considered her his next of kin. Ansley was embarrassed that he did not include Kevin or his parents. However, she was grateful that she was allowed to hear, firsthand, what the status of his condition was.

Sunday the Colebridges were to leave for the U.K. That morning they were all assembled in Nick's hospital suite for the farewells. Nick tapped his tray table, and they all turned to listen.

"I have an announcement. You've probably all guessed, but this is the woman I plan to spend the rest of my sorry life with." He held her hand in the air in a victorious gesture.

Ansley blushed. Anne was first to give the congratulatory hug.

"I'm at a loss for words," Ansley said, giving Nick an evil eye after hugs from the rest of the family. They had vowed their love and talked of not parting again over the days of his recovery, but there had been no official determination of a wedding.

"How can you be officially engaged until you give her a ring, Dad?" Kevin said, beaming.

"Ah. That was taken care of a long time ago. She simply has to put it on."

"I think it's a superb idea. Ansley, my dear, you are a welcome addition to the Colebridge line," Victor said.

After the clan departed, Ansley sat down by Nick's bed. "You might have warned me that you were going to make that announcement."

"And give you the ability to stall me? Not a chance. You're going to marry me this time if I have to get you pregnant to ensure it."

"I'm not going to deny that, but before you reserve the church, there are some things I have to tell you about me."

"Not going to change anything," he said, shaking his head from side to side.

"Please, just listen." Tears were starting to well in her eyes.

"Okay. I'll cut the tomfoolery. But, my love, there is nothing you can tell me that will
change my mind about you."

She was holding the corner of his bed sheet and twisting it. She wouldn't look at him. "I'm not sure that I can tell you this. I've never told anyone—not my parents, not Elaine, not even Dennis."

His face took on a serious look. "Ansley, my love, I do not believe you could damage my love for you if you told me that you did away with Mark and have his body in your freezer. We all have skeletons in our history. Whatever happened was to another person. You don't have to tell me."

"Yes, I do. It could affect our life together. I may not be able to have children."

"That would be okay. I would be disappointed for you, but I don't have to have more children to make my life complete."

"Listen to me." She was shaking. "I was pregnant once."

He looked at her but gave no indication of surprise.

"I gave the baby up."

"Adoption?"

"No . . . . Abortion."

"And you're afraid that would affect my feelings for you?"

"It's a pretty big thing."

"I know you, love. Whatever you did, you had no other choice. I'm not judging you. You're judging yourself."

The rest of the story came tumbling out nonstop. "It was only a few weeks before I discovered Mark with his lover. When I found out that I was pregnant, he said that we could not afford a baby—that it would ruin his chances of graduating. He said that he would leave me if I didn't get rid of it. I was scared and stupid, thought I loved him and that we were a family. I destroyed my baby because he threatened to leave." Her face was soaked with tears.

"Come here." He pulled her onto his bed and drew her wet face down to his chest. "You did what you believed you had to do. Mark was an even bigger bastard than I thought. But, you can't torture yourself. I know the teachings of your faith run deep, but Ansley, they're not necessarily mine. I make no judgment. You were a committed wife and torn

236

between conflicting beliefs of your own faith. Put it in the past where it belongs. We're starting a new life, and I see babies in our future." His arms closed tighter around her.

When she composed herself, she left his embrace and sat at the foot of the bed. "There's something else you need to know."

"Don't tell me you actually did murder Mark and have his body in a freezer somewhere."

She couldn't help but laugh. "I *wanted* to, trust me, I wanted to. But he's alive and well and living in misery with the bounty of his gathering, so I'm told."

"Good. That means that there's no deal-breaker for you to confess."

"I hope not. This is a little hard to talk about, too, but maybe not as bad as what I just told you. . . ."

"Spit it out before it chokes you."

I've been seeing someone."

He looked her in the eye and said, "I can't be surprised or upset. We've been apart quite a long time."

Before he could say more, she added, "I haven't slept with him."

"I didn't ask, love."

"But, I want you to know. I was going to. We had planned to go away together this weekend."

"Not to Florence, I would hope."

She gave his leg a playful shove. "Hardly."

"Good that I made a pass at death's door in the nick of time."

"Not funny . . . But a clever play on words. You will have to admit that you did go to extremes to reunite us."

"This chap . . . the one who has missed his golden opportunity . . . have you told him about me?"

"Not yet. I didn't think it was fair, or appropriate, to do it in writing, or even over the phone. He doesn't know where I am or who I'm with—"

"Poor bastard. I almost feel sorry for him. Come here." He beckoned with his hand.

"Still a controlling chauvinist, aren't you?"

"I own it. Now come here."

"Nick, someone could walk in."

"So?"

She moved up to lay her head on his chest. "You slept with Claudine?"

"That's what we men do, my love."

"And Fury?"

"Fury? Who the hell is Fury?"

"The redhead on the cover of whatever tabloid."

"Oh, the writer."

"That one."

He laughed. "Is that why you stopped taking my calls?"

"I have to ask, even if I don't want to know."

"I've never lied to you. I haven't been celibate, but about that one, let me put your mind at rest. My sole relationship with the young woman was professional. We optioned one of her books—that's all."

"I guess there were a lot of misunderstandings."

"I guess there were. Now that we have the confessions out of the way, do you think you could find me a decent steak in the great state of Texas? Since making love is off the table in this asylum, you can at least satisfy one of my carnal pleasures."

"Only if your doctor approves and you don't want a bottle of Dom Perignon to wash it down with."

CHAPTER THIRTY-NINE

Contrary to Nick's desire, Ansley left Houston three days later, arriving back in Florida on the day she would have returned from the getaway with Andy. Before leaving Texas, she made the dreaded call to Andy from her hotel room.

"I'm coming home tomorrow."

"I've almost forgotten the sound of your voice, but I'm happy to hear it and even happier to know I'll see you soon."

"Make me feel bad, why don't you?" *As if I don't feel bad enough.*

"I've been miserable to live with since you've been gone. Grant would probably fire me if he could."

"I'm sorry."

"I'll let you make it up to me."

Ansley cringed. *This is horrible. How am I going to tell him?* "I'll have to get home first."

"What time does your flight get in?"

"If it's on time, it gets in at three-fifteen."

"Did you leave your car at the airport?"

"No." *Why did I say that?*

"Good. I'll be there when you arrive."

"Andy, you don't have to do that. I can take a cab."

"Are you out of your mind? You're not taking a cab when I'm dying to see you."

"But it's a workday."

"I'm one of the bosses—remember?"

Get it over with, Ansley. Buck up. You've got to tell him, and putting it off won't make it go away.

"Okay. If you're sure Grant won't fire you."

Before driving her to the airport, Ian took Ansley to the hospital to say goodbye to Nick. He was showered, shaved, and sitting in the lounge chair in fresh pajamas and robe when she arrived.

"Are you trying to impress me?"

"Guilty as charged, counselor! You Americans don't miss a thing. How could I let you fly back to the hometown boyfriend with an image of a scruffy bum in a hospital bed? So, how did I do?" He held his arms out as though to show off his clothing.

"You did good—absolutely *GQ* quality."

"Then get the hell over here and show me."

She crossed the room and he pulled her down onto his lap.

"Whoa. Did they spike your IV with Viagra?"

He tickled her ribs and said, "That's two you're going to answer for when I'm out of the asylum."

"Two? What's the other?"

"Cutting that beautiful hair. Which, I might add, you'd better not do again."

"Yes, sir, your majes—"

Before she could finish, he covered her lips with his.

Ansley dissolved. He was Nick again, even down to the aroma of Green Irish Tweed.

"You sure you want to catch that plane?" he whispered in a sexy manner.

"No. 'But I have promises to keep and miles to go before I sleep.'"

"'The lady doth protest too much, methinks.'"

"I give in. Shakespeare trumps Frost," she said, pointing her finger into his chest. "And, I'm not playing that game with a man who has the entire Shakespearean lexicon committed to memory."

"Well, not quite the entire lexicon."

"You know every line of every play."

"Can I help it if I was inculcated in British prep schools where the letters in your cereal spell out Shakespearean quotations in the milk? I missed the memo that said we were only to read it, learn it, and teach it—not perform it."

She reached her arms out and began to dramatically recite, "'O Romeo, Romeo! Wherefore art thou Romeo? Deny thy father, and refuse thy name; or if thou wilt not, be but sworn my love, and I'll no longer be a Capulet.'"

"And all this time, I thought you were just a dumb blonde." He began tickling her, again, and she jumped up.

"Robert Frost or William Shakespeare, I've got to go."

"One more kiss before you leave."

She moved back closer to him and he grabbed her hand, pulling her back down. Her arms went around his neck and they kissed passionately.

"I love you," he whispered in her ear after their lips parted. "Now get out of here before my adrenalin kicks in to back up my raging libido, and I ravage you on the floor of this sterile chamber."

"I'm gone."

From the time she boarded the plane in Houston, up until landing in Jacksonville, Ansley stressed about facing Andy. *How did I get in this situation? What if I can't tell him?*

She had to get it over with. When Nick called that night, he would ask if she had broken the news to Andy. She couldn't lie to him. She also couldn't let Andy go on thinking that they were building a relationship—that she would go away with him. *He's going to expect to kiss me when I get off the plane. What am I going to do? I can't just blurt out in the airport,"Hey honey, I have news. My former lover and I are back together."*

Her connecting flight from Atlanta to Jacksonville was fully booked. Watching passengers pass her in the first class section, she wanted to say to the apprehensive that they were on the safest flight in the sky. *There's no way that I'm going to get out of facing the music by this plane crashing.*

When she exited the secured area of the airport, Andy was waiting with an enthusiastic expression on his face. Dressed in khaki slacks and a Ralph Lauren plaid shirt, he looked especially handsome as Ansley walked toward him.

He's the American provincial version of Nick. This is going to be so hard.

When she was within ten feet, his arms opened to greet her and enveloped her in a hug so overpowering that she almost dropped her tote bag.

OMG, I remember what it was that attracted me to this guy.

"I am so glad to see you," he said, squeezing her even tighter.

"It's good to be back." She couldn't quite bring herself to say that she was glad to see him, even though she was. It seemed to her that to say so would be misleading and wrong.

"How was your flight?"

"Smooth, but exhausting."

"You were in Houston?"

"Yes. I had to change planes in Atlanta."

"I have to admit, I'm really anxious to hear about what took you away so abruptly. It must have been an awfully close friend."

"Let's wait until we get to my house, and I'll tell you the whole story."

The drive from the Jacksonville airport to her condo took nearly an hour. Ansley was miserable and said very little. Andy reached over and squeezed her hand a couple of times but didn't push her to talk. It was all she could do to not react to his touch, but even his hand touching hers made her feel as though she were cheating on Nick.

When they entered the condo, it was as cold as Ansley's heart.

"I forgot to ask," he said. "What did you do about the cats while you were gone?"

"Mom picked them up. The condo seems like a tomb when they're not here."

"It's not empty with me here," he said, releasing the luggage and pulling her close to him.

Ansley stiffened and pulled away. "Let me get us something to drink. I am really thirsty."

"Why didn't you say so in the car? I could have stopped." A slight frown formed on Andy's face. "I'm not getting good vibes, sweetheart. Is something wrong?"

"I'm fine. What would you like? Pepsi, water, coffee?"

"Maybe I need something stronger."

"I have wine or Canadian Club—my dad's drink."

"A shot of the CC with 7-Up, if you have it."

"Have Sprite. Will that work?"

He nodded.

"Make yourself comfortable."

With a Pepsi for herself and his drink in hand, she walked to the sofa where Andy had settled down.

As she handed him the drink, he looked at her and said, "There's more to this mystery trip than a sick friend, isn't there?"

Dreading the release of words, she nodded. "We have to talk, Andy. And you've got to believe me, this is not easy."

"Your friend—it was a guy, wasn't it?"

She nodded. "Please listen. If I had met you first, we'd probably be married and have three kids by now. You are everything I could have wanted in a man."

His expression turned hostile and then quickly faded into sadness.

"There's so much you don't know about me, Andy. No one knows.

242

I never thought anything like this would happen in a million years. In fact, my whole life is something I would never have expected."

"No one was sick. He called and you went."

"No, no, no. He was sick—is still recovering. He nearly died. In fact, *he* didn't call. Someone called for him. He was unconscious when I got there."

"Where was *there*? I suspect that it wasn't Texas."

"I did come home from Texas. But, you're right. It was Mexico at first."

"He's Mexican?"

"No. He's actually British, but he was taken ill in Mexico. He was transferred to Houston as soon as the doctors believed it safe to move him."

"Does this guy have a name?"

"Of course. Unfortunately, it's one that you would recognize. I can't tell you who he is right now. No one in Jacksonville knows that I was ever involved with him. Probably only a dozen people in the world know. We've been apart for over two years."

"He must have hurt you a lot for you to avoid dating for two years. How could you let him back into your life now?"

"We hurt each other. It was as much my fault as it was his, maybe more."

"Ansley, I thought we had something pretty special happening."

"Andy, Andy, I did too. Honestly, I did, and if I am being honest, there's still a part of me that feels something special toward you. Please believe me when I tell you that you would have been the guy for me for life if I had met you first."

"Who is this mystery man and why can't you give his name? It's not Prince William is it?"

She laughed and a tear slid down her cheek. "Almost, but not quite."

He gulped down the remainder of his drink and stood up. "I'm not giving up, Ansley. I'm not fond of being part of a triangle, but I was falling in love with you, and if this guy walked away once, he'll do it again."

"Andy, don't. Don't let me hurt you any more than I have. You're an incredible guy. I would have fallen in love with you, believe me, I would—maybe I did."

Ansley stood and walked him to the door.

"May I call you occasionally?"

"It's probably not a good idea, but I'm not going to say no. Just please don't get your hopes up. I'm probably going to marry him."

"You're not married yet. Can I kiss you goodbye?"

"Not a good idea for either one of us."

"I will call. You can bank on it."

After Andy left, Ansley was emotionally drained. She plunged into unpacking and doing her laundry, hoping to shake the guilt-induced depression. When she finished the last load, she turned on her TV, trying to erase the image of the disappointment on Andy's face. *I never thought it was possible to be in love with two men at the same time, but maybe it is. What do I mean, maybe? I am in love with two men.*

Watching an Independence Day special, Ansley fell asleep on her couch. The phone woke her.

"I miss you already, love," Nick said in his sexy British accent.

"Me, too." The sound of his voice, even a thousand miles away, was thrilling and reaffirming that she had made the right choice. Her eyes sparkled for the first time since leaving Houston.

"Was your journey comfortable?"

"It was. I had forgotten how nice it is in first class, not that I've traveled much in the past two years."

There was a pause before Nick spoke again.   "Are you going to tell me, or do I have to ask?"

Ansley smiled. "Don't tell me the famous Nicholas Colton is feeling threatened?"

"Giving me a hard time, are you?"

She laughed. "As if I could. Yes, I'm going to tell you." She swung her feet off the couch and onto the floor. "He met me at the airport, and it was brutal. Do you know how despicable I felt having to tell him that I had been off with another man when I was supposed to have spent the weekend with him?"

"But, you did tell him?"

"I told him. But, I'm going to take the high ground, Nick, and not give you details. He didn't do anything wrong except fall for the wrong girl, and I owe him that respect."

"I'll defer to that. All I need to know is that he is aware that you're taken."

"That statement is true on many levels. I told him about you, but not who you are."

After talking to Nick, she forced herself to go to bed in an attempt to acclimate to the time zone.

CHAPTER FORTY

Ansley was at her desk the next morning an hour before her secretary. Telephone messages filled the spindle on the corner of Olivia's desk. Several were from Elaine. It was too early to return calls, so Ansley began reviewing the correspondence and documents that Olivia left stacked in her chair.

"Hey. It's good to have you back," Olivia said when she arrived at eight-thirty. "Is your friend better?"

"Yes, thank you—much better. It's going to be a slow road to complete recovery, but all is looking well." She had almost let it slip that the patient was male, but Olivia appeared to not notice.

"I bet Andy was glad to see you."

Ansley turned her face away. *I should have known that was coming.* "He was."

"You guys are really hitting it off, aren't you?"

If I give any hint that it's over, she's going to dig like crazy. "Yeah. We seem to be." Changing the subject, Ansley flipped through the stack of papers and asked, "What is the top priority today? Any fires to put out?"

"There are several discovery requests that you need to review for objections and a request for admissions that's due on Monday. Do you want me to prepare a motion for extension of time in which to respond?"

"No. I think that I can get it done."

"There have been three requests for consults by potential clients. You might want to return those calls first."

"Have any of them been served?"

"No, which is good. There are two divorce cases and one paternity, but nothing is urgent. I told them that you were away on a family emergency and that I expected you back any day."

What do I do? If I'm really going to marry Nick, I shouldn't take a new case.

"Thanks. You are golden. I couldn't run this practice without you."

Olivia smiled. "Just doin' my job." The secretary turned to go back to her office.

"Olivia, have we heard from the court on the visitation of the Langston children?"

"Not yet. Fran calls every day. I feel so sorry for her. She's really terrified of that guy."

"I know. It's scary. I think he's dangerous, but he stays just under the radar. The problem is the law can't lock someone up because others think he might commit a crime."

"I know he's crazy," Olivia circled the air around the side of her head with her finger. "I watched him in court. There's a weird look in those eyes."

"I tend to agree with you, but he fooled Dr. Sinclair. Too bad there's not an MRI or a blood test to detect psychotic sociopaths."

Although coming in that morning had felt strange, by ten a.m. she was mentally immersed in her work, seldom thinking about either Nick or Andy.

Shortly before three o'clock, a dozen roses arrived.

"Well, look what you got," Olivia said, coming in with the arrangement.

Nick. Ansley smiled and took the card that Olivia handed her.

"Where do you want me to put them? On your desk or the table?"

"The table. This desk is so messy that there's no room left," she said, reading the card.

> I am in love with you and willing to wait.
> Love,
> Andy

Ansley felt the color drain from her face, but fought to hide her distress.

"Who are they from? Andy?"

Ansley nodded, trying to smile while wanting to break down in tears. The beautiful flowers had turned obnoxious in four letters—the wrong four. *How can I sit at this desk and look at these? But, if I throw them out, Olivia will want to know why. I'm not ready to explain.*

At five o'clock, Olivia walked into Ansley's office. "Want me to stay late to help you catch up?"

"No. You've done enough the past two weeks. Besides, I'm only staying 'til six-thirty. One of the potential new clients, Sonia Nelson, is coming in between five-fifteen and five-thirty for an hour consult, and then I'm leaving—having dinner with my parents and picking up Shadow and Skye. You go ahead. I'll see you tomorrow."

After the consultation, Ansley closed the office and took the flowers to the garbage dumpster at the back of the parking lot before getting into her car. *I'll tell Olivia I took them home.*

"I'm so glad you're home, honey. I was a little worried about you," Laura said as Ansley walked in. "You acted so mysterious about your trip." She untied the apron from around her waist and laid it across a chair. "Have a seat. Dinner is in the oven, but we can talk for a little while first. Dad's not home, yet."

Both cats and the Sheridan shih-tzu, Candy, were lying scattered among the sofa and chairs of the living room.

"I'm not sure there's anywhere left to sit," Ansley said, looking around the room. She went to the sofa and wedged in between the throw pillows and Skye, who didn't relinquish an inch of space. Laura sat with Candy in an adjacent, wingback chair.

"You were visiting that man, Tony Col . . . something or other who you brought to Christmas dinner several years ago?"

"I was."

"I know you're an adult, and I want you to find someone and get married again. But, who is he, Ansley? Did you have some kind of relationship with him? And what about Andy? He's a really nice man."

"Can we take things one at a time?" Ansley hesitated. Avoiding eye contact, she said, "I did have a relationship with Tony, Mom. I was in love with him."

"Why did you keep it a secret? He seemed to be a nice enough fellow." Laura's brow was furrowed as she stared at her daughter. "He wasn't married, was he?"

"He wasn't married, at least not when we were dating."

"He's married now?"

"Yes and no."

"That's not possible. Either he is or he isn't."

"Mom, the first thing you need to know is who Tony really is."

A look of alarm registered on Laura's face. "Who he is? Is he a drug dealer?"

Laura's remark struck Ansley funny, breaking the tension that had held her hostage from the moment she walked out of the office.

"He's never even played a drug dealer to my knowledge," Ansley said, smiling and remembering that Nick's beard and mysterious appearance could have allowed for that quantum leap of presumption.

"What do you mean played? What is he? An actor? Ansley, you haven't gotten mixed up with an actor, have you?"

"Mom, you know him as Nicholas Colton."

"I don't know a . . . . You mean he has the same name as tha—" Laura went silent before looking Ansley in the eye with a serious expression and saying, "You're not telling me that he is Nicholas Colton?"

Ansley nodded.

Laura sat speechless, staring at Ansley as if she couldn't get the words out to ask questions.

"I met him in New York in 2001, right after I graduated from law school. Remember when I went to see Dennis dance?"

Laura nodded. "You met Nicholas Colton five years ago, and he sat at a table with me, and I didn't know who he was?"

Ansley nodded. "I think I'm going to marry him, Mom."

"Marry him? You can't. He's married. I saw it on one of those celebrity TV shows." Laura was shaking her head in bewilderment.

"I can, Mom. That marriage was not really a marriage. They only spent one night together. She's engaged to someone else. I met her in Mexico."

"You were in Mexico?" Laura had stricken look on her face.

Ansley thought for a minute that her mother might have a stroke or a heart attack.   "That's where Nick was taken ill. He nearly died. That part is all true. But he came through it. He's in a Texas hospital now and will probably be released soon."

Laura leaned her forehead forward, holding it with her fingers as though it ached. "This is all a bit much for me to process, Ansley. My daughter not only had some kind of relationship with a movie star, but also kept it a secret for what—five years?"

Ansley nodded. "And please don't tell anyone, yet. I've got to be sure of a lot of things and will have to close my practice if this is going to happen. In the meantime, I don't want to be the center of attention over Nick. You understand that the press would turn my life into a nightmare, don't you?"

"Do your father and I get to meet him—the real man?"

"You know you will. But I don't know when. He has to recover, and I don't know what they're going to do about the film he was working on when he got sick. There're a lot of unknowns at this time. Help me impress upon Daddy that this has to stay between us for a while. I'm not even going to tell Elaine."

"Did anyone know?"

"Dennis knew. Nick's family in England knew, some of his staff. But neither of us wanted to 'out' me, at least not until right before we broke up. He wanted to go public then. I never thought it would last—it was my little 'fifteen minutes' of walk on the wild side in fantasyland."

And that nice young man, Andy—how does he fit into this? Are you just tossing him into the garbage?"

I think that's exactly what I did a few minutes ago, flowers and all. "I told him most of the truth, Mom, but not who Nick is. It was hard. I did really like him and probably still do."

"But you like the movie star better?"

"Not because he's a movie star. It's way, way more than that."

"Ansley, are you sure you're thinking straight? Movie stars are notorious for cheating and divorce—and he's a foreigner. You need someone reliable, someone like Andy."

Foreigner? "Mom, he's British."

When Michael got home, Ansley went through the entire story again—Laura editorializing. Michael's reaction was the polar opposite of Laura's.

"Go for it, sweetheart. Take all the gusto you can from life. You only go around once. Let her be, Laura. If this guy makes her happy, which is obvious from the smile on her face when she says his name, then she should do it."

"Michael Sheridan, how can you encourage her? Didn't Mark hurt her enough? This movie star will end up breaking her heart again, only she'll be thousands of miles away and maybe have two or three babies. Are you going to drive to England to get her when it happens?"

I guess I know where I get my paranoid cynicism. It's in my DNA.

CHAPTER FORTY-ONE

Arriving home from work, eight days after returning from Texas, Ansley found a full mailbox and a note indicating a delivery had been left next door.

"It's been a while since I've seen one of these deliveries," Jeanette said, handing Ansley the single rose and a small, blue box.

"It *has* been a while." *Please don't start an interrogation.* "Forgive me for being rude, Jeanette, but I've got to dash. I'm expecting a very important call . . . from an opposing counsel. Thanks for taking this in for me, and tell Melissa, I said hello."

Returning to her unit, she tingled with the same excitement she had when the first gifts arrived five years earlier.

Once in her living room, she untied the elastic bow on the box, smiling and picturing him in her mind. Inside, a gold angel, with a halo of diamonds, rested on a bed of velvet. The card read:

> For the angel who healed me—
> heart, body, and soul,
>
> 'Doubt that the stars are fire;
> Doubt that the sun doth move;
> Doubt truth to be a liar;
> But never doubt I love.'
>
> Forever yours,
> Nick

A tear of joy rolled down her face as she ran a finger over the tiny charm. However, the joy vanished when she noticed a piece of mail bearing Andy's return address on top of the stack.

Picking up the envelope, her mood abruptly changed. After studying it for a second, she put it aside while she flipped through the remaining bills, letters, and advertisements.

Catching her attention were two pieces of mail bearing postage with the familiar likeness of Queen Elizabeth II.

The first was of thick, ivory vellum, sealed with wax, and bore the Colebridge crest—as elegant as a formal wedding invitation but rectangular. Retrieving a letter opener from her desk, she sliced through the paper. Inside was a handwritten letter.

> My dear Ansley,
>
> Victor and I wish to convey our deepest appreciation for your expeditious and devoted response to Nicholas in his time of peril. We are deeply indebted.
>
> Further, we wish to welcome you to the Colebridge family. Recognizing the bond you and Nicholas have forged, we look forward to hosting you at the manor often.
>
> Very truly yours,
> Katherine

I think I just put on the glass slipper, and it fits. The second envelope was pale-blue, smaller, and also handwritten.

> Dear Ansley,
>
> I write to say how being with you at my brother's bedside provided a great sense of comfort and satisfaction. To see the love the two of you have for one another is inspiring. Our parents find you enchanting, and it is obvious that my nephew adores you—nearly as much as does his father.
>
> You are, indeed, a valued addition to our family.
> Fondly,
> Anne

After reading Anne's note, Ansley laid it aside and hesitated a minute before reaching for Andy's communiqué. When opened, it displayed a white Persian kitten with blue eyes starring quizzically from the paper. The image evoked a smile.

He would remember how much I like cats.

Inside, the printed message read: "You are as intoxicating as catnip."

It was simply signed, "Andy."

She wanted to throw it away, but something held her back. Instead, she stowed it in the bottom drawer of her desk and then sank back on her sofa to savor the warm feeling of acceptance into Nick's family.

When Nick called that night, she read him the letter from his mother.

"So the lady of the manor has conveyed the Colebridge seal of approval on our impending nuptials. Well, we'll allow her to bask in the erroneous illusion that she has a say." He was steadily gaining strength, which brought with it the temperament of a caged animal.

"My, but you're in a testy mood tonight."

"Sorry, love. I'm ready to leave here—return to the real world, you, and my work. I am fine and may just walk out."

"Playing a doctor did not give you a license to practice medicine, Nick Colton. Be patient and wait for your physicians to give you a green light."

"Rather than argue about my judgment, or lack thereof, let's talk about what you're doing to close your practice."

"I'm working on it."

"Would you kindly define that for me?"

"I'm wrapping up cases as fast as I can. Don't forget, your divorce isn't final, yet."

"It will be soon, and you know it. Has your friend attempted to contact you?"

"By friend, I assume you're referring to Andy?"

"Andy. Yes."

"He has sent me a couple of cards—nothing inappropriate. He just signs his name."

She didn't mention the voice mail Andy left on her cell, saying that he missed her and hoped that she was well. Although she never responded, she had made no overt attempt to halt his pursuit.

"I should probably detest the fellow, but I actually feel sorry for him."

"You have no need for concern."

It was inevitable that Ansley would run into Andy in Jacksonville. His office was across from the courthouse, and his firm did forensic work for a number of attorneys. It happened ten days after her return from Texas as she left the building. Spotting him crossing the street, she wanted to retreat. However, she was trapped in a conversation with a client. Upon seeing her, Andy approached with a broad smile. She acknowledged him but turned her attention to the client. The woman recognized that Ansley and Andy knew one another and excused herself.

Reaching where Ansley stood, Andy hugged her briefly, stepped back, and said, "What a pleasant coincidence. Grant asked about you just this morning."

Taking a deep breath, she said, "I hope his family is well."

"They are. The girls want to know when we were going to get together again."

"That's sweet. Tell them I said hello." Ansley started to move away.

"I have to say, you look radiant this morning."

Ansley smiled. "Thank you." Her arms were loaded down with her purse and a hefty file. A gentle breeze had tousled her hair, which was starting to grow out. She wore a red-silk scarf that blew across her face, along with stray strands of her hair. Andy reached over and gently cleared both away. Within seconds, his blue eyes had locked with hers, and he seemed to penetrate her thoughts.

Those eyes—they're hypnotic. He is handsome.

Ansley froze. She neither wanted to create a scene nor have physical contact.

Why is my heart racing and part of me tingling? Think Nick. Think Nick.

"Maybe we could have lunch one day," he said. "I promise to be on my best behavior."

Don't even think about it, Ansley.

"I know you would be. But—"

"But, Mr. Mystery Man wouldn't approve." He nodded with a knowing expression on his face and then looked down at her left hand.

He's looking to see if there's a ring.

"Something like that," she said, and then added, "I've got to run—appointment at my office. Good to see you."

Walking to her car, she fought tears as her mind was swirling with images of Andy's blue eyes, the memory of his face when she told him about Nick, and the feel of his arms around her.

I can't have feelings for him. I love Nick. I made the right choice. Despite her attempts at conviction, anxiety plagued her.

When released from the hospital, Nick had first moved into a Houston hotel to recuperate. Within two weeks, he was in California, easing back into work. Fortunately, when he had collapsed on the set in Mexico, the majority of the film was done. They had continued production around his scenes, but a few remained unfinished.

"We were able to shoot a couple of soundstage scenes, but the rest will need to be done in Mexico and will involve a bit more physicality than I have at the moment," Nick said, in a telephone conversation to Ansley.

"So, is there a plan?"

"I'm going back to the manor to build up stamina before the producers attempt to reassemble the team needed to complete the film."

"Oh." Ansley was disappointed that he would return to England before she could see him.

"I want you to come to the UK. Can you work that out?"

"I'll do my best. You know I want to come."

On Friday that week, Ansley was in her office at six o' clock, working late on a complicated motion. Olivia was gone for the day, and the building was deserted. The two-story facility contained multiple executive suites with a central entrance that was supposed to be locked each day at five o'clock.

An uneasy feeling that she was not alone interrupted her focus. Looking up, her heart stopped, her hands went weak, and a cold chill streaked through her body. Standing in her doorway was a bedraggled man. He was tall, unshaven, and wore a cowboy hat, angled to one side of a head full of thick, scruffy hair. Dark glasses masked his face, and he wore a faded-black sweatshirt and tattered jeans.

Frozen with fear, she stared at the intruder, but he didn't move. Neither spoke.

Where's my cell? I've got to call 911.

Suddenly, Ansley shrieked, "What are you doing here?" and scrambled across the room, throwing her arms around him.

"Recognize me, do you?" he said as he kicked the door closed.

"You may look like a bum, but the homeless don't smell like Creed colo—"

His mouth covered hers before she could finish the sentence. When he pulled back, still holding her at the waist with one hand, he took off his glasses, looked around the room, and said, "So, this is where they keep you chained when you're away from me? Where's my photo?"

"This is the office that you helped me open three years ago, and you know darn well that I can't display your picture."

"You mean my money created the monster that holds you in captivity?"

"Stop it. You helped me open this office to give me flexibility so I could come running every time your fingers snapped."

"Apparently that didn't work out too well for me." He picked up a frame from her desk that held a picture of Skye and Shadow. "I'm relieved to see this isn't a photo of the other man."

She gave him a dirty look. "What are you doing here? Why didn't you tell me you were coming?"

"Answer number one: I'm here because this is where my woman is. Answer number two: Why would I have told you and missed the Kodak moment I enjoyed just now?"

"You are terrible. That was cruel, scaring me like that. Are you by yourself? Surely you're not alone."

"Ian is outside in the car, waiting to be certain that you are here. Since I'm going home with *you*, he'll get a room. How fast can you close up? I'm as randy as British law allows." Grabbing her again by her waist and squeezing, he said, "If I have to wait much longer, you might be arrested for sexual neglect of a Knight Commander of the Most Excellent Order of the British Empire."

"Commander of the what?" She frowned.

"You've been AWOL too long. You may now address me as Sir Nicholas."

"Ahh . . . impressive—working your way up to king?"

"Very funny. If you don't get ready to leave, I'm going to have my way with you on that desk."

"Your subtlety fails to become you, *Sir Nicholas*. Planning to leave a hundred dollar bill on the table?" she said, giving him a mischievous look. "And what does one call the wife of a sir?"

"My lady."

"Oh, my, gosh. That could be a deal breaker: Lady Colebridge. That's your mother, not me."

"You'll make it work. Now, get ready to go."

"You are so bossy." Her face bore a mock look of consternation.

"It's in my job description," he said, with a slight tip of his head and a wink.

"By what authority?"

"The authority bestowed upon me by way of being bigger and

stronger," he said, one eyebrow raised.

"Ahh, but I'm faster."

She no more than got the words out when he grabbed her. "But not fast enough." He then dipped her back and kissed her hard. Bringing her upright, he slapped her playfully on the derriere. "Now, let's go?"

"That hurt," she said, rubbing herself. "I think you were faking that hepatitis."

He laughed. "Believe me. I'm in a lot more pain than you."

As she cleared her computer screen and took out the thumb drive, the phone rang. Ansley glanced at the caller ID. "Blake and Blake" appeared on the small screen.

Nothing like cold water on a hot moment.

"Unless that's God, or the fire department, don't even think about answering."

She looked up at him, some of the merriment having faded from her face. "Not a chance."

In the parking lot, Ian was leaning against a black SUV, drinking a soda.

"Good to see you," Ansley said as they neared him.

"For me as well." Looking at Nick, he said, "I'll transfer your bag to Ansley's car."

"You're welcome to join us for dinner," she said.

Ian lifted the rear door of the Lexus but glanced at Nick before reaching for the luggage. Shifting his focus back to Ansley, grinning, he said, "Probably not a good idea. I think Nick's therapy requires privacy. But, thank you the same for the invitation."

"You've acquired a new car since I was here," Nick said as Ian loaded his bag into the trunk of Ansley's red Solara.

"The other one finally begged to be put out of its misery. The bank will let me have the title to this one in about three years."

Ian gave a goodbye flick of his hand and got into the SUV while Nick opened the driver's side door of the Toyota for Ansley.

Pulling out of the parking lot, Ansley said, "I still can't believe you're here."

"I'm here for the next two days and expect your undivided attention," he said, reaching over to squeeze her thigh.

At the first red light, she turned to him, smiling. "You look almost like normal—no more yellow eyes and skin, but I'm surprised that they let you on the plane in that outfit. Where did you get those clothes?"

"I'm close to one-hundred percent, which I plan to demonstrate shortly, and for your information, no one commented on my attire. However, there were a couple of looks as I boarded and took a seat in first class. As for my stylist, Ian went shopping for me in a Salvation Army store."

"That explains it."

When the light changed, she turned left and headed for the Interstate. "I've got to call Elaine. We were supposed to have lunch and see one of *your* movies tomorrow."

"If you like, you can tell her that I'm performing live at your flat— but it's a limited and *very* private run."

"I believe that your near-death experience has turned you into a comedian. Should Leno watch his back?"

CHAPTER FORTY-TWO

When they reached the condo, Ansley attempted to help him with his bag, but he refused. "Regardless of what you think, I'm no longer an invalid, love."

The door of the condo was barely closed when Nick grabbed her hand, pulling her back to him.

"Let me go change, and I'll be right back," she said, looking up, her eyes locked in his gaze.

"I'll help you with that," he said, scooping her up and heading for the bedroom.

"Nick, you shouldn't be lifting me."

"Will you shut up and relax? I'm fine, and I'm going to be even better shortly." His tone was barely above a whisper.

Putting her down next to the bed, he held her around the waist by one hand while the other began unfastening her blouse and unzipping her slacks. She yielded to his embrace, lifting her face to meet his, knowing that the wheels of passion were moving too fast for the brakes.

Two years dissolved away as he slid away her clothing, letting it fall to the floor, and then shedding his with the ease of a snake leaving a layer of skin behind. His hands were everywhere, exploring every inch of her body.

It was over quickly, courtesy of his extended period of abstinence.

"I'm sorry, love. I promise to do better next time," he whispered, gently brushing the hair out of her face.

"I'm not complaining."

They lay intertwined until both dozed. Waking after fifteen minutes, Ansley tried to ease out of the embrace and off the bed. Nick woke and held her back. "Where do you think you're going?"

"Promises to keep and miles to go," she whispered, putting her index finger across her lips.

"Hell, no. *Here* we shall stay until Monday morning."

"As utterly tempting as that idea may be, we're not John and Yoko, my love. You need nourishment; I need to make a call or two."

"Why did I have to fall in love with a practical woman?" he said, pulling her closer and kissing her briefly. "Do what must be done."

She gave him a mock salute and said, "Why don't I meet you in the shower after dinner?"

"Now that's a capital idea," he said, smiling and watched her as she left the bed and retrieved their clothing, placing his items across a nearby chair. "It will not offend me if you choose to remain unclothed."

"Yeah? Well, I'm not quite that brazen, even with you."

While she slipped on a knit top and pants and brushed her hair, Nick remained on the bed looking around the room.

"I'm relieved to see you at least display my photo in your boudoir."

"If you don't behave, I'll put it back in the drawer."

"Over my dead body, you will. I want that photo aimed at this bed at all times. I might put super cement on it."

She walked back to the side of the bed. "As if you had anything to worry about."

"Well, there is that other chap—Andy?"

"Yeah? Well, he never saw the inside of this room. I told you that he knows you are the only man in my picture."

She turned to walk away, and then changed her mind. "There is something you do need to know."

"Somehow, I don't like the sound of that."

"You don't have to worry, but you need to know that he still contacts me sometimes. He might even call."

"Really, now."

"Nick, he's a nice guy. You still talk to Penelope and Claudine. There's no possibility of me having a date with him, or anything like that, but I do talk to him. If I have to trust you with all the temptation that you're exposed to, you have to trust me as well."

"Relax, princess." He took her hand and pulled her down to a sitting position next to him. "I do trust you. Just be careful—for his sake. Out of a sense of guilt, you might give him false hope."

She nodded. "Not to change the subject, but I've been thinking. Since you're here, and not meaning to interfere with your planned orgy, I think you should meet my parents again—this time as Nick Colton. Do you mind?"

He smiled. "Excellent idea. I relish the idea of getting to know your family. And, there's something I need to discuss with your father."

"Be warned. My mother may go into an apoplectic fit. She vacillates between awe and fear where you're concerned."

"I'll be gentle."

They slept in the next morning. A night of trying to make up for two years left them exhausted, plus Nick's biological clock was still on PST.

It was nearly ten o'clock when Ansley slipped from bed, put on the gown that had logged no mileage and a robe. The coffee brewing brought Nick conscious.

"Continental or full English breakfast?" she asked as he staggered into the kitchen, wearing only his briefs. *That body should be against the law.*

Taking her by the waist, he pulled her close and kissed her forehead. "I'll spare you the morning kiss until after coffee and toothpaste."

She smiled and hugged him. "So which do you want?"

"I have a plan."

"And don't you always?"

"Watch the insolence. You're addressing royalty—remember?"

"You're not likely to let me forget," she said, holding her hands up in mock surrender. "What is your majesty's plan?"

"I'm thinking coffee here and breakfast out—then a trip to the bank where you say the ring is currently housed."

After breakfast at the Wild Flower Café, Ansley drove Nick to the bank where she took the small, satin pouch from her safe deposit box.

"Here it is."

"So I see," he said, taking it from her. "I'll keep it if you don't mind."

She looked at him with a bewildered look. *What is he doing?*

"Wipe that wounded-puppy look off of your face. I'm not going to keep the ring. I just want to hold onto it for a short while." He tucked the pouch in the breast pocket of his shirt. "Let's go meet the parents!"

What is he up to?

"O . . . kay. Let me give them a call. Mom's heart couldn't take having you just show up at her door."

Nick reached for her hand and took the phone. "No. If you call, and your mum is anything like her daughter, which, I suspect that she is, she'll kill herself between now and our arrival trying unnecessarily to make the house perfect."

Walking up to the Sheridan's front door, Ansley said, "Mom is not going to be happy that we're surprising her."

"Do you call every time you drop by?"

"No, but that's different. I'm family."

"Like it or not, so am I."

She smiled, shaking her head, and said, "Not to my mother."

Laura opened the door, dressed in jeans, old sneakers, and one of Michael's discarded dress shirts, all smudged with green paint. Her face registered immediate shock when she saw that Nick was with Ansley.

"Oh, my . . . . You're—"

"Nick, Mrs. Sheridan, and forgive me for not being honest when I was here before."

Laura stared at him for several seconds and then turned to Ansley. "Why didn't you call?"

"He," she pointed at Nick, "didn't want you to go to a lot of trouble getting ready for us. Can we come in?"

Laura nodded, opening the door wider to allow them entry. "The house is a mess. I am painting the guest room green."

"I can tell," Ansley said, smiling and looking her mother up and down.

"Do not apologize. Ansley's right, it was my idea to not call because I don't want you treating me as a stranger."

"Your accent . . . . You didn't have an accent when you were here last time."

Nick laughed. "Blame that on your daughter."

"Where's Dad?"

"He's watching TV in the bedroom."

"I'll get—"

"I thought I heard someone," Michael said, coming down the hall that led to the bedroom wing of the house. "Nick, it's nice to see you again." Michael extended a hand and they shook.

"The pleasure is far more mine than yours."

"Come on in the den where we can be comfortable," Michael said. "I hear you were pretty sick recently."

"It had its bright side," Nick said, winking at Ansley.

"Glad you're well and looking fit now."

Laura stood in place, watching Nick. Her expression indicated that she was self-conscious and not yet at ease with having a celebrity in her home.

"Laura, can we get these kids something to drink?"

"Of course. I'm sorry, Nick. That was rude of me not to ask."

"I don't want to put you to any trouble."

"Mom, I'd love a cup of tea, and I'm sure Nick would too," she said, looking at Nick.

He nodded.

"I'll help you. It'll give Dad a chance to get to know the real Nick."

As Michael led Nick to the den, he asked, "How are you feeling now? I understand you had quite an ordeal in Mexico."

"I've recovered. Just need to build a little stamina."

When they were settled in the two leather, wing-backed chairs, Nick reached into his pocket and took out the pouch. "Mr. Sheridan—"

"Call me Mike, son."

Nodding, Nick smiled. "Mike, first, I want to apologize to you for the secrecy that has surrounded my relationship with your daughter. I assure you, it was intended for her benefit. I would have liked to have been honest with you and her mother when I was here before, but Ansley was paranoid about anyone finding out that we were dating. There are negative sides to my profession."

"You don't have to apologize, Nick. I watch TV and read the papers. I know that the press hounds fellows like you. I appreciate your keeping Ansley out of that circus."

Nick opened the drawstring bag and took out the ring. "I bought this ring for your daughter over three years ago. She's never worn it on her left hand. I want to put it there, and I'd like your formal permission to marry her, even though I certainly don't deserve her."

"No mortal man does, son. I respect your asking. I don't really know you, but if my daughter is in love with you, that's good enough for me." He glanced over at a photograph of Ansley, taken when she was about twelve. It was a recital picture, and she wearing a tutu and pointe shoes. "However, her mother might be a tougher safe to crack."

"I sensed that."

"The thing you need to understand is that Laura and I stood by, helpless, when our Ansley's heart was broken by that bastard she married. We never want to see her hurt like that again." Michael leaned forward, took the ring, and looked at it. "I imagine that my permission is only a courtesy, considering you're both mature adults, but I would ask you, man to man, to be careful with her heart. But if you need my permission, the answer would have to be, 'of course.'" He handed the ring back to Nick. "Put it on the proper finger."

Nick beamed. "Thank you. I recognize that words are cheap. However, you need to believe that I am deeply in love with your daughter. I made the mistake of letting her get away once and learned the hard way that were no substitutes. You have my word that I will never betray her and will do my best to give her the life *she* deserves.

At Michael's insistence, Nick and Ansley had dinner that night on his membership at the Ponte Vedra Inn. After dinner, they went for a walk on the beach.

"Your dad and I had a lovely chat this afternoon."

"Daddy likes you; I can tell."

"I hope Laura likes me as well."

"She does, but I think you still make her nervous on two levels."

"Two?"

"She's in awe of your celebrity, and she's terrified that you will hurt me. It's the mother thing."

Nick stopped and turned to face Ansley. The moonlight lit her face like a spotlight. He reached in the pocket of his slacks and drew out the bag. Taking her left hand in his, he said, "Ansley Collier Sheridan, it's time that you accept my proposal of marriage and my promise to love you forever. Will you say that you will marry me and allow me to place this ring on your left hand?"

Tears began to run down her face. She put her right hand over his and with her head bobbing up and down, said, "I will. I will. Yes."

They embraced, kissing, oblivious to everything but one another.

CHAPTER FORTY-THREE

Sunday was a lazy day with the shadow of Nick's impending departure casting a trace of gloom over both of them. Having a quiet day in the condo seemed to be a good choice and he had not objected. Although Nick had tried to hide it, several times during the weekend, Ansley knew that his stamina was compromised. He had taken a nap after returning from her parents' house.

"I'm going to miss you," she said.

"You had better," he said, looking over the newspaper.

Changing the subject to avoid tainting the day, she said, "What's Ian been doing all weekend? I feel sorry for him in a strange town, alone, and not knowing anyone."

"Don't feel too sorry for him. Ian knows how to find the craic wherever he is. I'm sure that he's been none the worse for wear the past couple of nights."

"And what would that mean, if I may be so bold to ask?"

"He likes his pint or two when he's off Nick duty. As a matter of fact, he told me that he found a great local place to hang out and asked if we would join him there tonight."

"What did you tell him?"

Nick reached for his mug of coffee and said, "That I wasn't sure I wanted to share you."

"Let's do it. I like Ian. He's been great for us over the years."

When they went to meet Ian that evening, Nick drove Ansley's car with the GPS set for their destination.

"Did Ian give you the name of the Pub?"

"As I recall, he said it was called Culhane's. As I told you, he said the food is the best he's had in the States. An Irishman will always find a good pub."

Oh, my, gosh. Why didn't I ask earlier? Culhane's Irish Pub is at Atlantic Beach—Andy's neighborhood.

The blood ran cold in Ansley's veins.

Should I say something? No. Stop worrying. What are the chances that Andy will be there, especially on a Sunday night?

Ian was there when they arrived, seated in a booth at the back of the restaurant, intentionally chosen to give Nick the least amount of public exposure. He stood as they approached the table.

Glancing around the room, she couldn't help but look for a sign of Andy before giving Ian a friendly hug. "I hope Jacksonville has been kind to you this weekend," she said.

"'Has been the good experience with a share of what we Irish call the craic," he responded, a twinkle in his eye. "The same for the two of you, I'd be hoping?"

Ansley smiled and nodded.

"Other than the Guinness, what do you recommend, since any craic for me does not include alcohol?" Nick said, picking up the menu left by the hostess.

"I do not think that you would go wrong with anything on the list, but I can personally vouch for the Guinness beef stew, the fish and chips, and the shepherd's pie." The light reflecting off Ansley's ring caught his attention. "I see that the two of you have made it official—there's to be a wedding"

"There's to be a wedding," Nick said, with Ansley smiling.

"About time, I'd say."

"I agree." Turning his attention to Ansley, he said, "I think I'll go with the stew. How about you, love?"

"Sounds good."

"You won't be disappointed with that. The cook does it right here," Ian added.

While they were waiting for their food, Ian finished his beer—Ansley and Nick each had a cup of tea. Ian had just asked for a refill when Ansley flinched, almost spilling her tea.

I don't believe this. The color drained from her face as Andy Blake walked into the pub.

Sitting in the center of the booth, she was in his line of sight. He looked around as though searching for someone.

Nick sat to Ansley's left with only his profile partially visible. With his facial hair and a pair of fake glasses, Nick's identity was not obvious. Ansley wanted to duck behind him.

266

Maybe he won't see me. If the does, surely he would be discreet enough to avoid us.

Reaching under the table, she tapped Nick's leg to interrupt a conversation between him and Ian, who sat across from him. "Nick. Don't turn around, but Andy just walked in."

Nick turned his face toward her, eyebrows raised. "*Your* Andy?"

"He's not my Andy anymore. . . . Darn it. He's coming this way."

Addressing Ian, Nick said, "Her former inamorato." Turning toward Ansley, he asked, "How would you like me to introduce myself?"

"I don't care what name you use, just don't use Nicholas Colton or expose your British accent."

Reaching their table, Andy had a broad smile, his eyes focused on her, seeming oblivious as to the two men. "Ansley, how radiant you are. Aren't you a long way from home?"

"Hi, Andy! You never mentioned you liked Irish food." *He knows I'm lying.*

"You must have forgotten. I told you that I liked this pub when I learned that you were Irish-American. But, truth be told, tonight, I was out to pick up a burger and saw your red Solara. Curiosity got the better of me, and I thought I'd pop in here for a bite."

Damn me for getting a red car.

Noticing the two men, Andy's gaze settled on Nick, who rose halfway and extended a hand.

"Tony Colebridge, here." No trace of accent was in his speech. Gesturing toward Ian, Nick said, "And this is Ian Shaughnessy. I'm his driver."

Ian nodded, his eyes registering a slight look of surprise.

Although choking on Nick's unexpected fabrication, Ansley kept her expression steady. "Tony, Ian, this is Andrew Blake."

Looking down at Ansley's hand, Andy said, "Engaged? That's a new status, isn't it?"

"Officially, it's very new," she said.

"Impressive ring! I assume that one of you is the lucky man."

"It's Ian," Ansley said.

Turning his head away from Andy, Nick looked at her with a mischievous expression. Ian's eyes grew larger, but he said nothing.

"Congratulations, Ian. You've snagged a very special lady. Well, folks, enjoy your dinner. Good to see you, Ansley, and nice meeting you both," he said, nodding toward each man. With that, he turned and walked toward the exit.

"That was awkward," Ian said, when Andy was out of earshot.

"Good way to throw cold water on the evening," Ansley said, frowning.

Nick was silent.

"I'm flattered by the elevation of me status," Ian said, fiddling with his empty glass, "but I wonder how it is that the lad didn't question why she be sitting the closer to you, Nick."

CHAPTER FORTY-FOUR

Monday morning came too soon. Ansley's radio came on at five a.m., reminding her that Nick's departure was imminent. She eased out of bed to go to the bathroom, allowing him to sleep a few more minutes. Returning, she found him propped up on his pillow, wide-awake.

"Come here," he said, patting the bed.

"We've got to get ready to go. You told Ian to meet us at my office at six-thirty."

"Hush," he said as he pulled her onto the sheets, rolled over her, and pinned her in place. "He will wait." His mouth tasted of mint as it covered hers, his manliness on full alert.

The only sounds following were those of intense passion.

Lying in the wake, Ansley's hands tingled as every nerve ending throbbed—her body depleted.

"When can I expect you in Cheltenham?" Nick whispered.

The tears she swore not to let happen glistened in the early morning sunlight streaming through her bedroom window.

"Soon, I promise, soon."

Turning his body back toward Ansley, he gathered her in his arms, wrapping a leg over hers. "I'll try to be patient, love, but be prepared for me to ask everyday what progress you've made toward closing your practice."

Forty-five minutes later, they were driving to her office. Although Nick was taking a private plane to New York, he had to be at Kennedy to board a commercial flight to London by eleven a.m. Ansley had wanted to drive him to the airport, but he insisted that they part in the privacy of her office.

They arrived early and went inside to wait. In the silence of the empty building, neither spoke as they sat together on the love seat in the reception area, Nick's arm around her shoulder.

Ian arrived promptly at six-thirty.

"Stay here. I want our parting to be between only the two of us," he said, holding her close, kissing her, and then quickly picking up his bag and exiting the building.

Tears flowing, she stood at the window and watched as Ian met him, took the luggage, and stowed it the SUV. Nick did not look back as he got into the vehicle.

When they were out of sight, Ansley went to the restroom, patted cold water on her face, and walked down the hall, into her office. She turned on her stereo and plunged into the stack of work abandoned only three days before. As she moved papers, she realized the ring was still on her finger and removed it. Staring at it for a second, she put it in an envelope, folded the paper into a small size, and put it in a zippered compartment of her purse.

CHAPTER FORTY-FIVE

Three weeks passed and Ansley was little closer to wrapping up the practice. She had not told any of her professional associates about her intentions. However, she avoided taking new clients. While she was confident that she could work her way out of her current caseload, she worried about Olivia. They had grown close, working one-on-one. Olivia had left her job with the law firm, where they had both been employed, to follow Ansley. In recent days, Olivia had begun asking questions that gave Ansley cause to believe the secretary was suspecting something was amiss.

"How much closer are you today?" Nick asked as, true to his promise, he did every night.

"It's coming."

"Didn't ask if it was coming, my love. I asked how much closer."

"You sound like a zealous lawyer on cross examination. I didn't take a client who called today."

"I admire that decision, but you've got to get rid of the ones you have."

"Okay, okay. You've made your point."

"When are you coming over here? Martha is about to burst, wanting to tell everyone that we're to be married."

"Have you told anyone in your family that it's official?"

"I told you that I want Kevin to know it is official before the others, and I want you and me to tell him together. . . . So, when are you coming?"

"Next weekend is out. I've got a contested hearing early on the Monday after. I'm pretty sure I can get away the following weekend."

"Pretty sure? You make sure, or I'm going to think that you're dodging again. Do I have to come over and get you?"

"I'm not dodging. Nick, I told you that I'm going to come. I want to come when I can stay more than two days. You promised to be patient."

"I'm a man. We lie—and celibacy isn't working for me."

"Very funny. But if you'll calm down, I'll give you my word that I'll come within two weeks."

"And you'll come permanently, when?"

"By the first of the year. You know that I want to spend one last Christmas with my parents."

Ten days later, Ansley was working furiously to get the office in order before leaving for the U.K. on Friday.

"I can't believe that you're going to England for a week. I wish I could go," Olivia said. "I'm sorry that things didn't work out for you and Andy, but maybe you'll meet some sexy guy with a great English accent while you're over there."

Ansley grinned. "If I do, I might stay."

"Who is it that you're going with?"

"An old friend from my days in New York—Nicky."

"Do you want me to stay and help you finish up tonight?"

"No, no. It's five o'clock, and you need to get home to your kids. I'll be fine. I just want to make sure that I have all my dictation done tonight so that you can get it typed up before I leave, Friday."

After Olivia left, Ansley immersed herself in work. At eight, her cell phone rang.

"Where are you? I called your house."

"What time is it?"

"It's three o'clock here, so I guess it's eight over there."

"Nick, what are you doing up at three a.m.?"

"Trying to speak with my financee."

"Nick, I'm working late, trying to get everything ready to come. I guess time got away from me."

"Then, I'm not going to keep you on the phone. Get it done and get out of there. Is your door locked?"

"Yes, Nick. My door's locked. Funny, I can fly, alone, all over the world to meet you, but you're worried about thirty miles from my office to home."

"Just humor me. Go home! I love you. Talk to you tomorrow night, and you'd better be in the flat at a decent time."

"Love you, too."

After hanging up, Ansley worked another hour and then packed up for the hearing she had early the next morning.

Leaving the building, the parking lot was isolated. She didn't like walking to her car after eight o'clock, but had done it many times. With her briefcase on wheels in tow, she had her purse over her shoulder and keys out. Reaching her car, she popped the trunk open and lifted the heavy case. She was about to put it in when she felt the jab of a hard object in her ribs.

Her heart felt like it stopped. Her hands went weak, and the case fell into the vehicle with a thud.

Oh, God!

Shock and fear glued Ansley in place as she waited for what would come next.

Stay calm. Think before you do or say anything. Please, God, help me.

"Close the fucking truck and walk back in the building," the raspy voice said. "And don't think about making a sound, or I'll blow your fucking head off, bitch."

Where did he come from?

"Move," the hostile voice said.

It's not a robbery—too much anger in his voice. Stay calm—lose control and you're dead.

"I said, move!" His tone was escalating, the object still pressing against her body.

It's a gun. I know it's a gun. He said he'd blow my head off. Think. . . . Think!

Ansley closed the trunk and turned slightly toward the building.

I could push the panic button on my remote—no, I'd be dead before anyone could respond.

Her knees felt like Jell-O as she took the first step toward the building.

Is this random, or someone I've angered in a case? Is he crazy?

As she started to walk, the man gave her a shove. She shivered and stumbled, catching herself before completely losing balance.

He touched me! Oh, my, God. Calm down. Don't make a wrong move.

She could hear his heavy breathing.

I could scream but no one would hear.

From the corner of her eye, she saw the automobile at the back corner of the parking lot that she had not noticed when leaving the building.

Why didn't I look around? How could I be so stupid? My mind was on going to England—the hearing tomorrow. Am I going to die without seeing Nick again—telling him?

They reached the door and the gun pressed, once again, against her back.

"Open it."

I could say I don't remember the code. No. That would make him madder.

Struggling to keep her hand steady, determined not to show her assailant how terrified she was, she punched in the entry code. The click of the lock releasing echoed in her ears.

"Open it," the stranger commanded.

I know that voice.

Once they were inside, she knew that if she turned, she could see him in the light of the hallways, but decided not to take a chance on exacerbating his hostility.

"Where is *your* office?"

Not trusting her voice, she raised her hand and pointed to the hallway on the left.

"Move."

When they reached the end of the corridor, a plaque on the wall read, "Ansley C. Sheridan, Attorney at Law." He reached around her to open the door and discovered that it was locked.

"The damned door's locked."

What did you expect, you bastard?

He was so close that she could smell the repugnant odor of stale sweat, sour clothing, and smoker's breath. She almost gagged. Without speaking, Ansley took the keys, still in her hand, and unlocked the door. Her handbag remained over her shoulder.

If I could just get to my phone.

Her cell phone was in an outside pocket of her purse.

The office was dark, but Ansley waited for him to tell her to turn on the lights, fearful that any wrong move would cause him to pull the trigger.

"Turn on the lights."

She obeyed and stood motionless.

"Get it."

What does he want?

She turned, instantly recognizing him. Oh, God! It's Jack Langston, Fran's husband.

I am dealing with a violent psycho.

"Get what?"

"You know what I want, bitch."

She took a deep breath and said, "If you will tell me what you want, I'll get it. I can't read your mind."

"Her address, damn it! Her fucking address. You have it. I know you do, bitch. You let her take my kids. You and all your fucking questions in front of that fucking judge." He began making motions in the air, wiggling his shoulders, twisting his head, and speaking in a mocking voice. "'Have you been treated for any mental or emotional condition, Mr. Langston?' and 'Isn't it true, Mr. Langston, that you struck your wife?' Sure it was true. The fucking bitch had it coming, just like you. GET ME THE FUCKING ADDRESS!"

Think Ansley. You have to stay calm and think. If I could just get to my phone.

She was now facing him. Their eyes were in direct contact.

Olivia was right. He has a crazed look in his eyes. He won't respond to reason.

"Hurry up." The hand holding the gun began shaking. "You want me to kill you right now?"

He plans to kill me regardless of what I do.

"I'll have to pull Fran's file." She held her voice steady—monotone. She motioned toward a side room.

"Keep your hands where I can see them."

Olivia, I pray that you purged Fran's file from the active cabinet.

"If you kill me," she said in a monotone, "you'll have a hell of a time finding what you want."

Hostility flared from his eyes, but he did not respond.

Opening the drawer labeled "J-M," Ansley flipped through the files. Langston wasn't there.

Thank you, God.

"It's not here," she said, turning to the man and then pointing. "See."

"Where is it?" he demanded.

"My secretary may have put it somewhere else. If you'll let me, I'll call her. Here, my cell phone is in my purse."

"Don't pull any funny stuff," he said. "I've got my eyes on you."

"Watch. I'm unzipping the compartment and taking out the phone."

Give me strength, Oh, Lord. Please give me strength. Don't let him realize what I'm doing.

CHAPTER FORTY-SIX

Holding her breath as she grasped the phone, Ansley hit the speed dial for Elaine. Holding it close to her ear, she said, "I'm not getting service. I'll have to use the landline." She tried to scrutinize his expression to see if he suspected that she had not done what she said. He appeared clueless.

Casually holding the phone face down, she walked out of the file area, Langston still behind her brandishing his weapon. She went to the instrument on her desk. Picking up the receiver, she pretended to be looking at the number on her cell and hoped that he could not see that the prior call had engaged. Speaking in a slightly louder tone, she said, "I'll call Fran if I can't reach Olivia and ask her to tell me her address."

"You'd better not let on that I'm here."

"I won't."

"I'm calling Olivia first."

Picking up the receiver, Ansley dialed. After a relevant interval, she said, "Olivia, I need Fran Langston's file, and I can't find it. Do you know where it is?"

She made herself maintain eye contact with Langston. The cell phone lay on the desk, face down.

Nodding, as if she was conversing, Ansley said, "I looked there. Please help me."

"Hang up," Langston ordered.

Ansley put the phone down.

"Why did you make me hang up? She was trying to think where the file is."

"I don't trust you. Call Fran. Make her give you her address and don't let her know why."

Ansley picked up the phone and dialed again. When the person on the other end of the line answered, she said, "Fran, this is Ansley

Sheridan. I know it's late to be calling, but I'm in my office and need your address. You know it's unlisted to make sure your husband doesn't find you."

Taking a pen from the top of her desk, Ansley wrote down an address and held it up for the man. As he grabbed it out of her hand, a flicker of light came through the window.

Langston saw it too. "What the fuck did you do?" he screamed at her, grabbing the phone, slamming it down, and waving the pistol at her face.

"Nothing. You saw me. I did what you said."

Did someone get the message? Please, God. Let there be someone out there to help me.

Langston grabbed her by the arm, threw her onto a chair, and began pacing. "I should kill you right now. You filthy whore. You ruined my life—took my kids."

Ansley watched him, afraid to speak. *I've got to trust my prayers. The police are here. I'm going to get out of this.*

The phone on her desk rang, causing both of them to jump. "Don't answer that," Langston commanded.

It continued to ring. Langston was becoming more and more agitated. "Answer it," he said, completely reversing his position.

Ansley eased up and walked to her desk.

"Hello," she said, meekly.

"Am I speaking with Ansley Sheridan?" the stranger said.

"Yes." She kept her eyes on Langston, terrified as to what he would do next.

"Are you being held hostage?"

"Yes."

"Hang up," Langston shouted.

Ansley did as she was told.

"What did you do?"

"Nothing. You saw me."

"Call Fran. Get her over here."

The phone rang again. Ansley didn't move her body, her eyes following Langston.

"Answer it," he commanded.

"You want me to answer?"

"That's what I said, damn it, bitch. Answer the fucking phone."

She moved slowly back to the desk and picked up the receiver, but didn't say anything for fear of saying the wrong thing.

"Ms. Sheridan, this is Sergeant Carlyle of the Jacksonville Sheriff's Office. Does your captor have a weapon?"

"Yes." She tried to keep her voice calm to keep Langston from suspecting the question she was answering."

"A gun?"

"Yes."

"Is there more than one assailant?"

"No. I am working on that file right now."

"Stay calm and do as he says. Don't make any sudden moves. Can you get him on the phone?"

Before Ansley could answer, Langston grabbed the phone.

"If this is the cops, get my wife down here if you want this bitch to live."

Ansley's heart was racing, but she managed to hold herself together.

Langston's eyes grew wilder as he talked to the Sergeant. "There's no negotiating here," he said, hysterically. "Bring Fran and my kids here, and I'll trade you this bitch. I want my family, one-hundred thousand dollars, and a flight to Cuba, otherwise, this is a dead lawyer." He slammed the phone down.

"Now, we'll see how much they care about you," he said, sneering at Ansley.

Neither Langston, nor Ansley, moved. She silently prayed to survive.

The phone rang again. Ansley jumped.

"Don't answer it," Langston shouted.

"I wasn't going to," she responded.

It continued to ring, repeatedly going to her voice mail after four rings, and then it would ring again. Langston was becoming more and more agitated. Ansley feared he would snap and start shooting. When he appeared about to break, he shouted, "Answer the fucking thing."

Ansley eased back to the desk and picked up the receiver.

Before she could speak, from outside, the sound of loud music began playing. *Where is that coming from?*

Echoing Ansley's thoughts, Langston said, "Where in the hell is that music coming from?" He looked at Ansley as if she had the answer. She shrugged her shoulders and raised her eyebrows in a bewildered expression.

Swallowing hard, she said, "Hello."

"Ms. Sheridan."

"Yes."

"Are you in front of the door to your office?"

"No."

"Is your captor?"

Ansley took a deep breath. "Yes."

"When I say *now*, fall down on the floor. Can you do that?"

"Yes. Mr. Langston says that he will release me if you bring his wife down so that he can talk to her."

"Ms. Sheridan, did you understand me?"

"Yes. Absolutely."

"Talk to me as though you're describing his wife."

"Yes. Her name is Frances Seymour Langston." She fought to keep the quiver from her voice. "She lives in Arlington." Ansley paused, stalling for time. "She's a nurse and works—"

"Now!"

Hardly aware of what she was doing, Ansley dropped the phone, covered her face, and folded her knees, collapsing to the floor. Simultaneously, three SWAT team members stormed the room, shooting. Langston never fired.

The shooting stopped, but Ansley didn't move. She heard voices, but stayed crouched behind the desk, unable to look at the results of what she had heard. Then a strong hand was on her shoulder. She flinched, took her hands away from her face, and looked up at a red-haired officer of about thirty, clothed in SWAT gear and still holding his weapon. He reached under her armpit to help her up, saying, "Do *not* look. Just let me lead you out. You're okay. It's over." The music had stopped.

Adrenalin kept her steady until she was out of the building. Elaine was standing with Greg beside a police car and rushed toward her. The two women embraced. It was then that Ansley collapsed, shaking in a state of near convulsion, tears flooding her face.

"He was going to kill me."

Elaine hugged her tight and whispered, "I know, sweetie. We were terrified."

"You heard me?"

"I heard you and so did the 911 operator."

"You understood?" Ansley asked, her voice still trembling and her eyes looking like a rabbit coming face to face with a fox.

"I wasn't sure what was going on, but I knew something was terribly wrong."

"When I called you, I pretended that the call didn't go through. Then I dialed 911 and kept dialing so that he would think that I was calling Olivia and Fran. He kept waving his gun at me." Between sentences, she choked but appeared desperate to tell the story, unaware that a detective stood near, taking notes as she spoke.

"I didn't know whether I would reach a dispatcher because I had to dial four more numbers to keep him from suspecting." Looking back at the building, she said, "Is he dead?"

An EMT came up before anyone could answer. "Ms. Sheridan, come with me. Let us check you out."

"I'm okay. Is he dead?"

"I believe he is. Two medics are in there, but the officers shot to kill—they couldn't take a chance with your life."

"He's dead, Ms. Sheridan," the detective interjected.

"Let's get you over there where you can sit down," the EMT said, pointing to the ambulance. "We need to check you, Ms. Sheridan."

Ansley nodded and asked, "Where's Detective Carlyle?"

"He's debriefing the team," the detective taking notes said.

Elaine and the EMT walked her to the ambulance where she sat while her vital signs were recorded.

"I'm not shot. I'm okay."

Another detective joined the group clustered around Ansley.

"We need to take your full statement, Ms. Sheridan. I'm Detective Frank Luther with the Jacksonville Sheriff's Office."

"Can't this wait, Detective? Don't you see that she's in no condition to talk right now?" Elaine said.

"We need to transport her to the ER," the emergency technician said.

"I don't want to do either. I just want to go home. Why was that loud music playing?"

"It was to provide a distraction," Luther said.

"I think you ought to let them take you to the hospital, sweetie. You've been through a lot," Elaine said. "Do you want me to call your parents?"

"No, they're out of town, thank goodness. This will scare them to death."

"Ms. Sheridan, your friend is right. You need to let them check you out at the hospital. If you can just answer a few questions, we can wait until tomorrow to go over all the details," the first detective said.

"Can someone get my purse and cell phone? I can't go back in there."

"Of course, you can't," Elaine said.

"I can't ever go back in there."

CHAPTER FORTY-SEVEN

Elaine and Greg followed the ambulance to the hospital and took Ansley home when she was released. She sat in the back seat of the Davis vehicle and did not speak during the entire ride. When they arrived at the condo, Greg saw the women safely in and returned home alone. Elaine insisted on staying, over Ansley's protests that she was fine. The emergency room physician had stressed that Ansley was still in shock and should not be alone.

As the two women entered the condo, Skye and Shadow were waiting at the door. Ansley picked up Skye, who was closest, and hugged the ball of fur. Turning to Elaine, she said, "Thank you so much for everything you did tonight."

"Don't give it a thought. I'm just thankful I got the call and had enough sense to know that you were in trouble. Do you want me to stay in your room with you?"

"I don't mean to be ungrateful, but I think I would like to be alone to try to make some sense out of all this."

"I understand. I'll sleep in your guestroom. Call me if you need anything."

She felt her way to the bathroom, without turning on a bedroom light. She stripped off her clothes and purposely stuffed them into the trash basket instead of the clothes hamper. After taking a hot shower, she put on a gown that was hanging on the back of the door and went to bed in the dark. It was as if she thought darkness could blot out the horror.

Elaine went right to sleep and woke at six the next morning. Worried about Ansley, she went to the bedroom door and eased it open. Ansley was on her side, facing the opposite way. Elaine tiptoed around the bed to confirm that her friend was asleep.

Light, filtering through the curtains, dimly lit the room, but the photograph on the bedside table was obvious. Elaine looked at it and was immediately surprised to see an 11 x 14 image of a man. She could see a signature, but couldn't read the handwriting. Even without her glasses, the face was vaguely familiar. It was definitely not Andy Blake, whom Elaine had met when she and Greg had dinner with the couple one night. Curiosity got the best of her, and she eased the photograph off the table and took it to the living room.

Once in the light and with her glasses on, Elaine was astonished to see that it was a photograph of Nicholas Colton.

"We both have crushes on him, but an 11x14 photo by the bed is a little extreme," she whispered to herself.

Reading the inscription, Elaine gasped. "Oh . . . my . . . God."

My dearest love,
    May my love and devotion free you of the shadow of doubt haunting you.

Forever yours,
Nick.

Elaine was in shock and flinched as Skye jumped up on the sofa next to her. She rubbed his back without taking her eyes off the image. "This can't be the movie star—can it? How could Ansley know him? She would have told me if she did." Thinking for a minute, her expression changed. "I bet she bought it on eBay. It's not addressed to her."

She stared at the photo for several minutes more and then returned it to Ansley's bedroom. Back in the living room with a cup of coffee, she noticed a small photograph of a couple on Ansley's bookcase. Walking over for a better view, she saw that it was Nick and Ansley with two horses. Her hand trembled as she picked it up, causing a few drops of the hot beverage to mar the glass.

At seven-fifteen, Ansley came out of her room, her hair disheveled—eyes swollen. Elaine was watching *The Today Show*.

Turning the TV off, Elaine said, "Are you okay?"

"No. But, I'm going to be."

Ansley immediately spotted the photo next to her friend.

"I guess you discovered my secret life."

Elaine looked at the picture and up at Ansley. "I don't even know what to say. Is this for real?"

Ansley smiled. "For real."

"You know him?"

"I do."

"How long?" Elaine's brown eyes grew larger.

"Off and on for about five years."

"Are you serious?" The pitch in Elaine's voice rose an octave. "You've known him for five years and *never* told me?"

Ansley nodded.

"You sat next to me with my mouth hanging open, drooling over that hunk, at how many movies—and you *knew* him?"

"Was sleeping with him to put a fine point on it." Ansley wrinkled her nose and shrugged her shoulders.

"Oh my God. I don't have a word strong enough to describe how flabbergasted I am."

"You've met him."

"Like hell, I've met him. You don't think I would have noticed meeting Nicholas Colton."

"It was Christmas time about three years ago. You came to the condo, and Nick came out. He introduced himself as Tony Colebridge."

"What?" Elaine almost screamed. "That was Nicholas Colton?"

"One and the same. His real name is Nicholas Anthony Colebridge. We just used the Tony Colebridge part."

"Why in the name of everything sacred would you keep this a secret—and from your best friend?"

"Can I have a cup of tea and I'll try to explain."

Before the women finished having a bagel and tea, the phone rang.

"Do you mind? I can't talk right now," Ansley said.

"Got it," Elaine said, jumping up from the sofa.

No sooner than she said, hello, Elaine's expression went dramatic. "This is Elaine Davis her best friend. She's right here."

Ansley shook her head and raised a hand in defense as Elaine started toward her.

Extending the phone, Elaine mouthed, "It's *him*," pointing toward the photo.

Ansley's face brightened, a smile flashing across her face as she took the instrument.

"What's going on, love?" he asked. "I couldn't help but be surprised at your friend answering."

"It's a long story." Her exuberance melted into emotion as tears welled in her eyes. She started to tremble. "Something happened last night after you called, but I can't talk about it right now. I'm okay."

"Something told me to call. You can't leave me hanging like this. What happened? I don't like the sound of it."

Ansley bowed her head and covered her face with her free hand. Elaine watched. A few seconds of silence passed, and then Nick spoke again.

"Ansley, sweetheart, put your friend on the phone."

Without saying a word, Ansley handed the phone to Elaine and left the room.

"This is Elaine."

"What has happened?" Nick asked, urgency in his voice.

"She is okay, at least physically, Mr. Colton, but she had a horrible experience. I think you need to come here if you can."

"I'm on my way, but please tell me *something*."

"Ansley was accosted in the parking lot of her office as she was leaving last night. A crazy man held her captive at gunpoint. He was the deranged ex of one of her clients. The SWAT team broke in and killed him."

"My, God. Will you stay there with her until I arrive?"

"Of course."

"Please let me talk to her again."

Elaine took the cordless phone to the bedroom where Ansley sat balled up in a chair, her face soaked with tears.

"He's coming. He wants to speak to you."

Ansley accepted the phone and took a deep breath. "Nick."

"Don't talk, my love. I want you to know that I'll be there tonight. I am so sorry for what you must have gone through. I love you more than my life."

"I love you, too." She clicked the button and handed Elaine the phone. "I'm going to stay here and try to calm down, if you don't mind."

"Whatever you need," Elaine said. "Is there *anything* I can bring you?"

Ansley shook her head, closed her eyes, and put her face between her knees. Both cats were on her bed, watching as if they were aware that something was wrong.

The morning TV news had carried the hostage story, as had the local newspaper. Elaine shielded Ansley from both. The phone began ringing a little after eight a.m. with the concerns of friends and associates. Olivia was first to call. She told Elaine to assure Ansley that she would clear her calendar and take care of whatever was necessary with the practice as soon as she could have access to the office.

"We better let your parents know something before they hear a news report," Elaine said at eight-thirty when Ansley came out of her room for another cup of tea.

"I know. I've been thinking about that. I'll make the call and tell them that I'm okay. Can you tell them the story? I just can't go over it. I know I need to get myself together, but I'm not there, yet."

"Maybe you should take one of those pills the doctor gave you."

"No. I'd rather not. I can't take pills to cope with life. I'll get a grip on this."

The Sheridans were naturally upset upon hearing the account and wanted to immediately return home from Virginia. Ansley took the phone when she heard Elaine trying to discourage them.

"Please don't come, Mom. There's nothing you can do. It's over. I'm okay. Elaine is here, and Nick is on his way. I'm fine."

For most of the morning, Elaine answered phone calls, including the local media. Ansley stayed in her room with the bedroom phone unplugged. Shortly before noon, she came out, freshly showered but without makeup.

"I hope you're feeling as good as you look," Elaine said.

"I'm better. I still have flashes of the nightmare, but I feel a little calmer inside."

Elaine smiled and went over to her friend and gave her a hug. "I hope you don't mind, but I found a photo album and have been looking at pictures of you and Nick. I'm dying to know more. Do you feel like talking?"

"It might take my mind off everything else."

The friends spent the remainder of the day looking at photos, memorabilia, and gifts Nick had given her as Ansley described some of the places and events of their relationship. They ate ice cream and potato chips and giggled like a couple of teenagers. Sharing stories about the glamorous affair was a therapeutic distraction.

"I still can't imagine how you kept all this secret—even from your parents?"

Ansley rolled her eyes, smiling. "It was brutal. Do you know how much I wanted to tell you and how many times I almost let something slip? But I couldn't, because I never thought it was real or would last."

That eveing, Elaine insisted on making Ansley's favorite casserole, a curried chicken, for dinner. "This recipe makes enough for a small army but it keeps well. We'll have plenty if he is hungry." Elaine chopped onions while Ansley cut up fruit for a salad.

"I'm guessing the *he* you're referring to is mine and not Greg?"

Elaine gave her a don't-play-dumb-with-me look. "Give me a hard time if you like, but, I still don't believe that Nicholas Colton is actually on his way here—and could eat something I've prepared."

Nick had called from Heathrow and said he expected to reach Florida around nine p.m. Greg was coming for dinner after he stopped by the Davis house for a quick nap.

The doorbell rang at seven-fifty. The casserole was in the oven; Ansley was on the couch, playing Solitaire on her laptop; and Elaine was reading a magazine.

"Want me to get that?" Elaine asked. "It's probably Greg."

"Do you mind?"

Tucking her shirttail in her jeans, Elaine crossed the living room. As she opened the door, she choked on a gasp. She was face to face with Nicholas Colton. Unable to speak for a moment, Elaine stood motionless.

"Elaine, it's nice to see you again." Gesturing toward a man standing slightly behind him, he continued, "This is my friend and driver, Ian Shaughnessy. . . . Ian, this is Ansley's close friend, Elaine—Davis, right?"

"She nodded."

"May we come in?"

Still speechless, Elaine opened the door wider to allow them to enter.

"Ian's headed to a hotel but wanted to be certain that Ansley is—"

Hearing his voice, Ansley bolted from the sofa, almost dropping her laptop on Shadow.

"You're here!"

Elaine had to step aside quickly as Ansley passed, her arms outstretched toward Nick.

He immediately embraced her. "Of course, I'm here. Thank God, you're here."

Releasing her, he brushed tears from her cheek and kissed her warmly on the lips. He then hugged her once again.

"I'd be thankful, as well, that you're safe," Ian said, stepping inside the condo.

Ansley looked past Nick at the big Irishman and smiled. "Oh, Ian, thank you." Turning back to Elaine, she saw that her friend's face had gone white. "I don't have any ammonia, so don't faint." Ansley reached out and touched Elaine's arm.

Slightly flustered, Elaine responded. "I don't meet movie stars every day of the week, so forgive me if I'm a *little* starstruck."

Nick grinned. "Forget what I do for a living. I'm just an ordinary chap who happens to be your friend's fiancé."

"That might take a little time," Elaine responded.

"You'll get used to him," Ansley said and then turned to Ian. "We've got a huge casserole of Elaine's famous chicken curry. It's not corned beef and cabbage, but it's excellent. Would you stay and have dinner?"

"I'll have a rain check, but thank you for the invitation." Putting Nick's bag down, he gave her a brief hug and then turned to leave. "Nick, I'll catch up with you tomorrow."

Closing the door after him, Elaine addressed Nick. "My husband is on his way. I can't wait for him to meet you."

"It will be my pleasure." He looked down affectionately at Ansley. "But, if you'll excuse me, I'd like to have a quick shower and change out of these travel clothes."

"Of course," Ansley said, taking his hand and leading him to her room. Still in awe, Elaine watched until Ansley closed the door, and then returned to the kitchen.

Dropping his travel bag, Nick took her in his arms. "I do want to freshen up, love, but before I do, are you up to telling me what happened? I don't want to pressure you, but I want to know." He looked into her eyes, his filled with concern. "I saw a gut-wrenching, newspaper head-line at the airport." He gently brushed hair off her forehead.

"It was pretty bad—horrible, but probably no worse than the media played it. Thanks to Elaine, I haven't watched the news or seen a newspa-per. She's put the paper away for me to look at later—much later."

Nick watched her intently with a serious but compassionate expression.

"In a capsule, a client's ex-husband caught me while I was put-ting my briefcase in the car. He had a gun and was angry *and* crazy. He wanted me to give him his wife's address, but I think he also wanted revenge for my representing her. I don't know how I managed to trick him with phony phone calls, but that's how the police came." She took a deep breath and began to tremble. "They . . . killed him."

He pulled her head against his chest, holding her tight around the waist. "Say no more, love," he whispered. "You escaped. Thank God, you escaped." They stood, not moving, nor speaking for several minutes, and then she pulled away and wiped her face.

"Take your shower and then come out. I know Elaine is dying to get to know you."

Greg arrived as Nick came into the living room. After exchanging greetings and handshakes, Elaine announced that the food was ready.

Dinner conversation went well. Greg was comfortable with Nick and found common ground discussing the political leaders of their respective countries. They were just finishing dessert when the doorbell rang.

"Who in the world?" Ansley said, frowning. "It's after nine o' clock."

"I'll go," Greg said.

As he opened the door, Ansley heard a voice and gasped. Turning to Nick, she whispered, "It's Andy. Go in the kitchen. I don't want him to see you."

With a firm look on his face, Nick said, "No, love. Not this time." He patted her leg, got up, and walked to the door where Andy was telling Greg that he had been out of town the night before. Grant had called, informing him of what had happened.

Watching Nick, Ansley cringed in her chair, having no idea what to expect.

"I probably should have called, Greg, but I had to see for myself that she's all right," Andy was saying.

"Come in," Nick said, interrupting. "She's right here." His theatrical voice and British accent were clearly recognizable. He motioned toward Ansley.

Taking a deep breath, she stood up and walked toward the door— her hands clammy.

As she approached, Andy looked at Nick with a flash of stunned recognition. "Are you who I think you—"

"Nick Colton." Nick extended his hand to shake Andy's. "And I apologize for the deception a few weeks ago at the pub."

"Andy, I'm fine," Ansley said, coming forward, but stopping slightly behind Nick.

Greg eased his way back to the dining area whereupon he and Elaine discreetly moved into the kitchen.

Andy looked at Ansley. "Thank goodness." His eyes then went back to Nick. "It was *you* who said he was the other guy's driver?"

Nick nodded. "Not my finest moment."

"You're the fiancé?"

"I am. I assure you that the charade was not performed with ill intent. You can understand that if Ansley's relationship with me became public, the press would make her life hell."

Andy looked toward Ansley. "I guess this accounts for the part of your life that you refused to talk about."

"Andy, I sincerely appreciate your concern for Ansley. We are all thankful that she's safe," Nick said.

Ansley had moved to Nick's side, but out of respect, neither made a move to exhibit affection.

Andy looked back and forth between them. "Well, this explains a lot. I think I see why you were so evasive about his identity. I *never* had a chance."

"I beg to differ," Nick said. "You were formidable competition. Ansley has a very high regard for you. I was the fool who nearly lost *my* chance."

Taking Nick's lead, Ansley moved forward, opening her arms. "Thank you for caring, Andy. I'm sorry, too, that we weren't honest with you at Culhane's. You caught us off guard."

After they hugged for a moment, there was a pregnant pause when no one appeared to know what to say or what would come next. Andy's body language indicated that he was processing what he had just discovered. Breaking the silence, Nick said, "May we offer you something to drink, Andy?"

Looking at Ansley, and then back at the actor, Andy shook his head. "Thank you, but I'll be going—now that I've seen she is okay. I wish you both the best."

When he was gone, Nick said, "The man has substance. I like him. In fact, I hope he finds someone worthy of him."

"Me, too," Ansley said. "I hated seeing him standing there and finding out that you're the man I'm engaged to. I'll always feel awful about what I did to him. He was nothing but good to me."

Nick put his arm around her waist and pulled her close. "It wasn't intentional, love. I'm feeling a little remorse for my role in his disappointment—but not quite enough to step aside."

After the Davises left, Nick and Ansley sat silently on her sofa, his arm around her shoulder—her head against his chest. Only a dim lamp illuminated the room.

Breaking the silence, Nick said, "I'm going on record. I'm not leaving here without you."

She nodded, her face rubbing against his shirt.

Stroking her hair, he said, "Traveling here, all I could think was how easily I could have lost you last night."

"I had those same thoughts about you in Mexico," she whispered.

He squeezed her arm. "Whatever it takes to close that law practice—*make* it happen."

"I'm not arguing."

Taking her shoulders with both his hands, he moved her to face him. "That was way too easy." He tipped his head to one side, an eyebrow raised. "What am I missing?"

For a minute or two, she just looked at him. "What do you mean?"

"Don't be coy with me. For how many weeks have you been stalling with excuses about closing your office, spending a last Christmas with your family?" His eyes squinted. "I know what happened last night was life altering, but I also know you, love. You wouldn't walk away from your clients because of that. . . . What?"

"I have no idea what you mean," she said, a smile creeping across her face as she moved slightly away from him and sat erect. "I could never go back in that building."

"Ansley, there's more. I know it."

She didn't speak and turned her upper lip inward, trying to mask her smile.

"You are *going* to tell me."

"I am, but this is not how I planned it."

"What are you hiding?"

She reached out and took his hands in hers. "Remember when you were here a few weeks ago?"

He nodded.

She took a deep breath. "Well. . . . You made good on the threat you made in Houston."

"Threat I made in Houston?" he asked, furrowing his brow and not catching on to what she was referencing.

"Have you forgotten?"

"Apparently, I have."

"You threatened to get me pregnant so that I would have to marry you."

He froze for a second, a wide smile on his face, and then pulled her to him. "We are going to have a baby?"

"More like, I'm going to have your baby."

"Damn! That is perfect."

"Are you sure?"

"What do you mean, am I sure? There's nothing I could be more positive about. I love you, Ansley Sheridan, and on all I hold sacred, I vow that having a family and sharing my life with you will make me the happiest man on either side of the Atlantic."

EPILOGUE

Within two weeks of the assault, Ansley found a colleague to take over her cases. Nick provided Olivia with a year's severance pay and an autographed photo. Like the others close to Ansley, she had been in momentary shock meeting him.

The couple returned to the U.K. for an intimate wedding in a small, Anglican church. Only family, the Davises, and Nick's staff were present. Ansley wore a demure, Victorian dress, the Irish crucifix, and carried a bouquet of white roses with baby's breath.

Six months later, Katherine Collier Colebridge made her entrance. She had her father's dark hair and golden-brown eyes. K.C. was followed a year later by a blond, mini-Ansley named Ashley Sheridan Colebridge, and the family was completed with the birth of Nick, Jr. in 2010.

With their marriage, Nick made drastic changes in his career, vowing to be a better father to their children than he had been to Kevin. Limiting film appearances, he concentrated on his first love—classical theater—and worked primarily in London.

Skye and Shadow stayed in the United States, moving in with the Sheridans. It was a hard choice for Ansley to make, but she could not bring herself to put the cats through the requirements for admission to the United Kingdom at their advanced ages. Her most treasured wedding gift from Nick was two Persian kittens.

Although they visited Florida frequently, she never saw Andy Blake again. She heard through Elaine that he had married and took comfort in the knowledge that he had found love. In memory of Dennis, Ansley and Nick established a substantial scholarship for aspiring dancers at the School of the National Ballet Company.

AUTHOR BIO

Judith Erwin is an author and attorney, residing in North Florida. Shadow of Doubt is her second novel. As a freelance writer, she has published numerous articles in local, regional, and national publications. She is currently finishing her third novel, Shadow of the Past, and working on a non-fiction book that questions the future of marriage.

www.juditherwinofficialwebsite.com

WHAT READERS HAVE SAID ABOUT
SHADOW OF SILENCE . . .

"I couldn't put it down."
     --Katherine O. Birnbaum, Attorney

"Annie's dilemma keeps you wondering how you would handle her situation and makes Shadow of Silence an engrossing read."
     --Judy Wells, Novelist/Journalist/Travel Writer

"I would love to read to read more books by the author."
     --Elizabeth Lee, Reader

"Excellent! I enjoyed this book. Ms. Erwin writes an engaging story with unexpected twists!"
     --Ron Woods, Engineer

"I was spellbound."
     --Shirley McCoy, Reader

"I couldn't wait to turn the page and see what would happen next."
     --Karen Baltovski, Reader

"I could not put it down."
     --Diane Taylor, Mediator

"A real page-turner—loved it. Can't wait for others to follow."
     --Cynthia Klusmeyer, Reader

"It reads well and once started it is difficult to put down. Strongly recommend and look forward to future books from her."
     --Carlos Sotolongo, M.D.

"I loved the book and fell in love with Annie."
     --Cheryl A. Cobb, Reader

SNEAK PEEK

In Judith Erwin's third novel, Shadow of the Past, the fiery, red-haired daughter of Irish immigrants, Fury O'Quinn, has fashioned a successful career writing romance novels. Having failed to find a flesh and blood man who can live up to the attributes of her fictional men, Fury is content to remain single. In her quest to find subject matter for a new novel, she stumbles across suspicious matters from her family history and becomes obsessed with investigating why her great-uncle was permanently committed to an insane asylum at the same time that her grandmother, as a teenager, relocated, alone, to the family's homeland.

As she digs into the past Fury encounters not only shocking details, but also the unorthodox great-grandson of the man who was the central figure in the events that affected her ancestors. Gray MacGregor is a mysterious, wealthy, domineering and handsome bachelor who challenges the wit and wisdom of the audacious young writer.

Was Fury's uncle unjustly doomed to a miserable existence in the asylum by his powerful and unscrupulous employer? What happened to cause a sixteen-year-old girl to leave her family and all she cared about to cross the Atlantic alone, never to return? Will Gray MacGregor, heir to his family's fortune, stand in the way of Fury's quest?

COMING IN 2015

Preorder at:
www.juditherwinofficialwebsite.com
www.olbbooks.com

Dedicated to all women forced to recreate their lives following a failed marriage, Shadow of Doubt tells the story of Ansley Sheridan who sacrificed her career as a member of a world-class ballet company to marry a graduate student at the University of Florida. When her husband betrays her after only two years of marriage, Ansley is left with no career and little education. In returning to school and obtaining a law degree, she vows to never gamble another career on marriage. However, when a chance encounter with the suave and handsome British actor, Nicholas Colton, jolts her resolve, she finds herself floundering between doubt and desire.

Living a dual life, Ansley keeps her relationship with Nick a secret from friends, colleagues, and family, fearing the humiliation of being labeled the former lover of a superstar. In her world, only her former partner in the ballet company knows about the affair.

As Nick becomes serious, Ansley knows that to take the relationship to the next level, she will have to abandon her law practice and move to England where he owns a massive manor house in the country.

Can she be seduced by the temptation of a life of luxury and take a chance on a high-risk relationship, or will she honor her vow and walk away?